Everybody's loving
My Hero

"Marianna Jameson has hit the jackpot with *My Hero*. This book has it all: wit and charm, along with a wonderful heroine and a hero to die for, both of whom sizzle. Undoubtedly, Jameson is a rising star on the romance horizon."
—*USA Today* bestselling author Julie Kenner

"Few writers can make me laugh and cry within the pages of the same book. Talented newcomer Marianna Jameson is one of them."
—*USA Today* bestselling author Deirdre Martin

"Sharp, witty, wonderful! This sizzling, sexy debut novel by Marianna Jameson is destined for the bestseller lists!"
—Karen Kendall

My Hero

Marianna Jameson

A SIGNET ECLIPSE BOOK

SIGNET ECLIPSE
Published by New American Library, a division of
Penguin Group (USA) Inc., 375 Hudson Street,
New York, New York 10014, USA
Penguin Group (Canada), 10 Alcorn Avenue, Toronto,
Ontario M4V 3B2, Canada (a division of Pearson Penguin Canada Inc.)
Penguin Books Ltd., 80 Strand, London WC2R 0RL, England
Penguin Ireland, 25 St. Stephen's Green, Dublin 2,
Ireland (a division of Penguin Books Ltd.)
Penguin Group (Australia), 250 Camberwell Road, Camberwell, Victoria 3124,
Australia (a division of Pearson Australia Group Pty. Ltd.)
Penguin Books India Pvt. Ltd., 11 Community Centre, Panchsheel Park,
New Delhi - 110 017, India
Penguin Group (NZ), cnr Airborne and Rosedale Roads, Albany,
Auckland 1310, New Zealand (a division of Pearson New Zealand Ltd.)
Penguin Books (South Africa) (Pty.) Ltd., 24 Sturdee Avenue,
Rosebank, Johannesburg 2196, South Africa

Penguin Books Ltd., Registered Offices:
80 Strand, London WC2R 0RL, England

First published by Signet Eclipse, an imprint of New American Library,
a division of Penguin Group (USA) Inc.

First Printing, June 2005
10 9 8 7 6 5 4 3 2 1

This book is dedicated with love to my father.
He was an officer and a gentleman, and
taught me about truth and honor
as much through his actions as through his words.
I miss you every day, Duffy.

And to my husband,
who is my world-without-end hero.
Grá mo chroi,
Grá mo bheatha.

ACKNOWLEDGMENTS

For their much-appreciated help, support, and information, I would like to thank:

Joanna Novins, Karen Kendall, Jerrilyn Hutson, and Deirdre Martin, the smartest, savviest, most savagely funny women I know. They are wonderful writers and even better friends.

Eloisa James, whose elegant wit and graceful candor have provided much wisdom and guidance, and Julie Kenner, whose generosity and willingness to help me are gratefully appreciated.

Kevin and Carol Smith, for many hours of conversation and laughter, many, many glasses of wine, and exceptionally few but inevitably well-founded requests for me to stop talking about cops. *Go raibh maith agat.*

The Romance Writers of Southern Connecticut and Lower New York, for their unflagging enthusiasm and support, and bottomless well of talent.

Former Chief Louis DeCarlo, who graciously provided me with access to the Stamford (CT) Police Department; Lieutenant John Forlivio, commanding officer of the Crimes Against Persons unit of the Investigations Bureau, who was generous with his time as well as the information about how the department operates; Officer Michael Duffin, who provided exceptional, candid insight into a police officer's mind-set; and all of the members of the Stamford Police Department whom I observed and with whom I came in contact in the course of writing this book. Their patience, coutesy, and professionalism were and are greatly appreciated.

Officer Michael Skelly of the New Castle (NY) Police Department, who not only provided great information and much entertainment during our interview; he taught me the intricacies of handcuffing a suspect, or in this case, a curious writer, and demonstrated the "command attitude" in a way that still sparks a laugh when I think about it; and most expecially the *mucho macho* Lieutenant Michael Hutson of the Shaker Heights (OH) Police Department for being candid, humorous, and incredibly generous with his time as he shared his knowledge, experience, opinions, and insight with me. He not only gave me a guided tour through the mind of a *real* alpha male—*he read a draft of my book*. Without being threatened or bribed, and without flinching. I'm not sure a guy could *be* more courageous than that. . . .

My editor, Laura Cifelli, who has fabulous taste and terrific instincts, and my agent, Coleen O'Shea, who bravely read several of my earlier manuscripts and took me on as a client anyway. Thank you for seeing whatever you saw in those, and for having faith that I would improve.

And, finally, my husband, who now *prefers* take-out food to home-cooked, and my children, who exhibit endless patience and understanding when I zone them out to write "I-love-you books."

Although the City of Stamford and the other places mentioned are real, all characters and their names are works of fiction. Some elements of the facts and technical information imparted by the police officers interviewed had to be reshaped to fit my story. All mistakes are my own.

CHAPTER
1

Professional oblivion or a month in the blustery cold of a New England autumn?

Romance writer Miranda Lane wasn't sure which would be the easier fate to accept. Of course, pondering the question in front of a weathered stone fireplace in a borrowed beachfront condo in Stamford, Connecticut, rendered it sort of moot. But there was always room for a dignified retreat to her own cozy little nest in mid-town Atlanta.

Yankees and frosty mornings. She sighed. Surely such intensive culture-shock therapy would jolt her into productivity. Surely it would.

"By God, it has to," she muttered to the empty room. Accepting her college roommate's invitation to spend a month amid the fall colors of Connecticut to recharge her creative batteries had seemed like a good idea a few weeks ago. However, good ideas were no longer the mainstay of Miranda's mental diet. Nor had they been for the last several months. *Okay—year.*

Her creative dry spell wasn't just a career hiccup. That was the first place she'd felt it, but it had sprawled just as quickly and in more directions than an Atlanta suburb and now touched every aspect of her life. She had done nothing to deserve it nor to warrant so severe a remedy but, at this point, she knew the texture of her personality had gone from silk to sandpaper. A few close friends and a city full of strangers were the only people she was fit to be around. She couldn't hang the reason for her lack of imagination on her tanking sales numbers, her breakup with Josh, or the ticking of her biological clock. Her finances were fine, her health was good, and menopause was at least ten years away. She had never *needed* a man and didn't particularly want one right now. Nor did she want a child or even a best seller, although she'd take the latter without an argument. What she really wanted was some inspiration and *that* was in short supply.

She lunged for the cell phone before it completed its first chirp, thankful for the distraction. "Amy, bless your heart. How are you?"

"Exhausted," her agent snapped without any preliminary niceties. "I just finished meeting with Ellen Barber."

Miranda closed her eyes. Ellen was her new editor. She had a big name and a big reputation. It wasn't for being warm and cuddly. *This can't be good news.* "But, Amy, honey, it's Saturday night."

"Thanks for the update, Miss Scarlett." Amy let out an annoyed breath. "I've been trying to get in to see her for weeks and she calls me *this morning* asking if I'd meet her for tea. *Tea.* Not a drink. *Tea.* I missed the first period of the Rangers–Islanders game, *for which I have center ice seats*, to sip green tea with *your editor* at the Plaza."

Miranda winced. Amy was strictly a single-malt, Scotch-rocks woman. "I've heard that green tea is good for you. It's full of antioxidants."

"Save the Southern charm for when I'm in a better mood, Miranda. The only tea I drink is the kind in a G and T, and then only when I have to. For your information, the stuff is putrid. Despite that, I drank a half gallon of it to help further *your* career. Do you have any idea how much you owe me for that?"

"My firstborn?"

"For a start."

"Where are you now?"

"In the back of a cab approaching Madison Square Garden. I've got a lot of news and not a lot of time to tell you about it, okay?"

"Okay." Taking a deep, silent breath, Miranda glanced through the windows and beyond the deck to the rocky shoreline fifty feet away. Her good friend and fellow writer Molly Crandall once described working with Ellen as being only slightly less painful than sitting bare-assed on a hot barbecue —then denied ever saying it when her book hit number two on the *USA Today* best-seller list after just three weeks. Molly now drank green tea by the gallon and worshipped at Ellen's feet. And had just signed a four-book deal for a healthy six-figure advance.

"So how much does she love the book?" Miranda asked, pressing her forehead against the cold glass. "Please say 'lots.' It's been sitting on her desk for weeks."

"She loves it—"

"Thank God."

"—but."

Her stomach turned inward and began consuming itself. "I don't want to hear this, do I?"

"You know how things operate, Miranda. When Tina left, all of her authors were left hanging loose for a while. You were lucky to get reassigned to Ellen and you know it. You know her reputation."

"She's opinionated and tough. But you just said she loves it."

"She's opinionated, tough, and usually right. And I said, 'She loves it, but . . .' I'm not going to tell you the 'but' until you're sitting down."

Wishing she'd had the foresight to invest in a pair of asbestos underpants, Miranda lowered herself onto the couch. "I'm sitting."

"She wants you to make some revisions and she wants them before Thanksgiving."

Miranda caught her breath. "Thanksgiving is in three and a half weeks." *And I'm on vacation.*

"I know."

"What does she want me to change? Will she send me a markup?"

"No." Her agent's voice softened slightly. "She wants you to change the plot, the setting, and the hero."

Miranda's spine whiplashed into rigidity. "*What?* That's not a revision. That's a rewrite."

"I know."

"And she wants this in three weeks," she repeated.

"Yes. Can you do it?"

"Do I have a choice?" *I'll just find time to eat, sleep, and breathe in December.*

"You always have a choice. This time it's just not a good one."

Miranda grimaced at the finality in Amy's voice. "Did she tell you what's wrong with what I sent her?"

"Yes. She doesn't want it set in Atlanta; she wants it set in the North. And she doesn't—"

"Wait a minute. My books are always set in the South. I'm a Southern writer." Miranda waited for a reply, and when three seconds passed without one, her blood pressure plummeted. Amy *never* hesitated. Even when the news was bad.

"That's what I told her, kitten," Amy said as gently as her Brooklyn upbringing allowed. "You know what she said to me? 'Eudora Welty was a Southern writer. Harper Lee is a Southern writer. Randi Rhodes is a romance writer. She's generic. Plug and play.'"

"Generic?" Miranda repeated, breathless from the sting. "She said I was 'plug and play'?"

"Look, she's still adjusting to the genre. She came from a literary imprint—" Amy let out a hard sigh. "Yes, Miranda, she did. Just before she pointed out that your last few books haven't sold as well as your early ones."

Miranda rose to her feet and took another calming breath, willing away all the bad words she didn't ever want to be quoted as having said about an editor. "My third book didn't sell well, Amy. All the others have done just fine. And the biggest reason that one didn't sell was that it came out on September 12, 2001. People had other things on their minds that day. A publisher can't hold that against me. The two that followed did okay."

"We all know that, Miranda, but the numbers are what matter. It's been a while since you've had a book out. It's kind of like the bakery business, kiddo. Freshness counts."

Miranda felt her eyes widen. "She said I'm not fresh?"

"I'm paraphrasing."

"What did she really say?"

Amy took a resigned breath. "The other F-word."

Miranda could swear she heard a death knell sound in the distance. "Formulaic?" she whispered.

"Yes. I'm really sorry to have to be the bearer of bad news, but you know this business. The bottom line is that you can make her changes and keep your March release date, or return the advance and shop for another publisher. We're at the wire."

You mean the abyss. Miranda lowered herself onto the cushions again and closed her eyes, wondering how long it would take the lump in her stomach—or just her stomach—to dissolve. "What does she want?"

"She wants it set in the North, ideally New York City, but someplace else would be okay. And she wants your hero to be a tough, dark, alpha-male cop."

Miranda could hear Amy breathing on the other end of the phone, waiting patiently for the second wave of shock to wear off and incredulity to set in. Licking her very dry lips, she tried to sound normal. "You're not serious, are you, darlin'?"

"As a bounced check."

Finding another publisher won't be that difficult. "I don't write alpha males, Amy," she said gently. "You know I don't. And I sure as sugar don't write cops."

"You know that, I know that, and she knows that. But Ellen Barber thinks you *can* and that you *should.* Given her track record, I don't recommend arguing with her. You know the score. Look, she likes you, Miranda, and she likes your writing. However, she also likes alpha

males, and she loves cops. She has an autographed picture of Edward Conlon on her office wall, if that gives
you any insight."

Holy cats. Miranda swallowed hard. "You don't think
she wants me to use him as—"

"No." She paused minutely. "I mean, probably not.
But the thing is, Miranda . . ." Amy paused again. "She
thinks your heroes are wimps."

"That's because she has no taste, bless her heart,"
Miranda replied, striving to remain calm. "My heroes
aren't wimps. They're just not alpha males. They're beta
males. They can think without scratching their privates.
They can talk to a woman without trying to look down
her shirt. And they don't carry a pseudo-penis strapped
under their arms." She swallowed hard to control the
desperate quaver she heard in her voice. "For pity's
sake, Amy, I can't write about something I prefer not
to think about. If I were a vegan, would she make me
write about a butcher?"

"Okay, you're losing me here, hon."

Miranda took a deep breath. "I'll put in a villain and
make *him* an alpha cop. I swore I'd never do it, but I'd
rather compromise on that. Would she go for it?"

"She wants an alpha hero who's a cop, Miranda,"
Amy said firmly after a meaningful pause that was by
no means hesitant. "Her exact words were 'I want a
hero who's a hero.' She wants him dark, broody, sexy
as hell, and deeply flawed. 'A dark knight redeemed by
love,' and that's another direct quote. Personally, I think
she needs to stop reading the copy her marketing department sends her. Anyway—"

"Amy," Miranda interrupted quietly. "What do *you*
think?"

"I think she's right. On all counts." She let out a
heavy sigh. "I know this is a lot to absorb, Miranda.
Take some time to think about it and give me a call
back."

"No, no, I'll do it. Tell her I'll do it. Thanks, Amy. I
appreciate it." She ended the call and slid sideways to
the cushions, closing her eyes on the way down. An
alpha male. A cop. *Sweet Jesus, just take me now.*

*   *   *

It took two hours before she could bring herself to turn on her computer. Two hours that included an hour on the phone whining to Molly, a dinner consisting mostly of carbohydrates, salt, and saturated animal fats, and a long, hot bath. Only then did Miranda bring her laptop to the dining room table, sit down, and boot up. A fresh wave of despair ambushed her, stinging like a cloud of Alabama horseflies feeding on naked, sunburnt flesh, as she looked at the first page of her latest manuscript, the one on which she was about to commit a sacrilege. She stared at the cursor blinking cheerfully beside the first letter of the first sentence and fought the pointless dread and remembered anger that had been churning through her since Amy's call. She fought the urge to turn her hero into her antihero, to change perfection into pain. *No. No matter how tempting it may be, I am not turning Brad into Walter. That's a door best left closed, and Walter a man best left forgotten.*

She shook her head, squared her shoulders, and brought her hands to the keyboard.

"Ellen, honey," she said out loud, half hoping the strong, sure sound of her voice would chase away the memories of her once-upon-a-time father. "I wish you the dubious fortune of having to deal with a *real* alpha male someday. I promise you that it will send you running for a beta, and then you'll change your editorial tune." She took a long sip of her iced tea and flexed her fingers before settling them gently on the home keys. "Okay. Here goes. Good-bye, Brad. My sweet, loving, cuddly Brad. I'm just so sorry, darlin', but you're about to become a Dirk."

An hour later, after using her word-processing application's find-and-replace feature, the first round of rough changes had been made. Every reference to Atlanta had been changed to Stamford, every reference to her hero's neat blond hair had become wild and windblown black curls, and every reference to his profession had changed from lawyer to cop.

Every *lithe* became *brawny*, every game of chess became poker, and every glass of fine, smooth bourbon-

and-branch had become a bottle of Bud. His sleek Buck-head condo was now a small, messy one-story house near the interstate with windows that rattled every time a semi went past, and his sexy red Beamer had morphed into a white Dodge Ram.

She stared at the screen, fingers suspended above the keyboard. A smile that felt caught between devious and triumphant drifted across her face. *Go for it, honey. This is fiction. Get it out of your system.*

She found the first entry that described Dirk's truck and began adding details—wonderful, rich details her readers would not only identify with, but that would make them shake their heads in sympathy for her hero-ine. He drove a *mud-spattered* white Dodge Ram four-by-four, she decided. With an aging muffler and a gun rack hung against the back windshield. She squinted at the screen. The gun rack hung against a back windshield that was covered with . . . She searched her brain for a suitably revolting substance. *Dried dog drool.* She smiled wider. And just to make sure not a single reader would miss her point, she dropped the hint that it wasn't from *his* dog—the subtext being that Dirk wasn't worthy of owning a dog. She nodded her head in appreciation of her own genius as her fingers flew over the keys. *He isn't even worthy of owning a one-eyed, crop-tailed mutt like Walter's old hound, Barney. No, Dirk rents the dog to go hunting.* She paused for another moment. *Rabbits. The man hunts rabbits.*

Nope, not good enough. She backspaced over the word. The man hunted *bunnies.*

She clicked her mouse to save the mess she'd made and sat there perfectly still, holding her breath. A mo-ment later she closed her eyes and laid her head on the richly polished surface of the dining room table, reeling from the unexpected adrenaline rush that followed the massacre. She stayed there for several minutes. *Okay, so he's more good ol' boy than Yankee. She's not going to let me get away with it anyway. I might as well have fun while I can.* With a defeated sigh, she sat up and faced the ruins of her story. "Whatever you turn out to be, I hope you give Ellen the right kind of jollies, you lousy

Neanderthal," she muttered as she closed the document. "You've got balls the size of boulders and all the charm of a cabbie from Queens, but *I'm* the boss—and *you* won't be getting anywhere near your lady friend's silk panties until the last page."

On the way back to headquarters, Detective Chas Casey picked up the radio handset and told the dispatcher they would take the call as his partner, Fritz Gruber, flipped on the lights and siren and took a hard right onto Broad Street. Moments later they pulled up in front of a well kept condo in downtown Stamford.

The sound of shouting was faint but detectable from the curb. A clutch of more curious than concerned neighbors had gathered on the street. They stepped back as Chas crossed the small lawn. Positioning himself slightly to one side of the door as Gruber stood opposite, Chas unsnapped his holster with his right hand and pounded on the door with his left. It was pulled open by a flushed, angry young woman wearing a UCONN lacrosse jersey and a pair of wind pants. Behind her was a near-clone in a U CONN field hockey sweatshirt and a pair of biking shorts. Both women were blond and barefoot, and both were holding lacrosse bats.

"I'm Detective Casey from the Stamford Police Department," he said, flashing his badge. "We received a call about a domestic disturbance. What's going on?"

"God. I'm sure. I can't believe anyone called the cops. We were having an argument." The one who answered the door let out a harsh breath and brushed a fall of hair from her forehead. "Everything's fine." She started to close the door.

He stopped the motion with the flat of his hand. "Not so fast. If it was just an argument, why are you holding that?"

The woman looked at the heavy wooden bat in her hand, then back at Chas. "She picked hers up first. It's not like we were going to hit each other or anything. I'm sure."

"I think we should have a little chat. Can we come in?"

"Do I have to let you in?"

"Not if you'd prefer to step outside." He glanced meaningfully at her bare feet. "But unless you want all of your neighbors to know your troubles, letting us come in would be the sensible thing to do."

Chas watched her glance over his shoulder at the blatantly interested crowd on the sidewalk; then she stepped aside and let them enter the condo. As he walked past her, he gently took the large, heavy stick from her hand. The other woman quickly set hers on the floor and moved into the center of the living room.

It was a well-furnished condo with all of the most necessary equipment for the upscale student life. A large-screen plasma television hung on one wall; Magneplanar speakers stood sentinel in each of the room's four corners. A large, open armoire held a DVD and a VCR player and numerous components of a high-end stereo system, displaying an array of lights, dials, and gauges that put to shame the console in a fighter jet. Two notebook computers hummed on the dining room table next to an empty pizza box and half a dozen opened Diet Coke cans. A basket of laundry sat in the corner next to a pair of beaten-up backpacks and a pile of high-heeled shoes.

Chas spared a glance at Gruber, whose eyes had narrowed in disgust. The women were tall and slender, and their long golden hair had been artlessly streaked by a summer of sun and salt water. They were no older than twenty, but wore the aura of a privileged upbringing as casually as they wore their clothes. And that was why, despite radiating anxiety and guilt, they were regarding the detectives with a mixture of well-concealed irritation and less well concealed condescension. *Spoiled brats.*

Chas casually swept back his sport coat and put his hands on his hips. As intended, both young women's gazes were drawn to his gun, and some of their attitude deflated. "What are your names?"

"Sarah Chamberlain," mumbled the one who answered the door, watching sullenly as Gruber wrote it down.

"Victoria Chamberlain," said the other.

"Nice to meet you. Are you sisters?" Chas asked easily.

"Cousins."

"You both live here?"

"Yes."

"Is anyone else in the house?"

"No."

"Okay, what seems to be the problem? Victoria, you first."

The one who had not answered the door folded her arms and leaned abruptly onto one hip. "She took my leather pants without asking me, and she ripped them. They were Donna Karans."

Christ. It wasn't even a catfight. The neighbors called in a kitten fight. He concealed his disbelief and looked at the one who had answered door. "Did you take them, Sarah?"

"No. I *borrowed* them. *With permission.* She was just too drunk at the time to remember that she said I could."

"I was not, you liar."

"You were too. It was at that party—"

"Enough." He folded his arms across his chest, and looked at the one who'd answered the door. "Sarah, did you rip them?"

"No. *I* didn't rip them, but they got ripped while I was wearing them. Some guy—"

"Then apologize and promise you'll buy her a new pair," he said calmly.

"They were four years old. New ones cost, like, six hundred dollars? There's no way—"

Chas let her enjoy the full force of his glare until her arguing subsided. "At the moment, both of you are subject to arrest for a number of violations, beginning with disturbing the peace and ending with attempted assault," he lied. "If you choose to be arrested, Detective Gruber and I will handcuff you and lead you to our car in front of all of your neighbors *and* the photographer from the *Stamford Advocate* who pulled up when we did. Then you'll be fingerprinted at police headquarters, and you'll spend the night in jail because I guarantee we won't have enough manpower to process you no matter how fast your parents or their lawyers arrive. And on Saturday night, the jail is a pretty ugly place full of people who would consider it the opportunity of a lifetime to spend a few hours scaring the living hell out of you." He paused and watched the last of their bravado melt away.

"With a felony arrest on your record, you'll never get into law school or med school, and your names will definitely get in the paper. And I don't mean in the social column." He paused again. "So, Victoria? Sarah? What do you want to do? Apologize to each other and settle this like adults, or take a crash course in real life?"

"Nice touch about the photographer," Gruber muttered as they walked back to the car a few moments later.

"Sometimes I think it's a pity that spanking children has gone out of style," Chas replied under his breath.

A robbery in North Stamford consumed the rest of his shift and an hour beyond it, so it was nearly two by the time Chas walked through the door of the restored Victorian he called home. He picked up the mail that lay scattered on the floor below the door's old-fashioned mail slot and carried it into the kitchen as he pulled off his tie. Bills. Junk mail. More bills. Bank statements. He stopped as his eyes came to rest on a thick envelope of heavy, cream-colored paper with *Brennan Shipping* as its return address.

He swore under his breath and flicked it away, only to watch it land faceup in the center of the heavy, old, scarred wooden table. Impossible to miss. "But not impossible to ignore," he muttered, and left the room. Ten minutes later he returned, freshly showered and wearing a pair of faded jeans. Grabbing a beer from the refrigerator, he picked up the letter and walked into the small, cozy den at the front of the house. Sitting in one of the two large wing chairs, he put his feet on the low table in front of him and opened the envelope.

Dear Chas . . . He gave a silent laugh. *Nice familiar greeting.* He glanced at the bottom of the page. Dalton B. Harrington IV. Vice chairman of the board of Brennan Shipping and, inconveniently, Chas's great-uncle. He skimmed the letter.

. . . great pleasure to offer you . . . chief security officer . . . annual salary and bonus structure . . .

Chas raised his eyebrows. The base salary was six times what he was making as a cop. *Too damned bad they can't take no for an answer.* He tossed the letter on the table and grabbed the television remote. After twenty minutes of surfing through the late-night mix of re-hashed news, tape-delayed sports events, and old movies, he shut it off and picked up the letter again.

The board had been on his case to take the job for a year, and heavily on it for the last two months. Hell, one way or another his mother and grandparents had been bugging him to work for the company since he'd been in high school. They'd put up every roadblock, hit him from every angle, pulled every emotional string they could find.

It was a five-generation family tradition. As the eldest son, he had to carry on the legacy. It was his obligation.

His duty.

His responsibility.

He took a long pull of his beer. They were right about all of it. The problem was, he didn't want to be a businessman. An executive. All he'd ever wanted to be was a police officer. He'd told them that from day one.

What he found baffling was that they kept trying to get him to change his mind, even after he'd put in fifteen years on the force. As if something, some combination of material things, could make him want to leave. He shook his head. They were smart people. Very smart people. So why they couldn't understand that no high salary or plush office or use of the corporate jet would change his mind was beyond him. His decision had nothing to do with wealth or power. He didn't have anything against either, but he already had the first by virtue of being born into the right family, and he didn't covet the latter. Maybe it was just so simple that they missed it. He'd decided to become a cop when he was six years old, at the moment the honor guard lifted the flag from his father's casket, the moment hundreds of white-gloved hands rose in a solemn salute and the chief of the New Haven Police Department placed that tightly folded American flag in his small, outstretched hands.

He'd made up his mind about a lot of things that day, and had stuck to them all. In a matter of weeks he'd be promoted to lieutenant, the same rank his father had achieved before his death. From there he'd aim for the rank of captain and eventually chief, or maybe run for mayor. The only significant difference in their career tracks so far was that Chas had made sure he had no wife to widow, no kids to orphan, no long-term commitments to encumber him. Everything about his life was clean and simple and straightforward by design.

It was going to stay that way.

CHAPTER
2

The stranger strode into Miranda's line of sight with an easy, confident grace: shoulders back, dark eyes continually surveying the area, even the area in which she sat, well hidden. Watching him greet the others, she could tell he was at home in his surroundings. In fact, she thought, he looked like he'd feel at home anywhere, like a king of the jungle. Or king of the beasts, which was probably the more appropriate title.

She knew she didn't have to do what she was about to do. She probably shouldn't do it, but she needed to, if for no other reason than to perk herself up. After all, she'd spent entirely too much of yesterday slaughtering her manuscript. She hadn't seen sunshine in nearly a week. She'd spent all of last night watching the entire *Lethal Weapon* series instead of the restored *My Fair Lady*. And, as if all of that weren't enough, her period was two days late. The sooner she got this over with, the sooner she could go home and take a well-deserved nap.

Moving so slowly that her muscles ached from the tension, she snugged the cheap rifle tight against her shoulder and lowered her head until the curve of its wooden stock was cool and smooth and familiar against the flesh of her cheek.

Lovely.

She let out a slow, measured breath, blinked once, then focused on the center of the beastly king's chest and gently squeezed the trigger.

The impact knocked him off balance but not off his feet, and he looked down in horrified surprise at the dark red stain spreading across the front of his camouflage jacket. Miranda didn't really care about the stain or his surprise on seeing it. What she cared about was that he was out of her line of sight now and she had a clear shot at each of his similarly macho pals, who reacted fast, but not fast enough. By moving the scope quickly, smoothly, she sighted in his companions and nailed them with one shot each, in rapid succession. Liver. Heart. Stomach. They never saw her, and only one was able to fire a shot, which missed her by a good eight inches.

When the last man was covered in red, she lowered the gun and let out a pent-up breath as she slipped out of the area. She felt much better.

"Where the hell did you learn to shoot like that?" Jane demanded with a hint of high-pitched panic in her voice as she burst into the otherwise empty women's locker room.

Intuition wins again. I should have surrendered, Miranda thought with a tickle of regret. She knew the triumph had felt too good to last. She finished pushing her head through the round neckline of her cashmere shell and gave her friend a playful smile. "Honey, I grew up in the rural South. Shooting at moving targets was a daily chore. Shooting at things that just stood there was what we did afterward for fun."

Jane took a deep breath and crossed her arms. "Did you have to nail *all* of them?"

"Okay, Janey, I admit I was being a show-off. But they were just standing there like a bunch of turkey buzzards pestering fresh roadkill. It wasn't like they didn't deserve it." Miranda gave a one-shouldered shrug. "They'll get over it."

"I wish I had your confidence. They won't take it lightly."

"I imagine they won't." She fought back a satisfied smile.

"Miranda, I *know* those guys. They come in here all the time and, at this point, they're the closest thing I have to best customers." Jane's slim, athletic body eased away from the bank of lockers she was leaning against. She shook her dark blond head, pushed her green-framed glasses farther up her nose, and smiled her crooked smile. "You're a loose cannon. And you should have stayed on the floor and introduced yourself afterward."

"I think I'm better off having delayed those introductions. Those boys need to settle a spell," Miranda murmured to the woman who was the next best thing to a little sister. She lifted her long curls out of the neck of her twinset, tossed them over her shoulder, then reached for her long, soft corduroy skirt. "I just gave them an opportunity to practice being gracious losers, bless their hearts."

"I'm not so sure that's in their skill set," Jane muttered. "But I'm going to quote you when Team Testosterone demands to know what happened."

Miranda smoothed the skirt over her hips and picked up one sleek riding boot. "Team Testosterone, huh? Well, precious, I imagine I've just done you a favor. They'll be back even more frequently now that we've given them a run for their money. They'll never let the record stand if it shows they've been bested by Team Estrogen." She pulled on the other boot, stood up, and slipped into her leather bomber jacket, then surveyed herself in the mirror. She was a catalog image of the dressed-for-autumn New England thirty-something, a natural blend of rich forest hues: browns, golds, and deep greens. "Thanks to L.L. Bean, I at least look the part. If I lost my drawl, I'd fit right in."

Jane shuddered. "Why would you want to? I'm surprised you even came back for a visit."

Miranda turned to her with a smile. "I came to see my adopted family, honey. That means you. Besides, I'm the one who should be surprised to see you here. I didn't think you'd ever come back."

"I grew up here. You can take the girl out of Connecticut, but it's impossible to scrub the Connecticut out of the girl. As you can see, I've tried." She waved her hands toward her baggy camo gear and Doc Martens. "So here I will remain, playing the only role left to me: the ungrateful prodigal daughter who's not quite apologetic enough to suit the family and who is bent on wasting her lovely, cocktailable education that was guaranteed to open so many doors."

"You have nothing to apologize for, Janey. You finished college, then eloped with the man you loved. It's not a crime and it's not a sin. I happen to think it's quite romantic."

"So do I, but Paxton and my mother would argue that point."

"Well, your sister and your mother would lose the argument. And your education did open doors. You own your own business."

"That's right. I do." Jane grinned and threw her petite body into a dramatic pose. "After a short but successful stint as a curator of a museum of desert art, and a few months in the New York art scene, I now run a gallery in Stamford. *Daaaaarling.*"

Miranda paused. "You don't really tell people that, do you? With a straight face?"

Jane raised one blond eyebrow. "Of course I do. Well, okay, without the attitude. This is called a paintball *gallery*. It's a converted warehouse with movable walls that are covered in paint. The paint just isn't framed." She winked. "I have it all worked out. I mean, I have to put that Smith education to use, don't I?"

"Do tell."

Jane grinned. "I serve a niche market. I'm a leading supplier of postmodern, new-wave primitive, urban-industrial murals. Very new. Very chic." She lifted her chin and lowered her voice. "They're not for everyone."

"That works," Miranda said with a smile. "Why don't you try to sell one of your 'primitives' to those dead white males outside? It would probably fit in charmingly alongside their neon beer signs and velvet Elvises."

Jane choked on a laugh. "God, Miranda, you're such a bitch. I've really missed you."

"It's one of the secrets to my success. Listen, don't worry about them. This afternoon will give them something to think about." Miranda fluffed her dark hair out of the collar of her jacket, letting it fall loose down her back, checked to make sure her nail polish was intact, and reached for her lipstick. "I think I'll be back, Janey. This is way more fun than yoga. It's constructive, cathartic, and you get instant results."

"Yeah, well, what I actually came in here to tell you is that those instant results are waiting for you in the parking lot."

"Are they hoping for a rumble?" Sarcasm effectively hid the sliver of panic that shot through her and was gone. She unconsciously straightened her spine.

Jane shook her head with a silent laugh. "I'm guessing they want to meet the *man* who took down their team in ten seconds flat."

"Well, they're in for a little surprise from Dixie, aren't they? They should have known better than to cluster like that. What were they thinking?" Miranda asked, lifting her chin.

"Maybe they were thinking the game was over and they'd won," Jane replied dryly.

"Why would they have thought that?" Miranda shot her a sideways glance. "Do you mean *they didn't know* I joined the game? Good Lord, Janey, I probably scared the bejesus out of them."

"I'd say so. But I told them there *might* be an addition to the other team. You came in late." She shrugged. "In all honesty, it probably wouldn't have saved them if they'd seen you ahead of time. They would have taken one look and thought, 'Great, a chick.' I wouldn't have held it against them. How was I to know you were some sort of sharpshooter with an attitude? Anyway, what are you doing later?"

"Having dinner with Paxton and James."

Jane rolled her eyes at the mention of her sister and brother-in-law. "Sounds awful. What did you do to deserve that?" Then she grinned. "Well, say hi to James for me. He's the only family member who will appreciate it." She reached over and gave her a quick hug. Miranda tried not to tense but knew she failed when Jane started to laugh. "Can't you grant me some sort of a dispensation? One hug per sighting?"

Miranda gave her a sheepish grin and shrugged. "I'm working on it."

"You've been *working on* that look-but-don't-touch issue for as long as I've known you. Anyway, let me know what they say. I have to go get another group suited up." She walked through the locker room door and turned toward the reception area, leaving Miranda alone.

Taking two deep breaths and one last look at herself, Miranda grabbed her handbag and headed outside to pay her respects to the dearly departed.

There they were, just as Jane had promised. Four of them, laughing and talking and obviously waiting for someone as they clustered around the hood of an SUV. They could have been just dumb jocks. Or plumbers. It was a weekend; they could have been accountants or stockbrokers. But they weren't. Their eyes, their stance, their attitude gave them away. It—all of it—was indelibly stamped on her brain due to eighteen years of daily exposure.

They were cops.

Miranda pushed open the door and started to cross the parking lot fronting the transformed three-story warehouse.

"Well, I'll be damned. It must be Lara Croft in disguise."

Whoever said it didn't sound annoyed. She glanced at the men without breaking her stride and gave them a smile and a slight nod. "Good afternoon, gentlemen."

"Aw, c'mon, Hotshot. Don't be like that. We don't bite. In fact, we might want to recruit you," the short, swarthy one called.

She stopped and gave him a half smile, but didn't reply. Instead she just absorbed the tableau he presented. He had a great smile set in a face that looked like it had achieved intimacy with a few too many fists, and had a rock-star mane of curly dark hair that ended below his shoulders. The rest of him was solidly edge-of-middle-age New England suburban: straight-leg jeans, leather running shoes, navy blue North Face windbreaker over a golf shirt. *Attractive, but trite. He would never do, even as a secondary character.*

He and his buddies were openly studying her. The one she'd shot first, the one she'd caught totally off guard, did so most intently. He was the tallest of the group and the most conventionally handsome, but unappealing despite that. He was too big, too dark, too cocky. Too coplike, and, therefore, too much like Walter. The guy next to him was closer to being the poison she preferred on the page and on the hoof: a lithe, lanky blonde. He had been her second target.

She'd gotten him square in the liver through a small gap in his padded vest as he'd been reaching to give one of the other guys a prematurely triumphant high five. His side was probably aching already, building toward the tennis ball-sized bruise that would appear by evening. Though watching her just as carefully as his friends were, he didn't have their macho, in-command attitude. Frankly, he looked too bookish to be a cop. But she'd be willing to bet that, unlike the rock star, the chubby one, or Victim Number One, Blondie could order from a wine list, that his vocabulary included more four-syllable words than four-letter words, and that he couldn't name every team in the NFL. Better still, he probably didn't care.

Knowing her perusal of them had lasted long enough to assure them she was no pushover, Miranda decided to let them have their fun. Hiding her smile, she walked toward them with her back straight and her eyes meeting theirs. She came to a stop a few feet away from them, just outside the testosterone zone. Deliberately at ease, she cocked her head just enough to the left to indicate curiosity without flirtatiousness and made sure her hands hung at her sides, relaxed and open.

Only someone used to assessing people in a hurry

would have glanced at her feet, and that was exactly
what Victim Number One did. With a silent hitch of one
dark eyebrow, he acknowledged their placement, one
slightly behind the other, in the classic stance of a person
ready to respond rather than run. Then his eyes met
hers. His look stopped just short of being invasive.

Miranda felt the hint of a challenge ripple between
them and fought back another smile. *You just keep right
on dreaming, big boy. You are* so *not my type.* She
glanced away as the blonde extended his hand.

"Brian Murphy."

"I'm pleased to meet you, Brian. I'm Randi Rhodes,"
she replied in her silkiest drawl.

He didn't have much of a grip, but he cocked his head
and gave her a lazy, confident smile anyway. "Randi
Rhodes? That sounds familiar."

"That's what everyone says. You're probably thinking
of that wrestler." She deflected further discussion by
widening her smile and her gaze to include the other
men, who introduced themselves. Tony Pellegrini owned
the hair; the short one who looked better suited to ac-
countancy than police work was Fritz Gruber. She didn't
catch the dark-haired one's first name, but his last was
Casey.

"Where did you learn to shoot like that?" the first
victim—*Taz? Jazz?*—Casey asked.

She met his eyes as she devised then dismissed several
answers as too sarcastic, too flirtatious, or, worse, too
honest. "My daddy taught me. He thought hunting was
more interesting than needlepoint and more practical
than tap dancing." She paused, smiled again. "It seems
he was right."

He bit back a laugh and let his eyes drift over her
face, obviously pleased with what he saw. She looked
away without acknowledging it.

"Do you come here often?" Brian asked, appraising
her less subtly.

From the corner of her eye, she saw the dark one arch
that eyebrow again, this time posing a silent, unmistak-
ably male question involving territorial rights.

Sweet Jesus. This is turning into a Yankee pissin' match. And I'm what they're aiming for.

She pretended not to notice him and flashed a brighter smile at Brian Murphy. "I take it y'all are regulars. No, I don't come here often. As a matter of fact, this is my first visit."

"You just felt the urge for a quick, solitary game of paintball on a gray Sunday afternoon?"

Her eyes slid back to the speaker, Officer Tall, Dark, and Persistent. "Something like that." She paused. "I imagine you've had similar urges on occasion."

The corner of his mouth twitched again with suppressed laughter.

Nope. I'm not even tempted, honey, she replied by way of a deliberate blink. "It's been lovely talking with y'all, but I really do have to get gone. Y'all have a nice day. 'Bye now." She turned and walked slowly to her car, feeling their eyes on her every step of the way.

They were talking and laughing again by the time she drove past, giving them a polite little wave. From her rearview mirror, she watched them climb into their cars. His was the big navy blue pickup. *It figures.*

She turned out of the parking lot and headed toward the beach and her luxurious waterfront condo.

Indoor paintball had never struck Chas as a pastime worth much thought. He went to Jane's with his buddies to play a game; it was like tag football except there was less running involved and the floor was padded. That made it perfect for aging jocks with bad knees and tight lungs. After today, though . . . He let out a slow breath. After today, he'd think about it differently. *Christ.*

Randi Rhodes's lucky shot hadn't scared him; it had shaken him to his very core. Every hot childhood nightmare and cold adult dread had coalesced into one thick bullet of fear that had lodged in him the instant that gelatin cap exploded on his chest. As coincidences go, he'd come uncomfortably close to repeating history. He was thirty-eight, and he'd taken one shot to

the heart that came out of nowhere, just like his father had.

As he stood with his colleagues and watched her walk
away, Chas knew he would recover from the effects of
Randi Rhodes the woman pretty quickly. His recovery
from the effects of Randi Rhodes the sharpshooter was
going to take a bit more time. His body had already
reabsorbed the adrenaline rush, but a shadow had been
cast over his brain and it remained, haunting him. Chas
intended to shrug it off. He had to. He'd focus instead
on the shooter.

Randi Rhodes was attractive, and intelligent if the expression in her hazel eyes was any indication. After her
first hello, he added *dangerous* to that list. Her words
were like honey-dipped hollow-points delivered in a soft
Southern accent so smoky and lush it would make a
man break a sweat under the right circumstances—or the
wrong ones. Despite that smooth femininity, her posture
bespoke the confidence of a trained fighter, which had
a sexiness all its own. She'd been careful to keep her
arms free, her hands visible and unclenched. Relaxed
but ready. Her wariness was to her credit, given that she
was a lone woman interacting with four strangers, and
men at that. But there had been something else in the
back of her eyes as she'd held each of their gazes in
turn. Chas wasn't sure if it was the man in him or the
cop in him that wanted to know what that something
was, but he knew that was what he wanted.

"I think she liked me," Murphy said, as they all pretended not to watch her sit down in her green Mini
Cooper and swing her legs in the way etiquette books
prescribed.

"I don't think she liked any of us. That broad's got a
stick so far up her ass you could practically see it when
she opened her mouth," Pellegrini muttered.

Shaking his head in amused disgust, Chas watched his
colleague push a lock of that ridiculous hair out of his
eyes.

Gruber adjusted his glasses. "I think she has the hots
for Chas. She had a clear shot at each of us and she

nailed him first. Love at first sight—through the crosshairs."

"No wonder you can't get a date, Gruber. Get a grip," Chas said, hiding a smile as he watched Murphy frown. "That woman can't stand any of us. Probably can't stand men, period. We're just lucky that she remembered some of the rules and didn't nail every single one of us in the gonads."

"Shit, don't even fucking joke about that," Murphy shuddered, rubbing his right side.

"Nah. That broad's no lesbo; she's just uptight. I wouldn't mind trying to loosen her up. I mean, she's got no discernible tits, but that accent could give a guy a stiffy. Hey, anyone up for going to O'Grady's for a beer?" Pellegrini asked, flipping his keys from one hand to the other. "The women's pool teams start playing at two thirty. One of the teams doesn't wear underwear."

Chas couldn't help but laugh. "Christ, Pellegrini, you're a hound."

"Like you're not?" Murphy muttered, and Chas sent him a sideways glance.

Pellegrini shrugged. "Yeah, but I'm a purebred Italian hound. It's in my blood."

"I'll come down for the scenery, but I'm on duty at four," Gruber replied, sliding his wire-rimmed glasses back up to the bridge of his nose again.

"Can't. I told my mother I'd stop by before my sister heads back to Philly," Chas said, straightening from where he'd been leaning against Murphy's Explorer. He nodded at Randi Rhodes as she rolled past them with a dismissive wave.

"We should have asked her if she wanted to go out for a beer."

Chas grinned. "Give it up, Murph. She might sound like she grew up dusty and barefoot, but she's Champagne and foie gras now. Not beer and pretzels."

"And you would know."

Ignoring the implicit challenge, Chas clapped his resentful colleague on the shoulder. "I would, indeed, pal. Trust me. She's probably living in Darien with some retired investment banker twice her age and just came here to go slumming. Listen, I've got to go. Gruber, I'll see you later." He climbed into his pickup and pulled slowly out of the parking lot, heading toward Greenwich and his mother's house.

CHAPTER
3

Miranda pulled into the parking lot, stopped in front of her condo, and sighed. While the shiny black Hummer with vanity plates parked in her reserved space was obnoxious enough, the way her college roommate had parked the beast was what truly impressed her. Paxton had carelessly angled the huge, boxy vehicle across at least three spaces, precluding anyone else from parking anywhere near it. And it wasn't because she wanted to protect the paint job; it was just the way Paxton did things sometimes: thoughtlessly. But, Miranda reminded herself, Paxton balanced that talent with rare but genuine acts of thoughtfulness, like this trip, which rendered all frustrations moot.

She pulled her car into the condo's guest slot and jogged quickly up the broad front steps.

"Hunter, if you don't stop jumping on the couch, I will have to give you a time-out. And Bailey, don't you dare copy him. Now, please, I want you both to just sit still while Mommy finishes—Hunter, I told you to stop. . . ."

Paxton's well-bred New England voice carried to the foyer, and, taking a deep breath, Miranda pushed the already open door to the condo. She greeted the assembled group with a friendly smile and knew she wouldn't have to worry about any stray hugs coming her way.

Though sisters, Paxton and Jane were like different candies from the same box. They were both sweet in their own way, but Paxton hid her soft center beneath a crunchy, tart exterior, while Jane, younger by two years, was soft all the way through.

The tall blonde balancing precariously on top of a dining room chair in front of the two-story windows turned to look at her. "Oh, Miranda, I'm so glad you're back. I know I promised that I wouldn't bother you while you're staying here, but I just needed to get some measurements. I'll be gone in a few minutes. I'm rethinking the vertical blinds along the sliding doors. The last tenants kept asking for them, but I think drapes just work better. Hunter—"

"I prefer drapes, but since you're going to sell it anyway, blinds are probably the better choice." Miranda scooped up the four-year-old blond hurricane as he ran past her, and gave him an awkward hug. She concentrated hard on enjoying the mingled sticky-sweet smell of baby shampoo and apple juice that clung to him and ignored the cold shiver that babies always inspired. "How are you, precious? Are you giving your mama a headache?"

"That's not the half of it," his mother replied, watching them with an amused lift to her mouth. She turned back to the windows. "Listen, I hate to do this, but I have to cancel tonight. You'll be okay on your own, won't you?"

Miranda smiled and set the squirming child on his feet. "Of course I will. What's up?"

"Oh, everything. James is stuck in the city and won't be home until about ten, and I have to sign off on a bunch of drawings before the contractors will set foot in here." Paxton climbed off the chair and faced her, her flawless face contorted with something resembling concern. "You know they're starting on Wednesday, right? And you're sure you won't mind?"

"Like I've said every other time you've asked, Paxton, I don't mind at all. My schedule is flexible, and I keep odd hours anyway. And living in a luxury beachfront condo for free for a month is not what I consider a hardship."

Paxton waved a dismissive hand. "I had to get you up here somehow, and I knew if I invited you to stay at the house, you'd refuse. Rightly, I suppose. It's a madhouse most of the time. Anyway, since the children arrived, the only time I get to see you is when you're up here on a book tour or for some Smith College thing. Now, are you positive the builders and the painters—"

"—are not going to be in my way. Yes, I am, and if they are, I'll take my laptop and go into the dining room, or my bedroom. Or onto the deck."

"Forget the deck. It's the third of November. It will be snowing in a few weeks."

"Whatever." Miranda tossed a handful of dark hair over her shoulder. "You offered me the condo because of the workmen, right? You wanted someone to stay here while it's being renovated, and I wanted to come up for a visit. Nothing has changed. Stop worrying and stop apologizing. It's a win-win situation."

"Okay, okay. Now, just because we had to cancel tonight, that doesn't mean that we're not still on for Tuesday."

"Feel free to cancel that, too." Miranda set her purse on the high table behind the couch and walked into the kitchen.

"Oh, no, I most certainly won't," Paxton said briskly, carelessly dragging the Chippendale—*real* Chippendale—chair back to the dining room, where it joined its nine siblings around the oval table. "You're going to be here for four weeks, and you might as well have a companion."

"You make it sound as though my mystery date is a cocker spaniel."

Paxton flashed her a smile. "His eyes are just as dark and dreamy, but no, he's all male."

"Human?" Miranda asked with a sideways glance.

"Intensely."

Great. Miranda leaned against the polished granite countertop as she sipped Coke from a heavy crystal tumbler. "I appreciate your interest, honey, but I don't need a boyfriend."

Paxton glanced pointedly at the stack of Mel Gibson videos ready to be returned to Blockbuster. "I'll neither argue nor concede that point. But I will state for the record that sixteen-year-olds have boyfriends, Miranda. You're thirty-two. You need a companion, an escort, and probably an L-O-V-E-R. You broke up with Jack over a year ago."

"Josh. Despite that, I neither need nor want any of the above. As of yesterday, this vacation became a working vacation. I need some girlfriend time, lots of writing time, and a little time off for good behavior."

Paxton arched an elegant blond eyebrow. "Nonsense. We're heading into the holiday season. If you arrive at parties without a date, you'll be at the mercy of people who want to rub shoulders with someone famous and men who want to hop into B-E-D with you."

"Hop into what, Mommy?"

"Shh, Hunter, I'm talking to Miranda," she replied without taking her eyes off her quarry.

"I'm quite adept at keeping mercenary men out of my B-E-D, but if it will make you happy, I could carry a G-U-N," her quarry replied lightly. "I'm a decent shot."

"Good heavens, Miranda, don't even joke about that. You're not in Georgia anymore."

She swallowed a smile. "I appreciate your concern, Paxton, but I won't be invited to anything because I don't know anyone up here. And if I ever actually *was* famous, I no longer am, so you have nothing to worry about."

"You're wrong on both counts. Lots of people remember your name. It's not as if you've stopped writing. Your books are still in the stores. And you know my parents and us, and you know Jane." She made a face. "Not that she'll be invited to anything A-list. But as my guest, you'll be invited to *everything*. The invitations started coming in a month ago. And that's what Tuesday night is all about: being prepared."

"In that case, I need a Boy Scout, not a boyfriend." Miranda crossed the room to sit on the sofa. "What's the matter, Bailey?" She reached for the fussy two-year-old but immediately pulled back. "Oh, mercy. Paxton, do something about this child. She's well beyond toxic," she said, turning her head away from the source.

A grin crossed Paxton's cameo face. "You're just as maternal and cuddly as ever, I see. Come here, baby," she crooned. She carried the earthily aromatic miniature likeness of herself across the room to the large, well-used Louis Vuitton satchel that served as her diaper bag.

"So what's his name?" Miranda asked casually, looking away as Paxton nuzzled the platinum-blond wisps covering her daughter's head.

"I'm not telling you anything about him."

"Why not?"

"Because I know you," Paxton replied flatly. "You'll research him and find at least four things about him that you won't like before you ever meet him."

"You won't tell me anything? Why, that's hardly fair, Paxton. I'm sure you've told him things about me. At least tell me if he's taller than me. What about a criminal record?" Miranda teased, knowing her only hope of getting anything out of Paxton was by stealth or by mistake.

"Honestly, Miranda. Of course he's taller than you, and he's much more worthy of you than that insipid Jake ever was. *He* was a total drip."

"His name is Josh, and he *is* a total drip. He said he's going to wait for me."

Paxton swung her head sharply and fixed her laserlike blue eyes on Miranda. "He said that *when*? And he's going to wait *where*? You're not still living with him, are you?"

"No. I moved out in January. He just e-mails me every time he gets—"

"Horny?" Paxton asked with an edge to her voice. "That's when they usually get in touch."

"What's horny?"

The blonde rolled her eyes in despair. "This is a grown-up conversation, Hunter. Go find your truck. We're going to be leaving in a minute."

Miranda laughed both at Paxton and at the thought

of Josh getting horny. He would never have used that term. *Aroused,* maybe, or *amorous,* but never *horny.* "I never bothered to ask about his motivation, but I doubt it was that. I was going to say that I think he wants me back every time he gets his mortgage statement, bless his heart. We used to split the bill."

"See what I mean? Mercenary men. Now—" Paxton caught herself before she uttered even the first sound of The Mystery Date's name. "That was close. He's nothing like Josh, in any respect, so I can guarantee you won't be bored. As far as criminal behavior is concerned, I know that he and James were arrested when they were fifteen for streaking along Greenwich Avenue on New Year's Eve while under the influence of some rather expensive Champagne they'd filched from his grandfather's wine cellar. As for the rest, I'll only say that he's gorgeous and charming, smart, straight, single, and employed. The latter is optional. None of us can figure out why he does what he does, but he insists. He grew up in Greenwich," she added. "Old money. *Lots* of it."

"Thank goodness for that. I just can't stand dealing with new money," Miranda said lightly. "It's so stiff and crinkly and hard to separate."

"Go ahead and make fun, Miranda. It may not mean anything to you, but it does to others. He's a darling. He went to Dartmouth and has a degree in comparative literature."

Great. "He'll dismiss me the minute he finds out what I do. Why put either of us through it, darlin'?"

"See? That's exactly why I said I wasn't going to tell you anything." Paxton shrugged. "Just don't tell him what you do."

Miranda shook her head. "It's unavoidable. 'What do you do for a living?' is the most frequently asked question in this nation. People use it to establish personal value and social rank. It's like dogs on the leash sniffing each other."

"Good God, Miranda, that's vulgar."

"I know it is, honey, but it's true. I think it's a little bit more difficult for you to understand because your answers to that sort of question were always the right ones. You're the blond, blue-eyed, tennis-playing, cocktail-partying Anne Paxton Shelby Clarke of the New Canaan Paxtons and the Westport Shelbys, and you married into the Greenwich Clarkes, and you were an eight-hundred-dollar-an-hour Wall Street lawyer until two years ago."

"Honestly, Miranda. I never billed out at more than six. And that was standard for the Street. I mean, for what I did."

Miranda rolled her eyes. "I apologize. But my point is that I'm Randi Rhodes, a rootless Southern orphan who writes romance novels for a living. Paxton, honey, people don't smirk at you when you introduce yourself. They curtsy."

"They don't have to smirk at you, either. You don't have to introduce yourself as 'Randi Rhodes, romance novelist.' That's just a pen name, after all. It's not really you. Just introduce yourself as 'Miranda Lane, writer.' After all, one of your books did rather well. It was on *The New York Times* list, wasn't it?"

"The extended list, and only in paperback," Miranda replied in mock apology.

"Well, that's still pretty good. And saying you're just a writer is perfectly respectable."

Miranda blinked twice to deflect the insult she knew was unintentional. "I suppose it is, Paxton. But I don't lie about what I do. I love what I do, and I'm not embarrassed by it. I just wish other people wouldn't be embarrassed for me."

Paxton paused in her diapering operations and glanced over her shoulder. "Sometimes I just don't understand you, Miranda."

"I know, sugar. It's part of your charm."

Chas laid his keys on the faded Formica countertop and pulled open the refrigerator to grab a Coke. Tilting the bottle to his lips, his gaze swept the kitchen out of sheer habit. It hadn't changed much from his childhood, nor from his mother's childhood for that matter. The painted wood cabinets and drawers had been white for as long as he could remember, and the black-and-white checkerboard floor had been laid during the last major upgrade—sometime in the late 1950s, well before he was born. Starched white see-through curtains still hung at every one of the old wooden windows. Above the sink there was a photograph of his father, taken in that very kitchen. Two little boys dangled by their arms, which were slung around his neck, and a lace-swathed baby lay in his arms—

Don't.

"Chas, is that you?"

"I'm just grabbing a soda, Mom. I'll be right there," he called through the propped-open door that led into the butler's pantry and, beyond that, into the dining room.

Bottle in hand, he strolled through the house, stopping when he reached the doorway of the large chintz-filled, hardwood-floored living room. "It looks like Mattel exploded in here."

"We're playing Barbies," a little voice chirped as a small dark head popped up from the far side of one of the couches. His mother, his sister, and his nieces, Corinne and Emily, aged five and six, were smiling up at him from their places on the floor. They all sat cross-legged in a semi-circle amid a sea of miniature pink satin ball gowns, faux-fur stoles, impossibly high heels, and black vinyl biker duds.

"I don't see Ken," he said with a frown.

"We don't like boy dolls."

"They don't have pretty clothes."

He nodded with a gravity to match his nieces'. "I agree. Boys' clothes are never as much fun to play with as girls' are." He glanced at his sister, Julie, who had trained her dark, lecturing eyes on him, although above a smiling mouth. Her small glasses had been pushed past her forehead and were nestled in her short, dark curls. "What gives? I thought you would be packed and waiting next to the car, tapping your foot because I'm ten minutes late."

"We decided to leave tomorrow. Mitigating circumstances." She nodded toward the dolls and their wardrobe. "Care to join us?"

"Mom, no!"

"He's a boy."

"Thanks anyway. Maybe another time." He eased himself into a wing chair at the edge of their world and set his drink on a coaster in a small sea of framed family photographs. He glanced away from the one partially obscured by the bottle. It was his father in dress blues, much too young to look so stern. It had been taken the day he graduated from the police academy. Chas knew without needing to see it that his own graduation picture was just behind it. The physical resemblance between them was unnerving at the best of times. Right now, with the dull ache of Randi Rhodes's impact still throbbing in his chest, he could do without the reminder.

"I just met someone whose name sounds familiar, but I can't place it. Do either of you know a woman named Randi Rhodes?"

His mother and sister looked at each other, and something flashed between them before they looked back at him. His mother slid her reading glasses off her nose to let them dangle at the end of their gold chain against her dark turtleneck. Her bright blue eyes held amused curiosity. "How does she spell her name?"

Uh-oh. "I don't know."

"What does she look like?"

He shrugged. "She's about five-eight, slim, long dark hair, hazel eyes. Attractive. She's Southern, with an accent you could cut with a knife."

"You *met* her?" Julie asked, scooting up from the floor onto the chair behind her. "Here in Greenwich? Today?"

"Well, in Stamford, about half an hour ago. Do you know her?" he asked again.

Julie blinked at him, then smiled, and Chas braced himself. He knew that look. It was trouble.

"Not personally," she replied. "She's one of my favorite authors. Where did you meet her?"

"*How* did you meet her?" His mother stood up and brushed off her dark gray slacks.

This was getting serious. Even his nieces were watching him intently, their dolls temporarily forgotten. "What does she write?"

The women looked at each other, matching smiles breaking on their faces. "Romances."

Taking another pull at his Coke, he let this sink in. A full minute later he still couldn't picture the attractive woman with a fighter's stance and bad taste in men—if the looks she gave Murphy were any indication—writing steamy, flowery fluff. "You're kidding."

"No, we're not."

"Why is she in town? How did you meet her?" Julie repeated, then looked at her mother innocently. "Maybe she's on a book tour. Does she have a new book out?"

"No. Not until next spring, I think."

They were stalling, and not even trying to lie convincingly, which meant they were waiting for him to break the information deadlock. "I met her at Jane's paintball gallery," he offered. "She's a hell of a shot."

"Language," his nieces chided him in unison, then returned their attention to their dolls.

"My most profound apologies, ladies."

"What's profound?"

"Paintball?"

"It means special, Corey, dear," his mother said. "Whatever was she doing at a paintball gallery?"

Scaring the hell out of me. "Target practice," he replied dryly. "Anyway, we met her outside afterward. Are her books any good?"

"You can determine that for yourself. There are copies in the library."

His sister raised a dark eyebrow. "You're full of questions, Chas. She must have made an impression on you."

"In a manner of speaking." Wearing a grin that wasn't entirely authentic, he strolled out of the room. "Which shelf would they be on, Mom?"

"Next shelf down, to the right."

Chas glanced over his shoulder to see his sister lounging in the library's doorway, an amused tilt to her lips. "Thanks."

He found the books and slid them off the shelves. The dust jackets showed dreamy pastel renderings of sunswept beaches and shady, moss-draped bungalows. The back cover held a photograph of her nestled on a low, crooked branch of a gnarled but majestic magnolia wearing slim-fitting jeans, a thick turtleneck sweater, and a sly half smile. She was barefoot. Bare fingered. Toe ringed. Sexy as hell. *There's no way a woman like her would go for a guy like Murphy.*

"So is she the same woman you met?"

"Indeed she is," he murmured, glancing up at his sister. "What?"

She walked into the room with a triumphant hint to her growing smile. "I just don't ever remember you researching a woman before. At least not openly."

"That could be because you live two hundred miles away."

"Mmmm, could be. But I haven't always lived two hundred miles away, and you've gone through a *lot* of women." She perched on the back of the deep leather sofa.

He was not about to take the bait. "It says here she went to Smith."

"She did."

"Do you know her?" he asked again.

"No, but Paxton does. They were roommates for a couple of years. Her real name is Miranda Lane."

So this is the mystery woman Paxton set me up with. He returned his eyes to the picture. Something about her was irresistible. He looked back at his sister. "Why haven't I met her before? Was she at Paxton's wedding?"

"She lives in Atlanta and didn't make it to the wedding. Medical emergency, as I recall. What do you mean that she's a hell of a shot? Did she win the game? Or did she just shoot you?"

"Both. She took down four of us with four shots."

Julie raised her eyebrows in admiration. "That's good shooting."

"That's damned good shooting." Not realizing he'd

dropped his gaze to the photograph again, he brought his eyes back to his sister's face. "I'm sorry. What did you say?"

"My, my, Chas. It's not like you to let your attention wander."

He lifted one patronizing eyebrow and she laughed again.

"I said that had to hurt in more ways than one. Where did she get you?"

He waited a beat, then tapped the center of his chest. "I never saw it coming."

Her smile faded. "Chas," she started softly.

"Don't go there, Jules." He put the book on the desk and folded his arms across his chest. "I shouldn't have told you."

"But—"

"Julie, it was a game of paintball."

"This time."

Chas bit back a reply. The career choice he'd made was a common though unpopular topic in his mother's house and had been for fifteen years. Although Mary Casey had raised her children to respect everything their father had lived for and died for, she hadn't been pleased when, one by one, all three of them entered law enforcement. Julie and their brother, Joe, had gone to law school and, afterward, had taken jobs as prosecutors with different federal agencies. Only Chas had followed his father's footsteps exactly by entering the police academy.

"Have you even considered the board of directors' offer?" Her eyes flashed with anger.

"I reviewed it."

"That's not what I asked."

"Am I under direct or cross-examination, Counselor?" he asked mildly.

She didn't reply. She just glared at him.

Chas shrugged and gave her an easy smile, which belied the annoyance tightening his gut. "I have no intention of considering their offer. I don't want it. I'm not interested in a desk job."

"Oh, for God's sake, Chas, it's hardly a desk job. You'd have directors and vice presidents reporting to you," she snapped. "You'd be chief security officer of a Fortune 500 company. *Your* company."

"As I recall, the title comes with a desk," he replied dryly, determined not to get into it with her. He'd had enough run-ins with women in the last twenty-four hours. "Besides, I'm not qualified for the position. I'm not a businessman and I'm not a security expert. I'm a cop."

She dismissed the argument with an annoyed flick of her wrist. "You spent three years of nights and weekends driving up to New Haven to get an MBA. Don't tell me that was for fun."

Here we go. "That was for my résumé. I thought it would look good when I become Stamford's chief of police."

"I don't buy that for a minute. You're not going to let the family down, Chas. It's not your style. And you know you'd be an excellent CSO for a lot of reasons, not the least of which is that you have a vested interest in protecting the company's reputation and assets. Right now, Mom and Granddad are the only Brennans in the company. She'd prefer not to be, and he wanted to retire years ago, but you know he won't until one of us steps on board."

"Go for it."

"If I didn't live in Philadelphia, and have a husband with a job there, and have two small children, I would." She paused. "When are you going to give it up, Chas?" she asked in a deceptively soft voice. "Turn in the badge and give up your gun? Nobody but you thinks you have to finish what Dad started. And nobody wants you to get killed for it. That would sort of defeat the purpose, wouldn't it?"

Damn her. He counted to five. Then ten. "Julie, I'm not going to argue about it. It's my life, my career, and my choice. Drop the subject."

Julie closed her eyes and, a moment later, stood up. "Are you staying for dinner? Anna's making stuffed pork chops and the girls begged her for pineapple upside-down cake."

He shook his head. "Thanks anyway. I'm on duty at four."

*   *   *

Perched on the edge of his desk at police headquarters, Chas scanned the sheaf of papers in his hand. "Busy day."

"Pretty good for a Sunday," his day-shift counterpart replied as he logged off the computer and stood up. "One attempted armed robbery on the west side and one pregame assault down at Finnerty's again. Two broken fingers and a broken nose, one smashed TV. Same stupid bastards as last time."

"Happens every time the Jets play Denver," Chas murmured.

"I didn't know they needed a reason."

Chas gave a silent laugh.

"I heard you got nailed by a girl."

"Pellegrini can't keep his mouth shut, can he?"

The other detective chuckled. "It was Gruber, actually."

Chas looked up as his commanding officer walked in. "Captain," he said with a nod.

The older man smiled. "Heard you got nailed by a girl, Casey."

"Some girl," Chas muttered. "Four shots, four cops. She belongs on the goddamn SWAT team. Did you see the bruise on Murph?"

"Must hurt like a mother. Where the hell did a writer learn to shoot like that?"

How the hell did he know she was a writer? "She said her daddy taught her," Chas replied blandly, hiding his surprise. "She's a writer?"

The other detective nodded with a laugh. "Murphy's got the hots for her. Looked her up on the Web. She writes smutty stuff. Those porny romance novels."

Murphy. "Sounds like you're a big fan," Chas said with a grin, ignoring the ping of annoyance that came out of nowhere.

"Yeah, right. I put on my frilly slippers and read romance novels just before I take my nightly bubble bath," the other man said sarcastically. "Well, you guys should have some fun tonight. The weather's not going to keep them indoors."

The captain nodded as the detective left the room, then looked at Chas. "Scores came back."

Chas met his eyes. "And?"

"Yours were the highest. I'm meeting with the chief in about ten days to make recommendations. The commission meets a few days after that. O'Malley's decided not to retire, so there will only be one slot open. No reason that I can see why you won't get it. Keep your nose clean anyway."

"Who else is on the list?"

"Murphy, Daniels, and Colucci."

Piece of cake. "Thanks." Chas stood up and walked into the briefing room. He had the highest exam scores and the cleanest record of the four of them, and he'd worked the hardest for the promotion. He deserved it. Nothing could change that. He wouldn't *let* anything change that. It was the second goal he'd set for himself since joining the force fifteen years ago. The first one was staying alive.

As the day squad completed their reports and the night shift's briefing ended, the radios began to crackle. Chas and Gruber headed out to their car. Minutes later they pulled up outside a west-side sports bar, parking next to three marked squad cars and two ambulances. The shouting from inside could be heard on the street, where a crowd had gathered.

"What's up?" Chas asked a uniformed officer stationed outside the door.

The older man shook his head disgustedly. "Halftime pool game. Someone knocked someone else's quarters off the table. First one threw a punch, someone pulled out a chain." He jerked his head toward the stretcher being wheeled out of the building. "Caught a beer bottle in his cheek. The cutter dropped it and ran out the back."

As the detectives walked through the door of the dingy bar, Chas did a double take. *Not again.* Four burly women lay facedown on the filthy floor, hands secured behind their backs, shouting insults at each other. Other patrons were still gathered along the perimeter of the room. A few had returned their attention to the game.

Gruber looked at him, his eyes alight with a challenge. "Okay, is there some moon thing going on? Chicks don't usually fight this much. And never over football."

"Hey, asshole, don't call us chicks. And we were shooting pool."

"My mistake. You're obviously the flower of New England womanhood," he replied.

"You prick. This is sexual harassment."

Chas looked down at the eight thick, muscular legs visible between the tops of their Doc Martens and the bottoms of their workout shorts. His eyes continued up to the abundance of Lycra-covered backsides and over the volumes of flesh spilling out of tight shirts that had become untucked and hiked up during the fray. Long, beer-soaked hair clung to their heads.

Charming.

"No luck there, sweetheart," Gruber replied with a grin. "Believe me, there's nothing sexual about it. So what happened? You stopped for a few beers on the way home from cheerleading practice and the boys didn't want to let you play?"

"Shut the fuck up," the woman nearest him muttered.

One of the uniformed officers approached Chas. "Wagon's here."

Gruber reached down to grab the most talkative of the women by the upper arm to help her to her feet. Her booted foot shot out and kicked him in the ankle. With a curse, he reached for his foot and, in the process, dropped her on the floor with a thud and a whoosh as the breath was knocked out of her.

"You try that again and I'll put you in leg irons," he said, gripping his ankle.

"Kiss my ass," she gasped.

"No, thanks."

"I gotta pee," the one next to her stated.

"Me, too."

"You'll have to hold it," Gruber barked.

"I gotta pee, you prick. If you don't let me, my bladder's gonna explode, and then I'll sue the shit out of this fucking city," the first one shouted.

"You're violating her human rights," the other mouthy one yelled.

"Christ," Chas muttered, and pinched the bridge of his nose, then walked outside to see if there was a female officer available. It was going to be a long night.

CHAPTER
4

"Criminal Investigations Bureau. Officer Prescott."

Miranda glanced at her watch. It was five minutes after nine on Tuesday morning. She'd been waiting twenty-four hours for this officer's vacation to end and waiting five more minutes on hold just to hear his voice. Now that she heard it, she was even more depressed. It wasn't the smooth voice of a professional public relations guy, as she had hoped. Nor was it the happy, energized voice of a guy who had just come back from vacation. It was the unexceptional, no-nonsense voice of a cop in the public relations office, abrupt and heavy from years of arranging tours for elementary school children and scheduling public safety lectures at senior centers. And dealing with requests like hers. It would take a lot to make that voice sound enthusiastic.

Miranda stifled a sigh. It would take a lot to make her own voice sound enthusiastic. The whole situation sucked. She'd spent Sunday night and all of Monday and Monday night skimming the entire Stephanie Plum series, and every Suzanne Brockmann book she could find, and every Linda Howard, just to study their alpha-to-the-max heroes. And she'd rented an entire spectrum of movies this time, much to the amusement of the sex-on-the-brain high-school boys behind the desk at Blockbuster. She brought home Bruce and Arnold, DeNiro and Pacino, Dennis Quaid in *The Big Easy*—in truth more just to hear *that line* again—and two John Travolta movies. One was *Michael*, but she figured she deserved some sweetness and romance after all the blood, sweat, and tears she had already endured, and would continue to suffer through.

Between plunges into that steamy sea of testosterone, she'd spent a lot of time plotting and writing, then deleting and replotting again—in her sleep, in the shower, and at the keyboard since four this morning. It hadn't done much good. At the moment her heroine, Taylor, was elegantly posed in a chic suit and tasteful slingbacks, looking carefully at her manicured nails, back turned toward the hero. Her message, which Miranda was receiving loud and clear, was, *I am not interested in this hairy, oversexed buffoon. Find me a real man who can speak like an adult and isn't always looking at my behind.* Of course, Taylor, being Southern, was much too polite to reveal this in dialogue.

The hero-buffoon, a.k.a Dirk, on the other hand, wasn't Southern and wasn't subtle. This Yankee cop lounged opposite Taylor, tousled and unshaven, wearing not a thing other than sexily baggy, low-slung Levi's. His bare, hair-matted torso rose from the waistband of those jeans like an inverted triangle of boldly sculpted heaven. His pecs bulged, his biceps—cockily folded across those pecs—bulged, and his crotch bulged visibly from inside those bad-boy jeans. He was smirking at Miranda from the pages of her manuscript with dark, sleepy-lidded eyes and a full, pouty mouth, taunting her and telegraphing a message along the lines of *Yo, author-lady, find me a real woman, not some prissy, uptight china doll with profanity and body-hair issues.*

In short, neither of her characters was cooperating in the slightest, and Miranda knew her chances of getting them into bed with each other within a reasonable time frame were slightly lower than her chances of coming up with a workable peace plan for Northern Ireland. It was going to be a long, painful three weeks if she didn't get some serious inspiration. Soon.

With any luck at all, it was waiting for her on the

other end of the phone, in the very bored voice of Officer Prescott.

She forced a smile onto her face and into her voice. "Good morning, Officer Prescott. My name is Randi Rhodes. I'm an author doing some research for a book in which one of the main characters is a Stamford police officer. I'm wondering if it would be possible to arrange an interview with a member of your department so that I can—"

"Just a minute."

She heard some muffled conversation in the background, then papers shuffling. "I'm sorry, Ms. . . . . Roads, was it?"

"Yes, Randi Rhodes, R-H-O-D-E-S."

"Who do you want to talk to?"

"I was hoping you could arrange for me to speak with a detective in the vice squad."

"It's always vice."

"I'm sorry?"

"I said, it's always vice. What's with that?" She heard him sigh heavily and mutter something under his breath before he spoke to her again. "Anyway, we can't do vice. If the chief clears it, you can talk to someone in the Crimes Against Persons bureau or Crimes Against Property. What's your preference?"

Vice. "Um, Crimes Against Persons, I guess."

"Okay. You have a letter from a publisher?"

She looked at the phone in surprise. "What sort of letter do you mean?"

"A letter that says they're going to publish your book."

"As a matter of fact, I do."

"You'll have to provide us with a copy. New rules since nine-eleven," he muttered, clearly unimpressed with the rules, or maybe with her, or all of the above.

"That's fine. I'll bring a copy with me."

"When do you need to talk with someone?"

She closed her eyes and spoke softly through a hopeful grimace. "Well, sir, I would prefer to conduct an interview as soon as it could be arranged."

"Let me take your name and number and I'll get back

to you as soon as I can. Maybe this afternoon. Is there anything else you're going to want? Like a ride-along?"

Be still, my heart. "If that could be arranged, I would appreciate it."

"You'll have to sign a personal safety waiver. You'll also have to wear a bulletproof vest at all times and, no, you can't carry a gun, play with the lights or siren, touch the radio or computer, or yell, 'Freeze, dirtbag.' In fact, you stay in the car, in the backseat. And it won't be for a whole shift. Maybe a few hours."

"All right. I appreciate the information."

"No problem."

I'll bet.

Finally, he cleared his throat and asked her for her telephone number.

When the call ended, she drained the last of her coffee and stood up. "Good girl, Miranda. You get a reward for selling out so easily. Time to go shopping and spend the rest of that advance before they make you give it back. But first, coffee with Detective Murphy."

Purgatory, Miranda decided as she drove through downtown Stamford. It was the only fitting description of the hour she had just spent in the company of Brian Murphy. Not hot enough for Hell and not sweet enough for Heaven, the meeting had just been a serious waste of time that she thought would never end.

When his e-mail arrived through her Web site on Sunday night, she'd been in a rotten mood and therefore trolling for fan mail. Not that she received much anymore, but desperate times called for desperate methods of procrastinating. She'd thought his message was shy and sweet, almost naive. She realized now the correct word was *bumbling,* but, if nothing else, it had seemed sincere. She'd written back and a brief real-time chat had ensued, during which he'd suggested meeting for coffee after assuring her he was not some lunatic. He was a detective in the Crimes Against Persons unit of the Stamford Police Department, and *that* was why she had agreed to meet him. That and the very mistaken assumption that he was a sensitive, intellectual beta male

and by interviewing him and using the cop-related information she learned, she could keep herself, her agent,
and her editor happy.

Thoroughly annoyed with herself, she pushed her foot
to the floor and took off at the green light faster than
she needed to. *The only critical information I gathered
was that my male radar is seriously out of whack.* Far
from being sensitive or intellectual, Brian Murphy was
a dull, conceited, potty-mouthed boor and a seriously
unskilled flirt. And he hadn't shown the slightest inclination to talk about being a cop. He'd wanted to talk about
first-datish things. Only her Southern upbringing pre-
vented her from pointing out that meeting for coffee at
Borders and signing dog-eared copies of her books for
his mother was *not* a first date, in her opinion. The very
least he could have done was buy new copies. There
were several on the shelves. She'd checked.

The whine of a siren shook her out of her annoyed
fog. She glanced up to see flashing blue lights drawing
close in her rearview mirror. Slowing down, she pulled
to the side of the road to let the police cruiser pass, and
felt a sickening solidification in her belly as it, too,
slowed down and pulled in behind her. *Great. More
cops.*

"What is it with police officers in this town? If I get
a ticket, I'm writing it off as a research expense," she
grumbled, digging in her purse for her wallet. She
glanced into the rearview mirror again. "Well, for pity's
sake, son, get over here and say howdy. I haven't got
all day."

A few moments later she saw a young, fresh-faced
officer get out of the squad car and approach her vehicle
with that peculiar cop swagger. She lowered her window
and smiled. He didn't smile back, just skimmed at her
with that head-back, eyes-down look. *Typical.*

"Good afternoon, Officer."

"Good afternoon, ma'am. Do you know why I pulled
you over?"

"No, Officer, I sure don't," she replied, infusing her
voice with enough Southern sugar to put him into a dia-
betic coma.

He didn't seem impressed. "Your license plates are expired. You were also doing ten miles over the legal limit. It's thirty-five miles an hour along here."

Good Lord, he's trolling for a date. She blinked twice and managed not to laugh. "I'm so sorry. I'm new in town. I guess I overlooked the sign. There was a sign, wasn't there?"

"There's a sign about fifty yards back. How long ago did you move here?"

"Four days, but I'm just visiting."

"Welcome to Stamford. May I have your license, registration, and insurance, please?"

"Here's my license. The other documents are in the glove box." He nodded at her unspoken question, and she reached across the seat to open the compartment on her dashboard. He had just taken everything from her and was turning to take them back to his car when something behind her car caught his attention.

She glanced into the mirror to see a suspiciously familiar navy-blue pickup pull in behind the squad car. Tall, dark Paintball Victim Number One dropped out of the cab of the truck and walked toward her car with that same cop swagger.

Surely life isn't this cruel.

She watched him approach, coming to a stop next to Officer Friendly. He leaned against her car, one palm on her roof, the other on his left hip. His gray tweed sport coat gaped open, revealing his gun, dark and ominous against his Dockers-clad right hip, and the broad expanse of chest she'd assaulted two days earlier. He didn't bother to remove his Revos—naturally—but she could tell he was looking straight at her. Something about that smile begging to be let loose from behind serious but twitching lips.

He was proprietary and in control—and pure, unadulterated alpha.

She blinked and focused on the third button of his white shirt for a moment as she fought a wavelet of panic. *Be rational about this. You need one. He is one.*

She drew in a slow breath. *Why not?* All she needed was a face for Dirk—something to focus on. She didn't need to spend any time with him to get that. And she could get the other stuff from the cop she was going to interview, or from books, or she would just make it up. She took a shallow breath. *It could work.*

Three days ago she would have described him as her average nightmare. Today, however, by editorial decree, he was her greatest fantasy. She glanced up at his face. Despite being a cop, he was attractive: tall and dark, with a mouth made for laughter. She chewed on her lip thoughtfully. If she took some artistic license—made that mouth poutier, his attitude cockier, those shoulders even broader—he could probably fulfill another woman's fantasies. For instance, her editor's.

She smiled into the dark lenses that hid his eyes. *I dub thee my hero.*

"Hey, Hotshot. Do you go looking for trouble or does it just find you?" he asked in a voice she'd have to sand-paper to make it Dirk's.

"It just finds me, like you seem to," she replied with soft voice and a silky smile. "Or is this a coincidence?"

Both sets of male eyebrows rose. "Life is full of happy coincidences like this one," Alpha Cop said, with a glance at the officer who had pulled her over. He gave a curt nod. "Mick."

"Hi, Chas. So this is Hotshot, huh?"

"That's right. What's she been up to? Bank robbery? Drag racing?"

"Ten miles over and expired plates."

Chas laughed out loud.

Beautiful sound. Beautiful mouth.

"Were you bored?" he asked.

The uniformed cop smiled, not at all sheepish. "It's been a slow day. Besides, she's cute."

"I know," Chas replied meaningfully.

"It figures." With a defeated smile, the young cop returned the paperwork to Miranda. "Have a good day, ma'am. You should take care of those plates as soon as you can. See ya 'round, Chas."

Despite her best intentions, a fresh splinter of annoyance slid under Miranda's skin and began to fester at the easy assumptions that had just been made by both

men. "Excuse me, Officer," she said in the softest, most
polite, most Southern belle-like voice she could manage
under the circumstances. Both men looked down at her.
"I'm just tickled that I've provided y'all with an opportunity to catch up, but weren't you going to give me a
ticket?"

The patrolman glanced meaningfully at Chas, who
shrugged; then they both looked back at her.

"You want me to write you a ticket?" Mick asked.

She gave him a couple of wide-eyed blinks for good
measure. "You pulled me over because I broke the law;
isn't that right? Two of them, in fact?"

"Yes."

"Then it just wouldn't be right if you didn't write me
a ticket."

He smiled. "Nothing says I have to write you a ticket,
ma'am. Besides, you know Chas."

Not nearly as well as he's willing to have you believe.
She smiled. "Actually, Officer, I *don't* know Chas, and
he doesn't know me. We met once. Briefly."

A doubtful Mick looked again toward a highly
amused Chas.

"Excuse me, Mick; I'm talking to you," she said, a
touch of vinegar in her honeyed voice.

Mick returned his gaze to her face, his expression both
less indulgent and less amused.

Chas interrupted with a light slap on the roof of her
car. The sound it made was rich with finality. "Hotshot,
it's been a pleasure, as always. Mick, I think you should
just say 'thank you' to the lady for reminding you to
carry out your sworn duty." A smile tugging at the corner of his mouth, he reached into the car, plucked the
paperwork out of her hands, and handed it to the
younger man. Then Chas turned away and walked back
to his truck.

Minutes later, as Miranda sat in her car wondering at
what point the Stupid Bug had sunk its big, sharp teeth
into her brain and started to chew, Mick returned from
his car and handed a ticket through the window for
her signature.

"Here you go, ma'am. Together the violations come

to two hundred dollars, and it's double points for the first offense. If you don't pay the ticket or schedule a court appearance within ten days, there will be a warrant issued for your arrest. Do you understand that?"

"Yes, I do."

"Okay." He straightened up, then bent down again. "Ma'am, I heard about the paintball. I don't know what the deal is, but if you don't mind me saying, you can't do better than Chas."

Miranda smiled at him tightly. "That remains to be seen, Mick. Thank you."

"Drive safely."

By four o'clock, Chas had finished running his errands, had been to the gym, and was just finishing up an hour on the pistol range. He was free until tonight, when he would meet up with James and Paxton—and Miranda, the most attractive smart-ass he'd met in a long time. Despite her behavior to the contrary, he could tell she was interested in him. Both times they'd met, she'd been studying him and not flirtatiously. She'd been appraising him, as if he were a science experiment. It wasn't flattering, but he wasn't sure he minded. He just wanted to know what was going on inside her head.

He pulled the clip out of his Glock and set the gun on the shelf in front of him. Pulling off his protective headphones, he pressed the button that brought the shot-up targets back to him.

"How did you do?"

He turned to see Murphy lounging against the corner of the three-sided stall and shrugged. "Not bad overall. Twenty rounds, looks like six holes on this one." He gestured to the approaching target.

"Nearly as good as Randi Rhodes."

Grow up. "She's some shot," Chas agreed with a grin that implied he'd missed the underlying insult. He reached for the punctured papers. "She gave me something to think about."

"Yeah." Murphy paused. "I heard we're both on the short list for the promotion."

That list is shorter than you think, you prick. "May the best man win. How's your bruise?"

"Huge and sore as hell." Murphy shifted his weight to his other hip and gave Chas a lazy smile. "In the interest of fair play, Casey, I just thought I'd let you know that I e-mailed her. And asked her out."

"Thanks, Murph, I appreciate that. Did she say yes?"

"We met for coffee this morning."

Ignoring the stab of irritation the information generated, Chas forced another grin as he reached for a cleaning cloth and began taking apart his gun. "That's it?"

Murphy's eyes narrowed slightly. "For today."

"Well, don't get your hopes up. She's only in town for a few weeks. Visiting a mutual friend. But, *in the interest of fair play,* if you'd like me to put in a good word for you when I see her tonight, I'd be happy to." He concealed the satisfaction that surged through him as Murphy's smile faded.

"You're seeing her tonight?"

"Just drinks and dinner." He shrugged casually.

"How the fuck do you do it, Casey?" The other detective's voice was tight with annoyance. "We only met her two days ago. You didn't even think she was cute."

Chas considered telling him the truth, then reconsidered. Murphy was a good cop but a whiny, scheming bastard otherwise. He never passed up an opportunity to take a dig at someone, and Chas had been a favorite target of his resentment since their days at the police academy.

"Sure I did. But I didn't see any point letting you know." He shrugged again. "As they say, there are the quick and the hungry, Murphy. I've never liked being hungry."

Would this day never end? Miranda squeezed her eyes shut and pinched the bridge of her nose but made sure to keep her irritation out of her voice. "No, Officer Prescott, I understand your point perfectly. I didn't specify, so I know you couldn't know that I need to interview a man. I apologize for not being clear, but I'm afraid that the detective I interview has to be a man. My character is a man, and it just won't be the same if I interview a woman."

"I'll see what I can do, Ms. Rhodes. Are you sure there aren't more criteria you're going to remember later?"

She bit her lip. If Brian Murphy was assigned to her, she'd deal with it, but if Chas Casey was—

Hold it. He might not be in that group. He might not even be a detective, she told herself firmly. He could be a uniform on his day off. Or the chief of police. He might not be a real cop at all. He hung out with cops and acted like a cop and walked like a cop, but that didn't mean he *was* a cop. He could be an FBI agent, or a mall security guard. Or just a poser with a license to carry concealed. "I'm sure, Officer."

"Call back tomorrow afternoon."

"Thank you again, Officer Prescott. I'll do that."

Miranda ended the call and went upstairs to prepare for the next round of Yankee torture: her mystery date. After the events of the last few days, she wasn't particularly in the mood for a companion, an escort, or an L-O-V-E-R, regardless of what Paxton said.

Slipping into a blissfully hot bath, she tried to picture a man who combined the best qualities of an educated cocker spaniel and a wealthy Boy Scout, but it was just too taxing. At this point, she decided, closing her eyes, she'd be happy if her date had a clean vocabulary, a steady pulse, and the ability to take a graceful hint. But she wasn't going to hold her breath.

The huge old Victorian was quiet except for the hiss of the radiators and the creaks and groans that Chas had long since failed to notice. He glanced at his watch. He had time for one more paragraph; then he had to get into the shower. The trouble was, he was having a hard time putting down Miranda's book. Not that the story was that compelling—romance novels were the last thing he'd pick up voluntarily—but he was definitely intrigued by the author. *How could such a saber-tongued tigress write such slow, dreamy prose?* He shifted on the well-worn, cracked leather sofa and propped a hand under his head.

Draped in a dress woven of cobwebs and shadows, Laura stood before him, backlit by the watercolor smudges of a summer twilight. Cicadas thrummed an endless cadence to welcome the encroaching darkness. Lavender and old roses lined the path that led down to the boathouse, and the heady richness of their scent drifted on the sea air, intoxicating him. Reed's hands hung envious at his sides, longing to replace the sultry breeze smoothing the silver-blond strands from Laura's face. But to touch her now would be to destroy her. Thus he stood, and watched, and waited.

He set the book aside and stretched. Since Sunday, he'd finished two of her books and this was his third. Her heroines appealed to him for the same reasons she did—they were sexy and smart—but her heroes concerned him. They were emasculated dweebs who exuded as much animal magnetism as a tub of wallpaper paste. *Kind of like Murphy.*

The very notion that her heroines were attracted to them was a tribute to Miranda's obviously rich imagination, just as her sex scenes were an indication of an equally rich fantasy life. They were delicately written, but packed a punch. He'd never again be able to think of tapioca pudding as just a child's dessert.

He was looking forward to seeing her tonight—legitimately, this time. He'd never been attracted to a woman who seemed intent on dismissing him. Possibly because he couldn't remember any attractive ones ever doing that. Perhaps he was getting jaded after twenty-five or so years of dating and just needed a challenge, but he was intrigued by Miranda and the faint chill in the air around her. She wasn't uptight, like Pellegrini had said, but neither was she a hair-sprayed, marriage-minded, sugarcoated Southern belle. There was too much going on behind her eyes. That was why he knew there was no way in hell she'd fall for Murphy—he was an asshole, and obvious about it.

He glanced at his watch then and, with a muttered curse, bolted off the couch, out of the small den, and up two staircases to the shower. Fifteen minutes later he was back downstairs, slipping on his shoes and shrugging on his blazer. Grabbing his keys and overcoat, he headed out the door. If not for a date with destiny, he thought with a grin, at least for a date with Miranda.

"I can't believe you're going out on a blind date with someone you know nothing about."

"That's sort of the point, isn't it?" Miranda held the phone between her shoulder and her left ear as she tried to fit the gold post through the hole in her right earlobe.

"But, I mean, you know *nothing* about him. He could be a loser."

Miranda switched the cordless phone to her other shoulder and repeated her effort on her left earlobe. "Look, Janey, I know you don't get along with her these days, but you have to admit that if there's one thing your sister knows, it's men. Y'all grew up together. You know better than I do that Paxton only dated nice guys, and now she's married to the best of the breed."

"Okay, I'll agree with the last statement. But she didn't tell you anything? I mean, if Paxton told you something, I might be able to figure it out and tell you about him."

"He went to Dartmouth."

"Okay, that rules out a few men. What did he study?"

"Comparative literature."

"Oh, for heaven's sake, Miranda, he's probably gay."

She slid her feet into her new black pumps, bought that morning in the moments between blowing her schedule with police-related boredom and blowing her budget on police-related research. "She said he's not."

"What does a straight man do in Stamford with a degree in comparative literature? He can't be a professor, or she would have told you where he did his other degrees."

"She wouldn't dare fix me up with a professor. I just spent six years with one and she knows I'd go screaming into the night at the prospect of spending time with another. He and James have been friends since they were kids. If he were the type of boy who pulled the wings off flies and set fire to the cat, you know James wouldn't let her set me up with him." Miranda traded the confines of the huge walk-in closet for the bathroom that was as big as her living room in Atlanta. "She also said he's old-money and doesn't have to work but does anyway. I assume he's a day trader or an art collector or something."

"Oh, wait a minute. Dartmouth. I know who it is." Jane burst out laughing. "This is too good to be true. It almost makes me want to call to congratulate her."

Miranda stopped moving and met her own eyes in the mirror above the marble-topped vanity. "Jane, honey, tell me everything you know this minute."

"No way."

"You just said you would."

"I lied. You have to call me tomorrow and tell me everything."

"There may not be anything to tell. The evening could be a total washout."

"It won't be. Trust me."

Miranda paused, her lip liner halfway to her mouth. "After you just lied to me? I don't think so, darlin'."

"Trust me," Jane repeated. "I went out with him once."

"Only once? What's wrong with him?"

"Absolutely nothing. It was a very long time ago. But that's all I'm going to tell you."

"Thanks for nothing, sugar," Miranda said. "I have to get off the phone right now or I'll be late. Are you really going to send me into the unknown without any more information?"

"Well, I'd go out with him again, but I doubt he'd ask me. Feel better?"

She blotted her lipstick gently. "No."

"Okay, here's my advice. Don't fall for him. Everyone does. Where are you going?"

"Chez Jean-Pierre. It's on Bedford Street near the police station."

"Oooh, nice. Leave plenty of time for finding a parking space, though."

"Great. Now for sure I'm going to be late. I'll talk to you later."

Miranda gave herself a final, stern look in the mirrored wall of the bathroom. Her hair was upswept and soft; her makeup and jewelry were understated. Her black miniskirt wasn't too short, her heels weren't too high, and her sapphire-blue angora sweater was on the baggy side of sexy.

"Casual yet elegant. Professional. Grown-up. Nervous as a virgin in a whorehouse," she muttered, and spun away from the mirror. "I'm way too old for this nonsense."

At the bottom of the large, curving staircase, she grabbed her small black purse, slipped into her long black coat, and headed out of her borrowed condo to her illegally tagged car to meet a dark-eyed stranger she wasn't supposed to fall for.

CHAPTER
5

After driving around the block twice and getting tangled up in downtown Stamford's apparently random system of one-way streets, Miranda finally found a parking structure that she thought might be somewhere close to where she was headed. She eased her Mini into the first available space and turned off her headlights. Grabbing her purse, she glanced around, then swung her legs out of the car. She closed the door, clicked the electronic lock, and looked up to see a broad chest looming before her. A scream died in her throat as she met those warm, dark, laughing eyes.

My hero.

She crossed her arms across and stood her ground, recovering from the rush of unwarranted panic. High heels and all, she still wasn't at eye level with him. And he had that command attitude going, she noticed with a cross between annoyance and exasperation. Confined as she was in the small space between her car and the next, she felt dwarfed. "Well, now, I wouldn't have bet my granny's garters on this."

Both eyebrows rose as he smiled back, idly flipping his keys around his index finger. "You're just full of surprises, Hotshot. After that big Southern-belle routine you pulled on poor old Mick this afternoon, I assumed you'd be polite the next time we met."

Ouch. She cocked her head and met his eyes and, on principle, refused to back down even by a step. Or a word. "I, on the other hand, somehow knew you'd be condescending."

He winced. "Bull's-eye again. You're dangerous even when you're not armed."

A man who surrenders that easily can't be all bad. Deciding to cut him just a little bit of slack, she bit back a smile and gave him a slow, steady blink. "It's not nice to sneak up on women, you know," she said mildly. "You scared me to death."

To his credit, he looked contrite. Part of her wished he didn't. "I'm sorry. I didn't mean to sneak up on you or to scare you. Don't you look around before you get out of your car?"

"I did, but you were in my blind spot." She paused, hoping it would soften the challenge in her words. "Besides, I don't usually have stalkers after me."

"How would you know? Maybe you overlook them, too." Amusement tugged at his lips. "And, for the record, I'm not stalking you."

He really does have a lovely mouth. She tried and failed to completely hide a smile. "So I'm supposed to believe this is just another happy coincidence?"

"Seems to be." Shaking his head in amused exasperation, he slid his hand around her elbow. "Come on," he said, urging her away from the car to walk with him toward the exit.

She froze at his touch, but immediately forced her body to relax. *You need this man. And he's being polite, not possessive.* Nevertheless, her first few steps were stiff-legged.

He glanced down at her. His gaze swept her face, most likely missing nothing. "You look hassled."

"It's all those one-way streets."

He looked away and she saw that his grin stopped just short of laughter. "There are three of them around here, and one is one block long. Where are you going? I'll walk you there so you don't get lost."

She had, at best, two more minutes to get in the proper frame of mind for a date. What she needed was solitude, not a skirmish. She decided to find out if he was the kind of guy who could take a hint. "Thank you, but I can find my own way."

"Where?"

"Excuse me?"

"You can find your own way where?"

She glanced at him, both amused and annoyed at his persistence. "Where I'm going. Why do you want to know, anyway?"

"Just curious. Who knows? We might be going to the same place."

Jane's laughter on the telephone flashed through her mind, freezing her brain for a moment. The odds were against it, she assured herself. *No cop would have a degree in comp lit, and no trust-fund baby or Dartmouth graduate would become a cop.* She said nothing, but as they left the brightly lit shelter of the parking structure and walked into the cold, glittering November drizzle, she shifted her arm. It slid easily out of his grasp. She took a step away from him, then drew her pashmina shawl over her hair to cover the rudeness of the action.

"You're the first woman I've seen actually use one of those. Usually women just toss them over their shoulders, and I spend all night picking them up off the floor."

"How gallant." It came out sharper than she'd intended, and she didn't meet his eyes.

"I try." His hand slid around her arm again, and she didn't like it any more the second time. Before she could pull away, he brought her to a slow stop, and then swung her in a quarter turn to face him. Unless it was a trick of the light, his were the darkest brown eyes she'd ever looked into, dark like bittersweet chocolate, and deep. "Why are you angry at me?"

Because you're a cop and I don't like cops. Because you're Dirk and I don't like Dirk. Because I need you and I don't want to. She dropped her gaze to his chin and gave a small laugh that she hoped sounded genuine. "I'm sorry. That last comment came out sharp, and I didn't mean it to. I don't know you well enough to be angry at you. But I know we rub each other the wrong way, and I'm getting suspicious about all these coincidental meetings." She glanced up, offering him a smile and a truce—and the opportunity to turn into Dirk by making a comment about rubbing her the right way.

Instead, he folded his arms across his chest and turned back into a cop. "When I saw your car pulled over this morning I stopped in case something was wrong. It's called being friendly."

In the animal kingdom, it's called marking your territory. "And now?" she asked.

He shrugged. "We're both single adults living in the same city. Being near the nightlife on a Tuesday evening seems more predictable than surprising. Now, answer another question. Are you always such a smart aleck when you meet a man?"

She knew that looking away would be an entirely weak, entirely female thing to do. She did it anyway. "It depends on the man."

He tilted her chin up. She didn't have time to get annoyed before their gazes collided and held for a long, silent, unfathomable moment. Then he turned away and they started walking again. He'd regained custody of her elbow and she allowed it. He'd already accused her— twice, and with good reason—of being rude. Shaking him off wasn't worth the risk of losing her role model.

"What brings you downtown tonight?" he asked, his voice perfectly pleasant.

"I'm meeting some friends for dinner." She made sure the smile she'd forced onto her face could be heard in her words.

He glanced down at her. He wasn't fooled. "Blind date?"

The man unravels good intentions like a kitten playing with a loose thread. She took a calming breath. "Please don't let me keep you from—"

"It's no trouble. I'll make sure you get where you're going and then be on my way."

"No really, that's not—"

"I insist. So where are we going?"

Remain calm. "*I'm* going to Chez Jean-Pierre."

"Nice place. Have you been there before?" he said,

subtly changing direction and steering her across Bedford Street.

"No, I haven't." She let out a controlled breath. The man was truly fraying her composure, which was something she didn't need minutes before meeting another man she might actually like. "Truly, I appreciate your help, but I can find it myself. You're going to be late for your own date, and no woman likes to be kept waiting."

"Did I say I have a date?"

She glanced at the strong line of his chin. It looked smooth and soft, just like a man's chin should look sometimes. Her eyes flicked upward. Without a doubt, his eyes had worked a lot of magic on a lot of women. If he hadn't been a cop, she might have considered letting them work some magic on her. But he *was* a cop. She was sure of it. And she didn't get involved with cops.

"You shaved recently, and when a man shaves at night, it can only mean he has a date."

"Very observant." He smiled. "You're right, I do have a date, just like you do."

"I said 'friends.' You said 'date.' "

"Actually, I said 'blind date.' "

"Why do you care?"

"I don't. You just seem like the type that friends would set up on blind dates."

"Why do you say that?"

He dropped her arm and reached for the heavy wooden door he'd led her to. "Because you're so tightly wound. You probably scare the hell out of the average guy."

Usually well able to defend herself against candor, his words nevertheless surprised her and, to her intense annoyance, stung. As she flailed for a suitably sarcastic response, she felt hated, alien tears spring into her eyes. And that, *of course,* was the moment he glanced down at her.

Chas's smile faded the instant he saw the unmistakable crumple of her mouth, the wet sparkle in her eyes. *Paxton will disembowel me.*

Ignoring the watchful gaze of the doorman, he pulled Miranda back into the wet, chilly wind and turned her to face him. "Christ. Don't start crying. I didn't mean it." He let out an annoyed breath. "You're not that sensitive, Hotshot. You can't be."

She pushed away his hand, glaring at him with eyes now less wet than full of fire. "Stop touching me. I'm not crying. I never cry and, no, I'm not sensitive. You're just a clod. That was mean. Uncalled-for and mean."

"It was sarcastic."

"It was *mean*," she insisted. Her eyes glittered in the doorway light, as green as any cat's. "You don't know me or anything about me. How dare you talk to me that way?"

"I'm sorry."

"I don't give a damn if you're sorry. You ruined my afternoon and now you've ruined my night. Just leave me alone." She spun around and, head held high, reached for the door handle.

Oh, hell. This night was already unforgettable. "Miranda, wait."

Her hand froze in midreach. She slowly turned to face him. "How do you know my real name?" Her eyes had gone cold. Very cold. It wasn't a good sign.

"Could we talk over here for a minute?" He gestured to an area a few feet away from the door, under the marquee of the shop next door. She followed him stiffly, her gloved hands jammed into the pockets of her long black coat.

"Tell me how you know my name."

"Paxton told me. I'm your date."

Her eyes closed slowly as she absorbed the news. "Of course you are. How could I not have seen this coming?"

He paused. And frowned. "Believe it or not, there are worse fates in life than having dinner with me," he replied, unable to keep the coolness out of his voice.

She opened her eyes and met his squarely. "Name one."

Jesus, the woman has claws. "Explaining to Paxton why you don't want to have dinner with me."

She paused. "Okay, you win. But you need to agree to something right now." She narrowed her eyes and bounced a rigid index finger off the spot where she'd shot him two days ago. "We're going to play nice in there. I'll be delightful and you'll be charming, but don't you *dare* flirt with me."

On the next cold day in Hell. He tried to look sincere. "I'll do my best."

"You'd better." She bounced her finger off his chest again, at which point he brought his hand up slowly and closed it around hers. It was little, and warm, and covered in thin, soft leather. She stiffened, just as she had every other time he'd touched her, but she didn't pull away and some of her edge disappeared. "No sly remarks indicating we've met. If Paxton finds out, she'll take it out on Jane, who doesn't need the headache." She paused. "So what's your name again?"

Very, very sharp claws. "Chas Casey."

"And you're a cop?"

"You've seen my gun. Do you want to see my badge?"

"Thank you, no. And I don't want to know anything more about you. Not now anyway." She slowly slid her hand from his. "I'll go in first. Give me a minute. I think I'd like a stiff bourbon in my hand before I meet you again, Chas Casey." As she spun toward the door, her coat flared, revealing a tantalizing expanse of high-heeled leg sheathed in sheer black. He remained in the cold, wet night, watching the door close behind her. The soft thump seemed the appropriate punctuation.

There was something about her—not just intelligence, something even sexier, maybe disdain—that sent a challenge and, at the same time, a warning. When it all came together it was damned hard to resist playing with her, especially because she so clearly didn't want to be played with. Without question, pursuing her would be entertaining, but why—and whether—he wanted to undertake it were questions he wasn't in the mood to answer.

Five minutes later, suitably chastised, as well as damp and chilled to the bone, Chas walked to the heavy wooden door, pulled it open, and walked inside. His eyes found Miranda instantly. Dressed in casually sexy "date" clothes, she had her back to him as he approached the group. James, Paxton's husband and his oldest friend, glanced up and nodded his hello from across the crowded room, then tapped his wife on the arm.

Here we go.

"Chas. It's about time you made it," she called.

He forced a smile in response as he watched Miranda's hips straighten and shoulders stiffen. She turned to face him slowly, giving him his first real opportunity for a full appraisal.

She was reasonably tall and slim, with long legs and a long neck, and she had all that dark, tie-me-up-in-it hair twisted into some ornate braid thing. Her face was pretty. Her eyes were stunning. They'd been hazel every other time they'd met but, as he'd just learned, they went green when she was angry. And the expression they held now made it clear that it might take more time than he had left on this earth before his earlier comment was forgotten or forgiven.

"James, Paxton, good to see you." He went through the perfunctory handshake and kiss on the cheek, respectively, then waited for Paxton to introduce Miranda, which she did on cue.

"Miranda, this is Chas Casey. James and Chas grew up together. Got into heaven knows what sort of trouble. But he's put all that behind him, haven't you, Chas?" She turned her laughing, watchful eyes on him. "Miranda was one of my roommates at Smith, and she's going to be staying in Stamford for a while. She's a terribly talented writer of national prominence, and if you aren't perfectly charming to her, you'll have to answer to me."

Miranda extended her hand, smiled, and told him how nice it was to meet him. That was when he knew without a doubt that he would pursue her, and why: *She thought she was immune.*

"Well, I'd say the evening went well," Chas said under his breath as the couples split up at the entrance to the parking structure in which they had both parked. In truth, it had gone about as well as he'd expected. Miranda had despised him with silent grace, neatly side-stepping every opportunity for a private conversation that he or Paxton could manufacture, all the while keeping a smile on her face that assured him he didn't have a hope in hell of arranging a second date.

"If you mean because we fooled Paxton, yes. But you were flirting, and you promised not to," Miranda muttered through a casual smile as she gave one last wave to James.

"I said I would do my best."

They walked in silence until they reached her car. The electronic locks clicked open, echoing in the busy downtown silence.

"Well, good night," she said, meeting his eyes for a long, neutral moment. Then her glance fell to his lips.

Nope, she's not immune at all. He made those watched lips of his curve into a smile that was friendly and reassuring, but not at all triumphant and not at all indicative that he had tomorrow morning off. "You're heading back to the beach?"

She brought her eyes back to his. "You know where I live?"

"Between getting briefed by Paxton and seeing the ticket Mick gave you, you might as well have left a trail of bread crumbs."

She smiled grudgingly and looked away. The gesture might have been flirtatious under different circumstances.

"Have you paid it yet?"

"No."

"Good. Don't bother. It's all gone."

She cocked her head and her eyes searched his, giving nothing away. "Thank you, Chas. That's better than getting flowers."

"You're welcome." He paused for effect. "I'll follow you home, just to make sure you get there safely."

She dropped her eyes and turned toward her car. "Oh, that's not necess—"

"I know it isn't," he interrupted, keeping his smile easy. "But I'm going to do it anyway, so it would save time if you didn't argue. And just in case you need to hear it, I have no ulterior motives. Though you may not believe it, I was brought up to be a gentleman, and a gentleman sees that even a reluctant date gets home safely. Especially when she has expired license plates."

After a moment's pause, she surrendered with a silent laugh and crossed her arms, the embodiment of a flirtatious smolder held in check by prudish determination. "I'm agreeing under protest, and only because I apparently have no other choice. But just to avoid any misinterpretations, I'm not inviting you in, even for coffee, and I'm not going to kiss you, even on the cheek."

"Of course you won't." He bent down and picked up the soft gold shawl that had slipped off her shoulders and handed it to her, then opened her car door. "Good night, Miranda."

It was a quick trip to her condo. She drove like everyone did when a cop was following them, and he had a hard time not laughing at her very complete stops and religious use of her turn signal. It was a far cry from the way she'd driven into the parking structure earlier in the evening. He made eye contact every time her eyes flicked to the rearview mirror, but after the tenth time, he winked at her. She kept her eyes on the road ahead of her after that.

He pulled his truck into the parking space beside her and walked her to the only door in the row of condos that didn't have its outside lights on.

"Would you like me to replace that while I'm here?" he asked, pointing at the darkened lightbulb inside the fussy brass lantern above the door.

She glanced up as she reached the top of the three shallow steps. He remained at the bottom. "It's not burned out. I just forgot to turn it on. Thank you, though, for offering."

Paxton told him she'd just broken up with a guy she'd been involved with for six years, and it showed. Despite her early bravado, she had a bad case of the first-date good-night jitters and was trying to conceal it, which made it all the more apparent. An experienced dater knew five minutes into the date what was going to happen at the end of the night. It was the rookies who didn't plan ahead.

He knew he should cut her some slack by making light conversation but she was a big girl and she'd set the rules. So he merely stood there and tried not to smile as, head down, she fumbled for her house keys in a very small purse, then, sparing him a panicked glance, dug into her coat pockets. Chas bit back a smile as her shoulders slumped and her eyes closed in agonized disbelief.

"I can't believe it," she murmured. "I didn't put the house keys on my key ring. I kept meaning to."

"Did you lose them?" he asked, enjoying the opportunity to watch the scattershot light play on her hair as she shook her head.

"Dollars to doughnuts they're on the kitchen counter next to my other purse."

Chas remained silent. She eventually opened her eyes.

"I'll call Paxton. Maybe she has an extra set," she mumbled.

He hated the word, but it fit: she looked cute, all sheepish and nervous and uncomfortable. "That might not be necessary. Is the alarm on?"

She nodded warily.

"What's the code?"

"Why? What are you going to do?"

"I'm going to open the lock on that window, climb in, turn off the alarm, and open the door for you. The legal term for it is breaking and entering."

"You can't do that," she protested.

"Sure I can. Criminals do it all the time. It's easy."

"What will I tell Paxton?"

He shrugged. "Tell her the truth. She won't care."

"But the lock—"

He walked up the three steps, put his hands on her shoulders, and looked into her eyes. They were big and dark with concern, and every cell in his body was urging him to take advantage of the moment. "I know what I'm doing. You'll still be able to set the alarm when I leave. It has nothing to do with the lock. Tell me where the control panel is and what the code is."

"The panel is on the wall that the door opens onto, and the code is oh-nine-one-nine," she said uncertainly.

He gave her shoulders a squeeze before stepping away. "Relax, Miranda. And stay right here. I'll be back in a minute."

He returned to his truck to get a screwdriver out of the toolbox, then crossed the small lawn. Crouching behind the shrub in front of the window, he popped off the screen, then took the screwdriver he'd gotten from his truck and eased open the lock. He slid up the sash and climbed over the sill to the strident peals of the alarm. Seconds later the house was silent again and he was opening the door to a nervous, shivering Miranda. She stepped timidly over the threshold and he shut the door behind her. "Are you okay? You look shaky."

"I'm fine," she said quickly. "Never been party to a felony, is all."

"There's a first time for everything." When she didn't smile, he tipped her chin up. "I'm teasing you, Miranda. Despite what etiquette books might say about it, it's not a crime in Connecticut to invite someone into your home through a window. So, now that we're in, why don't you relax? The date's over," he said, easing her coat from her shoulders. He hung up her coat in the closet, then walked to the front door. He wasn't about to linger like a tenth grader hoping for a makeout session. She'd set the rules. She could change them.

With his hand on the curved brass handle, he turned to her with a smile. "Good night, Miranda."

Misplacing her keys had knocked the fight out of her. She closed the gap between them slowly, her earlier nervousness replaced by an amused acknowledgment of defeat. Once again, her gaze slid from his eyes to his mouth.

"Thank you, Chas, for everything," she said softly, lifting her eyes back to his. "I know I was less than delightful this evening, but you more than lived up to your end of the bargain. You were definitely charming, and quite the gentleman." She paused. "Would you like some coffee?"

*   *   *

"Yes, I would, thanks."

Plumb crazy. That was what she was, Miranda told herself as she smiled and spun away toward the kitchen before anything more than that "thank you" could happen. It had been too long since she'd flirted with anyone, and, given the crackle Chas put in her airspace, there was no question that she was headed for trouble. Especially since her decision to invite him in was for business rather than pleasure. She'd decided on the way home that she would interview him.

She let out a slow breath and reached into the freezer for the bag of coffee. It could be a sweetheart situation if she could keep it impersonal. Of course, she ran the risk that he might not want to help her if he thought there was no personal angle. She shook the coffee grounds into the filter and began pouring water into the reservoir. It was a risk she wouldn't run if she didn't tell him what she was doing. If this were a real first date and she had invited him in to get to know him better, she would certainly ask questions about his work. *After all,* she told herself, *I don't need much from him, just some background, some insight. I could do it subtly.*

She stopped mid-pour, leaving the water carafe tilted over the coffeemaker's reservoir.

If it were the right thing to do I wouldn't be trying to rationalize the decision.

She finished pouring the water, then set the carafe on the counter gently. As far as ethical decisions went, it wasn't *so* bad. In a day or two she would receive permission to interview someone anyway. Even if he were to read her book someday, which he would never do, there would be no way he would know whether it was his information she included or the other guy's.

That settles it. She turned to face him with a smile and found him leaning against the counter across the kitchen, studying her. The look on his face wasn't affectionate, or hopeful, or even romantic. It was that closed cop look, and it caused her stomach to plummet just as it had when she was growing up. She wondered if she looked as guilty as she felt.

"Is everything okay?" he asked.

"Just fine. Why?" Her voice was too breathy and her pulse was too fast. *Not good.*

His eyes remained neutral. "You went quiet all of a sudden and stopped in the middle of what you were doing. I thought I might be making you uncomfortable. Would you prefer that I left?"

She looked at him and blinked.

Saying yes would undoubtedly save her soul from eventual damnation.

Unfortunately, she had a book to finish.

She smiled and slipped into her most Southern manner. "Most definitely not, Chas. Don't be silly. I invited you in. It's just that I realized I was making a pot of regular and wasn't sure if I should continue. It's all I drink. Is that okay with you?" Not only would she become ill if she had to continue this nonsense all night, but he'd see right through her. She'd never mastered the art of chattering.

"It's fine," he replied. "Drinking decaf has always struck me as pointless."

She smiled and led the way into the living room, waving him toward the couch as she kicked off her shoes and curled up in a chair big enough for two. "Let's chat while that's brewing. Either I can tell you all about being a writer or you can tell me all about being a cop."

"Or you can tell me what made you change your mind about me," he replied easily, with a look that was amused but direct.

"Pure guilt," she replied without hesitation.

He raised an eyebrow, issuing an invitation for her to continue.

She settled her elbow on the chair's arm and her chin on her palm. "Unlike y'all, Southerners are brought up to be friendly to everyone and even more friendly to those we don't like, at least in public. But you just rubbed me the wrong way from the start, Chas, and I forgot my manners. It wouldn't have bothered me much if we'd remained strangers, but here we are with a mutual friend who is determined to have us like each other." She offered him what she hoped was a charming shrug. "I decided that I should give you another chance. I'm hoping you'll let me redeem myself."

He waited for a beat after she finished talking, then shook his head with a silent laugh. She wasn't sure if he believed her, but at least he wasn't going to pursue it. Miranda let out a slow breath and snuggled deeper into the chair, knowing she'd dodged a bullet.

"So tell me why you became a writer."

"The idea of telling lies and getting paid for it appealed to me," she said after a moment's thought.

"Interesting set of skills. No doubt useful. Was telling lies a talent you developed as a child and then you decided to go pro, like a skier or a pianist would?"

She laughed, not trusting his easy voice one bit. "Not in my household. I didn't develop the talent until I was eighteen and moved away to college. Toward the end of my first year I realized I could tell stories that people liked. The stories kept me company," she added, startling herself by doing so. Then she laughed again, as a talisman against the memories.

If he'd noticed anything, he didn't let on. "Smith is a long way from where you were raised. Do you go home often?"

Home. Her spine stiffened automatically at the word, and she smiled to counteract it. "No. Atlanta is home now. But Smith was a long way away from where I grew up in more than just miles," she said, trying to ease away from the subject that she knew would lead to questions about her family. "I was a big-haired Southern girl who wore makeup and high heels and accessorized like the economy would just wither and die if I didn't. Back in Alabama, where I grew up, that was normal, but at Smith I was the skunk at the garden party. I talked too funny to fit in among the New England intellectual elite, and the radical feminists took issue with the fact that I wore pink and shaved my legs," she said, and watched that beautiful smile cross his mouth as he laughed. It made her relax. The danger had passed. "I would have gone home the second day if it hadn't been for Paxton. I'm sure she wasn't thrilled to have drawn such an alien as a roommate, but she was very good to me. Kind of half big sister and half fairy godmother. She just breezed through life like she held the patent on it, and let me move in her wake until I figured out how to cope on my own. Well, I'd say that's enough about me. Tell me about yourself. How long have you been a police officer?"

"Fifteen years. I went to the academy straight out of college."

"Dartmouth, from what I hear," she said, trying to sound like an interested female instead of an interested writer. "Comp lit. There can't be many of y'all."

"You'd be surprised. How many Smithies are romance writers?"

She paused, surprise, guilt, and amusement colliding within. "Three that I know of. How did you find out what I write?"

His grin revealed that he was clearly pleased at having caught her off guard. "Paxton told me you were a writer, but Paxton and my sister are good friends, and my sister and mother are big fans of yours. They told me who you were." He paused. "Even if they hadn't, Brian Murphy found you on the Web Sunday afternoon. As you know."

Knowing the conversation was in danger of heading off course way too quickly, Miranda just gave a slight nod and ignored the mention of Brian Murphy. "Why didn't you say anything earlier this evening? I mean about knowing what I do and what I write."

With un-Dirk-like tact, he allowed her evasion. "I wasn't supposed to know. After all, on Sunday you introduced yourself as Randi Rhodes. Paxton only mentioned Miranda Lane."

He's too nice to be Dirk. He's discreet and thoughtful. Two things Brian Murphy isn't. Two things Josh never was. She felt something inside soften toward him and, not sure she liked it, she pushed herself deeper into her chair.

"Why do you use a pen name?" he asked.

"My first editor thought my real name sounded too sedate for the books I was writing. She suggested Randi

Rhodes because it sounded fun and sexy, it was a play on my real name, and it would put me on the same shelf as Nora Roberts."

"Who?"

Miranda rolled her eyes. "The romance writer's high priestess of productivity and talent. We all bow before her. She writes, I don't know, ten books a year and they all get parked on *The New York Times* list for weeks and weeks." She raised an eyebrow playfully. "You almost got away with that one, but it's not time to switch sides yet. How long have you been a detective?"

"Five years. I was a sergeant for three before that, and I should be a lieutenant by New Year's Eve."

A career policeman. One per lifetime was her limit, and she'd reached it years ago. No smile or pair of dreamy eyes could change her mind on that. She swallowed hard and smiled. "Have you ever done anything you consider heroic?"

He shifted his position on the couch, laying his arm along its back. "I'm sitting here now. That took some courage."

Caught by surprise, she laughed. "I'm not that scary, and you're not very subtle."

"Subtlety doesn't always bring the best results, Miranda."

Time to downshift. "What kind of crimes do you solve, soon-to-be-Lieutenant Casey?"

"At the moment, I'm in the Crimes Against Persons bureau, so I handle things like homicides and assaults. Robbery. All the good stuff," he replied with an ironic smile. "Before that I spent a few years in vice."

The ethical dilemma might just evaporate, she thought, relaxing a bit. She might get assigned to interview *him.* And even if she didn't, she was only going to be here for a few weeks. *It's the right decision.* "Why did you switch?"

He was silent for a moment. "I tolerate blood and violence better than I tolerate sleaze."

A guilty tickle crept up the back of her neck. She made sure she didn't look away. "What makes someone decide to become a police officer?"

He shrugged easily and the moment passed. "Lots of reasons, but I'd say most people do it because they want to make their world a better place."

"Is that why you became one? Paxton said no one can figure out why you did."

He flashed a lazy grin. "They know. They just keep looking for a different reason. I became a cop because my father was a cop."

Oh, hell. Not a legacy, too. Daddy would be so pleased. She pushed away the unwanted thought and smiled at Chas's words, however unwelcome. "That sounds reasonable to me. But why Stamford, if you grew up in Greenwich? Was he a Stamford cop, too?"

"New Haven."

She heard the coffeemaker stop burbling and stood up. "Okay, now you've definitely piqued my curiosity. How did you end up in Greenwich?" she asked, moving into the kitchen. He followed her casually.

"My mother's from Greenwich. They met when she was on her way home from a Yale football game. Her boyfriend had dumped her during halftime, and she was crying so hard that she ran off the side of the road. My father was on his way home at the end of his shift and saw her do it, so he stopped to help and ended up driving her home. She invited him to stay for dinner and they were married six months later. Is that romantic enough for you?" Arms folded across his chest, he leaned back against the breakfast bar. His smile was designed to seduce.

Just breathe. "It's charming. Is it true?"

"Every word."

"It has all the elements of a modern fairy tale." She glanced at him over her shoulder. "All that's missing is the happily-ever-after part."

She knew from the speed with which his smile faded that it was the wrong thing to say.

"It doesn't apply," he said coolly as he straightened and pushed away from the counter. "Would you like me to help with the coffee?"

Damn it, Paxton, why didn't you mention his parents?

Feeling more awkward than stung, Miranda fumbled a mug and it fell from her hand to shatter on the floor. She looked up from the mess to see him standing right in front of her. "Chas, I'm so sorry for being glib. I didn't—"

"Don't worry about it. You didn't hurt yourself, did you?"

"No. I'm fine. I'll clean it up in a minute."

"You need to leave the kitchen before you cut your feet. I'll clean it up." Before she could argue, he picked her up and deposited her on the breakfast bar a few feet away. She was still catching her breath—whether from the surprise of breaking the mug or the surprise of their sudden contact, she didn't want to know—when he emerged from the pantry closet with a broom and dustpan.

"Chas, please, I'm so sorry. Truly, I don't know what I—"

He cut her off with a look. "Don't apologize, Miranda. I was out of line. I assumed Paxton had said something."

Why hadn't she? Damn her again. "She didn't tell me anything about you. I never would have—"

"My father was shot and killed in the line of duty when I was six. It's not a secret or a sore subject," he added as she automatically brought a hand up to cover her shocked-open mouth. He swept the last of the broken crockery into the dustpan and crossed the room to dispose of it. "I should have realized that you couldn't have known. Please don't feel awkward about it. There's no point in both of us doing that." He recrossed the room to stand in front of her and gave her a contrite smile. "I had a nice time this evening, Miranda, but I think it's best if we call it a night."

Despite his smile, despite the tension in the room, his dark eyes were still seducing her, and for the first time in a long time Miranda felt the belly-clenching tug of something her Bible-thumping daddy and twelve years of Catholic education had assured her was sinful.

"I believe you're right, Chas. Good night," she said in a voice not far above a whisper.

Sliding hands that were strong and much too warm around her waist, he lifted her off the breakfast bar, set her on her feet, and dropped a light kiss on her cheek.

Self-loathing began pounding through her before he was halfway to the door. *He's a good man and the son of a hero, and I'm using him, secretly, for my own commercial purposes. Surely that falls under the heading of sleaze.*

CHAPTER
6

At seven o'clock, groggy from the effects of sleep-
lessness induced by a guilty conscience and one or two
overstimulated hormones, Miranda stumbled down the
stairs to the strident peals of the doorbell. A team of
carpenters greeted her, ready and willing to perform the
sacrilegious conversion of the condo's small, cozy library
and adjoining office into a home theater. Her day de-
graded from there. By seven thirty she had barricaded
herself in the loft with her laptop, only to be interrupted
an hour later by a pair of very chatty but incomprehensi-
ble stonemasons. They quickly began removing the slate
floor in the foyer, which would be replaced with traver-
tine marble at some indeterminate time in the near
future.

There was only one room in the entire residence that
provided an escape from the piercing scream of the table
saw and the irregular pounding of masonry hammers and
the swirling, choking, multimedia dust. She sat curled up
on her unmade bed, alternately tapping on and cursing
at the laptop nestled luxuriously on a pillow stuffed with
French goose down as she tried to resuscitate her once-
charming story and reinvent her once-charming hero.

"Okay, come on, *Dirk*," she muttered derisively.
"You're stuck in an elevator in the lovely new Stamford
courthouse with opposing counsel. No, that was last

week. Now you're a witness for the prosecution and she's the defense lawyer. Y'all aren't supposed to talk to each other. It's against the rules and could cause a mistrial, and *plenty* of people saw y'all get into the elevator together. You're as disciplined as all get-out but, ooh, honey, she's wearing those CFM shoes with the pointy toes and high, skinny, skinny heels."

She reclined onto the mountain of tasseled and beribboned pillows she'd stacked behind her and stared at the artfully faux-finished ceiling. "The power goes out and you're stuck between floors. It's getting hot in there. It's July. Taylor's looking nervous in her little gray lawyer suit, but you . . . oh, my, but you're sweating pretty, Dirk, getting all dark and glowy." She let out an exasperated breath and focused on the middle distance. "Come on, work with me, Dirk, honey. There's only one way you wear clothes, and that's commando. Right now those Dockers are getting awfully snug, seeing as you're only six feet away from heaven in high heels." She closed her eyes. "She's a jar of marshmallow fluff, all soft and sweet, and you're just dying for a spoonful." She stopped and opened her eyes. "You are not headin' down that road, today, Miranda. Get a grip. They have to kiss before they get to play with food."

She took a deep breath. "Okay, Dirk, honey, you're a gorilla in a tie. All that chest hair's gotta be getting itchy. What would a big, bad hunk o' burning love like you do, darlin'? Rip off your shirt? Declare your lust in a series of unintelligible grunts? Hoist yourself through the small opening in the ceiling that every elevator supposedly has but that *I've* never seen?"

She closed her eyes, trying to choreograph the scene, when, unbidden, Chas Casey's handsome face superimposed itself on the featureless, meaningless Dirk. With that maddeningly sexy smile, without looking at the heroine, without breaking a sweat, he reached into the call box, lifted out the handset, and spoke to the building's security guard.

"Oh, hell. *Duh.*" She smacked her palm to her forehead. "Of course *you'd* do that, Chas. But would Dirk?"

"Oh, hi. I didn't know you were in here. Who are you talking to?"

Miranda's eyes flew open at the sound of Paxton's voice. Perfectly made-up despite the early hour, and casually chic in faded jeans and a heavy silk shirt that probably cost as much as Miranda's monthly car payment, Paxton stood in the bedroom doorway. She was flanked by Liz, her underfed, context-free interior decorator, who was staring at Miranda through black-framed glasses only slightly larger than her pupils.

"I was talking to myself," Miranda replied evenly.

"You were talking to yourself?" Liz repeated, raising her perfectly sculpted eyebrows and turning to Paxton for direction.

Without trying too hard to hide her irritation at the intrusion, Miranda pushed herself upright and tried to look dignified in her baggy workout clothes. "I'm plotting."

"Miranda's a writer," Paxton declared, sweeping into the room. "She's hit every major best-seller list there is, including *The New York Times*. She's staying here while she's working on her next novel. Liz and I just need to discuss the color going on that wall."

Liz straightened her retro-'70s studded denim jacket and gave Miranda a sycophant's smile. Annoyed at the sight of it, Miranda closed her manuscript, closed her laptop, and scooted off the bed. "I'll just get out of y'all's way and go get some more coffee."

By the time she traversed the noisy, cloudy path to the kitchen, she was frustrated on several levels and gave up all hope of working for the next hour. Pulling on a loose sweatshirt, she walked to the small private beach to relieve her stress and annoyance in a beneficial way.

It had been at least two days since she'd exercised, so after a few deep, cleansing breaths that didn't really do much for her, she began moving through her tae kwon do patterns. She increased her vigor and intensity in proportion to her unsuccessful efforts at clearing her mind and figuring out when and where, not to mention how, she was going to get her revisions done. When she'd finished and bowed to her nonexistent opponent, she turned to go back to the condo. Only then did she notice the dark-jacketed figure sitting on the low stone wall that separated the strip of dormant sod from the strip of pebbly sand.

Sweaty, with her breath forming staccato clouds in the cold sea air, she walked toward him reluctantly. He looked like he'd been up for a while. Showered and scrubbed, unlike herself. What bothered her more than knowing she looked like something the cat dragged in was the simple fact of having to deal with him. It required energy, and she had just expended all of hers.

She came to a stop a few feet in front of him and he smiled at her. It was a good smile, sexy and amused, and it reached his eyes. She knew what it meant: *All was forgiven.*

Of course, she knew better than to think anything had been *forgotten,* and that was why that look was positively the last thing she wanted to see at the moment. She had to exorcise the guilt-ridden ghost of last night in her own time and in her own way.

"Good morning, Miranda." His voice held a hint of flirtation.

Oh, mercy. Here we go again. "Good morning, Chas."

"Did you sleep well?"

Those dark eyes of his were scanning her, absorbing her. Keeping her pulse rate high when it should have been dropping. "Fair to middling. And you?"

"About the same." He stood up, reached out one large, warm hand, and helped her step onto the wall. Before she could tug her hand away he dropped it, and they fell in step with each other as they crossed the lawn.

"This visit can't be written off as coincidental." She glanced at him out of the corner of her eye. "What brings you here so early? Don't you work?"

His eyebrows rose at her tone, and she knew she'd just put the conversation on a downward spiral. "I'm sorry. I didn't mean that to sound . . . It was sharp. I'm sorry." She let out a heavy breath and gave him an apologetic smile. "May I change my answer to your last question? I had a lousy night. There was very little sleep involved."

"Not because of our conversation, I hope."

She gave him a look that let him know she didn't need the coddling. "What I meant to say a minute ago was, 'When do you work?' But that's just as rude and just as much none of my business, so I'll start from scratch. Hi, Chas. It's just lovely to see you. What brings you here?"

He stopped at the edge of the deck. "You do. And I *do* work. As of tomorrow, I'll be on the day shift for five days."

Which meant he had the day off, and he'd chosen to spend the first part of it with her.

I should confess now and get it over with. It's my only hope of ever getting a good night's sleep again. She continued up the short flight of steps and dropped into one of the many chairs on the large deck. He stayed on the stairs, leaning against the railing and idly slinging his key ring around his index finger.

She glanced from those large, oddly elegant hands to his eyes. "You did that last night. Do I make you nervous?"

The corner of his mouth twitched with good humor as he put the keys and his hands in the slash pockets of his bomber jacket. "Not particularly. Wait. I take that back. Are you armed? Other than with your hands and feet?"

"My only other weapon is my wit, but that's been dull for months."

"Don't be so sure about that. What was that?" He nodded his head toward the beach. "It's impressive."

"Tae kwon do." *Get to the point. Why are you here?* "What level?"

"Nearly a black belt. And you?"

"What makes you think I know anything about it?"

His look was too innocent to be credible, and she let the shadow of a smile cross her lips. "We also established last night that I'm observant," she replied. "It's a balance issue. So?"

"Not nearly as far as you."

"Good. Expertise and speed provide a good counter-balance to height and weight."

He paused just long enough for her to feel her words hit the earth with a dull thud. "Are you expecting to have to fight me off at some point?"

Being on edge around him was one thing. Letting him know just how on edge was another. She tried to cover her mortification with a laugh. "Actually, no. That's not what I meant." She waved a dismissive hand, as if the motion would make the words disappear. "Now you're beginning to understand why I'm a writer and not a public speaker. I require heavy editing at all times. Let's back up a ways. You got up early on your day off just to say hello?"

He came to the top of the stairs, and she felt his presence encroach on her like a wave rushing the shore. "I thought you might like to go for a drive."

"At eight thirty?"

"It's ten fifteen." He stopped and leaned against the railing a foot away from her.

She needed air. Choking, dusty, indoor air. "Heavens, I didn't realize it was so late. Thank you anyway, Chas, but I have a ton of work to do." Giving him an apologetic smile, she stood up and took a few steps toward the sliding glass doors that led into the living room.

"It's not entirely a social call, Miranda. I thought I would drive you to the DMV to get temporary tags for your car. Before you drive it somewhere else and get a ticket I can't fix."

Oh, hell. She closed her eyes briefly, then, with her hand on the door handle, turned slowly and met his eyes. He was slinging the keys around his finger again and watching her with a look that was partly amused and partly challenging and very, very coplike. She heard the sound of the surf and the gulls and her own breathing for a moment. And she felt again that damning tug, low and hot and heady and guilty. "That's kind of above and beyond the call of duty, isn't it?"

"Just say 'thank you,' Miranda. Then go find your paperwork."

She knew if she demurred again, he'd go. Without a

fuss, of course, but probably for good. That would leave her with a less cloudy conscience, but with expired tags on her car, no clue where the DMV was, and no role model for the in-desperate-need-of-improvement Dirk. *And* she'd have to go back inside and deal with Paxton and Liz.

That primrose path to an eternal suntan had never offered a more enticing escort.

"Thank you, Chas. I'll get my purse and be down directly."

In record time, Miranda changed from her workout clothes into a long denim skirt and bulky sweater, put on mascara, and pulled her hair out of its messy chignon to give it a quick brushing. After calling a quick, generic good-bye to all present in the house, she hurried out the door and down the front steps. She faltered and slowed her stride considerably when she saw him leaning against the passenger side of a very sleek, dark blue Porsche parked nonchalantly in one of her neighbors' reserved spots, next to Paxton's rudely parked Hummer.

The situation was becoming troublesome. Chas was turning out to be less Dirk-like every time she saw him. Detective Dirk couldn't afford new mud flaps, let alone a second car. And he wouldn't have the car door open before Taylor ever got near it. Dirk wouldn't open it at all.

"Nice car," she murmured as she slid inside.

"Glad you approve."

It was clean inside and warm, and held a trace of the mingled scents of summer: sand and salt water, Cutter's and Coppertone, and him. It was a gift on such a cold, dark, late-autumn morning. He slid behind the wheel easily, put the car in gear and brought the engine to life, then spared her a glance. "Just what do you suppose Paxton was thinking when she set us up?"

Miranda merely smiled and turned her head to look out the window. Several minutes and several miles passed silently as she tried to reconcile herself to the alien thought of a kinder, gentler Dirk. It just seemed oxymoronic. Dirk was an alpha. He couldn't be *kind*.

He couldn't be *couth*. Which left her wondering if Chas was truly an alpha. It seemed almost traitorous to consider that he wasn't, but the evidence was compelling. It was time for a reality check.

Leaning against the headrest, she looked at him across the small cockpit. *No. It's time to start poking him to find his soft spots.*

"Explain something to me, Chas. You drove your truck last night. Given that we actually met before our date, why was I worthy of a shave, but not the car? I reckon you were either slumming last night or you're trying to impress me now."

She expected the laughter. She didn't expect the glance that stroked her, leaving a tingle in its wake.

"Oh, you're shave-worthy, Hotshot. I just needed to set the pace. You know, the sexy car, big gun, five-o'clock shadow, blue-chip pedigree—I didn't want you to fall for me too quickly."

Biting back laughter of her own, she turned back to watch barren trees flash past her window. "You're flirting again."

"A little."

"A lot."

"Okay, a lot. It was only against the rules for last night."

"Like that stopped you."

"So is it working?"

She glanced at him. "I'm not sure. It's been a long time since anyone's flirted with me."

"Sorry, I don't buy that. Just admit it's working."

She didn't hold back her laughter this time. "Ain't chasin' that rabbit, Chas."

He shook his head. "You're tough."

"It's about time you noticed."

"I notice a lot of things." He maneuvered smoothly around a lumbering SUV. "Do you have plans for lunch?"

The question was asked casually enough, but it caused a shift in the mood anyway. She looked out the window again, wishing she could rewind the situation by ten sec-

onds. Until she found out who she was going to be interviewing, she had to keep things with Chas strictly
business. Or at least impersonal.

"I have a standing date with my laptop," she replied
lightly.

He was quiet for the rest of the short trip, until he
pulled into a large parking lot next to a modern granite-
and-glass building and killed the engine. Then he rested
one forearm on the top of the steering wheel and looked
at her. His eyes were warmer than she expected them
to be.

"Tell me why you're so tough, Miranda. Your heroines aren't."

"You've read my books?" She should have been flattered, but she couldn't be. She knew the only reason
he'd read them was for research purposes. To research
her. "All of them?"

He was watching her with a slight frown. "The three
most recent. Does it matter?"

Her breath caught in her throat. He'd read *Like a
House Afire*. The caterer and the house painter. The
scaffolding at midnight. *Oh, God. The tapioca pudding*.
She smiled and tried to remain poised. "Of course not,
Chas. I'm flattered that you took the time. But please
don't make the mistake of comparing me to my heroines.
They're fiction. They're not me."

He smiled. "Damn."

The silence grew replete with suggestion, and she
couldn't stop the warmth from rising to her face.

"Okay, I'll quit flirting before I'm tempted to tell you
that you're cute when you blush." He glanced down and
reached for a stray curl that lay on her arm. He
smoothed it between his fingers idly, then let it drop.
Their eyes met again. She wasn't even sure if she was
still breathing.

"Why is it that you bring out the worst in me?" he
murmured.

She swallowed hard. "Don't be so humble, Chas. I'm
sure you can get worse than this."

Her words broke the mood and, glad for a reason to

look away, she leaned forward and picked up her purse from the floor. It was all she could do not to open the car door and jump out.

He laughed and removed the keys from the ignition. "You blow hot and cold faster than anyone I know. Would you like to know what I think the reason is?"

"Unequivocally *no*," she replied, and stepped out of the car. They fell in step as they crossed the parking lot, and he gave her a smile that could weaken the strongest knees. She braced herself. "You're going to tell me anyway, aren't you?"

"I think you like me."

She pursed her lips against her laughter. "Actually, I think you're an egomaniac."

"Every guy is. But look at the facts. You don't exactly shut me down when I—"

"I try, but you just can't take a hint, bless your heart."

"Last night you let me into the house—"

"You broke in," she interjected.

"—*and* you got in my car this morning—"

"I was coerced."

"—and not just because you wanted to ride in a Porsche."

She let out a sigh. "Now I'm the one who's slumming. I thought it was a Ferrari."

His smile widened. "You agreed to have lunch with me—"

"I most certainly did not."

"But you will, and furthermore, you'll enjoy yourself, because you already know that I can be charming. You said so yourself." He raised an eyebrow. "So am I right?"

She stopped as he reached for the heavy door and pulled it open. Stepping across the threshold, she looked past him, away from those eyes and that smile, and tried to ignore the long-dead spark that, of all people, a *cop* had ignited. "I'm not going to get into it with you now. Let's get the paperwork done and then I'll let you know how hungry I am."

CHAPTER
7

The longer Chas knew her, the more he wanted to know about her. Watching Miranda's moods shift was like watching a storm roll in across the sound, never knowing where the next lightning strike would be. She was hardheaded, inquisitive, hesitant, and flirtatious by turns, as if she just couldn't decide what she wanted—from him or from herself. Luckily one of them was clearheaded on the subject. He knew exactly what he wanted. He wanted her.

"Are you trying to get me drunk?" Miranda asked, watching him pour the last of the wine into her goblet.

"No. If you get drunk, you'll have done it to yourself. Why do you ask?" He leaned back in his chair. She'd definitely lost some of her edge, but that could have been a result of his deliberately light conversation or the cozy setting as much as the wine, which she'd only sipped.

"I don't usually drink. Especially in the middle of the day. When you asked me if I wanted wine, I thought you meant a glass."

"You can never get anything nice by the glass. So, no more cop stories. I get to ask some questions now."

"Check, please," she said, looking around for the waiter.

He smiled. "Excellent. Interrogations always go much better when the suspect is nervous."

"Can I quote you on that?"

"Nope. But I'll go easy on you." He picked up his wineglass and asked over the rim, "How long have you been writing?"

She sat as far back in her chair as it would allow and flipped a handful of long dark hair over her shoulder. "Seriously for about eight years. I dabbled before that. My first book came out six years ago. My sixth will be released in March."

"So you write one a year? Unlike—who was it who writes ten books a year?"

"Nora Roberts. I write one and a half to two in a year, actually. In between books there are things like revisions to do and book tours to go on and ideas to pitch. And downtime, both planned and accidental. I doubt I could ever do ten, but I could probably do two to three a year if I pushed myself." She shrugged. "It all depends on how much I love the story and what else is going on in my life at that moment." She smiled. Her hazel eyes were calm and deep for a change.

Chas leaned forward slowly, folding his arms on the table. "What's going on in your life at this moment?"

She didn't move, but he watched, intrigued, as her pupils dilated and her irises turned green. A second later she dropped her eyes and picked up her wineglass, then twirled it by the stem, making Chas wonder why the question—or the answer—made her uncomfortable. He added it to the growing list of things he wanted to know about Miranda Lane. It was already a damned long list.

"I came up here to work on a new proposal—"

"What's that?"

"The framework of a story that you send to an editor with the hope that she'll pay you lots of money to write the rest of it."

"You don't send a book?"

She shook her head. "I don't. I'm trying to pull together a synopsis and a few chapters."

"But . . ."

She glanced up at him, then went back to studying the

stem of her wineglass with a slight frown. The green had faded from her eyes. "But I have a new editor and she wants some pretty extensive revisions to the book that's coming out in March. It should be in production already, so I have to work on those first."

"How long will those take?"

"More time than I have to do them."

And yet, here we are. "In other words, I'm cutting into your writing time?"

She smiled and took a small sip of wine instead of answering.

"How long are you going to be in town?"

"Three more weeks. I'm leaving the day before Thanksgiving."

"And between now and then you'll spend your days writing?"

"And most of my nights. I have to if I'm going to hit my deadline." Vivid green eyes flicked to his, then away.

She was guilty as hell. But of what? He said nothing, and didn't allow his expression to change. It achieved the desired effect.

"I usually write from about eleven in the morning until about four, and then again from about eight until midnight or so. When I'm on deadline, it really can run straight through the day." Unable to put any more distance between them without leaving the table, she lifted the wineglass to her lips again but didn't take a sip. "Right now, I'm trying to write anytime that I'm not answering the door to let in workmen, or entertaining Paxton, or being stopped by Stamford police officers." She glanced up at him again. "Or being kidnapped by them."

He smiled and shifted in his chair, leaning back as if he were settling in. "Now who's flirting with whom?"

"I've heard that turnabout is fair play."

"You're honest. That's good," he lied with a smile. It was disconcerting how much he wanted her, but what was more disconcerting was that he wasn't doing more in the way of acting on it. Getting a woman horizontal didn't constitute much of a challenge these days. As skittish as Miranda was, he could have done that last night if he'd applied himself. He didn't, because, while it would have been enjoyable, it wouldn't have been satisfying. He wanted to get past the attitude, past the sarcasm, past the guilt—no, to the bottom of that, actually—and see what was real and what was bravado. How much might be shyness or insecurity hidden by overcompensating boldness.

That desire to learn her was part of the reason he'd chosen this restaurant. It was expensive, out of the way, and overrated, but, in the event a breakthrough occurred, it never hurt to be prepared. The other side of the building housed an historic inn with cozy, tastefully romantic rooms, an excellent wine list, and twenty-four-hour room service.

She gave a small, nervous laugh, then took a small sip of wine. He waited.

"Don't congratulate yourself too soon, Chas. My honesty may be situational. After all, you're trained to spot a liar, aren't you? Maybe I'm just not willing to be found out yet."

Something in her manner changed then, causing her to put down her wineglass and lean forward on her elbows. "Why did you agree to a blind date, Chas? Is Paxton trying to marry you off or help you through a broken heart?"

"Those are the only two possibilities?" He leaned forward on his elbows to put his face within a foot of hers and watched her immediately pick up her wineglass again, this time as a shield rather than a distraction. But she didn't lean away from him. "Tell me why you care."

"I don't care," she said with a forced smile. "I'm curious."

"Neither. Anymore, anyway."

"She's not trying to marry you off anymore, or you're no longer nursing a broken heart?"

"For someone who doesn't care about the answer, you're particular about its precision." He let his eyes roam over her face before continuing. She was beautiful. Aroused and beautiful and trying damned hard not to be sexy. Chas wondered if she knew just how miserably her efforts were backfiring. "I'm not interested in marriage, and my heart doesn't break. That makes me the quintessential 'spare man,' something every society hostess craves. In return for completing her table now and then, Paxton has introduced me to quite a few nice women."

"Do you end up dating them?"

Despite the boldness of the question, he smiled and shrugged. "I went out with some of them once or twice."

"That's it? Why?"

Still amused but getting annoyed by her line of questioning, Chas paused to take a sip of wine. "Not everyone is cut out to date a cop."

"So you don't want to get married and you don't have relationships, and it's all because of your career. How intriguing. Will that change when you become a lieutenant? Or is it a separate issue?"

He put down his wineglass and met her eyes again. "Forgive me for pointing this out, but your questions are becoming what my grandmother would call impertinent."

She laughed, which wasn't the response he was expecting or looking for. "What would *you* call my questions?"

"Nosy."

She laughed again and inched forward conspiratorially. "I apologize, Chas. Like I told you last night, I've totally abandoned my manners since I met you. Every Southern grandmother shelling peas on heaven's front porch is surely looking down upon me in horror and shame. But, heaven help me, I'm intrigued, is all. I've never met a man who was so up-front about not getting involved with women."

He paused, still torn between irritation and amusement. "It's only relationships that include certain expectations that I avoid. And the decision has nothing to do with my rank. Satisfied?"

She didn't flinch. "It sounds complicated."

"Quite the contrary. It's extremely simple, Miz Miranda," he replied in a deliberate parody of her drawl. "I avoid commitment. On purpose. Intentionally. Openly. What about you?"

"What about me?"

"According to Paxton, you've reentered single life fairly recently, but according to what you said a few minutes ago, it sounds like you don't have much of a social life."

She smiled. "Some girlfriend she is, giving you the lowdown like that. I'm going to have to remind her of the rules. Well, you're right. I don't have a social life when I'm on deadline."

"You're on a deadline now."

"Don't tell my editor, but I occasionally have to get things done. Like fulfilling my civic duty and eating lunch."

Enough is enough. The bill had been paid, the dishes had been cleared, the conversation had turned into sexual banter, and all he could think about was . . . He stood up and walked around the table to her chair. "It's time to get you back to the pumpkin patch, Cinderella."

"Scullery."

Bedroom. "Whatever."

He resisted the temptation to touch her as they left the restaurant, but by the time they had crossed the large, empty gravel parking lot, putting more and more distance between themselves and those deep featherbeds a couple could lose themselves in, touching her was all he could think about. He opened her door, then walked around to the driver's side. As he settled in his seat, it felt as though the inside of the small car had gotten smaller or their personal spaces had expanded. Either way, there didn't seem to be any room for withdrawal.

Knowing there was a very good chance he could end up with a black eye or worse, Chas leaned toward her slowly, captured her chin, and lowered his mouth to hers. Her lips were soft and parted in surprise. She tasted of Chardonnay and coffee, of warm, strong, passionate woman, and of infinite possibilities. After only a few seconds, she began to kiss him back, tentatively.

Tentative was fine. For the moment. He moved closer, slid his hand into that silky mane of hair, and was about to deepen the kiss when she stiffened. A second later he felt her hand against his chest.

"Stop," she whispered against his lips.

"Why?" he whispered back, then took her lips again, wet them, traced them.

"Chas."

He took his hand away and lifted his head, and she turned immediately toward the window. Then she took a deep breath and he knew two things: Everything she would say in the next thirty seconds would be a lie, and the game was over. For now.

"Chas, you're not my type of guy," she began haltingly, and he glanced at his watch. "I'm here on business, just for a short time. I don't want . . ." She took another breath. "With Paxton and all, things could get complicated and I don't want that. You were right this morning; I do like you, but not like that. Not like this."

All that in only twenty seconds. Not bad. He eased back into his seat, giving her some space. "Is that five reasons or six?"

It didn't surprise him when she didn't answer.

"Which is the real one?" *Twenty-eight. Twenty-nine.*

"My old boyfriend and I are sort of . . ." She sighed. *Thirty.* "I just can't, Chas. I won't."

He fought the urge to shake his head, to shake *her* for lying. He took a deep breath and decided to let her talk herself into a corner, or out of one. "If you're back with your boyfriend *sort of,* why did you return my kiss?"

"I'm not sure, but it won't happen again."

"I can guarantee it won't," he replied evenly. "I don't like women who cheat."

As expected, she bristled and turned those sparking green eyes on him. "I'm not cheating. *You* kissed *me.* I don't remember extending an invitation."

"You kissed me *back,* Miranda. It was an option. You exercised it." He pushed in the clutch and turned the key, gently bringing the powerful engine to life. "That's against the rules. If you're spoken for, you're obliged to tell me *before* anything happens."

She let out an annoyed breath. "I'm not *spoken for.* A *parking space* is spoken for. A *table at a restaurant* is spoken for. *I* am not spoken for. And I can make up my own mind about whom I kiss and when."

He turned to her, looking her straight in the eyes. He kept his voice low and calm and even. "Then make up your mind. Right now."

She didn't move an inch, didn't even blink. "What do you mean?"

"Me or him."

She didn't hesitate. "Him."

"Why was that so difficult to remember two minutes ago?"

"It wasn't."

"Good."

God Almighty, he wanted her more than ever. Putting the engine into gear, he pulled slowly onto Route 7. Silence reigned.

"What if I'd said you?" she asked ten minutes later.

You'd be naked and breathless, lost in a sea of French goose down. He slowed down into a blind curve, then shot forward as he cleared it. "I knew you wouldn't."

"Nonsense."

"You're not the devil-you-don't type of woman. You like things safe."

"There's no way Paxton said anything like that about me."

"She didn't have to. I read your books, remember?"

"I told you I'm nothing like my heroines."

"I'm not saying you are. But I've read three of your books, and all the heroes are the same guy. Obviously, that's the type of man you prefer."

"If you mean they're fully evolved, you're right," she snapped.

"I mean they're wimps." Not hiding his smile, he decided that rendering her speechless held a certain satisfaction.

"They are not wimps," she protested. "You're not qualified to say that anyway. My books aren't written for you—"

"That's irrelevant. Here's a newsflash, Hotshot: Men understand how romance works."

She paused and took a breath. "Tell me why—"

"Your heroes don't have a clue. They're totally passive. They feel your pain. They hug. They delay their own gratification. Hell, they're not only wimps, they're complete fantasies."

She swiveled her shoulders to face him. Her cheeks were flushed and her eyes held the full heat of a nicked ego, but her voice was smooth and cool. "Another cheap shot," she said with a forced smile. "Maybe that's what I should start calling you, since you call me Hotshot. Which, by the way, I wish you'd stop."

He could tell that his laughter surprised her. "You're absolutely right, Miranda. It was a cheap shot. I apologize."

She took another deep breath, which did nothing to calm her down. "Apology accepted. So let's get back on point. You have a degree in comparative literature, yet calling my heroes 'fantasies' is the best reason you can come up with for calling them wimps? All I can say in response to that is, *duh,* Chas. Of course they are. Fantasies, I mean. Do you think romance novelists write about reality? Who in their right mind would want to read about a potbellied boor who can remember the stats on every player in the NFL but can't remember his wedding anniversary? Or his kids' birthdays? Or the fact that his wife likes lilies and can't stand roses? Reality is what people want to escape, and with good reason." She turned back to the window.

"All men aren't like that," he said and let her settle for a minute. "It sounds like you're saying that you know all your books go over the top."

"What do you mean by that?"

"No man defers his own gratification as many times as that dorky Reed did."

She swung her entire body toward him this time, unbuckling the seat belt when it proved unyielding.

"Put that back on," he ordered quietly before she could get a word out. She snapped the buckle into place without argument, but she was as wired as if she had a high-voltage current running through her. Her eyes, which never left his face, were laser hot.

"Excuse me," she said in a voice low and aching with the strain of her control. "But women *love* Reed. Women from all over *the world* wrote to tell me how much they liked Reed and how they wished their men were like him." Turning to face the windshield again, she took a slow, deep breath and regained some of her composure. "Why should you care what kind of men I write about anyway, Chas? Is this conversation some sort of payback because I didn't want to kiss you?"

"No. You did want to kiss me. In fact, you did kiss me." Cursing the rugged Connecticut countryside for demanding his concentration, he swept his eyes over her face, then dragged them back to the curving road ahead. *All that passion going to waste.* "And I know you're lying about why you didn't continue kissing me, but I'm not going to lose any sleep over it."

"Good," she snapped. "By the way, it doesn't matter whether you think I'm lying or not, because I don't owe you a reason. I assume you've heard the expression 'No means no'?"

He knew it was a reasonable comment, but under the circumstances it sent a riff of annoyance shooting through him. "Oh, give me a break, sweetheart. This isn't prom night, and I'm not trying to get into your panties. It was just a kiss, and the only reason it bothers you is that I'm under your skin already."

She turned back to the window. "That's utter, ego-driven nonsense," she said tightly. "I suggest we call it a draw and just write off this whole exercise as a few bad coincidences and leave it at that."

He just shook his head as they sped down the entrance ramp to the Merritt Parkway.

Miranda heard her cell phone chirping with unanswered calls as she let herself into the condo. There was one from Amy, wanting to know how she was doing; two from Paxton, wanting her to call back; and one from Jane, wanting to know how last night had gone. But all Miranda wanted to do was rewind the last hour.

Stupid, stupid, stupid. That was what she'd been to argue with him. Especially about something as subjective as her books. No. *Her heroes.* There had been reviewers who had been more harsh. Heavens, her current editor was more harsh. She let out a heavy breath as she punched in Amy's office number.

At least she'd had the late-blooming maturity to calm down and apologize. He'd been perfectly polite about it, but she knew that was the last she'd see of him. With good reason. She'd behaved like an ill-mannered child. At best.

Grimacing against the hammering in the library and the pounding in the foyer, she took the phone onto the deck as she waited for her agent to answer. A few minutes spent shivering in an icy wind might blow some sense back into her head.

"Miranda, how are you? I know it's only been a few days, but how are the revisions coming along?"

"Hi, Amy. I'm doing okay. The revisions are going okay, too." *Liar, liar, pants on fire.*

"Do you have something you could send me today?" *No.* "Sure."

"Good. What's all that pounding?"

"Workmen."

"Where?"

"Inside."

"Inside your *house*? You have to work like that? Are you crazy? What's your friend up to? This is a rental unit, right?"

"She's putting it on the Christmas home tour. It's some charity thing. She's getting everything done at cost, and then she's going to sell the place."

"Why?"

"Because she's fallen in love with a simply darling little villa in Tuscany and needs a few extra dollars for restoration," Miranda replied, feeling her teeth start to chatter.

"How little?"

"Forty acres, eighteen rooms, a fountain, three out-buildings, and an olive grove."

"God Almighty. You sound like you're shivering. Did the workmen turn off the heat?"

"No. They're inside. I'm on the deck."

There was an incredulous pause. "I know it was a

freebie, but, Miranda, get the hell out of there. You can't work like that. It sounds like you're in a war zone. You only have a few weeks. Rent a little furnished apartment, or go stay at your friend's real house."

"She has two little kids, four big dogs, an Irish housekeeper, and a British nanny, and she doesn't have an outside job. Trust me, dealing with this commotion is the better deal," she said, hugging herself against the wind.

"Suit yourself. How are things going otherwise?"

"I'm going to hear from the police department today about interviewing a cop. If all goes well, I'll be riding along either tonight or tomorrow night."

"Good girl. Have fun. Listen, I have to run, but I wanted to let you know that Ellen called me today. They're going to be updating the Web site for upcoming releases and she'd like to put up an excerpt. Might as well start generating some excitement."

I am dead meat. Day-old roadkill. "Thanks. I'll pull something together."

"Great. Keep me posted. If you start getting into trouble, I want to know *immediately*."

"Right." She ended the call, then called Officer Prescott.

"He's in a meeting," the voice at the other end informed her.

"Oh, well, this is Randi Rhodes. He was setting up an appointment for me to—"

"You're the writer? Yeah, the chief said no."

Miranda stared at the phone in horror. "Did he give a reason?" she asked as calmly as she could manage.

"Let's see, it says here that his decision was based on the need to protect the security and integrity of ongoing investigations."

"So I can't interview *anyone*?"

"That's right, ma'am. If you have any other questions, you can call back. Officer Prescott should be available a little bit later. Have a good day."

I'll see if I can schedule one. Miranda back walked into the reverberating condo and headed for her laptop.

*   *   *

Chas walked into the austere, painfully hip restaurant in Manhattan's financial district and spotted James instantly. His oldest friend was standing in a well-dressed cluster of young Wall Streeters who had gathered near the artfully beaten stainless steel bar talking in earnest, heads bent toward each other. The women were sleek and the men were cocky. Their sense of superiority was palpable.

James glanced up, caught Chas's eye, and made his excuses to the group. The two of them sat down at a microscopic table and ordered a round of drinks.

"They never turn it off," James muttered behind his smile. "They'll all be old before they're thirty."

Chas smiled. "The new crop?"

James nodded and glanced back at the expensively besuited mid-twenty-somethings. "They have three topics of conversation: money, 'the deal,' and sex, and the order of precedence depends on the time of day. Right now they're still on 'the deal.' By the next round of drinks, they'll be onto sex." He met Chas's eyes. "They're ten years younger than me. Was I that much of an asshole ten years ago?"

"You were worse."

"Thanks, buddy."

Chas shrugged. "I still can't figure out why Paxton went out on a date with you, much less married you. She has such a low tolerance for them."

"I'm not sure. It was either the loan of your handcuffs, or she just ran out of ways to say no." James grinned. "Asshole or not, I was persistent. But her tolerance is still low and getting lower by the day. I have to stop bringing her to company parties. Either that or make her go back to work so she can expend her aggression in a more profitable way."

"What's she done now?"

"She mowed down half of the mergers and acquisitions department at a party a few weeks ago." He laughed. "I have to say, though, I love watching her in action."

Chas raised an eyebrow but said nothing as the waitress placed their drinks on the table.

James raised his glass. "Her return to Wall Street will have to wait another few years. How about a toast to a father of three?"

Returning his friend's grin, Chas lifted his glass. "Congratulations. When's the big day?"

"I'm not sure. She hasn't actually told me yet, but after going through it twice, I know the signs. The most obvious one is—"

"I don't really want to know," Chas interrupted.

"—she buys real estate."

He raised his eyebrows. "That's a new one. My sister rewallpapers her house."

"It's hormone poisoning, and it gets more expensive each time. With Hunter, she decided to sell the apartment in the city and buy the house in New Canaan. With Bailey, she bought that place in Vermont and a condo on Sanibel. A month ago we closed on that place in Italy and she decided to sell the condo in Shippan. She's got to be pregnant."

"Jesus. Sounds like she's having twins. If I were you, I'd seriously consider getting cut before she bankrupts you."

James laughed. "Where did you say you're going tonight?"

"Lincoln Center. Some Brazilian folk orchestra." Chas shrugged and glanced at his watch. He had an hour before he had to meet his date at a trendy bistro near her office.

"I take it you weren't in charge of the plans for the evening?"

"Not quite. The lady asked me out, and had all the arrangements made."

"Interesting strategy. Who is she? Another of your bachelor auction dates?"

"Got it in one."

"And you're seeing her again. It must be lust."

"Must be," Chas agreed dryly. "She's attractive, intelligent, and articulate, with no obvious bad habits." Despite that, he'd prefer to be waiting to meet a certain annoying brunette, but he wasn't about to admit that to James.

"Seen Miranda lately?"

Here we go. "Of course I have. We just went out last night. You were there, remember?"

"Nice dodge. Paxton said you showed up at the condo this morning and took her out. She wasn't back by the time Paxton left at one. Let me guess. Lunch at that inn on Route 7?" James asked, laughing.

Chas smiled benignly. "The Burger King on High Ridge Road, actually. We had to wait on line for a really long time. They were changing the grease in the french-fry machine."

"I'll bet they were. How does she like her burgers?"

"Raw." He took a sip of his drink. "Look, you can tell Paxton that I appreciate her efforts, but nothing's going to happen. Miranda Lane, writer of national prominence and your wife's college roommate," he said, gently mocking Paxton, "is also attractive, intelligent, and articulate, and she has a great voice. But she has one rather obvious bad habit, which more than unbalances the mix. She's a sarcastic pain in the ass who is unable to pass up an opportunity to behave like one." That she was maddeningly sexy, had eyes that bewitched him, and tasted like a slice of heaven didn't change that fact, either.

James took a sip of his drink. "As I recall, you called her a sarcastic pain in the ass the day she shot you, and you didn't even know her then. You still went out with her."

"Only because I'm scared of disappointing your wife. She'd reclassify me as an asshole, and I wouldn't get invited to her parties anymore. And, for the record, the fact that my opinion hasn't changed over a few encounters should be considered evidence that getting to know Miranda would be a pointless undertaking." Chas lifted his own drink with finality.

Amused but unconvinced, James changed the subject.

CHAPTER
8

Two corpses and a bureaucratic nightmare on an empty stomach was a bit much. His shift didn't even officially begin for another half hour, and Chas hadn't gotten much sleep last night. He rubbed his eyes, stifled a yawn, and tried to put a suitably sympathetic expression on his face.

"Mrs. Jensen, will you be willing to come down to police headquarters later today and give us a statement?" he asked the older woman, who was visibly and justifiably upset. Hers was the sort of neighborhood in which residents expected to look out the window in the morning to see birds in the trees, not dead hookers.

She nodded and glanced back at the tree. "My husband planted that in 1960. My grandchildren were playing in it after school yesterday," she said in a choked voice. "What were those women doing up there? What were they doing here? Where did they come from? Detective, *that's Greenwich.*" Her voice breaking, she pointed to the backyard that abutted her own. The bodies had been laid on the thick lower branches of a pine tree that hung over the fenced property line, creating a jurisdictional issue in addition to a macabre neighborhood spectacle.

"I know, Mrs. Jensen." He put his hand on her shoulder and gave it a little squeeze. "There are a lot of unanswered questions right now. All I can tell you is that it appears that the women were killed somewhere else and their bodies were brought here."

"But in my tree, Detective?" she wailed, and took a breath to try to regain her composure.

The absurdity of the situation, combined with hunger and lack of sleep, threatened to crack his own composure. *Two Dead Naked Hookers up a Tree on the Greenwich Line.* It wasn't a headline one encountered every day.

"I'll have to cut it down. I won't ever be able to look at it again. My husband planted that the year we moved in," she repeated, shaking her head and letting two tears roll down her cheeks. "He died six months ago."

"I understand, Mrs. Jensen. I'm very sorry for your loss. But you can't cut down the tree until we've completed our investigation. In fact, we're going to leave the yellow tape up for a while. You need to stay away from it and keep others away from it." He reached into the breast pocket of his sport coat and pulled out a card. "Here's my number. Please call me if you remember anything. Noises in the night, unusual phone calls in the last few days. Anything. And we have an appointment later today, right?" he asked gently.

She nodded. "Are the . . . the . . . are they going to be taken away soon?" she asked, pointing to the closed body bags lying on her lawn.

"Yes, ma'am. Just as soon as the crime-scene unit is finished. Thank you, Mrs. Jensen. I'll see you later."

He left her on her back porch and walked back to the tree to join Gruber and three uniforms and the crime-scene unit. And a matched set from the Greenwich PD.

"She hear anything?"

Chas shook his head. "Did anybody else?"

"A lady down the block said her dog started barking at about four this morning. Three other people said they were out jogging at around five and didn't see anything. That's about it."

One of the crime-scene analysts walked over from where he'd been stooping in the grass. "Looks like they backed up the car right under the tree. Tracks are fresh.

This is one for the books, huh? Have we decided who gets the bodies?"

The members of the group looked at each other and then away, choking back gallows grins.

"We could cut 'em in half," cracked one of the Greenwich detectives.

"Christ, Willis, keep it down," Gruber growled, glancing over his shoulder at the clutch of worried, whispering neighbors gathered across the street and the two news vans parked nearby with their satellite masts up. "Twisted bastard."

"Lighten up. What the hell are we supposed to do? A guy calls us telling us there are two dead bodies draped above his side of the fence, and the lady calls you because they're in her tree. Somehow I don't think there's a policy in place to cover this one."

"Nothing like a nice, early start to the day. Listen, Tommy, she wants to cut down the tree. I told her she can't, but you might want to make an impression on her. Start talking about body-fluid residues or something," Chas said to the crime-scene analyst, then looked at Gruber. "Anything else?"

Gruber shook his head. "Let's go. I gotta get something to eat. The lieutenant called me at five. Got me out of bed. Were you up?"

Chas nodded his good-byes to the others as he turned to walk to the car. "Hell, no. I was in the city last night and didn't even get back until one thirty."

"Tough life." Gruber slid behind the wheel and started the car. "Were you out with that writer again?"

"Not last night," Chas said casually, glancing out the window at the bare autumn neighborhood. "She's a nice woman, though. Interesting. We went out to dinner Tuesday, and yesterday morning I took her to get temporary tags for her car; then we went out to lunch." He felt a little bad about the implication that they'd spent the night together, but the more important thing was to make sure that word got back to Murphy and that he backed off.

"Shit, Casey, you have some fucking luck," Gruber

muttered. "Dunkin' Donuts or the diner on High Ridge?"

That was Murphy taken care of. "I don't care where we go; I just need some coffee and some food." Chas leaned back against the seat and rubbed his eyes. "Why would someone put dead hookers up a tree?"

"That sounds like the opening line of one of Pellegrini's jokes."

"All we need is the punch line."

"Where's her husband?" Gruber asked.

"Died six months ago."

"What did he do?"

"President and CEO of an electronics supply company in Bridgeport. Three kids. One in Chicago, one in New Haven, one in college in Boston."

"Living the American dream," Gruber muttered, and turned onto the parkway headed toward breakfast. "Except for the hookers."

Miranda walked along the deserted beach kicking pebbles and shooing away seagulls. This week had gone straight to hell in a handbag. Chas was gone and wouldn't be back, thanks to the very un-Southern charm she'd displayed the other day. The cops had turned her down. She'd lied to her agent. And yesterday she'd gotten her period.

She stopped and looked out over the water. Yesterday, today, every day this week had been sucky writing days. *Type, read, delete. Type, read, delete.* She might as well be running on a giant hamster wheel, for all the good she was doing to the manuscript. Dirk—or Dork, as she'd begun calling him—was totally misbehaving. At the moment, her heroine thoroughly hated her so-called hero. Miranda knew she should call Amy, especially since she'd had the temerity to send the increasingly nervous agent two chapters as a test run. There was no way she could send an excerpt to Ellen to put up on the Web site.

All in all, there were only two good things that had happened this week, and one was only halfway on the list. Two naked hookers had been found in a tree near Greenwich yesterday. It had been the lead story on the local news both last night and this morning. Chas was quoted by the paper and gave a quick statement on TV, but that wasn't why the story grabbed her attention. It had saved her plot.

At least now she had a reason for her hero and heroine to get together on the page. He was investigating the case and she was defending the suspect. Unfortunately, how they were supposed to get from glaring at each other across the table in the interrogation room to sweaty and naked on top of it was something she hadn't quite worked out yet.

The other good thing was that the weather had finally cleared. The blue sky was meant to last only a few hours, but the rain of the last few days was gone, leaving behind a sky clear of smog and full of sunshine that crystallized the air. She could even see the smokestacks of Long Island. It wasn't terribly scenic, but it was *something* on the earthly horizon. Unlike her career horizon, which at the moment was an endless, empty wasteland utterly devoid of creativity and, therefore, opportunity. She dug the cell phone out of her pocket before it could chirp twice.

"Hi, Amy."

"Hi."

Miranda looked at the phone warily. Amy never used greetings. She said they were only used by people who were afraid to get down to business. "How are you?"

"Unimpressed."

It's what I pay her for, Miranda told herself. *Honesty, candor, and the ability to inflict gut-wrenching pain.*

"It's not working. Dirk's not an alpha male, Miranda. He's a Neanderthal," her agent began. "Ellen wants primal, not primitive. You've made him a cave dweller with no fire except the one burning beneath his loincloth. Trouble is, this is the twenty-first century. He's not supposed to be the one drooling. Your readers are."

Miranda winced. "He doesn't drool."

"He might as well. Come on. Women are supposed

to want to crawl into bed with him, but the way you've written him, I can practically smell the fresh blood of a woolly mammoth on his breath. I mean, he's vivid, but he's no cupcake."

Miranda took a long sip from her bottle of nearly flat Coke. "So he needs an inner child *and* a feminine side?"

"For a start. And while we're at it, get rid of his beard. I can see where you're headed with it and it won't sell."

"What do you mean 'where I'm headed'?" she asked innocently.

"I've read everything you've ever written, Miranda, and I know what you do to characters you don't like. Get rid of the beard before you even get started. And give him tear ducts in addition to sweat glands. You're great at making guys cry and you know it. Miranda, you have to put *good* things in Dirk. He's your *hero*," she said emphatically. "If you can't find something to love about him, neither will your heroine and neither will your audience. You know all this, babe. I shouldn't have to remind you." She paused. "Look, you can't afford to have this book tank. Find a role model. I mean that literally. Who did you interview at the Stamford cop shop? Anyone you could use?"

"That's not going to happen."

"Why not?"

"The chief said no."

"So find a cop on your own. Start running red lights or smoking in elevators. Or call a police department in another town." Amy paused. "Tell me straight, kiddo. Are you going to be able to do this? Because if you can't, I have to tell Ellen—"

"Yes," Miranda said firmly. "I'll have something for you in a few days. Something really good. You'll swoon."

"Something I'm well-known for," the born and bred Brooklynite said dryly. "Keep in touch."

It's going to be a long two weeks. Miranda slid the cell phone into her pocket and lowered herself to the shell-strewn sand, then rested her elbows on her knees. She closed her eyes, pressed the pads of her thumbs against

the inner corners of her eyebrows, and made herself fight
the sense of defeat tearing at the edges of her confidence. *The revisions are going to get done. They have to.*

Faking her way through the rewrite by doing second-
hand research wasn't an option. Not for an editor who was
a self-proclaimed cop slut. Figuratively speaking anyway.

Her only viable option was to make up with Chas,
even though that would be as dangerous personally as
faking it with Ellen would be professionally.

He'd kissed her.

She'd let him.

She'd kissed him back.

That put the attraction pretty much out in the open.
*Which would be terrific if I engaged in hit-and-run ro-
mances as easily as I write them.*

She could deal with him one of two ways. She could
be honest and ask him if she could interview him, or she
could continue to interview him surreptitiously. Either
way, she'd be using him. Either way, she'd have to deal
with the personal situation that was developing. Either
way, she'd get what she needed: a cop in her head. Either way she'd get precisely what she wanted to avoid:
a cop in her—

She stood up hurriedly and walked to the water's
edge, then reached down and splashed some cold water
on her face. It didn't clear her mind any. *Heart* and
bed were still the only two words available to finish that
thought. Neither was appropriate. Neither was viable.
But both were becoming distinct possibilities.

Oh, hell. Why now? I have a book to finish. She sank
back to the sand, rested her forehead on her drawn-up
knees, and forced her mind back into production mode.
As much as she'd tried to convince herself in the past
few hours that Chas wasn't the perfect Dirk, he was.
He'd worked his way up the departmental ladder. Any
of his stories could be tweaked from being strange truth
into believable fiction. And he was physically attractive
without being perfect. A small scar on his chin and another over his left eye added some intrigue to his face,
and it looked as if his nose might have been broken once
and set properly. The kink was only noticeable close-up.

His behavior gave her a good base to work from, too. He was attracted to her and annoyed with her at the same time. His manners fluctuated with his mood. And she knew how he kissed. Not that she'd let him really get going, but at least she wouldn't have to start from scratch on that detail. That smooth maneuver in the car would translate well to a book, too. It had taken her completely by surprise. A nice surprise, if unwelcome.

She lay back on the sand. It *was* unwelcome. *It was.*

"Okay. I'm switching into book mode. Dirk's character traits. Personality," she said calmly to the empty sky after a deep, cleansing breath. "Quiet. Cynical. Watchful. Angry at Taylor for defending scumbags. He hates lawyers. He likes sex. He thinks sex with lawyers violates the natural order of things. Oh, sweet Jesus, this is not working." She shut her eyes against the glare and sought a safer topic.

Habits. She smiled. Chas definitely had some habits she could lift. The key slinging was a good one. And she'd recently discovered that he could weave a pen through the fingers of his left hand while his right remained relaxed and open. It had to be a sign of ambidextrousness or something. He'd done it while they were at the DMV waiting for her paperwork to be processed. It could be a habit Taylor found terribly annoying until she realized just what else those limber fingers could—

Miranda opened her eyes and blinked in the bright sunshine. *No, no, no, no. No limber fingers.*

Chas reached for the phone without taking his eyes off the report in front of him. "Detective Casey."

"Julie's been crawling up my ass for nearly a week, and you know if she's pumping *me* for information she's damned near desperate. Tell me what's going on with Paxton's writer friend and I'll hang up."

Chas laughed and shook his head at the thoroughly disgusted voice of his younger brother. "That's some greeting."

"I didn't have time for this shit in high school or college, and I sure as hell don't have time for it now. Can't you just make up something? Send her an e-mail so she'll quit calling me," Joe Casey complained from just over three hundred miles away in Washington, D.C., where he'd recently begun working as assistant general counsel for Brennan Shipping.

"I don't have to make up anything. She's beautiful but a complete pain in the ass."

Joe paused. "I like her already. How many times have you been out with her?"

"Twice. Dinner and lunch." Chas put down his paperwork and leaned back in his chair.

"In that order?"

"Don't go there." Chas watched Murphy walk by too nonchalantly to be doing anything other than eavesdropping. "Tell Julie there's nothing going on."

"You're shitting me. You? *Nothing?*" Chas could hear the amusement in his brother's voice. "You just said she's beautiful. Julie says she's beautiful. And she went to Smith, so odds are she's intelligent."

"She is intelligent."

"So why isn't there anything going on? It can't be because she's a pain in the ass. Half the women you date are colossal pains in the ass."

"Some of them have redeeming qualities."

"She doesn't?"

"The jury's still out."

"Bullshit. I'll bet she's not interested in you. That's a new one."

Chas frowned. "Of course she's interested in me, you prick. But she lives in Atlanta and she's going back there in two weeks."

"Sounds like a great opportunity."

"Grow up."

"Julie and Paxton already have you married and living in New Canaan. In fact, I think there might be a baby on the way."

"You first."

"Hell, no. Why do you think I'm in D.C.? I'm out of range. You live in the crosshairs."

"Well, tell Julie to hold off on buying the monogrammed towels. It's not going to happen." Chas listened to the sound of his brother's laughter. "What else is going on?"

"She said you're going to turn down the board's offer."

"That's right," Chas said coolly.

"Why?"

"It's a desk job. I don't like desks."

"We need you," Joe replied, his voice equally cool.

"Who does?"

"The board. The company."

"What the hell are you talking about?"

Silence greeted his question, making the hairs on the back of Chas's neck rise. "I asked you a question."

"I'm sorry. I thought—Never mind. Listen, I have to fly."

"Not so fast. What's going on?"

"Sorry, Chas. It's need-to-know. Talk to Mom. Or call Dalton. I've gotta go."

Chas stared at the dead phone. "Fucking right I'll talk to her," he muttered, and glanced at his watch.

"Yo, Chas, you up for some paintball tonight?"

Chas glanced up to see Pellegrini leaning too casually in the entrance to his cubicle. *Christ. How long has he been there?* "No. Thanks anyway."

"C'mon. Why not?"

Chas clicked his mouse to begin shutting down his computer and stood up. "I have plans."

"You going out with that writer again?"

He shrugged into his sport coat. "No, as a matter of fact, I'm not. But I'm beginning to think you're a wimp, Pellegrini."

"Fuck you. Whadda you talkin' about, anyway? I asked you if you want to play paintball."

"If you want to see her, you should just ask her out. Or has the Italian stallion been gelded?" Chas grinned. "She's nice, and she isn't dating anyone as far as I know."

"Who the hell are you talking about? I never said anything about a woman."

"Jane."

"The chick who runs the paintball place? I never said anything about taking her out. She's not my type. She's kinda, you know, too nice." Pellegrini gave a one-shouldered shrug and looked behind him to check who might have overheard him.

Chas shook his head. "I know. I just said she's nice. Look, Pellegrini, I've known her for years. I even took her out once. Jane Shelby is a nice kid. She's sweet and a little on the . . . she's kind of shy." He slid his paperwork into the top drawer and met the other man's eyes. "Bottom line is she'll never ask you out, so if you want to get to know her, you're going to have to get over—"

"What's with the 'Shelby'?" Pellegrini's face turned wary and a little alarmed. "Holy fuck, you're not talking *the* Shelbys, are you? I thought her name was Johnston. Jane Johnston."

"What's wrong? They don't bite. They're nice people."

"Yeah, they can afford to be. They own half of Fairfield County. Holy fuck." He closed his eyes. "Where'd the Johnston come from?"

"Johnston is her married name."

His eyes popped open. "She's *married*?"

Chas grinned. "Why should you care? You just said she's not your type."

"She's really married?" Pellegrini slowly shook that wild mane of hair in disbelief. "Shit."

"Get a grip, Pellegrini. She's widowed. She got married young and he died a few years later. That was a while ago. She's a sweetheart. But . . . look, I have to go," Chas said, reaching for the keys to his truck. "You've been drooling over her for months. Quit fucking around and ask her out. You never know how desperate she is. She might say yes."

Miranda had intended to stay on the beach long enough to ensure all the workmen would be gone by the time she got back to the condo. But as she stepped across the threshold, the carpenter came out of hiding to deliver a long-winded monologue about his schedule.

This was followed by the stonemasons, speaking in high-speed, colloquial Spanglish, telling her when they'd be back and warning her to be careful not to trip over the uneven surfaces. It was all she could do to smile and nod and shoo them all out the door.

Finally alone for the first time in what felt like forever, Miranda leaned against the front door, absorbing the sudden, pulsing silence and surveying the wreckage around her. In the space of twenty-four hours every available surface, including those that had been draped, was covered in dust. Plaster dust from the drywall that had been ripped down. Sawdust from the paneling that would be put up. Stone and mortar dust from the floor that had been dislodged.

Miranda picked her way carefully to the master bedroom, the door of which she had kept closed, and stepped out of her running shoes. Stripping off her clothes, she turned on the bath taps and, fifteen minutes later, practically fell into the deep, steaming tub. Lacking bubble bath or anything more glamorous, she squirted in some body wash and turned on the air jets.

After time for only one big exhale, she reached an arm out of the silky, drugstore-scent foam and answered another call from Amy.

"What's that noise?"

Miranda switched off the jets. "A Jacuzzi."

"You know, I'm having a really hard time feeling sorry for you. I heard seagulls during our last call, and two hours later you're in a Jacuzzi."

"After the day I've had, sugar, it's a necessity. What's up? Has Ellen decided she wants him to be a cowboy instead of a cop?"

"Down, girl."

"Sorry."

"Did we ever discuss sex?"

Miranda's eyes fluttered shut in anticipation of the deep and twisting pain she was about to endure at the hands of this woman to whom she handed over 15 percent of her blood, sweat, and tears. She slid into the water until the foam tickled her chin. "Can you give me a context?"

"With regard to Ellen."

"No. Is she for it or against it?"

"Definitely for it. More of it. She wants it hotter and she wants it earlier."

"Don't we all," she muttered, but the silence on the other end of the call indicated that even gallows humor was unappreciated. She sighed. "How much more and how much earlier?"

"At least two more scenes, and the first should be around page thirty."

"Page thirty?" Miranda yelped, sitting straight up in the water. "They've barely met."

"That's why they call these revisions."

She took a deep breath. "Amy," she said in a deliberately calm, quiet voice, "I feel it's only fair to warn you that I'm thinking of quitting this profession and doing something that doesn't make me feel like I have to rationalize every fucking decision or apologize to every fucking person on the planet."

Her words were met with a short but reverent silence. "Did you just say 'fuck'? You never say 'fuck.' You're not about to go postal on me, are you? It would be really bad for your career, Miranda. Just calm down."

"I am calm, and I'm not about to do anything more dangerous than shave my legs. And I said 'fucking,' as in I'm sick of this *fucking* story and I'm sick of these *fucking* revisions. Once upon a time, I thought writing was *fun*, Amy. Not anymore. I want to write something else. Something that no one can look at and tell me I'm doing it the wrong way."

This time Amy's hesitation was barely discernible. "Listen, kitten, get these revisions done and we'll talk. In the meantime, just keep thinking about earning the rest of your advance so we can get this baby on the shelves and start selling some books. That will let everyone know you're doing things the right way."

CHAPTER
9

Chas stood near the wall, surveying the high-end, cocktail-partying crowd at Shanna Pendergast's yearly holiday gathering, held earlier and earlier each year so that the first lady of the social-climbing set could claim her party launched the season. After the last two days of dealing with dead hookers, distraught suburbanites, and the press, the last place he wanted to be was at a cocktail party. But he'd accepted the invitation a month ago and in the end thought it might be entertaining.

Shanna's were the kind of parties attended by "everyone"—local Greenwich residents, representatives from the Manhattan art world, the theater, and Wall Street, a *few* members of Long Island's elite, and the occasional politician or ex-president—everyone with the right amount of fortune or fame to elevate them above the masses. The only element missing was the criminal, although based on the corporate scandals of the last decade, that point was open to debate.

Shanna's parties were usually a good time. The crowd glittered in every sense of the word. There were nearly as many security guards, bodyguards, and chauffeurs loitering outside the massive house as there were guests inside. The men—both guests and employees—wore dark suits or tuxes and were full of hearty greetings and lots of bullshit. The women were expensively dressed, some tastefully, like Paxton and his mother, and others less so.

As if on cue, a pair of much-discussed Los Angeles breasts with permanently surgically erect nipples, sheathed in a shirt made from shrink-wrap, came to a rolling stop in front of him.

"Hi, Chas. It's fabulous to see you." The new and obviously improved Baxter Sumpter pressed herself against him to effect an air kiss near his cheek. The breasts didn't give much against his chest, and he wondered what material the surgeons had used as struts. Just like Enron, entities that size couldn't be self-supporting.

"It's been a long time, Baxter. What's new?"

"And you're usually so subtle, Chas," she purred.

"Sorry. Freudian slip."

"Mmmm-hmmm. I'll only believe you because you're one of my favorites."

He had no desire to hear the details, and began his departure with a smile. "It's always nice to see you, Baxter." Her answering look left him wanting a shower. A hot one. Lots of soap.

He glanced past her to see the crowd parting for a cane-wielding octogenarian and knew he was the target. "I'll have to catch up with you later."

He met the white-haired terror halfway and led her toward an alcove that was conveniently vacated by the mismatched married couple that had slipped into it moments before.

"What do you think you're doing, turning down our offer?" Stella Maris Windsor-Dolan demanded, looking up at him with her deceptively sweet face.

He knew she would wait until hell froze for his answer. As the reigning matriarch of a large family, she was related by blood or marriage to half of the shipping concerns in the world, from yacht designers and stevedores to freight lines and cruise ships. Stella Maris had broken gender barriers to become a marine engineer in the '40s and a maritime lawyer in the '60s before retiring in the '90s to sit on the boards of several major multinational corporations, including Brennan Shipping. She terrified everyone, proudly. Except her godson.

"Can I get you a drink, Aunt Stella?"

"You can give me an explanation, you troublemaker."

"I heard that Shanna is stashing some Macallan behind the bar." Chas gave her a smile that he knew could melt her if she were in the mood to let it.

She wasn't. "Answers, Charles. I may need a drink after I get those. You may, too." She sat down on the small settee and looked up at him expectantly.

With a grin, he leaned in the doorway. "I have an aversion to desks, Palm Pilots, and corporate vice presidents. And I like carrying guns and catching bad guys."

"You'll have plenty of opportunities to do the latter when you take this job. Just ask your brother."

His radar surged out of suspended operation as he remembered Joe's comment from this afternoon. He hadn't had a chance to corner his mother yet and follow up on it. He raised an eyebrow. "Ask Joe about what?"

"The company's computers have been hocked."

He paused. "You mean 'hacked'?"

"That's right." Her eye held a gleam of satisfaction.

"When?"

"It was discovered a week ago."

God damn it. He kept his voice calm. "How do you know?"

"I'm on the board. If you were, you'd know too."

He ignored the comment. "Why is this the first I'm hearing about it?"

"Your mother and Dalton decided it would be a need-to-know situation. And they thought you didn't need to know."

"Why are you telling me?"

She fixed a cold glare on him. "*I* think you need to know. And *I* think it's high time you stopped playing cops and robbers and took your place at your mother's side. Your grandfather's an old man, Chas. He's tired. Your mother is running more and more of that company and leaning too heavily on Dalton, if you ask me. Get in there, boy. That hotshot brother of yours isn't ready yet, and your sister can't, though I think she'd do a hell of a job."

A tidal surge of anger and guilt pounded him.

"Thanks for your vote of confidence. Tell me more about the problem," he said coolly.

"Joe has a team of whiz kids working on it. I can't understand half of what they're talking about, but it doesn't seem like they know much. Even whether it's coming from inside the company." She made a motion to stand up and he instantly helped her to her feet. "Enjoy the party, Charles. Which bar has that Macallan behind it?"

She leaned heavily on the ancient, gold-headed cane and headed back to the party without a backward glance. Chas found Shanna and made his excuses unobtrusively, then left, reining in his impatience as he waited for the valet parking attendants to find his car. He would have preferred to walk to it himself, but it would have taken longer to argue with them than to wait for it.

He drove down the long driveway and away from the property before pulling over and reaching for his cell phone.

"What's up?"

Chas could hear voices in the background. "Plenty. Get someplace you can talk," he snapped at his brother. His fingers tapped a harsh tattoo against the steering wheel as the car idled on the side of a road in backcountry Greenwich. Across the miles, he heard a door close and the background noise fade.

"Okay, what is it?" Joe's voice held an edge of defensive wariness.

Son of a bitch. "Why didn't you tell me what was going on?"

"Pick a topic, Chas."

"Take a fucking guess what I'm talking about, Joe. I just had a conversation with Stella Maris. She told me about the company."

"What did she tell you?"

"Probably as much as she could. The woman uses a slide rule to plot her flower gardens, for Christ's sake. But you, little brother, are going to tell me just what's going on or I'll come down there tonight to persuade you."

"I'm not at liberty to discuss it with you. Ask Mom," Joe replied coolly.

"The fuck you're not. Tell me."

There was a long pause that ended when Joe swore under his breath. "A week ago, some new kid in the IT department actually started looking at monitoring data instead of just filing it. There was a lot of traffic going out at night when most of the traffic should have been inbound. This kid is smart. He's done his share of hacking and he knew what hc was sccing. He bypassed everyone and went straight to Granddad."

"What do you mean, went straight to him?"

"I mean he drove from the office to LaGuardia and got on a plane to Palm Beach that afternoon. With his laptop."

Chas let out a heavy breath. "He thought it was an inside job?"

"Yes, and he was right. Most of the data was junk, but every night there were a few files coming out of the R-and-D group."

Chas curled his fingers into a tight fist, then flexed them before he hit something. Brennan's research division was renowned for both its innovation and its tight security, which was why the government contracted it so frequently for highly classified work. "Which project group?"

"You know which one."

"God damn it."

"To put it lightly." Joe let out an annoyed breath. "We've assembled a team. They've been working their asses off, but so far all we've traced are a few dead ends. We're still trying to figure out what's gone out and how long it's been going on."

"And?"

"At this point it looks like they got in six months ago."

Chas closed his eyes, pinching the bridge of his nose. "Why didn't you tell me?"

"Need to know, Chas. You weren't on the list. You're still not, and I've just broken about six federal laws by telling you."

"Quit whining. Who's on the list?"

"Granddad, Mom, Dalton, Stella Maris, and me. As far as I know."

"Why wasn't I put on it?"

"You fucking know why," Joe snapped. "They don't want you here part-time, Chas. And they don't want you waltzing in like some sacrificial fucking hero to save the day. If you want to know anything else, ask Mom. Don't ask me again."

Chas stared at the small phone in his hand for a few moments after his brother disconnected. A faded line from a college course flashed through his mind. Something about Fate leading the willing and dragging the unwilling.

God damn it. The familiar guilty pull he'd grown used to had just escalated into a tight squeeze. He put the Porsche into gear and pulled away from the side of the road. It was just after nine on Friday night. He was in no mood for a party, in no mood for company, but in no mood to go home and try to ignore the situation.

He barely noticed the familiar landscape as he drove slowly along the unlit streets. Of course he cared about the company. They—all of them—were crazy if they thought he didn't. It was what had made everything in his life possible. It was a four-generation legacy that he would do everything in his power to maintain and enhance. Everything except sacrifice his life to it. That didn't mean he deserved to be shut out of the investigation. He shook his head, still not quite believing his mother had done that. It was a stunt he wouldn't have thought her capable of pulling. He'd rectify the situation soon enough.

He slammed the car down a gear, stood on the accelerator, and shot down a road that he knew was a two-mile straightaway with no driveways. *Why is it so fucking difficult for them to understand that I don't want to grow old sitting behind a desk all day?* He was a cop. Like his father he was a damned good cop, and he had every intention of becoming a high-ranking cop, *not* a corporate officer. The only title he wanted anytime soon was Lieutenant. His name had already been formally presented to Chief Drucker and would be sent to the Police and Fire Commission next week. He'd know within a few weeks whether he had the promotion or not. He had the best shot of anyone at getting it. The two high-profile cases he'd been involved with this week wouldn't hurt either.

He reached the end of the road and pulled in at the stop sign, then lowered his window as the Greenwich patrol car following him turned off its rooftop lights and pulled alongside his car. The uniformed officer lowered his passenger window and leaned across the seat.

"You been drinking?" he asked.

"No. What did I do?" Chas replied, feeling some of the adrenaline in his bloodstream dissipate.

"I clocked you at one forty-two."

He grinned. "Not bad."

The cop laughed. "You've done better, Chas. You must be getting old."

"Hardly. The road's wet."

"How've you been?"

"Doing okay. You?" Chas replied. "You a father yet?"

"Any day now." The cop straightened up as the radio unit began to crackle. "Damn. Gotta go. Where are you coming from?"

"Shanna Pendergast's."

The cop rolled his eyes. "That's where I'm headed. Later, buddy."

"See you around."

A short while later, his anger temporarily spent, Chas found himself turning off U.S. 1 and heading toward the beach—and the other part of the reason he'd been quiet tonight: Miranda Lane. She'd been invited to Shanna's, all right. Paxton had made sure he knew that. But, pleading work, she'd stayed home. It was just as well.

He was restless, bored, and not in the mood to deal with anyone. Except Miranda. Not that it made sense. She was beautiful, but that had never been the only thing that attracted him to a woman. But this woman . . . He let out a hard breath that was nearly a sigh. This one was annoying and appealing in equal parts. Blunt when he least expected it and secretive without necessity. She was glib, snide, and downright cocky—or flirtatious—when she had no logical reason to be, but she wasn't afraid to admit defeat or back down when it was called for. He was tempted to label her an enigma, but it could be that she was just fickle. Or premenstrual, for that matter. Whichever condition was the right one, it didn't change the fact that he may have blown his chance with her by being such a hard-ass the other day. And it didn't change the fact that he still wanted to get to know her. Hell, he just *wanted* her.

He engaged the Porsche's hand brake and looked at the façade of her condo, still the only one with its outside light off, wondering if he should bother ringing the doorbell. Wondering just how annoyed at him she still was. Wondering why he couldn't stop thinking about that kiss.

Taylor wandered alone through the dark, third-floor hallway of the old mansion, looking around in wonder at the sheer luxury surrounding her. The lavish, catered cocktail party she'd abandoned was in full swing two floors below.

"The man was raised in a trailer park and has been on the bench since he was thirty-five. How can he afford this? Being a judge doesn't pay that well," she murmured, lifting a Baccarat flute of Champagne to her lips.

"Accepting bribes helps."

Her heart rate exploded in panic, and she spun around at the sound of the low, familiar voice that was too close to her. He moved even closer, his dark, brooding eyes and moody mouth filling her field of vision. His hand came up to her face, and before she could pull away, his thumb, surprisingly gentle, smoothed against her lower lip and into her mouth, brushing the tip of her tongue. She tasted Champagne, and him. His hand fell away. His gaze remained locked on her, intoxicating her.

Miranda closed her eyes in despair. *She* tasted *him? How gross was that? Not to mention grammatically dull.*

With a sigh, she opened her eyes and continued the scene, knowing she'd have to scrap nearly all of it.

"When are you going to stop asking for continuances?" His voice sleeked along her nerves like ice cubes in a hot frying pan.

She rolled her eyes and grimaced. *What sort of a moron tries to fry ice?* She backspaced over the line.

His voice sleeked over her nerves like cool water on sun-warmed flesh, leaving a tingling wake that was as delicious as it was dangerous.

"We shouldn't be here. We shouldn't be talking to each other. You know that," she protested in a panicked whisper.

He leaned his forearms against the wall above her head, and even her four-inch Jimmy Choos didn't bring her to his eye level. He looked down at her, his dark eyes hot and amused. His heat, his scent enveloped her, short-circuiting every defense without a touch. Sparks were colliding in her bloodstream, causing a firefight of forbidden desire.

"Don't you worry, Counselor," he said, his words a low growl. "No one knows we're here. I'm not going to risk a mistrial. Your client is as guilty as the night is dark, and I want to see him put away for good. Let's put this case to bed."

Bed. Just the word made her shiver.

"Quit asking for continuances. You're not doing it to try to save your client; you're doing it to avoid facing me. To avoid facing what's happening between us." He lowered his face until his mouth brushed the delicate rim of her ear. Her eyes fluttered shut. She could feel each word as he said it. "Do you need to hear it, Taylor James? Every time I see you, I want to strip you down 'til it's just you and those high heels you wear. I want to pull down that tight little lawyer hairdo and use all that gorgeous hair to tie you up. I want your mouth beneath mine, Taylor. I want your body beneath mine," he whispered.

No. A caveman with bondage fantasies would not whisper.

—he growled.

She squinted at the screen. He'd already growled once in this scene.

—he squeaked.

She typed the words in disgust, then clicked to save it, although she knew she shouldn't have bothered. From her position on the floor of the loft, she turned to stare into the designer flames of the pressed sawdust log burning in the fireplace, listening to the pulsing hum of her laptop and the roar of the wind on the other side of the arched windows.

It was almost nine thirty on Friday night. She'd spent the entire day thinking about sex. Straight sex. Kinky sex. Playful sex. Angry sex. Rip-off-your-clothes-and-hump-on-the-stairs sex. She had a stack of self-help books on one side of her, with all the relevant chapters tagged with Post-its and paper clips. On the other side, she had an even taller stack of romance novels. Some were by her favorite authors, and others were there just because they contained hot sex scenes. Nothing was working for her, though. Not the vintage Sting playing in the background, not the sexy underwear she'd put on after her bath, hidden though it was beneath her sweats, and not even the two glasses of wine she'd drunk or the candles and sandalwood incense she'd lit.

She *hated* writing love scenes. She always did them in one huge effort at the start of a book just to get them out of her way, and then she'd fit them into the book as needed. She never had more than three significant ones in any book, and she had her own style of writing them. Nothing kinky, no anatomy lessons, no purple prose. Lots of euphemisms and dreamy adjectives. The occasional toy or foodstuff.

It worked.

That is, it worked when the hero was a tender, sensitive lover. But Andy—the hero formerly known as Dirk—wasn't that. He was sweaty. He was earthy. He wanted to get rowdy and loud and do it on the kitchen counters, and frankly, Taylor was appalled.

Miranda put her head in her hands. The situation was

approaching hopeless. Other than occasional walks on the beach, she'd been holed up in the condo for two solid days and nights breathing marble dust and fumes from the wood stain, ingesting massive quantities of caffeine-laden drinks—and writing and deleting and re-writing. That her hero and heroine still hated each other and she was beginning to hate them both was only part of the problem. The real problem was that she'd given herself a deadline the first time Amy had called about the revisions. She'd said it out loud. She'd written it down and taped it to her file folder of notes and onto the screen of her laptop. If she wasn't on track within a week, she'd surrender.

It had sounded good at the time, but her week ended at midnight tomorrow. There was only one thing Miranda hated more than writing love scenes, and that was admitting defeat.

Two stories down the doorbell pealed, and she brightened at the thought of the pizza she'd ordered more as a time-wasting diversion than dinner. Money in hand, she jogged down the stairs and arrived at the door out of breath. She opened it to see Chas standing in the splash of light, his dark hair and long dark coat sparkling in the rain. *Sexy* barely fit as a description. He was gorgeous. *My muse is obviously a merciless bitch with a warped sense of humor.*

Miranda blinked, then looked at the box in his hand. "Is that my pizza?"

"I'm fine, thanks," he replied.

"How did you get it?"

"I met the delivery guy on the way to the door."

"Did you pay him?"

"No, I pistol-whipped him. The tide's coming in, so I'll drag the body to the beach after we eat." He paused, looking at her closely. She could see the little bump on his nose. "Yes, I paid him. Can I come in?"

She blinked again and stepped back. "Of course. Thanks. That was nice of you."

"Not really. It was self-serving. Now you have to share it with me," he pointed out as she lifted the box out of his hands.

"Um, okay, I suppose. Watch out. They're not grouting until Monday," she said, balancing the pizza box on one hand while trying to shut the heavy wooden door behind him. He crossed the threshold, stepping gingerly onto the boards covering the new black marble floor, then lifted the box out of her hands. She looked up to find him studying her intently. "What?"

"Are you okay?" He reached past her to push the door shut. She heard the lock click. Loudly.

"I'm fine," she replied, taking the pizza out of his hands again and picking her way across the foyer to the kitchen. "What brings you here? Has Stamford run out of criminals?"

She set the flimsy box on the counter and pulled a large knife out of the wooden block on the counter, only to have one strong, slender hand come around her from behind and close around her wrist. His other hand gently took the knife out of her fingers and laid it on the counter, out of her reach.

Only vaguely aware that she stood within the circle of his arms, enveloped by the rich, earthy scents of wet wool, cold rain, and warm man, Miranda looked up at him over her shoulder. His mouth was the first thing she saw. It was soft and sexy, and twitching with suppressed laughter. *Where had it been ten minutes ago?*

She frowned at the thought and glanced up to his eyes, which were focused on her face. "What are you doing here, anyway?" she demanded again, and turned around to fully face him.

"I'm not exactly sure," he replied, and she was sure she heard laughter in his voice even though he still wasn't quite smiling. "Why don't you sit? I'll slice."

She folded her arms across her chest. "Excuse me, darlin', but don't you think you've been overbearing enough, not to mention insulting, *every single time* we've met? This is *my* house and *my* pizza, and *you're* an uninvited guest. In fact, I think that makes you a trespasser. That's twice you've broken the law over here. No pizza for rude men or felons, honey." She poked a finger into his chest. "Arrest yourself and get out."

He wrapped one hand around hers, lifted that rigid finger to his lips for a light, shiver-inducing kiss, then dropped it. "I'm the good guy; you're the bad influence. Besides, trespassing isn't generally a felony, and you invited me in both times, remember? How much have you had to drink?" he asked, turning her around and steering her by the shoulders to a stool at the breakfast bar. "Sit."

"A little bit of wine." She watched him shrug out of his long cashmere overcoat and drape it over the back of the bar stool next to her.

"I thought you said you didn't drink."

"I said I didn't drink *much*."

He peeled off the dark tux jacket and tossed it over a different bar stool. "So how little have you had?"

"Two glasses, not that it's any business of yours, soon-to-be Lieutenant Casey."

"There's no need to get formal. We've kissed, remember? I know what you taste like. Are you alone?"

"Of course I'm alone. I'm on deadline. Why are you laughing at me?" Her eyes slid down the length of him. He looked awfully good, casual and relaxed even while dressed up. "And where have you been?"

"A cocktail party. 'Tis the season," he replied, pulling off the bow tie that was hanging open around his neck and slipping it and the top two studs from his shirt into his trouser pocket. She couldn't tear her eyes away from the graceful, economical movements of those long, strong fingers as he removed his cuff links, pocketed them, and began rolling his sleeves up over solid, almost sculpted forearms. He recrossed the room and reached for the knife he'd taken away from her. "And I'm not laughing at you. So you ordered a large pizza just for yourself?"

She made herself look away and take a deep breath. It was all those hours thinking about sex that had her noticing things like the shape of his hands, the width of his shoulders, and the way his pleated trousers emphasized his slim hips and— It had to be. She never noticed things like that about men. Well, not since Josh, anyway.

But, then again, Josh hadn't looked particularly good in pleated pants. He didn't have the right kind of behind. It drooped.

She glanced back at Chas and tried to remember what they'd been talking about. "Why are you laughing at me?"

"You asked me that already."

"Well, what did you say?"

"I asked you why you ordered a large pizza."

"Because I'm hungry. You look nice, by the way," she added grudgingly.

His shoulders shrugged with a silent laugh. "Thank you. You look"—he glanced up to study her with a small frown—"thinner. And pale, except for your cheeks. That's probably from the wine. Your eyes are all sparkly, too, which I have to say is rather fetching."

"*Fetching?* Who are you pretending to be, Cary Grant?"

He laughed out loud, and she had to look away. Sometimes looking at him was like staring at the sun too long. It did things to her. Distracting things.

"How much wine did you say you've had?"

"I could swear you just asked me that. Are you quizzing me? If that's the case, I don't recall saying how many glasses I've had. Enough to make me sparkly and fetching, apparently."

"At least we're talking in plurals. So how's the book coming along?"

She lifted her chin. "Swimmingly, thank you."

"*Swimmingly?* Who are you channeling, Doris Day? Anyway, I'm glad to hear it."

"I'm not nearly blond enough at the moment to be Doris, but I'm glad you're glad. Plates are in the cabinet above the dishwasher. Where did I leave my wine?"

"I don't know. Where did you leave it?"

"Oh. Upstairs. I'll be right back."

"I'll join you."

She spun around and was surprised to find him so close. She pressed a hand against his chest to stop him from following her. It was warm and very solid, and the starched pleats that covered it were still crisp and nearly silky, and she wondered how the fabric would feel against her cheek. She blinked herself back to reality and looked up into his eyes. They were dark and warm, and he seemed closer than he had been even a minute ago. It all added up to trouble. She wasn't sure if she minded.

"I'm going to the loft, not my bedroom. You stay here. I'll be back directly."

He slid his hand over hers and smoothly lifted it away from those stiff, silky pleats. He let it fall gently away, but not before his thumb had brushed across her palm in an innocuous stroke that she nevertheless felt everywhere.

"I've always wanted to see the loft," he said easily. "What makes you think I'd be interested in seeing your bedroom?"

She rolled her eyes, then turned and continued walking toward the stairs. "Because you kissed me, then got all snarky because I wouldn't let you kiss me again. It doesn't take a rocket scientist to jump to the conclusion that you probably want to sleep with me, too, Cary."

"Just a romance writer?"

"What does that mean?"

"Not a rocket scientist, just a romance writer. You were talking about who was better qualified to jump to the conclusion that I want to sleep with you, Doris."

She turned around on the stairs, and wobbled. His hands shot out, settling on her hips to steady her. She ignored them. "Don't put words in my mouth. That's not what I said and it's not what I meant. Why are you following me?"

"Because you're in front of me."

"Don't get cute, Chas. You don't do cute."

"Okay. I want to see the loft."

"It's up here." She turned back and continued up the stairs. "So why are you here? Or do you moonlight as a delivery man for Giovanni's Pizza?"

"You know, Miranda, you have a really nice ass," he said matter-of-factly.

She spun around again. "That's it. You and your stupid macho, alpha-male comments are not welcome. Go home."

"If you keep doing that, you're bound to get dizzy and go right over the banister," he said with a laugh, then turned her around again and pushed her gently up the last few stairs, keeping his hands on her hips for no good reason at all. "We'll get your wine and then I'll leave."

"Okay, fine. Here's the loft. Now leave."

CHAPTER
10

Miranda watched as Chas looked around the small, cluttered room in disbelief.

"You left candles burning unattended?"

She stuck her hands on her hips and her chin into the air. "I wasn't intending to stay downstairs this long. I was going to get my pizza and come right back up here."

"For what? What the hell were you doing, having some sort of a ritual ceremony?" he demanded, coughing as he crossed the room to open the windows. "It stinks in here."

"It's sandalwood incense, and I happen to like it," she said, watching the flames in the fireplace flare as a cold, wet draft swept through the room.

He turned away from the windows and began blowing out the candles. "You won't when you sober up. Sit down. I'll bring up the pizza."

"I thought you were leaving."

"I'd be breaking my sworn duty to protect and serve the citizens of Stamford if I left you now. You'd burn down half of Shippan Point. Now just stay here."

She watched his back retreat, and as soon as he was out of sight she quickly cleared away her work, piling it in the least noticeable corner of the room and pulling a potted plant in front of it. Then she stood near an open window inhaling as deeply and as often as she could without making herself dizzy, and berated herself for drinking alone, for opening the door, for not being able to maintain a clear head around him.

"Here, this will help, too."

She whirled around to see him cresting the top of the stairs, balancing the pizza box in one hand and holding out a large tumbler of water with the other.

"Thanks," she murmured, taking the water. Her eyes flicked over the contents of the flat tray on top of the box. Plates, napkins, a bottle of wine, and two fresh glasses—

"That's not mine."

"What isn't yours?" He glanced down. "Oh, the wine. Don't worry about it. The stuff you were drinking could take the paint off a car. And it will give you a nasty hangover. This stuff should be easier to drink and to deal with later."

"Did you bring it with you?"

"No, I found it in the wine cellar." He set the box on the low marble coffee table and looked at her. "Relax. James and Paxton will never miss it. There was at least a case of it in there. And judging from the dust, they've forgotten about it."

"It looks expensive."

He picked up the bottle and looked at the label. "It looks ridiculously expensive," he agreed as he began to peel off the heavy foil wrapper covering the top of the bottle. "Let's hope that means it's drinkable. Could be some plonk they picked up after several hours of sitting in the cellar of some château eating foul cheese and drinking their brains out, a pastime otherwise known as a tasting tour." He looked up and grinned at her. "Come on, don't look like that."

"Like what?"

"Guilty. I promise I'll replace it, if that makes you feel better. Have some pizza."

She turned away and sat down on the far end of the couch. "I'm not guilty of anything. You're the one opening their wine."

He poured a small bit of wine into a glass, swirled it

for a moment, and then drank it. "It should be okay if we give it a minute."

He poured two glasses, handed her one, then walked over to the opposite end of the couch and sat down. "The wine is not what you're feeling guilty about. I think you've sobered up a little and now you're embarrassed that I saw a side of you I wasn't supposed to see. And you're feeling awkward about our kiss. And you're feeling guilty that you lied to me about being back together with your boyfriend."

"Very good, Detective. Game, set, match," she said lightly, watching the wine swirl along the inside of the heavy crystal goblet.

"So what were you working on?" he asked a moment later.

Too tired and frustrated to lie, even to him, Miranda sighed heavily and pushed herself deeper into the corner of the couch. "The rewrite from hell."

"I thought it was going swimmingly."

"I lied again. I've turned into a bad but prolific liar around you, Chas, as I'm sure you're well aware. Add that to the catalog of my sins." She rubbed her eyes, distracted and suddenly restless, then turned her gaze to the storm pounding against the windows. "Nothing's working."

"Writer's block?"

"No, nothing like that. I don't even believe in that. I just . . . No matter," she muttered. "I'll figure it out."

"I thought you only had to change the location of the story," he said, sliding a slice of pizza onto a plate and handing it to her.

"Thank you. Well, not exactly. The location is one thing I have to change."

"What are the others?" he asked, helping himself to a slice. She watched him fold the slice in half the long way and bite off the end. He was such a Yankee.

"The plot, the hero, and the sex."

"So what's the problem?" He settled himself against the cushions of the couch.

She glanced at him. "What? No snide comment?"

"Nope. I'm on sabbatical for the next few minutes."

"Let me guess. One of your rules for dinner conversation?"

He just flashed that charming but, at the moment, annoying half smile.

She sighed again and shifted her gaze back to the window. "Apparently my revised hero is a jerk of megalithic proportions." She glanced at him. "Perhaps I should rephrase that. I haven't figured out his proportions yet. He's just a jerk. According to my agent, no woman, real or fictional, would ever want to sleep with him, despite his good looks. He's mean, uncaring, selfish, brutish, snide, and has less natural charm than a cannibalistic troglodyte. And, no, he's not based on you. Much."

Chas laughed. "Thank you for that. At least he's not your usual wimp. Are you branching out?"

"For the record, I've completely discounted your evaluation of my heroes. That's not why he's different. He's different because my new editor wants me to write about a different kind of hero."

"What kind would that be?"

She settled a hard glare on his face. He didn't seem to notice. "You're enjoying this, aren't you?"

He nodded with a grin as he finished swallowing. "Immensely, but not for the reasons you think. I'm not enjoying your distress. So what kind of hero does your new editor want? Not one that's mean, uncaring, and all those other things, I take it?"

She shook her head. "An alpha male."

He laughed out loud. Miranda rubbed her eyes again, took a sip of wine, and waited for the moment to pass.

"Sorry," he said after one or two false attempts to stop laughing. "So the mean, uncaring one is your attempt at creating an alpha male? Who is he based on? Your ex?"

"Hardly. He's not based on anyone. Not even you."

"You already said that. If you tell me again, I'll know you're lying," he said with a grin.

What a flirt. "He's not based on you, I swear it," she replied, fighting back a smile of her own.

"Great." He reached for another piece of pizza. "So come on, no one dreams up a guy that bad, who's supposed to be good, without a romance gone wrong somewhere in the past."

Just when I was getting comfortable with Chas, Dirk comes roaring back. Thank heaven. She set her wineglass down and folded her arms across her chest. "You are *not* allowed to come in here and play amateur psychologist with me, Chas. For the record, I'm no tragic figure, and nothing bad has happened to me."

He shrugged. "Whatever. So how are you going to go about putting New Age sensibilities into a Neanderthal mind?"

Miranda picked up her slice and took a bite. "If I knew that, I'd have done it already."

"Why don't you model him on someone you like?"

"I thought about that. But the men I like aren't like him. The editor demanding all these changes wants him to be brooding, dark, and in control. I like openness and easiness and—"

"—wimps," he finished for her.

"Are we back to that?"

"Well, that's the problem, isn't it?"

"No."

"Was the last boyfriend a wimp? The one you broke up with a year ago?"

She frowned at him. "Just how much do you know about me? And who's been talking?"

"Paxton, James, your Web site." He shrugged. "Some things I've just surmised."

"What? No undercover police work?"

"Well, if you want me to run a criminal background check on you, I can do that."

"You wouldn't find anything. I don't even have any outstanding traffic tickets."

"Anymore," he said, and winked at her.

She rolled her eyes, unable to smother an involuntary smile. "I know I'm going to regret asking, but just what exactly do you know about me?" she repeated.

"I know that you're thirty-two and you graduated from Smith with a degree in English literature. That you worked in an advertising agency for three years, until you sold your first book, and then you began writing full-time. During that time, you were living with a professor of philosophy who taught at Emory. You broke up late last year after being together for about six years. You've had one pretty big best seller, and most of your others have done respectably well. And you're bright and brainy and beautiful."

Uh-oh. "My goodness. That's what I call doing your homework. Thank you." She unfolded her legs and stretched them out along the cushions, putting a barrier between them.

"Do you regret asking?"

"Yes and no. Everything but the last sentence was fine."

"What was wrong with the last sentence?" He looked lazy and content and perfectly comfortable leaning against the pile of cushions in his corner of the couch. She had to shake off the small, unexpected burst of warmth the picture generated, and remind herself that she was using him. Just using him. That was *all*. Nothing more.

He set his plate on the table, then wiped his hands with one of the paper towels he'd brought up instead of Paxton's starched, monogrammed linen napkins. A moment later he stretched out on the couch, sliding farther along the cushions, the length of his legs pressed lightly against hers.

I'm just using *him. Really.* "You're a troublemaker," she stated.

"You're the second woman who's made that observation tonight. The other one was about eighty years old and has known me since I was born. And you're both wrong." He nudged her thigh gently with his foot. "I don't make trouble; I just make trouble fun." He held her gaze with a smile that was both a crime and a sin, and for just a moment the heat of eternal hellfire wasn't stronger than what he ignited inside her. Lifting her wineglass to her mouth with both hands, she took a nonchalant sip to cool herself down.

"And speaking of fun, you didn't look like you were

having much fun when I got here. What were you doing up here alone with candles, wine, firelight, and a stack of books about sex?"

So much for concealing the evidence. "They aren't books about sex; they're books about relationships."

A pause built as he considered the wine in his glass; then he took a thoughtful sip and set it on the table. "Does that mean you were doing research?"

"Can we talk about something else?"

"No. You're having trouble with your alpha-male hero and your sex scenes. I'm just trying to think if there's anything I could do to help you. It's that 'knight in shining armor in need of a damsel in distress' thing. Must be a throwback gene."

She narrowed her eyes as she watched him try to keep a straight face. "We call them *love* scenes. And I'm so glad you find this amusing. Thanks very much for your offer, but I don't need your help." *Shut up, Miranda. Yes, you do.*

"Don't you think your readers would rather think you were doing research on lovemaking in a bed with a man instead of alone with a stack of books and a laptop?"

She started choking on the wine she was trying to swallow. "If that's an offer, I'll pass."

He grinned. "Suit yourself. So why isn't writing sex scenes easy? I thought romance writers just sat back and remembered and wrote."

Oh, Lordy. She took a deep breath and looked at the ceiling, but still couldn't keep a laugh from escaping. "They're called *love* scenes. And they're difficult to write precisely because you *can't* do that."

"Because it's not ethical? It would violate that statement in the beginning of the book about nothing being based on actual persons, living or dead?"

She knew he was baiting her, but it was one assumption about her field that she had always despised. "No. It's difficult for several reasons, but one of them, obviously, is that what we write about isn't what real people do."

He raised an eyebrow. "It isn't?"

"You can give it up, Chas. I know you're just trying to rise me. I haven't had that much wine."

"Okay. So everything you write is pure fiction?"

"Well, maybe some people do some of those things, but mostly I think people just like to boast and exaggerate and fantasize." She took another sip of wine. "Wild sexual behavior is just not part of the average person's reality. Sex is one of the top sources of dissatisfaction in a marriage, second only to money. Don't you think if people were actually doing all of those wild things instead of just thinking about them, their love lives would be happier?"

"Is that what was wrong with your relationship? The sex was bad?"

She sat up straight, as though he'd poked her with a cattle prod. "I am *not* discussing that with you."

He shrugged. "Relax. Sometimes people want to be asked."

"I'm not one of them."

"Got it. There's no need to get huffy. I just thought we were starting to bond, that's all. You know, like girlfriends." He nudged her thigh again with a playful sock-covered toe. "My mistake. You know, if you hadn't had all that wine sloshing around inside you when I got here, I probably would have tried to put the moves on you by now."

She pushed herself further into her corner of the couch and reached for her slice. "For your information, if I hadn't had all that wine in me when you got here, I wouldn't have let you in. Furthermore, I've sobered up."

"Pretty much. Does that mean I should try to put the moves on you now?"

She took another bite of pizza. "No, it means you can tell me why you opened another bottle."

"Self-restraint, I suppose." In a deliberately casual, almost idle move, he slid a hand over her foot and began rubbing it lightly. Toes. Instep. Arch. Pure pleasure. Sheer danger. "Taking advantage of a tipsy woman is against the rules, so if I keep you in a vulnerable position, that means we're both safe."

"That's not even fuzzy logic; it's just plumb crazy. And you have a lot of rules," she said, keeping her voice steady. The man knew what to do to a foot.

"Nothing says *you* have to follow them," he said softly with a smile that was an engraved invitation to trouble.

"And yet I'm not even tempted to break them," she replied with a very Southern toss of her head. "So getting back to the subject we were discussing—"

"Sex?"

"I believe we were talking about doing research." She glanced at him. "I've done a bit of research on you, Chas, as much as I'm embarrassed to admit it."

He studied her for a long moment, and she felt a flicker of regret as the amusement in his eyes faded. His hand came to a stop, fingers draped lightly around her ankle. He refilled his wine glass before replying. "Okay, Miranda, as you said the other day, turnabout is fair play. Tell me about me."

She pulled her knees up and tucked her feet beneath her once again. "I saw the pictures in the paper this week. Very nice."

"Thank you." His voice had gone not quite cool, but flat.

"They're what made me go sleuthing. According to an older article I found online, it sounds like you single-handedly saved a neighborhood."

"Nope. I bought a gorgeous, dilapidated old Victorian in the worst part of Stamford and started restoring it. That's all."

She heard a thread of defensiveness running through his deceptively easy words. "So it's all fiction? All those neighbors praising you? Saying that your presence brought police patrols back into a neighborhood that had been forgotten by everyone but the crack dealers? Come on, Chas, the last thing I expect from you is false modesty." She stretched out a leg and nudged him with her toe, knowing it was a hollow attempt to lighten her words.

He ignored it. "False modesty is the last thing you'll get from me. That article was nothing more than some heavy-handed propaganda placed by a congressman who wanted to get some federal funding for the area. It was mostly hype."

"But your family has a long history of philanthropy. The redevelopment effort seems to be your primary method of engaging in it."

"Not true," he said lightly. "I participate in a lot of bachelor auctions. I'm always a big seller."

She yawned and stretched her arms over her head in a pantomime of unconcern. "Another article dropped some not-so-subtle hints that you might be aiming for a career in politics. By ignoring a lucrative family business in favor of public service but still getting an MBA from Yale, it almost seems as though you might be waiting around until the Democrats run out of Kennedys."

She saw his jaw tighten, but his words were still easy. "I'll neither confirm nor deny. How's that for a political answer?"

"I like it. Now, I hope you won't be disappointed to learn that—just like you—I'm not averse to engaging in a bit of amateur psychoanalysis."

He lowered his eyes and shook his head in mild disgust. "Fire at will, Miranda."

She leaned back against the cushions, her arms wrapped around her pulled-up knees. "You've gone out of your way to lay out your conditions for a relationship, and yet you keep flirting with me."

"Standard male operating procedure."

"Isn't it obvious that I'm not seeking the same things you are?"

"What do you want that I don't? You don't strike me as being marriage-minded," he said bluntly. "And you don't seem impressed with the résumé or the portfolio, so I think you're probably just out for a good time."

"Does that bother you?" she asked with a smile.

"That you're not out trying on wedding dresses or running a Dunn and Bradstreet report on me?" He shook his head slightly. "It's a nice change. Now that we're clear on what you don't want, what do you want from me?"

She kept the smile on her face as she looked past him to the fire that was starting to flicker and fade. It was a question she would have welcomed under other circumstances, but this was not the time or setting for confessions. "Nothing, actually."

"I thought you gave up lying to me."

She brought her gaze back to his face. The conversation was getting strained, but something perverse within her wanted to push it, to see how far he would let her go. "We were talking about you. Why are you doing all of this?"

"Flirting with you?"

"No. Everything else. Being the perfect cop, making the world a better place one brick at a time, being a mentor to ghetto kids. Is it really what makes you happy or are you searching for your fa—" As they left her mouth, her words snapped the last boundary of the conversation, moving it beyond a point she'd never intended to reach.

"All right, Freud. Knock it off." His eyes were hot, his jaw set, his body tense.

She said nothing, but felt every muscle in her body clench and prepare.

"Who the hell do you think you are, questioning my motives? I'm a cop because I want to be one. I bought a house because I liked it. I got to know my neighbors because it's the polite thing to do, and I went to graduate school because I felt like it. That's it." He set his wineglass on the table and stood up.

She was on her feet immediately. His gaze slid down her body, making her aware that she'd assumed a fighter's stance, legs braced, hands open and rigid. The realization burned through her, and she forced herself to relax even as the air between them grew heavy.

He watched her with those eyes, once again cool, once again cynical. Cop's eyes. Too long ignored, an old pain seared her as she looked into them. She knew they were Chas's eyes and not her father's, but the look was interchangeable, and fifteen years ago she had learned to hate it: its dispassionate detachment, its ability to observe without feeling.

She closed her eyes and willed away the memory. He was still watching her when she opened them.

"We're some pair, aren't we, Miranda?" he said quietly, then turned to the stairs. "Thanks for dinner and the conversation. I hate to make you come downstairs, but you'll have to lock the door behind me. I hope your muse returns soon." His words trailed him as he jogged down the stairs. When she heard him turn at the first landing, she followed slowly, feeling exhausted by the visit and depleted by the sudden loss of his presence.

He was waiting for her beside the front door, coat on, keys in hand, looking calm and easy.

"Thanks for dropping by," she said automatically. He smiled at the irony and she shrugged with a contrite smile.

"Good night, Miranda." He waited for a beat before turning toward the door.

"Chas, I'm sorry," she said in a quiet rush.

He stopped at a quarter turn and looked at her, his eyes assessing her with an expression she couldn't define.

"I shouldn't have said any of those things. I had no right. I was being bitchy and defensive and stupid and—" She stopped when she realized her voice might break. "You didn't deserve it."

Without questioning the impulse or arresting it, she took a step toward him. She reached out and slid a hand around his neck, and pressed herself against the hard, broad length of him, hips to hips, chest to chest, hot, seeking mouth to hot, seeking mouth. His hands slid around her waist, one fisting in the loose fabric at the back of her sweatshirt, the other sliding, warm and flat, up her bare back to pull her close. The heat between them dizzied her as their kiss deepened and became ravenous.

Moments later, still breathless from the raw passion of his kiss, still trembling from the hunger incited by his touch, she watched him walk away and knew she'd made a mistake. Her mistake wasn't that she'd kissed him, and it wasn't that she'd let him leave.

She closed the door and leaned against it, and let herself slide to the floor. Stretching out facedown on the icy black marble, Miranda closed her eyes and wondered how she could have dared to break the fragile camaraderie they'd achieved, and what she'd have to do to rebuild it.

CHAPTER
11

Coffee mug in hand, Miranda stood in front of the doors leading to the deck, watching the sun try to burn its way through one more gray, watery Connecticut sky. She'd endured another long, sleepless night full of self-chastising thoughts and story ideas that would never work—and memories of that kiss. She shook her head. *No man should be able to amass that much talent.* It had ended more than twelve hours ago, but it still made her toes curl.

For an entirely different reason, her stomach was churning just as intensely as those painted toes were curling. She'd passed her self-imposed deadline, and her story was still as dull as the paint on Andy-the-hero's dirty truck.

Fortunately, she knew what she needed to do to bring the story to life.

Unfortunately, bringing herself to do it would be pushing the limits of her pride.

As if I have any left after last night. Cringing, she recalled her high-handed talk about fictional sex and the real thing. *What in creation was I thinking, talking about* that *with* him*, of all people?*

"Sweet Jesus, if the man is thinking about me at all, he's thinking I'm plumb crazy. There's no way he'll help me now," she murmured.

"Did you say something?"

She spun away from the windows to face the thin, bearded Englishman who was there to paint a sylvan fantasy on the walls and ceiling of the first-floor powder room. He was en route to the front door, cigarettes and lighter in hand.

"Hi, Paul. No. I mean, yes. Just thinking out loud." She smiled. "How's it going?"

"Told her off this morning," he replied with a grin.

"You what?"

"Told her off. Paxton. While you were out."

Thank God for Starbucks. "I didn't even know she stopped by."

"Aye, she did, with that infernal desecrator."

Miranda bit her lip to hide her smile. "Liz?"

"That's the one. Stood behind me telling me to add more shadow here, more sunlight there. More nymphs, fewer fucking fairies." He shook his head. "Then Paxton floats in asking when was it going to be finished. I told her in an hour, because that's how long it would take me to cover the whole bloody thing with a coat of white paint if she didn't get the buzzing fly out of my ear." He grinned and resumed his lope to the door. "Works every time." He stopped abruptly. "Oh, yeah. A guy stopped by for you. Big bloke. Cop. Left his card. Said you should call him." He patted his coveralls absently. "I think I left it in the kitchen."

"Thanks," she said slowly, both liking and not liking the little leap of fire in her belly. It could only have been Chas.

She decided to take it as a sign.

"What are you doing?"

Chas looked up from his monitor to see Gruber leaning in the opening of his cubicle. "Reviewing that armed robbery at the Glenbrook diner two years ago. I'm testifying this week.

"Feel like taking a drive?"

Chas leaned back in his chair and stretched. "Anything to get away from this damned paperwork. Where are we going?"

"Scenic downtown Bridgeport. Those two hookers matched some missing-persons reports filed there late last week. There's a briefing and press conference at one thirty. I invited us."

"What about Greenwich?"

"They'll have to get their own invitation."

With a laugh, Chas stood up and shrugged into his sport coat as they walked toward the stairs. Murphy passed them in the stairwell, giving them a curt nod. *Prick.*

"It's Saturday. What the hell is he doing here? I thought he was taking the day off."

Gruber shook his head as they rounded the landing. "Who the hell knows what goes on in that guy's head. He's been acting like a fucking prima donna for days."

Chas grinned. "I'll tell you what's wrong with him. Randi Rhodes blew him off."

Gruber looked at him. "He said he went out with her."

"Once," Chas repeated meaningfully.

"Shit. Don't tell me you're dating her."

"We've seen each other a few times."

"Lucky bastard. See, now, if it was me, he wouldn't give a shit."

"If it were you, he wouldn't have to."

"Thanks a hell of a lot, Casey. I'll remember that next time you're first in line for a bullet."

Chas grinned as they emerged from the rear of the building and headed toward their car. "So what's the topic?"

"Drugs, sex, and electronics. It appears that Jensen was trying to expand into the importing business. He also invested in some real estate conveniently located near the port and was quite the up-and-coming slum landlord in Bridgeport until his demise. He was the hookers' landlord and their employer."

"Couriers?"

Gruber nodded. "Illegals. Autopsy results aren't in yet but it looks like they were delivering a message. Probate on Jensen's estate was settled about ten days ago, and Mrs. Jensen decided to liquidate his holdings. Several buildings went on the market Tuesday. It seems the tenants' association isn't pleased."

"I suppose it beats sending a letter," Chas said. "Unfortunately, we're about to lose jurisdiction."

"To who?" Gruber demanded. "Bridgeport already—"

"All of us are. I just got off the phone with—"

"God damn it. Not the feds."

Chas slid behind the wheel of the unmarked cruiser. "Apparently the dearly departed Mr. Jensen has been under investigation by the FBI and DEA for two years for trafficking in counterfeit electronics and the occasional opium shipment. I got in touch with the lead investigator on the case. He's e-mailing some documentation to me now."

"Shit."

"I think we're going to have to pay a little visit to the widow Jensen before we head up to the briefing," Chas replied with a grin. "She's not quite as helpless as she seems. She was the company's chief financial officer for ten years until the board of directors asked her to step down nine months ago."

Gruber's smile returned. "It's only polite to bring a gift to a grieving widow. In this instance, I think handcuffs might be a nice touch."

Chas tried to keep his mind clear as he cruised down the Merritt Parkway toward Greenwich. He'd just ended his shift and was heading to his mother's house to have a little chat. Last night had started off mediocre and had gone straight to hell from there. The initial conversation with Miranda had almost compensated for Stella Maris's revelations, but even that kiss—which had left blood roaring in his ears—didn't counterbalance the way the conversation with Miranda had ended. The woman wielded words like she would a stiletto in a street fight.

He'd been at his health club when it opened at six this morning and put himself through a punishing routine to burn off the lingering irritation. But now, after he'd finished a shift that had included a trip to Bridgeport, chasing a seventeen-year-old assault suspect for six blocks, and having to help wrestle 250 pounds of blood-

spattered, angry, drunk, biting woman into the back of
a patrol car, all the anger was back and comfortably
settled in his brain. Cursing under his breath, he pulled
off the parkway and continued the trip to his mother's
house along the back roads.

He pulled into the parking area next to the kitchen
door and, after stopping in the kitchen to grab a Heineken from her refrigerator, walked toward the library. He
wanted to get the conversation over with and get back
to his place so he could decompress in peace. Walking
through the door, he unclipped his tie and put it in his
jacket pocket, then opened the top two buttons of his
shirt.

"Busy?"

From her place behind the elegant desk in the corner
near the fireplace, his mother looked up with a smile
and idly tapped her silver pen on a pile of handwritten
notes. The light from the lamp next to her turned her
short hair into a silvered halo. "Well, hello. This is an
unexpected surprise. You didn't just get off work, did
you? It's nearly six."

Chas nodded and remained standing, leaning on his
folded arms along the back of the big leather chair opposite her. "Busy day."

"Nothing too bad, I hope."

He shrugged and gave her the shadow of a smile. "Depends on how you define 'too bad.' "

"You left Shanna's party early last night. Was anything wrong?"

"I had to meet up with Miranda." It was a half-truth,
but it worked.

She raised an eyebrow. "I'd like to meet her. And not
just because she's captivated you. Why don't you invite
her to dinner on Wednesday? Joe will be in town for a
quick visit. I'm sure he'd like to meet her, too."

*Okay, so she knows why I'm here. That will make it
quick, if not easy.* "I'll ask her. Why is he coming up?"
He took a casual pull from his beer.

She shrugged. "He called it a business trip."

"What would you call it?"

His question hung in air suddenly as heavy and still

as the look in his mother's eyes. She laid the pen on the
polished surface of her desk and leaned back in her
chair, clasping her hands loosely in her lap, elbows on
the armrests. Her entire attitude shifted from maternal
ease to the cool confidence of an executive. "I had a
feeling that Stella Maris would say something to you.
Can I presume you've already talked to your brother?"
She paused and waited for his nod. "What did he tell
you?"

"Not everything. Why are you keeping me out of it?"

"You haven't been singled out, Chas. Julie doesn't
know. Neither does most of the board."

"I don't give a damn about the board, and Julie's a
lawyer, not a cop. A crime is in progress. In my jurisdiction," he replied tightly.

"But not in your area of expertise. It is, however,
within Joe's. And it's actually federal jurisdiction, as
you're well aware," she replied calmly. "Nevertheless,
we'll be bringing in the Stamford Computer Crimes Unit
tomorrow. Naturally, we'll expect you to attend the
meetings, but as a family member and a stockholder,
Chas. Not as a police officer. You will not be part of
the team in that respect."

"Damn it—"

"Don't even start, Chas," she snapped, and stood up
in one fluid movement. "I grew up eating, sleeping, and
breathing the international shipping industry. It still
didn't prepare me to run the company, even at my father's side, but I'm doing it."

He took a slow, silent pull from his beer, keeping his
gaze locked on her face.

She smiled grimly. "That's not a dig about you turning
down our offer. What I mean is that it's a little late in
the day for me to start learning the intricacies of digital
security on top of everything else. It's a field I barely
understand. I need to know that the information I'm
getting is the best there is and that the investigation is
progressing properly and quickly." Her one-shouldered
shrug was nonchalant. "Joe is already on that side of
the table, although I'm not convinced that he should be
involved too deeply. I've requested that he not be made

part of the investigative team. He doesn't know that yet, and when he finds out I'm sure he'll raise holy hell. And when he does that, I'll tell him the same thing I'm going to say to you right now: Get a grip."

She slid her glasses off her nose and let them dangle from the loose gold chain she wore around her neck. "I want you on my side of the table, Chas. Right next to me. I want you helping me to make the decisions, not investigating the crimes. If your ego can't handle that, I'd like to suggest that you rethink the situation and get back to me when it can."

The silence in the cozy room vibrated as their eyes met and held.

"Do you want me there as your son or are you asking me to resign from the force and be there as your employee?"

She didn't flinch, and, despite his anger, he felt a surge of respect for her. "I would never ask you to do that."

"Then what are you asking me to do?"

"I'm asking you to accept the situation as it stands. I know you despise the term as nothing more than media hype, but the simple fact is that you and your brother and sister are the heirs to Brennan Shipping Industries, even if you refuse to acknowledge it. I want you to help me in that capacity. Work with *me*. Not with the police, not with the FBI. With *me*. Help *me*. Will you?"

Leave it to her to ask the simplest questions—which were inevitably the hardest to answer. "Why didn't you tell me what was happening?"

"I intended to tell you as soon as we had the meeting confirmed, which will be in a few hours. Up until a short time ago everything was chaotic, and your grandfather, Dalton, and I made the decision to keep the list to those who needed to know."

"Why was Stella Maris higher on that list than I was?"

"Stella Maris happened to be having cocktails with your grandparents and me when that young man walked into the house a week ago. No one had any idea what he was going to tell us so no one thought it would be a problem." She folded her arms and leaned one hip against her desk elegantly. "I'm serious about inviting

Miranda to dinner, Chas. We're going to be immersed in the problems all day, and I intend to keep the discussion to strict business hours so that Joe's team can get into the building that night and do what they have to do. Once they're in and have set up whatever equipment they have to set up, we'll all be on edge until this situation is resolved. Miranda's presence Wednesday night will ensure that the three of us drop the subject for a few hours."

"I'll ask her," he repeated coolly, straightening up and finishing the last of his beer. "When is Julie getting here?"

"I'm going to call her tonight and ask her to come up on Thursday morning."

Chas could feel the weight of her gaze on him, and met her eyes.

"I know this has nicked your ego, Chas, and I'm very sorry for that. I would have preferred to tell you about it myself." She paused briefly. "But let me make one thing perfectly clear. I don't want you accepting our offer because of this. I don't want you there short-term, nor do I want you there harboring any regrets. I want you there when you want to be there, body and soul. Not before."

Chas sounded surprised, Miranda thought again as she studied the two pomegranates in her hands. That one small fact had been chewing her brain since she'd hung up the phone Sunday afternoon after a very brief conversation—a conversation it had taken her twenty-four hours to script and rehearse and actually work up the courage to initiate. He'd told her he was working, which was why he hadn't been able to chat, but why would he have been *surprised* that she called him? *He'd* made the first move by stopping by and dropping off his card on Saturday. Not that Paul had been able to find the card, but that didn't really matter. She'd gotten his cell phone number from a quietly amused Paxton. *Perhaps it really didn't matter that he sounded surprised. He accepted my invitation without hesitating.*

"Excuse me. Could I get past you?"

The question startled her, and with an apologetic smile she put down the fruit—too messy to prepare— and moved along the aisle in the upscale natural-foods market in Greenwich.

Obviously he'd stopped by because he wanted to see her, and when she wasn't home he'd left his card. Surely that meant he expected her to call. Unless he thought she was too petty or immature or just plain too embarrassed to call him?

None of those assumptions would be out of place, she thought, feeling a fresh wave of humiliation wash over her, but they weren't very flattering. She took a deep breath. If that was what he thought of her, well, then, by placing that call she'd shown him that she had backbone. Squaring her shoulders proudly, she charged over to the poultry counter.

Two hours later she was back at the condo and up to her elbows in dinner preparations when the doorbell rang. She paused, frowning. Paul had already left for the day, and no other workmen were scheduled to arrive until tomorrow morning. Paxton would have just walked in. As she walked to the door, Miranda glanced at herself in the ornate mirror in the foyer and grimaced. *Surely he has better manners than to show up several hours early.*

A glance through the peephole sent her jumping back, a sick shimmy rippling through her belly. Brian Murphy stood there, looking grim and coplike, staring straight at the peephole. He'd obviously just gotten off work. His tie was off but he still wore his gun.

She took a deep breath to tame that momentary burst of panic, then plastered a smile on her face and pulled open the door. "Well, isn't this a surprise," she said brightly.

His expression changed immediately and he smiled back, letting his eyes do a full sweep of her figure. She fought off a shiver and decided, perversely, that she was glad she was a mess. He just might take the hint.

"Hi. Sorry to drop by unannounced, but I don't have your phone number, and my e-mail has been down for a few days."

"Oh, I'm sorry to hear that. Technology can be so annoying sometimes." She hesitated for a split second, hoping he would notice how busy she seemed and behave against type by leaving. "I'm absolutely up to my eyeballs in cooking, but why don't you come in out of the cold for a moment?"

"Thanks. If you're sure I won't be in the way."

"Heavens, no," she lied, and stepped aside. Closing the door, she led him to the kitchen.

He looked around with interest, and eventually took a seat at the breakfast bar. "Nice place."

Nice? She looked at the large open space, which was straddling the line between hunting-lodge coziness and postmodern sterility. *It's dreadful.* "Thank you. It's in a state of flux right now. My college roommate owns it and is putting it in some charity home tour; then I believe she's going to sell it. Since I was coming up for a visit anyway, she offered to let me stay here and babysit the workmen and decorators while I finished my book."

"Nice friend." He was watching every move she made with a mixture of male interest and professional curiosity. The feeling it left her with wasn't a good one, certainly not a tingly one, like a similar perusal from Chas would create.

"Yes, she certainly is. What can I get you?"

"A beer would be fine."

She pulled a Heineken out of the refrigerator, then reached above the sink to get a glass.

"The bottle is fine. Thanks," he said, taking it from her. He glanced at the label, then at her. His eyes cooled slightly, letting her know he knew it was Chas's preferred brand.

"I dropped by on Saturday to see if you wanted to go to lunch. Some guy said you'd be back soon. I left my card."

The strain of smiling grew proportionately with the alarm his words inspired. No wonder Chas had sounded surprised when she'd asked him over for dinner.

How many more ways can I dig myself a deeper grave?

"Well, wasn't that just the sweetest thought?" she said, hearing the saccharine in her voice. "That was Paul, the painter. Well, artist is more like it. He does the most spectacular murals. Now, in fairness to him, he did tell me you stopped by, but he misplaced the card, so I didn't have your number."

He nodded, barely. "How is your book coming along?"

Like this conversation: slow and painful. "Very well, thank you. I'm nearly done. Probably only a week or so left to go."

"What's it about?"

"It's set in Stamford and it's about a criminal defense lawyer. She's defending a real bad guy whom she knows is guilty as sin—"

"Of what?"

She blinked at the terse interruption. "Murder."

"Tough subject for a fluffy book. What's the hero do?"

Fluffy? She swallowed the lick of irritation the word generated. "Well, I try not to shy away from tough subjects. Romance novels aren't just about romance, you know. More and more frequently, they're about topics that—"

"What's the hero do?" he repeated, looking her straight in the eyes.

You mannerless boor. "He's the arresting officer."

"He's a Stamford cop?"

She felt her spine stiffen ominously, and it was an even larger struggle to maintain a friendly countenance. "At the moment he is. My editor is nudging me to set it in New York City, which would really put me into a deadline crunch. My hero started out as the prosecuting attorney when the story was set in Atlanta, but my editor wanted some changes—"

"Is that why you came up here? To research Stamford cops?"

Miranda paused, but before she could take a calming breath, the phone rang and she picked it up, sending him an apologetic smile. A quick glance at the caller ID revealed nothing.

"Hello?"

"Hi."

Miranda felt her face freeze at the single syllable. Brian Murphy's intrusive eyes hadn't left her face. He didn't even pretend not to be listening.

"Oh, hi, how are you?" she replied, trying to affect a casualness she was far from feeling.

"Are you okay?" Chas asked after a slight pause. The question was terse. Abrupt.

She forced a smile onto her face and into her voice. "Fine and dandy. Just up to my eyelashes, what with making dinner and visitors stopping by and all."

"You don't sound okay. Tell me again that you're all right or I'm sending someone over."

Great. Just what this party needs. The SWAT team. She forced a laugh. "Don't be silly."

"Randi, where's the bathroom?" Brian asked loudly, standing up.

She met his gloating eyes and let her smile dim just enough to let him know she wasn't amused. Or intimidated. "Right down that hall, first door on your left, *Brian.*"

"Murphy's over there?" Chas asked, disbelief evident in his voice.

Brian sauntered away, and she took a deep, open-mouthed breath before addressing the incriminating silence on the other end of the phone. "Yes. I'm sorry about that," she said softly, hoping that Brian would not overhear, although, given her luck, he probably had supersonic hearing. "He's not here by invitation, and I'm not being held hostage, so just stand down." She resumed her normal volume. "What's on your mind?"

"I just wanted to let you know that I'm running late."

"All right. How late?"

"Probably not more than an hour. There was a pretty good stabbing on the west side and we've still got paperwork to finish up."

"Well, thanks for letting me know."

"I'll let you get back to—"

"Please don't finish that sentence," she said in a low voice. "Can I call you back in ten minutes?"

"Miranda, you don't have to. I know what Murphy's up to. He's just an . . . a jerk," he said, catching himself, and she couldn't help but smile. *How many men made a point of not swearing in front of a woman?*

"All right. Thank you.'Bye now. I'll talk to you soon." She ended the call and set the phone down as she heard the powder room door open.

Looking cocky, Brian strolled into the kitchen. "I have to get going. Thanks for the beer. Enjoy your evening. Don't forget to say hi to Chas for me," he said with a cold, snakelike smile.

She smiled back warmly, just like her mother had taught her. "I'll be sure to do that. Thank you so much for stopping by."

A business dinner. That was what Miranda had said on the phone when she'd called Saturday, but she hadn't elaborated. Chas smiled as he pulled into the guest parking space in front of her condo. Given that they didn't have any business in common, anything she really needed to say to him could have been said over a casual drink. But she hadn't invited him for a drink. She'd invited him for dinner. He'd intended to get more information out of her when he called her this afternoon, but having that asshole Murphy present precluded that. He'd obviously been listening to every word.

To hell with Murphy. He had better things to think about, like what awaited him on the other side of the front door. Shutting off the engine, he grabbed the two bottles of wine he'd brought—Champagne for tonight and a vintage Bordeaux to ease her conscience about the one they'd drunk the other night—and started up the short walk. There was a blend of adolescent anticipation and thoroughly adult desire running in his veins.

The door opened and she stepped aside with a nervous smile and intoxicating green eyes. Her hair was loose and her long, dark green velvety dress clung to her softly, stopping a small distance above her bare feet. She looked like some delicate creature just awakened from a woodland nap, and everything about her indicated that she had decided to do more than just talk. *Like surrender.*

The dust was gone, the new marble floor and hearth

shone softly in the firelight, and the aromas from the kitchen were tantalizing. The lights were muted, the dining room table was formally set, and a Chopin étude played softly in the background. *The woman certainly has a head for business.* He made a point of keeping his smile friendly rather than triumphant.

"Hi," she said, easily sidestepping what was intended to be a hello kiss and shutting the heavy door behind him. "Come in. Thanks for coming over. Oh, heavens, you didn't have to bring anything. If anything I . . . well, I apologize again about Friday night. I was—" She barely stopped for a breath. "No excuses. I was just out of sorts and out of line, and I hope you've forgiven me." She kept a respectable distance between them as she avoided meeting his eyes. "I'm just finishing something in the kitchen. If you don't mind, you can come in there and we can have a drink. I wasn't sure what you'd like, so I thought I'd leave it up to you. Everything is in the wine cellar. It's pretty well stocked. I—"

"Miranda?"

She stopped short and turned to him. Her dress flared out around her legs, then came softly to a swaying rest. Her eyes were huge and luminous, and very, very green as they watched him from within that forest of dark hair.

"Yes?"

"What are you doing?"

"What do you mean?"

"You're chattering like a squirrel."

"Am I really?"

"Yes." He paused. "Why are you nervous?"

"I'm not. Okay. Yes, I am. But only because I . . ." She took a deep breath and her words came in a rush as her fingers tangled themselves together near her waist. "Because I know this looks like a date but it isn't, and I just don't want to give you the wrong idea."

"What would be the wrong idea?"

"That this is a date."

As her words registered, he glanced around the room. "Why would I think this was a date? You've prepared a meal that smells wonderful. You've set the dining room table. You have a fire lit, music on, and you're looking more beautiful than I've ever seen you look. There's no way this could be a date. It's definitely a business meeting."

"You're a worse liar than I am," she pointed out.

"You're rubbing off on me."

She smiled, then turned and continued walking toward the huge, gleaming industrial range. "I knew it would look bad. But I couldn't invite you over for cold fried chicken and sweet potato pie. Not if I'm going to ask for a favor. So first I thought I'd come up with a nice, casual menu. By the time I'd decided on one, it wasn't casual anymore, because I like to cook and don't get the chance to much." She lifted the cover from a pan and a cloud of fragrant steam rose around her. "So then I thought, we can't eat this kind of food sitting on the floor in front of the TV, or in front of the fireplace, and the breakfast bar is . . . well, I think the whole idea of them is just plain stupid. So I had to set the table. And Paxton put all that gorgeous china and whatnot here for me to use. So I used it."

Done stirring and sniffing her creations, she turned to face him. Flushed and dewy from the steam, she leaned against the countertop, picked up the glass of Coke at her elbow, and met his eyes. "Then I thought that if you walked in looking nice, like you just did, and I was in jeans or sweats, that wouldn't be good, so I threw on this. And it seemed like a good night for a fire, and—" She stopped. "So that's how it happened. Go ahead and laugh. But I really did invite you here to discuss something related to my book, and not for any other reason."

He knew she thought she was telling the truth, but every bit of her body language—from the pedicured toes that were slowly rubbing up and down against her ankle, to the way she kept wetting her lips so delicately with the tip of her tongue—every bit of her body language was saying she had other reasons for inviting him over. Reasons she wasn't ready to admit to having.

"Okay, it's not a date. Cut to the chase. Tell me what you want before the suspense kills me."

"I want you to be my hero."

*   *   *

Chas recovered almost immediately, but as the request left her lips, Miranda knew it was the last thing he was expecting to hear. She held up a hand before he could speak.

"I need to make a few things clear. I already more or less told you that I'm in danger of losing my career if I don't write about some dark, moody, alpha male. What I haven't told you is that the character is a cop, by editorial decree." He hitched one eyebrow and she took a deep breath. "I've never written about a cop before, but I've known some. Can't say as I liked them much, but I knew them pretty well. Anyway, I've done a decent job of making my hero real, but he's not fully there yet." She hesitated, wishing she didn't have to say it. "Neither are the love scenes," she added in a low, penitent voice.

Chas folded his arms across that chest she was already too well acquainted with and leaned against the granite counter. "The cop is the mean, uncaring Neanderthal who's absolutely not based on me?"

I should have prepared crow instead of quail. "I know that sounds incriminating," she admitted. "I was having a bad day."

"*Days.*"

She acknowledged his correction with a weak smile. "He's much nicer now."

"Glad to hear it. What about the sex? I thought you didn't need my help with that, either. After all, you have all the expertise a writer needs stacked in the corner of the loft."

She licked her lips and looked at her freshly painted toenails, wondering how long he would persist in torturing her. "To be precise, I don't need your help with the sex so much as help with his approach to it."

"He's not approaching it effectively?"

"I'm in no position to spoil your fun, Chas. I realize I'm asking for a big favor despite having done nothing since we met that would give you any reason to help me. I hope you will anyway." She glanced at him, seeking some assurance of his help, but none was forthcoming. He just watched her with those amused, exultant, backbone-melting eyes. "The point is that my editor wants me to put in more sex, put it in earlier, and make it hotter. She's known for it. You know how they say that some books 'sing'? Well, hers have been known to 'singe.' "

"And that bothers you?"

"Let's just say she likes her books to have the kind of love scenes I don't usually write."

"Okay, you've persuaded me. When do we start?"

His quick capitulation caught her by surprise, and she felt herself begin to blush. "I figured I'd have to spend all of dinner trying to convince you."

"We're both just full of surprises tonight. When do we start?"

"After dinner?"

He shrugged. "Why not now? I'm ready."

Sweet Jesus. She took another sip of her Coke and wished he would stop looking at her as if she were dessert. "I'm not certain you understand the parameters of your input, Chas. In academic terms, this is a theoretical exercise, not an interactive lab session." She watched anticipation warm his eyes and she faced it down. "Don't smile like that," she said sternly. "I'm serious about this. Very serious. You saw what I was going through the other night. If you think sitting down to write hot love scenes is easy, then you've obviously never tried it."

"Not since I was twelve and trying to get something published in the *Penthouse* 'Forum.' But I'll take your word for it. It's a real drag." His grin was edging toward a laugh. "So tell me more about this moody alpha male that you think I am, and how you think sex with me is different from sex with your androgynous Nordic wimps."

"That's not the way it works. And we most certainly are not going to talk about sex *with you.* We're talking about *lovemaking* between two fictional characters. I just need some—" She stopped and looked at him, at those dark eyes that were too warm and too amused and too damned beautiful. "Why did I ask you? What in the Sam Hill was I thinking?"

"Please, go on. You just need some . . . what? Ideas?

Inspiration? Technical information? A demonstration of—"

"I must be insane. I need Heathcliff and the only guy in the house is a grinning Narcissus." She shook her head. "Let me get the appetizers out of the oven. You open a bottle of wine. Then we'll sit down and discuss what I need from you. *Seriously.* Okay?"

"What am I going to get out of this deal?"

"Dinner," she said over her shoulder as she opened the oven door. "The satisfaction of knowing you helped someone. And, if your ego requires it, thanks in the acknowledgments."

"You won't dedicate the book to me?"

"Don't even joke about that," she said, peering into the oven. "I don't dedicate my books to anyone. Ever."

"Why?"

"A girlfriend dedicated two books to the guy she was living with. After they broke up, he sued her for a cut of all past and future royalties. His lawyer said the dedications were proof of his contributions to the works."

"Are you serious? What happened?"

"She settled in order to keep a few deals alive. Let's go into the living room and discuss happier things," she said, hiding her amusement that the look in his eyes had become serious.

She set the tray of tiny filled pastries on the coffee table and watched him. "Champagne?"

"Absolutely. It's not every day that I get used by a beautiful woman."

It has been lately. She accepted the wine from him with a forced smile.

"To literary pursuits," he said. Their heavy crystal flutes collided gently and, as the ominously pure note of their bargain faded into the room, Miranda lifted the wine to her lips.

CHAPTER
12

"So what *exactly* do you need from me?" Leaning against the counter across the kitchen from her, Chas watched as Miranda put the finishing touches on the array of tiny quail. She'd relaxed considerably, but was still being too evasive. It was time to encourage some revelations.

"I've never written about a cop before. I've never written about this so-called alpha male before. There's only so much I can get from psychology textbooks, true-crime books, and Mel Gibson movies. I need to learn when the cop face happens, to learn how you know someone's lying," she murmured as she spooned a thin orange sauce over the birds.

"Oh. Well, I'm not telling you that. You'd be in on the secret, and then I'd never be sure when you were lying to me," he teased.

"You've caught me every time." She shot him a quick glance. "I've changed my ways."

"That's good to know, Miranda. I'll put it in my little cop notebook. Now that I can trust everything you say, I'd like to know how much the hero resembles me at the moment."

She froze for an instant, but recovered quickly. "What do you mean?" she asked, keeping her face turned away from his.

"The other night you said he wasn't based on me 'much.' That means 'some.' I'd like to know *how* much."

She straightened up, and her big hazel eyes met his with a look that was as guilty as hot, sweet sin, but she remained silent.

"You look like a deer trapped in the crosshairs," he pointed out.

"That's pretty much how I feel."

He smiled. "Confess to the crime, Miranda. You'll feel much better. I promise."

"Does that line work with criminals?"

"All the time," he lied.

She surrendered with a sigh. "His hair is darker. His truck is white, and it has a gun rack in it. And he lives in a small house. I wrote all of that before I met you," she added, then hesitated. "You don't hunt, do you?"

"Hunt what?"

She winced. "Rabbits?"

God Almighty. RoboCop meets Elmer Fudd. He frowned at her, biting the inside of his cheek until he was sure he wouldn't laugh. "He hunts *bunnies*? Christ, Miranda, I thought you were going to say 'bears' or at least something that can fight back. Just what kind of first impression did I make on you?"

"I thought you were kind of cocky. And a flirt."

"And because of that you made me a bunnykiller?"

She smiled, looking faintly ill, and seemed to shrink before his eyes. It was killing him not to laugh.

"Not you. Him," she said.

"It doesn't matter. He's a cop. We protect helpless things. We don't kill them." He folded his arms across his chest. "So tell me, were you using me all this time? Were all the conversations we had—" he paused for effect—"fodder?"

She looked away. *That answers that.*

"That sounds awful, Chas. And it wasn't like that. Can I plead the Fifth?"

"No."

"Okay, then, yes. Sort of." She closed her eyes with a grimace, then opened them and met his gaze slowly and painfully. "Not the whole time. I had a lot of him sketched out before I met you. I mean . . ." She let out a groan and raised her hands in surrender. "Okay, here's the whole truth. I really did have a lot of him sketched out before I met you, okay? I mean, I had the entire book *written,* but then I had to change him. And I met you, and I didn't like you much at first. You were sort of, um, presumptuous. But then—"

"When was I presumptuous?"

"When Mick pulled me over. You showed up and got all territorial. I didn't like your attitude one bit, but that's when I realized it was what my character had to be like and the kind of thing he had to do. The more I kept running into you, the more it just seemed like a sign."

"A sign."

"I know it sounds crazy, but we writers are pretty much a crazy bunch to begin with. So I just thought I'd use you as a basis from which to develop him—"

"Him, meaning the Neanderthal?"

She nodded after a moment's hesitation. "Just to give him a face and a starting point. But as I got to know you more, I liked you better and couldn't make the character work because you weren't as bad as he was."

"High praise indeed," he said, torn between being annoyed and amused. Amusement held a slight lead at the moment.

"Chas, please. The character is a good guy now. Three days ago I couldn't even get the heroine on the same page with him. At this point, they've already—" she hesitated for a split second "—kissed."

The nerve of the woman. She's been writing sex scenes about me without even having . . . He stood there, arms folded across his chest, and let her endure the full weight of the same stare he used in interrogation rooms. To her credit, she looked away only twice.

"Does he kiss like I do?"

It took her a minute to decode the question, but when she did, her hands returned to her hips and the sparks returned to her eyes. "You're not mad at me, are you? And this interrogation—"

"That was *not* an interrogation. You didn't even let

me get started before you confessed. You sang like a canary. Where's the fun in that? Do yourself a favor and don't ever go into a life of crime."

"Thanks for the career advice, but I don't think that's a switch I'll have to consider. If you'll help me. I mean, as you've already agreed to," she amended, her eyes turning greener by the moment. "I can't believe you, Chas. You were subjecting me to all this talk and all those glowering looks just to make me sweat? To teach me a lesson?"

"Only the latter. I'm hoping to do the former later on."

She shot him a dirty look that, this time, was underlain with amusement. "And all the while here I was thinking you were *almost* a gentleman."

Damned if she didn't still have claws and no fear about using them.

"After this little episode, I expect full cooperation from you, soon-to-be Lieutenant Casey. I need to learn the terminology, the attitude—" she continued.

"Toward what?"

She picked up the tray of quail and held it out to him. "Would you please carry this to the table? Be careful. It's hot. Your attitude toward everything. How you respond to things on duty and off—"

"Like women?" he asked, walking into the dining room.

"Among other things."

"So what's his name?"

"It's Andy now. It used to be Dirk."

Dirk? He walked back into the kitchen shaking his head in mock despair. "Okay, there's the first part of the problem. Other than the guy in *Boogie Nights,* how many men do you know named Dirk? Never mind. Your answer would probably scare me. But I'll tell you this: a hero has to have a normal name."

"He does. I just told you, it's Andy."

"Three-year-olds are called Andy."

"So are thirty-five-year-olds. What would be a better name? Charles?"

He shrugged. "Sure."

"I'm sorry to inform you, but Charles is not sexy. Of course . . ." She met his eyes as she passed him a bowl of thin, steaming French beans and picked up a crystal bowl filled with mesclun. "I suppose I could call him Chas."

"Don't you dare. What about Frederick?"

"Too stuffy," she said as she preceded him into the dining room.

"Mark?"

"Too short and too plain. You can't sigh 'Mark' or moan 'Mark,' at least in print. Short names need at least two syllables or some fluidity. Unless it's something sexy like Ty or Crash or Rafe." She paused. "Sebastian is a good one. Those terminal N sounds work well."

"You choose a character's name based on how it sounds when it's moaned?" he asked, pulling out her chair for her.

"Every trade has its tricks." She smiled and sat down, slipping a fall of curls over her shoulder and out of the way. "Well, come on, if I wrote something like, 'She was overcome with desire and wanted him to hold her, to touch her, to make her feel like a real woman. "Oh, Howard," she moaned, "make love to me now," ' would it work for you?"

"If you wrote something like that, I don't think it would work for anyone."

She laughed. "I rest my case."

"I still don't think any woman could convincingly moan, 'Dirk.' "

She looked at him, serene and superior, and held out her hand for his plate. "Why don't we let me handle the writing and you handle the technical information? *Bon appetit.*"

"When's the last time you used your gun?" she asked from her place on the floor next to the marble coffee table. She didn't look up from the notes she was making on the legal pad. Her china coffee cup and saucer were inches away from her elbow. The empty ramekins that had held crème brûlé had been moved to the floor with the rest of the coffee service. The entire surface of the table held tidy stacks of yellow sheets covered with neat, Catholic-schoolgirl script. Chas had been stretched out on the couch across from her for the better part of an hour, answering her questions and watching her fill those pages. Watching her laugh and frown and argue and explain and, only once, blush.

"For what?"

She looked up at him and blinked. "Stopping a . . . what do you call them? Perps?"

"Movie stars call them 'perps.' I call them 'bad guys.' It was three and a half years ago."

"Why did you ask 'what for'?"

"Well, I go to the pistol range a few times a year."

"Oh." She looked down and scanned some notes, then glanced at a different stack. "So how do you stop them, since you're obviously not kneecapping them?"

He shook his head in disbelief. Again. "For God's sake. That's what their own people do to them. Can I give you a piece of advice? Stop watching action films."

"Desperate times call for desperate measures." She looked up again. "So?"

"Most of the time we try to talk to them. When that fails, we have a few other methods of persuasion before we pull our guns. Pepper spray. Batons. There's the occasional tackle or punch thrown. Handcuffs help." He paused for effect. "Hey, there's a thought. Would you like to—"

"No," she said, deliberately keeping her eyes on her papers.

"Be sure to let me know if you change your mind."

"I'll do that," she said dryly.

He watched her for a few silent moments, bored with being interviewed and ready to get on to more interesting pursuits. "So how exactly do you go about writing the sex scenes? Other than getting drunk alone and trying to asphyxiate yourself, I mean."

"I wasn't drunk, I was tipsy, and they're called love scenes," she murmured.

"Whatever. How many have you written so far?" he asked.

She sighed. "I've started about twelve for this book

and have exactly half of one finished. At the moment, the hero is trapped in a state of advanced arousal. He'll be there indefinitely."

"I can sympathize."

She glanced up, eyes rich with laughter. Her smile had softened and her edgy attitude had all but evaporated over the course of the evening. She sat across from him now, backlit by the fire and just a foot out of reach. Miles farther than that, if he wanted to be honest about it.

It's time to close that gap.

She looked back to her papers and continued writing.

"Okay, based on your other books—"

"Which of them?" she murmured.

"All of them."

"You've read *all* of them?" she asked, looking up at him again, eyes wide with surprise. She pushed a thick curtain of hair over her shoulder and out of her way, then reached for the coffee cup she'd emptied the last time he'd made her nervous.

"Yes. I think the reason you're having trouble with the love scenes in this one is that guys like me—I mean, like your hero—don't do anything the way the heroes in your other books do. Particularly when it comes to sex."

"Well, I know, but— Wait a minute. What do you mean? My readers think my love scenes are *hot.* One really important reviewer said they were, and I'm quoting, 'Real and wicked. In fact, really wicked.' "

He raised an eyebrow. "I presume the reviewer was a woman?"

"Sex is universal."

"Thanks for clarifying that. I know you said all the things your characters do are things real people don't do—"

"I didn't say 'all the things,' " she interrupted, tucking her hair behind her ears.

"Okay, *much* of what you have them do. But tell me this: Who constitutes your market?"

"Women."

"Between the ages of . . . ?"

"I'm not exactly sure. Twenty-five to fifty?"

"With kids."

"What does that have to do with anything?"

He leaned up on one elbow. "Who but a woman with children would *not* question the fact that your single, twenty-something heroine had tapioca pudding in the fridge? Or Cheez Whiz? Or enough Chips Ahoy to scatter on the floor and roll around in?" He shrugged. "I've never met a single, childless woman who had any of those in her kitchen. Fat-free yogurt, maybe, or the occasional DoveBar, but *not* tapioca pudding. Come on."

She bit the inside of her cheek, mildly annoyed. "Well, I buy those things every now and then, Chas, and other single women do, too. I don't know any woman, single or otherwise, who exists on Evian and tofu. Or fat-free yogurt. Maybe we just eat the comfort foods when we're not dating observant men and worrying about our thighs." She brushed a strand of hair from her forehead. "Anyway, I didn't think it was that strange. But please, don't stop there. Tell me what else I'm doing wrong."

She was so easy to distract. Sometimes. "Everything. With your heroes, that is."

She let out a heavy breath and closed her eyes for a few seconds. "Of course I am. Why don't you just tell me what you do differently? And don't get smart."

"Everything. We talk to women differently. We hold them differently. We kiss them differently. Miranda." He paused, waiting until she looked up. "Please tell me that you don't actually know a man who would ask a woman's permission to take off her bra?"

"It worked with his character."

"Because his character was a wimp."

She sighed in exasperation. "He was not a wimp. He didn't demand things from a woman."

"Secure men don't demand, but they don't ask permission for things like that, either. Come on, would you want a guy to stop in the middle of some serious groping to—"

"Well, come on, then, Stud Bubba, tell me what a real man does," she interrupted, her ordinarily soft drawl sharp with sarcasm. "I can hardly wait to find out."

He smiled. "When necessary, they persuade. But only when necessary."

She stared at him for a moment, then smiled back, shook her head, and returned to her notes. "I don't recall you persuading me to kiss you that afternoon in your car."

"I didn't have to. You wanted to kiss me," he replied softly, and watched her shrug one shoulder in response. "Does that mean you agree?"

She waited a moment before answering. "I suppose." She straightened her posture, brushed some flyaway hairs from her forehead, and bit gently on the end of her pen. "Come on, Chas. Let's get back to work. This is serious. I'm on deadline."

"I'm being serious. We're talking about love scenes." He folded his arms and tucked them underneath the back of his head to give himself a better viewing angle. The atmosphere was definitely changing, and he wasn't about to miss out on an opportunity should one arise.

"No, *I'm* trying to talk about love scenes. You just want to talk about . . ." She looked down at her notes. "Actually, I wasn't talking about love scenes at all. I was talking about police procedure. You started this conversation."

"We'll call it hero procedure. How does he kiss?"

She kept her eyes trained on her notes. "Nicely."

"Well, there's another problem. He needs a decent name and he has to be a great kisser."

"He has a decent name, and there's nothing wrong with kissing nicely. You kiss nicely." She glanced up at him, and if she'd been any other woman, he would have sworn she was flirting. But Miranda wasn't just any woman, and he knew he was pushing her limits.

He raised his eyebrows at her in mock disbelief. "Excuse me? Twenty-five years of practicing every chance I get, and I only kiss *nicely*? Are you deranged? I'm a *great* kisser."

She started laughing and put down her pen. "Well, okay, your kisses—" She stopped and laughed again. "They were innocent kisses, not anything . . . I mean, they were nice, Chas."

"I think 'nice' falls a bit short of reality, but there's no way I'd describe them as innocent. There was nothing innocent going through my head either time I kissed you, Miranda. Or the many times I've thought about it. What was going through your mind?"

"I don't remember." She picked up the pen again and began tracing over something she'd already written. "Can we get back to work now?"

"Yes. Come here." He held out his hand and watched her eyes flick from it to his face. They were wary rather than amused.

"Why?"

"I want you to."

"Why?"

He didn't answer, nor did he withdraw his hand. A moment later she sighed and rested her forehead on the heel of her palm. He couldn't tell whether her eyes were open or closed.

"Chas," she said softly. "Don't do this. I'm leaving in two weeks."

"Two weeks is a long time. Look at me. What am I doing?" he asked just as softly.

She lifted her head and met his eyes again. Hers were dark and full of something akin to pain and desire and regret. He flexed his fingers in invitation and kept his voice low but insistent. "What I'm doing is what your hero would do in this situation. What would your heroine do?"

She hesitated and tried to cover it with a soft laugh. "It's a different situation, Chas. They're not real."

"You want them to be. How can you write about something you don't know?"

"What don't I know?"

"How we feel against each other. How we fit together." He paused. "Come over here and lie down with me, Miranda."

She closed her eyes again briefly, then stood up slowly and walked around the table, sat down on the edge of the couch on which he was stretched out. She took his hand, stroked it, covered it with both of her own, then brought his palm to her lips. A moment later her eyes, green and tentative, met his again. Her dark hair fell around them like a veil as, wordlessly, she lowered her mouth to his, and slid her body onto his.

That there was so little weight to her was his last conscious thought before he lost himself in the deep, slick softness of her mouth, the subtle, female fragrance of her skin. His hands slid around her waist, over her hips and back, drawing out the warmth from her, absorbing her quietness. He stroked the heavy fabric that was rough then smooth by turn. The minutes passed slowly as she returned his kisses with careful enthusiasm, never relaxing, never reaching the level of spontaneous combustion they had Friday night.

"This is one very long dress," he whispered against her mouth so as not to surprise her when, a moment later, his wandering hand finally reached its target destination and met her flesh. It slid up a smooth, firm calf to a soft, warm thigh. That was when she went rigid, and his hand stilled where the line of that thigh met the curve of her silkclad bottom. When she didn't relax, he removed his hand and smoothed the fabric of her dress back into place.

"What sort of assurances do you want, Miranda?" he murmured, sliding his mouth to the seductive hollow of her throat and his hands to the edges of her velvet-covered breasts. "What will make you trust me?"

She lifted her head and looked into his eyes. *Amorous* was one word he *wouldn't* use to describe her look.

"Listening to me and taking me seriously would go a long way toward it."

Christ. She didn't want him to persuade. She wanted him to beg. "You don't pull your punches, do you?"

She shook her head slowly, the hint of a smile gracing her lips, and he could practically hear the bedroom door slam shut. In his face.

"For your information I both listen to you and take you seriously. I just also happen to think you're sexy as hell, and being in your presence for extended periods of time brings out the Neanderthal in me," he murmured, brushing a hand over her cheek. He slid it around her neck and brought her mouth back to his.

She broke the kiss a moment later and sat up, swinging her feet to the floor. He picked up her hand, twined his fingers through hers. She waited a minute before pulling away.

This hasn't happened in a decade. "You're trembling."

"Too much adrenaline and nowhere for it to go," she replied, false lightness in her voice.

"I know a really good cure for that," he said, watching her avoid his eyes.

"I'll bet you do." Tilting her face to the ceiling, she took a deep breath and shook her hair until it tumbled down her back in a passionate tangle. The movement exposed the pure curve of her throat from her chin to the demure neckline of her dress. He traced it with a finger and felt a shiver move through her seconds before she rose and glided away, sinking gracefully to the floor a few feet from him. Her skirt spread out around her like a mossy, shaded moat that he wouldn't dare try to cross.

At some point during the evening, the music had stopped. The firelight had faded to golden flickers, and it was in this strange, silent light they sat, watching each other. She slid into a cross-legged position and, resting her cheek on her palm, looked up at him, her smile gone, her eyes dark and bemused.

"It's not going to happen, Chas," she said softly. "We've known each other a week. I'm leaving in two weeks. I used you and you forgave me. You told me I'm beautiful and sexy, and I admitted you're a great kisser. Please let's leave it there. I don't want complications."

He spent a moment deciding whether to retreat or push onward; then he stood up and smiled at her. "In that case, how about some more coffee? I'm sure you have more questions."

"Won't coffee keep you up?"

He let the comment pass unremarked and walked into the kitchen. "You asked me about attitudes earlier. Did I answer you?"

"No," she replied, following him into the kitchen warily.

"Okay, ask me again. What do you want to know?"

he asked, keeping his back to her as he shook ground coffee into the filter.

"Well, there's an attitude that comes with being a police officer, and I—"

He glanced at her over his shoulder. "How do you know?"

She met his eyes. "Experience. But we were talking about you. Does it spill over into your personal life?"

"Probably." He finished pouring water into the reservoir and turned to face her. She'd lifted herself onto the countertop across the room and sat with her legs crossed and dangling, watching him. "The longer you're a cop, the less you trust people and the more cynical you get.

"Did you trust me?"

He walked to her, then leaned both hands on the counter at her sides. She stiffened but didn't break eye contact and didn't look particularly alarmed. *Back on track.* "No."

She raised an eyebrow. "Why not?"

• "I knew you were up to something."

She licked her lips in a way that was unconsciously sexy. "You didn't make much of an effort to find out what it was."

"I didn't have to. I knew you'd tell me. Most bad guys fall into one of two categories: the kind that return to the scene of the crime to view their handiwork and the kind that let the guilt get to them."

"Well, I'm not a bad guy." She glanced away. "But I'm that predictable?"

"Most people are."

"You really are cynical."

"It's one of the things that keeps me alive." He leaned forward and let his mouth drift to a spot just below her ear. She leaned away just a little, but all it did was allow him greater access. He smiled against her skin and kissed her again.

"Chas, I thought we agreed . . ." she whispered in protest, but the hands that had come to rest on his shoulders weren't pushing him away.

"Agreed to what?" he murmured, trailing kisses along the line of her jaw.

"Not to do this."

"I don't know what you're talking about. Ask me another question." His mouth found hers, effectively ending the interview.

It wasn't until he had the zipper of her dress halfway down her back and her bra unhooked that she broke their kiss by jerking her head up and her body away from his. She pulled her arms from around his neck and snapped them tightly to her sides. "I think it's time you left."

He pulled back in surprise. Mild panic had opened wide her half-closed eyes.

"Why?" He paused. *Oh, hell.* "Don't tell me you think I should have asked permission."

Her cheeks went pink and she glanced away. "No. I just think that—"

"What are those?" he interrupted, looking at two rounded lumps that had settled near her waist inside her dress. She looked down.

"My breasts," she said in a small, pained voice.

He gently poked a finger into one of the lumps. "It feels like a breast." He flicked his eyes up to look at her. "Is there something I should know about?"

She folded her arms tightly across her considerably diminished chest. "They come off with the dress," she replied, lifting her chin, but her newfound defiance was undermined by her flushed face.

Oh, Christ. He swallowed, and kept his face neutral. "Cancer?"

"No." She flushed deeper. "Sheer vanity."

He had to bite the inside of his cheek to keep from laughing but couldn't hide his smile. "What's left?"

"Not very much."

"Can I see?" He hooked a finger over the neckline of her loosened dress and pulled it forward, only to have his hand slapped away a moment later.

"No, you certainly may *not.* I think it's time you left," she repeated, glaring at him.

"Okay, I'll go." Biting back laughter, he slid his arms around her, refastened her bra and zipped up her dress, then slid her off the counter and set her on her feet.

Two soft plops brought both of their gazes to the floor. He bent to pick up two warm, gel-filled half-moons and set them on the counter, then stood facing her, a strained but ridiculous silence filling the room.

"I appreciate the thought," he said at last, and watched her blink; then they both broke into laughter. He wrapped his arms around her as she rocked forward to bury her face in his chest.

"The part of me that isn't utterly mortified is already thinking this has to go into the book," she said a moment later, lifting her face to his.

"As long as you change the names." He kissed her lightly. "Still want me to leave?"

The look she gave him was edged with contrition. "Yes."

"Wonderful," he said under his breath as they walked to the door. "Good night, Miranda. It's been an evening like no other."

CHAPTER
13

"I thought you were going to send me something," Amy stated flatly.

"I was." Miranda was nearly finished with her two-mile walk on the beach and was wishing she'd chosen to bring her water bottle instead of her cell phone. Amy annoyed was an Amy she didn't like dealing with.

"Well? Ellen wants an excerpt for the Web site, Miranda. If we don't send her one, she's going to get nervous and start asking for chapters. Based on the last stuff you sent me, sending her chapters now would not be a positive career move. So, are you going to send me something or not?"

"Yes. Today. I was doubting everything last time I talked to you, Amy. But I think I've solved the problems. I promise you I will send you something before the close of business."

"What happened? Did you meet a cop?"

Miranda smiled. "Yes, ma'am, I sure did."

"You're going Southern on me again, and you know I hate that. Tell me why it's working all of a sudden. In English."

And they wonder why we call them "damn Yankees."

"Because he's the real thing, Amy."

"Now you're starting to scare me. Are you okay? You

didn't, like, find God or anything between last week and today, did you?"

Close enough. "Of course not."

"Okay, then what do you mean by 'the real thing'? You didn't find an alpha, did you? God help us. Don't tell me they really exist?"

Miranda stopped power-walking so that she could laugh without starting to gasp. "He's better than an alpha, Amy. And, thanks to him, my hero is getting pretty close to perfect."

"I hope so, kitten. I hope so."

At seven o'clock that evening, Miranda still wasn't exactly sure that she wanted to be doing what she was doing, which was driving to Chas's house for dinner. She'd rather be safely back at the condo writing. It wasn't the fact that she was traversing some less-than-scenic neighborhoods, which featured trash-lined streets and boarded-up and burned-out houses. It wasn't even the fact that the headlights in her rearview mirror had been there practically since she'd left the condo. No, what had her stomach in knots was her destination. More specifically, her host and his expectations. And, to be honest, her own as well.

As he was wishing her good-night last night—rather thoroughly, as a last attempt to get her to change her mind and let him stay—he'd managed to get her to agree to join him for dinner. A dinner *date*. Her answer had to have been induced by a combination of too much caffeine and too much Casey. It certainly hadn't been a rational decision. She shook her head. *A date.* For the last year, she'd avoided them the way she avoided green olives in martinis and babies with full pants. She hadn't been on one in seven years, give or take a few months, and she'd been an incredibly young, stupid, needy twenty-five at the time.

She'd gone from that first date with Josh to living with him within two months. But Josh had been predictable and compartmentalized and undemanding. And utterly boring after a very short while. But he'd been safe. Chas was none of those things, particularly the latter. She

shook her head again and drove through another intersection, skimming the red light. If it hadn't been such a
bad neighborhood and she wasn't being followed by God
only knew who, she would have pulled over and thought
about what she was doing—and then turned around and
gone straight home. *Chas was a cop*, for pity's sake, and
getting involved with a cop was something she'd sworn
she'd never do. Not after growing up with one in the
house. But what bothered her even more than the obvious attraction was the fact that she had to force herself
to remember he was a cop when she was with him, which
was crazy, since it was the only—okay, *main*—reason she
was spending time with him.

Heat flickered deep inside. Of course, when she *did*
forget he carried a badge, Chas was almost irresistible.
Warm and funny and flirtatious and charming enough
to slip past the emotional barriers she'd erected around
herself—and he'd done that despite being able to fire
sharp comments that struck true and deep. No one had
been able to come anywhere near hurting her since her
daddy—she caught herself and her smile faded; *he didn't
deserve the title*—since *Walter* had shown her the door.

After Walter had done his damage, she'd changed all
the locks on her heart and her soul and anything else
that might be in need of protection. In the fifteen years
since then, only Chas had made it past her defenses.
And not, she realized now, because she hadn't been vigi-
lant, but because she'd never tested those defenses.
She'd just made a point of avoiding men like Walter and
Chas, who threatened her equilibrium. Men in general,
except for Josh.

The light at the next intersection turned red. She
slowed down and tried to keep the car rolling, but the
light lasted too long and she had to come to a stop. The
car behind her also rolled slowly to a stop. Due to the
unseasonable cold snap, there weren't many people on
the street. Still, Miranda kept her eyes moving from the
shadowed faces of the two men in her rearview mirror
to the empty sidewalks visible in her side mirrors and
the deserted street to the front. She'd left the car in
gear, poised to rocket away if need be. But the light

turned green and she took off at a speed only slightly higher than she normally would. The car continued to follow her at a sedate pace, and her mind turned back to Chas.

"No complications," she muttered. "What was I thinking?"

Things were *already* complicated. The attraction between them was strong and mutual and out in the open. They'd known each other only a matter of days, really, but there was an electricity between them that had never existed between her and Josh. What she'd felt with Josh didn't qualify as a spark compared to what she felt with Chas. It didn't even qualify as static electricity. And that was why, despite what she might pretend, tonight was laden with possibilities, if not expectations. Casual sex wasn't one of her hobbies, but she'd prepared herself for the possibility by wearing a thong and thigh-highs and the push-up bra from hell just to lend herself some curves—although after last night, that was an unnecessary effort. She'd even bought some condoms and had thrown one in her purse. Then she'd thrown in a few more.

A glance at the house numbers indicated that Chas's house was beyond the next cross street, but she would have known it without knowing his house number. His block was far tidier than any other she'd driven along on this side of town, and in the middle of the row of small two-story houses sat an imposing Victorian grande dame, fully restored to an idealized version of her youth.

Every window on the first floor was lit up, although translucent coverings made it difficult to see inside. The wide front porch and driveway were well lit, too, and the sidewalks had been swept clean of the light smattering of snow that had fallen throughout the afternoon.

She pulled into his driveway and cut the headlights. Before she had shut off the engine or could indulge in any second thoughts, Chas appeared on the porch, barefoot and *not* freshly shaven, casually dressed in khakis and a white button-down, drying his hands on a dishtowel. She grabbed her purse and traded the warmth of the car for the bite of the wind as she hurried up the front walk. As her foot landed on the bottom step, she saw him look past her and raise a hand to wave at a passing car.

"That car followed me practically all the way over here," she said, as his hand slid around her elbow in what had become a familiar gesture. His smile was warm enough to make her forget about the cold. And the complications.

"What do you mean 'practically all the way'? They were supposed to follow you *all* the way," he replied, opening the heavy wooden door and ushering her over the threshold.

"Those were cops?"

"Yeah. Jamison and Cooper. This isn't the best neighborhood, and since you get into trouble just heading downtown, I didn't want you to take any chances. Let me take your coat."

His eyes skimmed her approvingly, and she was glad she'd decided to wear a skirt. It was long and black, stopping a few inches above her ankles, but it was slim, and therefore flattering. The dull camel-colored twinset also appeared demure, but it was cashmere, and shot with occasional strands of gold, and therefore sexy. She'd chosen the outfit deliberately, and, judging by the smile hinting at the corners of his mouth, Chas caught the symbolism. *Utter confusion.*

"Your house is lovely," she said, looking around the spacious foyer and into the rooms beyond. A large living room lay to the left, and from where she stood she could see the edge of an ornate fireplace, a few pieces of upholstered period furniture, and the shadow of a baby grand piano. To the right lay a much smaller, much cozier book-lined room with well-worn leather furniture and a smaller, plainer fireplace. A few magazines lay on the low coffee table, and newspapers were stacked near the hearth. A wide staircase swept up from the front edge of the living room, and next to it lay a wide hallway that led to the back of the house and the kitchen, which she could see through a swinging door that was propped open.

"Thanks. Why don't we get something to drink? Then I'll give you a tour, if you're interested."

As they walked down the hall, they passed a set of French doors on the right, which led into a large, chandeliered dining room. Two places had been set at the far end of the long table.

They entered a large, airy, carefully modernized kitchen that retained much of its period charm. The wood floor, tall, glass-fronted cabinets, and large red-brick fireplace, convincingly blackened with use, led the eye away from the modern, wood-fronted appliances. The countertops were wooden and old and cluttered with odds and ends, mail, and small appliances.

"Is Champagne okay with you?" he asked, taking her agreement for granted as he lifted the dripping bottle from its icy silvered bath.

She lifted an eyebrow. "Again?"

"You seemed to like it last night."

"Well, I did, but are we celebrating something?"

"Of course we are," he said, expertly twisting the cork so that it popped out with a little sigh. He poured out two flutes, and handed one to her. "I've never entertained—how was it Paxton put it?—a writer of national prominence in my home. Much less a beautiful one."

"Oh, heavens." Miranda set her flute down on the scarred wooden surface of the heavy table and flew out of the room, out of the house, and pulled open her car door. By the time she was retracing her steps across the lawn, he was halfway down the front steps.

"What's wrong?"

"Nothing's wrong. I just forgot something. Go back in the house. You don't have a coat on. You'll freeze."

"Neither do you."

"But I have a sweater on, and shoes," she pointed out, refusing to go into the house until he had crossed the threshold first.

"What did you forget?"

"These," she said, producing from behind her back a large bouquet of flowers in every color and variety she'd been able to find.

He stared at them, then at her, then took them from her slowly and broke into a grin. "You've caught me by surprise. I don't think anyone has ever given me flowers before."

She tried to ignore the burst of bright, warm pleasure his words elicited by resorting to sarcasm. "At your age? A first?"

"In more ways than one."

She looked away from the warmth in his eyes, which was stoking the unsettling heat within her. "That's what you get for inviting a writer of national prominence to dinner," she said lightly, walking toward the kitchen. *Save me, Jesus. I'm not quite sure I'm ready for this.*

"So if I were a vase and lived in this house, where would I hang out?" Miranda asked as she walked into the kitchen and glanced at the many cabinets lining the walls.

Chas watched the unpretentious sway of her hips as she walked away from him, highly entertained by her deliberate nonchalance. Just as she had last night, she'd neatly sidestepped at least two opportunities for a casual kiss and, therefore, the opportunity to reestablish any of the intimacy painstakingly achieved last night. On the other hand, none of her skittishness had reappeared. So far.

"There's a closet near the back door that my mother goes into every time she comes over. I have no idea what's in there, and frankly I'm scared to look, but feel free. If you find anything that resembles a body, give me a shout. Otherwise, I don't want to know." He took one last look at the way her skirt hugged her trim backside and turned to the vegetables he'd been washing.

He heard the closet door open with a loud squeak of the old hinges. "Oh, my. Your mother is quite a woman, Chas. It looks like someone robbed Tiffany's and stored all the loot in here."

"It figures. She's probably been cleaning out her closets. My sister refuses to let her into the house until she's signed an affidavit stating she isn't carrying in any castoffs."

Miranda crossed the room with a heavy crystal vase cupped in both hands, and began filling it with water. After placing the flowers in it, she fluffed them out a bit, then stood back and surveyed her work.

"What do you think?"

"Absolutely perfect," he said, his eyes on the arranger rather than the arrangement.

"I agree." She turned to face him. "Now, how about that Champagne?"

He handed her the flute she'd set down earlier, and topped it up to add some fizz.

"To research," she said, raising her glass to his and meeting his eyes.

"Where would the world be without it?" he added, and touched her glass lightly. The full, clear note carried through the room and melted away.

She lowered her eyes and took a sip. "I saw a piano in that front room. Do you play, or is it just a piece of furniture?"

"I play."

"Still? I mean, I presume you learned as a child?"

He nodded. "I still play pretty often just to keep in practice. Do you?"

"I never learned."

"Would you like to?"

She shook her head. "You know what they say about old dogs and new tricks."

"C'mon. It's kind of like typing. Your fingers are probably limber enough from that. Give it a try." Taking her free hand, he led her to the living room despite her token, laughing protests. They sat next to each other on the bench and he ran his hands over the keys in a light arpeggio.

"It's simple. You put your left hand here, and your right hand here. No, like this." He brought his arm around her and picked up her right hand, placing it on the keys. From the corner of his eye he could see her roll her eyes, but she was smiling. "Relax your hand."

She turned her face until their eyes met. Their lips were almost touching. "You're not being very subtle, Chas," she said, trying and failing to suppress her laughter.

"I know. I haven't resorted to tactics like these since high school," he murmured, brushing his lips lightly over hers.

"I'd be surprised if it worked then," she said, her voice barely above a whisper.

He brushed her lips again. "Kiss me, Miranda."

One heartbeat later, she moved forward that last millimeter and their lips met once, then twice before he felt one of her hands come to rest lightly on his back, the other rustling through his hair. Wrapping his arms around her, he moved her slightly off balance and deepened the kiss. Her lips parted beneath his and their tongues met in a hot, wet, passionate tangle.

God, she was sweet. Addictive. An intriguing combination of knowing and not knowing, of confidence and hesitancy, of passion and propriety. He drew her in closer, wanting to get past that line she didn't want him to cross. That was when her sense of propriety won out. She broke the kiss and turned her face just enough so he couldn't reclaim her mouth.

"Just like you let the punishment fit the crime, I have to let the reward fit the effort, Chas," she said lightly, breathlessly, and he let her slip out of his arms.

"Ready for the tour, then?" He stood up and joined her in the doorway, handing her the glass of Champagne she'd left on the piano. She was flushed and beautiful, and still a little out of breath.

He bit back a satisfied smile. The kiss had been deep and sexy and damned enjoyable, but not enough to put her in that condition—unless, of course, the cool and elusive Ms. Lane's defenses were crumbling.

Resolving to let her set the pace for the rest of the evening just to see where she took it, he led her through the house. She was quietly appreciative of his restoration efforts. She listened, asked questions, didn't gush, and somehow managed always to gravitate to the significant details, whether she ran light fingers over the hand-carved newel at the bottom of the staircase, or trailed her eyes along the dining room's ornate crown molding.

"You've seen the 'afters'; now I'll show you a 'before,' " he said, opening the door to a room on the second floor. She stepped into it and he watched her eyes widen as she took in the stained, graffitied wallpaper, the bullet-to-fist-to-chair-sized holes in the walls, and the scarred wooden floor covered with burn marks from cigarettes and larger fires.

"Oh, my heavens," she breathed. "Was the whole house this bad?"

He leaned against the doorjamb, enjoying the view as she did a slow, disbelieving twirl. There was a charm and a softness about her tonight that he hadn't noticed before. That she hadn't revealed before. "This room was one of the better ones, actually."

"Were you looking for a fixer-upper?"

He grinned. "No. I was quite happy living in a condo downtown."

"What made you buy this place?"

"It was a crack house. The city was days away from condemning it. A triple shooting brought me down here. Under all the grime, it was a beautiful old house, and I thought it would be a shame to lose it, so I bought it. I couldn't even live in it for a few months. It took two solid weeks to clear out the garbage and another three months to rewire and replumb the first floor. After that, I moved in and lived in the kitchen for six months while I worked on it room by room. By the end of two years, the first floor was finished and I started on the second. I just decided to leave this room as a reminder. I'll get around to fixing it one of these days, when I decide what to do with it."

"Other than this room, are you done?"

He turned out the light and closed the door as she exited the room. "Almost. The basement's pretty rough. One more floor," he said, steering her away from the large main staircase and toward a narrow door at the back end of the hall.

"Let me go up and turn on a light." He opened the door and started up the steep staircase that opened into his bedroom, which took up three-quarters of the high-ceilinged, dormered attic. Grabbing the universal remote-control unit, he pressed the buttons that turned on all the wall sconces, then opened the motorized blinds on the skylights. She appeared at the top of the stairs, looking around in something that stopped just short of wonder.

"This is magnificent." Her gaze swept the space, from the small fireplace and seating area at the far end, to the large period bed and the fireplace next to it near the top of the stairs. She came up the last two steps and stepped into the room, going nowhere near the bed. "It's bigger than several apartments I've lived in."

"It was the servants' quarters. There were about twelve small bedrooms up here—cubicles, really—and one small bathroom. I figured it would be a shame to let all that wiring and plumbing go to waste, and just leave it as an attic."

"Is that the bathroom?"

He nodded and watched her walk through the door, heard her gasp. She walked out a few minutes later.

"It's not quite what I'd call a true restoration, Chas."

"I had to weigh historic accuracy against the reality of a cast iron tub and no running hot water during cold Connecticut winters."

"Chas, there's a fireplace in there," she said, moving toward the stairs.

He let her descend two or three steps before joining her. "That's original. The rest is new."

Chas took her up on her offer to help with dinner. It was such a guy's menu, Miranda thought with a smile as she tore the Romaine lettuce into bite-sized pieces. Everything that needed cooking was being cooked on the grill, which was on the porch off the kitchen.

If it was going to happen tonight, he was setting the stage very carefully. As they prepared the meal, he stood just a bit closer to her than necessary, and would brush against her as they moved around the kitchen. It was kind of cute, actually, that he was being so careful not to come on too strong after testing her with that kiss. No doubt if she'd been agreeable, she'd be upstairs now getting a private tour of his sheets instead of casual glances across the sink.

"I think everything else is just about done. Time to

throw on the steaks," he said as he came in from the porch, bringing with him the summery scent of grilled food and the sharp tang of early winter.

She glanced at him over her shoulder. "I can't believe you're standing out there barefoot and without a coat on. Aren't you freezing?"

He smiled and shook his head. "Cold feet, warm grill. These won't take long. Why don't you take the rest of this into the dining room?"

She picked up the salad and carried it through the connecting door. The dining room was a beautiful room, as were all the rooms he'd redone. The walls were painted a rich, deep red, almost the color of the bottle of merlot he'd opened, and the dark wood and stained glass of the built-in china cabinets gleamed in the light of the chandelier.

She set the salad on the table and put the wine near his place, then turned to look at the many photographs clustered on the large sideboard. They were of his family, no doubt. A young woman who was in many of the pictures resembled Chas, with her dark hair and eyes, and her open smile. The young man who was in them, though, was blond and blue-eyed, and bigger, much bigger than Chas. Taller, broader. She wouldn't have known he was related except for his mouth. His smile was the same as Chas's. Just as sexy, maybe a little poutier.

Her eyes drifted to a wedding picture at the back of the group, and she found herself staring at it for a moment in disbelief. Chas's face looked out at her. His smile, his eyes, his dark, wavy hair. Only the dated clothing told her that it had to be his parents' wedding picture. The resemblance Chas bore to his father was almost eerie.

"I hope you're hungry."

She turned to see him enter the room bearing a steaming platter of seared tenderloin and tuna fillets, potatoes, and a rainbow of out-of-season vegetables.

"It smells wonderful." She met his eyes with a smile. "How many more people are coming over? You have enough for the whole neighborhood."

He smiled back and set the platter on the table, then pulled out her chair.

"That was a really lovely meal, Chas. And you were right. You *are* a pretty good cook for a Neanderthal. Even for a Renaissance man," she teased as she ignored his suggestion to stay seated. She picked up her plate and flatware and followed him into the kitchen.

"Thank you. What is it with you and archetypes? Men aren't made with cookie cutters, you know. There are a lot of things about me that might surprise you. I could turn the tables on you."

"You could try." She met his hitched eyebrow with a sideways glance and decided to scale back the flirting. It was too easy and likely too dangerous. "Do you want me to clear or wash?"

"Neither. You can entertain me while I do both."

"I'll clear," she said, and sailed back into the dining room, returning in a moment with the still-full platter of grilled food. "When do you find out about your promotion?"

"In about two months. Maybe less."

"And is this a big one? I mean, personally? Or is it a stepping-stone?"

"It's both," he replied after a slight hesitation. "My father made lieutenant before he died. I intend to climb higher than that."

Shades of Walter. She covered her shiver with a quick turn back toward the dining room. "How high?"

"I'm aiming for the top. Might as well. The only other option is retirement."

She could tell he was uncomfortable with the direction of the conversation, but decided she'd quit after one more round of questioning. "Most people dream of that. You'd be young enough to do something else. What do other cops do afterward? Don't a lot of them go into private industry? Security firms and the like?"

"Some do. I could do that now, if I wanted to. I turned down a good offer last week. It would be safer, and I'd make a hell of a lot more money." He shrugged to end the conversation.

Maybe one more round. "If the offer was so good, why didn't you take it?" she asked from the dining room.

"I like being a cop." His voice held a tone she wasn't about to ignore.

"That's reasonable. What does the rest of your family think about it? I mean, your being a cop," she said, returning to the kitchen. He didn't respond until she was nearly behind him.

"I'll say it wasn't a popular decision and leave it at that. Quit interviewing me, Ms. Lane, or at least switch research topics for a while," he said, capturing her unawares as his arms slid around her waist from behind. She jumped, and nearly dropped the salad bowl.

He caught it and set it on the counter, then turned her slowly within the circle of his arms. "Why are you so nervous around me?"

"You startled me, that's all," she replied, leaning as far back in his arms as she could. His eyes were too dark, too amused, and way too close.

"Why are you so nervous around me?" he said again, closing the gap she'd just created.

"One reason is that you keep repeating yourself." She put her hands against his chest and pushed. *Another is that all you want to do is get me naked and horizontal while I'm trying to keep this impersonal.*

He dropped his arms with a laugh and stepped back. "I get no reward for all the effort I put into dinner?"

"It depends on what you're serving for dessert."

Miranda had remained engaging during dinner and while she helped him clean up, but by the time they moved into the study with coffee, she'd grown quiet. She chose to sit in the chair farthest from the fire, and drew her feet up beneath her. Chas considered himself a pretty patient guy and, even if he hadn't been, there was something about Miranda that precluded any reason for impatience. He didn't know her well, but he knew her well enough to know that she made her own decisions. She didn't let herself be rushed or pushed around. Or seduced, apparently.

She intrigued him for a lot of reasons he could list

and a few he couldn't. He also knew there was no point even fantasizing about making love to her tonight. It wasn't going to happen.

He stoked the fire back to a healthy blaze and sat down on the end of the couch farthest from her. Bringing his bare feet up onto the table, he settled in, relaxed and comfortable and fully prepared for her next words.

"It was a wonderful evening, Chas. Thank you."

"That sounds like a preamble to 'good-bye' and 'good-night,' " he said easily, glancing at her over the rim of his coffee mug.

"I suppose it does."

"It's not even ten o'clock yet, Miranda. Surely your curfew is later than that."

"I have a lot of writing left to do, Chas, and not many days left to do it. If I don't keep going . . ." She shrugged convincingly, which meant she was lying.

He wasn't in the mood for it. They'd moved beyond that.

"If you don't keep going, you might have to talk to me about those complications you want to avoid," he interrupted quietly, keeping his eyes on her mouth rather than meeting her eyes, so as not to issue a challenge. "I like you, Miranda. I'd like us to trust each other. You already confessed about interviewing me, and I know that took a lot of courage, because you didn't have to do it. But there's something else beneath all of your lovely sparks and icicles that makes you seem fragile and vulnerable, and it makes me want to protect you. I know that may not sound very flattering, and I'm pretty sure it's the last thing you want to hear, but I won't apologize for it." He swirled the coffee in his mug and took another sip, then brought his eyes up to meet hers. "I let it drop last night, Miranda, but time's up. I want to know what you're afraid of."

His words hung in the air between them, having shattered the room's warm coziness as quickly as would a wintry draft through a suddenly broken window. Miranda hadn't expected this turn in the conversation, but she realized now she should have. Chas was a watcher.

An investigator. He didn't like leaving questions unanswered.

Feeling cornered, she watched silently as the burning log turned into little more than a glowing ember, and wondered why he didn't make some noise, start some conversation, change the subject. But he didn't. He didn't say a word, didn't shift his position, didn't let out an exasperated breath. He just waited. And Miranda was appalled that for the first time in her life, maybe the first time it really mattered, words were failing her.

In all the years of hurt, she'd never thought to form the words, because she'd never imagined saying them. She'd never considered that there would be a time she'd want to say them, or a person she'd want to hear them. Yet here she was in what might be the right time with someone who might be the right person and she didn't know what to say or how to begin. The only thing she knew for certain was that if they came out at all, they wouldn't be coherent.

"If I had an answer, what difference would it make? What do you want from me?" she asked.

"I want you to trust me."

She met his eyes. They were dark and warm and resolute. "That's it?"

"No. That's just the beginning, but it's enough for now."

"Why should I trust you?"

"You're the only one who can answer that. And you're the only one who can answer the question, 'Why shouldn't you trust me?'"

She counted six panicked heartbeats before she answered. "What do you want to know?"

"What man hurt you?"

"It doesn't matter."

"Was it your father?"

A bitter, amused smile crept across her mouth before she could stop it. "You got it in one, Detective Casey."

Concern creased his forehead for a moment; then Chas assumed his cop face: neutral, mildly interested, unshockable. She was glad for it. It was like talking to a stranger instead of someone who cared, or said he cared. "What did he do?"

"Nothing dire, nothing criminal, nothing even scandalous. The only thing I can charge him with is that he told me the truth after eighteen years of lying to me." She looked at him. His eyes gave her the barest flicker of encouragement. "His name is Walter. Walter Burrows. He was a career military man, the son of a military man and proud of it. Very strict. Very religious. He believed in doing the right thing. He was a pretty good father, too. He fed me, clothed me, housed me, educated me. He never touched me. In any way. In fact, he never even hugged me, as far as I can remember."

"Why not?"

"Because I wasn't his." She took a sip of her cold coffee to try to stem the tide of words swelling within her. "My mother had been feeling unwell on and off for a long time. She didn't talk about it much, and military doctors aren't the proactive sort. Moving around didn't help much, either. Around Thanksgiving of my freshman year at Smith, she finally felt sick enough to make a fuss. She went into the hospital, I came home, and two days later, she died. After the funeral, and after everyone had left the house, my father handed me a box of her things and told me to go through the house and collect what else I'd like of hers and pack it up. He said he was going to stay the night at a buddy's house. I figured it was because he wanted to get drunk to drown his sorrows, but then he told me it was because it wouldn't be appropriate for both of us to stay in the house. That's when he told me I was hers, not his."

She jerked her chin away from the hand that had been supporting it and looked with surprise at the dampness that had accumulated on her palm. She hadn't felt the tears begin. She closed her fist around them and continued.

"I don't know the circumstances of my conception, but Walter and my mother made a deal, apparently. Before I was born he agreed to marry her and raise me as his own, but the understanding was that I was really her responsibility, not his. In his mind, when she died, his obligation to both of us was fulfilled. I wasn't sure what to do, so I flew back to school the next day with two boxes of her belongings. I spent that Christmas with Paxton and Jane. One month later, a check arrived from a life insurance company. She'd listed me as her only beneficiary." She shrugged and checked her palm. It was dry. "The last time I communicated with him was when I thanked him for driving me to the bus station so I could catch a bus to the airport in Birmingham." She focused on the flames chasing across the burned logs just to keep her mind free of other images.

"Is he still alive?"

Her shoulders sagged with relief that he hadn't tried to offer her sympathy or comfort. No one could. It took her a minute to remember that he knew about that firsthand. "I don't know."

He said nothing, and eventually she had to fill the void. "It's not the standard Southern tragedy, Chas. I mean, it completely lacks any Tennessee Williams rage, there's no quiet Faulknerian despair, and the story line is fairly trite." She paused, then smiled tightly as she met his eyes. "I know the old adage is to write what you know, but if I did, it would depress the hell out of people, and the world already endures enough heartbreak and anguish. I don't want to put more out there. I've learned that people burn out on tragedy, but they always love a happy ending. So I defy tradition and write about what I don't know." *Like love and romance. Commitment. Trust.* She looked away, feeling his eyes still on her.

"How did you get to Smith?" he asked in that even, dispassionate voice.

She leaned her head against the back of the chair and closed her eyes. "Another tired story. A few teachers who saw promise and encouraged me to apply for scholarships, a mother who clipped coupons and went without a lot of things on my behalf."

"How did you stay there after she died? The insurance money?"

She flashed him a bitter smile. "God bless the innate

charm of the Southern woman. I relied on the kindness
of strangers." Not a flicker of surprise passed over his
face and she looked away, not pleased with herself for
trying to get one. "Paxton got drunk that Christmas Eve
and told her grandmother the truth about me instead of
the story we'd agreed on. The next morning, Grandmother Shelby summoned me to her room. . . ." She
watched his lips twitch and knew instantly that he'd encountered the old woman, probably more than once.
"She informed me, at seven o'clock on Christmas morning, that she had just gotten off the phone with the president of the college. A new scholarship would be in place
by the beginning of the next term, and it would cover
me until I graduated. To this day I don't know why she
did it."

"She never told you?"

"No."

"Does Paxton know about the scholarship?"

"No. You're the first person I've told." She gave a
harsh laugh to prevent herself from succumbing to other
emotions. "What did you put in this coffee? Sodium
pentothal?"

"Why, can you taste it?" he asked with the shadow
of a smile playing around his mouth.

She met his eyes. "Are we done?"

"No. Tell me about the guns and the tae kwon do."

"They're no big things. I grew up on military bases in
the Deep South. Everybody learned how to shoot. With
so many guns everywhere, it would have been dangerous
not to. And I took up tae kwon do a few years ago,
more for exercise than anything else. That's it."

"Are you afraid that I'll hurt you?" he asked after a
long moment.

She shifted her gaze to the fire and went silent for
a long time. "I'm not afraid that you will, but I think
you could."

"Physically?"

"No. I mean, of course you *could,* but you never
would. I know that much about you."

"Then how?"

She leaned back again, closed her eyes, and took a

deep breath. "I know this is going to sound awful, but I like you, Chas. I like you a lot, and I wish I didn't. I don't want to miss you after I leave, and I'm leaving soon."

A long time passed before either spoke again.

"What branch of the military?" he asked.

"Army," she replied, her eyes still closed.

"What did he do?"

She looked at him and fought the awful constriction in her throat. "Military police," she said in a voice that fought for normalcy, and watched Chas close his eyes as if in pain.

Another long silence built between them, and Miranda began to feel more empty than relieved. She started to plot her exit. Quick, clean, nothing emotional—

"May I approach you?"

He'd been so silent and still and unmoved through all her revelations and her silences that the question took her by surprise. She didn't dare move her eyes away from the few flickering embers lying amidst the deep, powdery cushion of ashes. An ungentle fear began to build within her, the fear she hadn't thought about in years, the gnawing fear she'd locked away in a safe-deposit box in Atlanta along with the papers and trinkets of a woman she'd loved and lost, and may never have known at all.

"I thought real men didn't ask permission," she said, but the attempt to shake the fear failed. Chas said nothing, just looked at her with dark eyes that didn't judge and didn't soothe. "Yes."

He swung his long legs to the floor and walked to her slowly. Stopping in front of her, he slipped his hand into hers, entwining their fingers. And waited.

She rose from the chair and moved into his arms hesitantly. She waited for him to try to kiss her, and when he didn't, she felt her throat tighten ominously. Slowly, she rested her head against a chest that felt warm and solid and alive and comforting.

It was terrifying.

CHAPTER
14

She wasn't sure how long they stood like that, but Miranda knew she had to go home. Lingering within a protective, comforting hug wasn't a practical strategy for eventual departure. It was the potential means to a very different end. As he'd pointed out to her days ago, no man delayed his own gratification for too long.

"Chas, I'm going to leave now. Thank you for a really nice evening," she whispered into the warm softness of his shirt.

His hold on her relaxed but his arms remained around her. "I'll go start your car and clean it off."

She glanced up at him. "What's on it?"

"It started to snow again while I was grilling." He dropped his arms and feathered a kiss across her forehead. "It will only take a minute. You stay in here and stay warm."

She walked with him to the front door and waited while he slipped his bare feet into a loosely laced pair of fleece-lined boots and shrugged into a jacket. When he pulled open the door, her mouth fell open in dismayed surprise. The neighborhood was slick and sparkling, as a heavy, gelid rain lobbed down from the sky.

"What in the Sam Hill is that?"

He glanced down at her. "Sleet. Welcome to winter in New England."

"Sleet?"

"Icy slush that falls from the sky. C'mon, you went to school in Massachusetts. You should remember it."

She glanced up at him. "That was over a decade ago, and, as far as I can remember, I stayed indoors in bad weather."

He smiled. "If you're nervous about driving in it, I'll be happy to drive you home."

She returned her gaze to the wild night outside the door. "I'd have to get back here somehow to get my car. I have to think about this for a minute." She stepped back into the warmth of the foyer and he closed the door.

"Would it be less complicated if you just stayed here?"

She looked up at him again. There was nothing suggestive in his eyes. "It depends."

"You set the conditions. It's your call."

"What is?"

"Everything," he said quietly.

As he stood before her, slightly rumpled, with a heavily shadowed chin but eyes still full of compassion and energy, Miranda knew without a doubt that he had breached every one of her defenses. She'd let him into her life and, from there, into her heart. It was a stupid mistake, and one she knew she would regret, but she also knew that she was about to make a much bigger one.

"Thank you, Chas. If you don't mind, I'd like to stay."

"Of course I don't mind," he said after a second's pause. "Let me turn off the lights and lock up, and I'll get you set up in one of the guest rooms."

She felt something inside her soften dangerously as she looked into his eyes, and she knew that if he so much as moved toward her, she would sleep with him.

He smiled and turned toward the hallway. "I'll be right back."

She watched him walk toward the kitchen. A few minutes later he returned to the foyer and stood framed by the shadows of the darkened house. They walked up the stairs in silence, and he showed her to the large, beautifully furnished guest room at the front of the house.

"Anything you need is probably in here. Extra blankets are in that chest. Towels are in the bathroom. Do you need . . . Would you like to borrow something to sleep in? A T-shirt?"

She stood a few feet away from him, feeling awkward but full of a disconcerting mixture of gratitude and warmth and desire. Nodding her head in response to his question, she stepped closer to him. "Thank you," she whispered, and reached up to place a light kiss on his lips.

Chas lay in bed, his palms supporting the back of his head, staring at the ceiling.

Miranda Lane was a paradox at best. The attraction had been between them from the start. All the interplay that had followed, up to and including this evening, had been leading in only one direction, and they both knew it.

He closed his eyes and conjured her face as he'd last seen it. Framed by dark, tousled curls, her eyes had been hesitant and warm, her mouth soft and waiting. Just like that old song said, she had him bewitched and bewildered. She trusted him and wouldn't admit it. She wanted him and wouldn't act on it. She was afraid of getting involved yet did nothing to stop herself. And she wasn't a tease. Not a deliberate one.

She'd been on the edge. Already over it, if his experience told him anything.

He wouldn't have had to flirt or persuade or even ask. He wouldn't have had to say anything; he could have just put out his hand. Instead of lying here now, alone and frustrated as hell, he'd be learning her, finding out if all that simmered beneath her cool, sharp exterior was as intense and passionate as he imagined it to be. He'd know already if she moaned or laughed when something felt good, if she allowed her hands to be as bold as her words, if she—

Damn it.

He hadn't put out his hand. Even though the woman had been clouding his brain for days, he hadn't issued the invitation part of her had been ready to accept. Because he didn't want part of her. He wanted *all* of her. Freely given. No fears lurking in the background; no projections of her father coloring her memories after she left town.

He knew she was deep into her writing and on a tight deadline. That didn't make it easier to stay away. Once she finished the book, her time would be less than limited. It would be finite. But no matter what happened, he wasn't going to make leaving difficult for her. He wouldn't break her heart. He didn't do that to women. Besides, he didn't want her heart. He just wanted her.

Rolling over and shutting his eyes was the only realistic solution.

Stupid. That's what I am. Miranda pulled her face out of the pillow, took a huge breath and plunged her head downward again. She hadn't done it on purpose. She knew revealing too much personal information too soon was totally against the rules of dating, but it had never been a problem for her. In six years, she'd never told Josh as much about herself as she'd told Chas over the last few days. Josh had never asked. *But it's not even a dating issue,* she scolded herself. *This is a business relationship. Business.*

Then why do I want to sleep with him?

She came up for air again and retreated back into the pillow, as if doing so would block out the truth. It didn't. The truth was there, crashing inelegantly through her brain like an elephant at a dead run. *Because he's nice. Everyone says so—Jane, Paxton, James. Because he gives a good impression of caring. Because he's sweet and funny and a flirt. Because he smells wonderful, he kisses like he invented the sport, and because being in his arms and against his chest felt divine—and I don't even like hugs.* She rolled onto her back and stifled a groan. *Pathetic just doesn't begin to cover it.*

The sound of footsteps jolted her upright. The squeak of a stair made her catch her breath. She'd been in bed for over an hour, all senses on full alert, waiting for just those sounds. Her rational side knew he wouldn't knock on her door. Still, she frowned when his quiet footsteps passed her door and continued down the main staircase.

He couldn't be thirsty. She'd seen a water glass and carafe on his bedside table. He couldn't be hungry after that dinner. That left only one reason he'd be up in the middle of the night: He couldn't sleep, either, but he wasn't about to bother her.

It's probably another one of his rules.

Which meant it was up to her. She closed her eyes in despair, knowing she was woefully underskilled in luring a man to bed. Josh had been her only lover, and he had always made the first move. Or what passed for it.

Time to grow up. She flung back the covers and dropped her feet to the floor. And stopped.

"I can't sleep with him just because he's nice and he smells good," she whispered to herself.

Why not? I've done worse things for stupider reasons, she told herself a moment later.

Giving herself a stern push toward the brink of what could well end up being sheer humiliation, she crept down the stairs, shivering in the T-shirt he'd lent her. The temperature in the house wasn't the cause of it. Not the sole cause.

The fourth stair from the bottom creaked when her foot touched it, and the sound brought him out of the small, cozy den they'd sat in earlier. His rumpled khakis had been donned carelessly. His white shirt was buttoned but untucked and his feet were still bare, and he looked at her with a surprised expression on his face. She smiled, hoping she didn't appear nearly as nervous as she felt.

"Hi, Chas."

"Hi. Is everything all right?" he said, unsuccessfully stifling a yawn.

Ignoring the flutters in her stomach, she walked down the last few steps, crossed the hall, and stopped in front of him. "I heard you come downstairs and figured that you couldn't sleep either. There's something I wanted to say to you. Ask you, actually," she replied softly.

"What's that? I'm so tired I'd agree to anything."

"Would you mind if I stayed with you tonight?"

He blinked at her in a split second of incomprehension. It was more than she could take.

"I mean with you," she repeated, imbuing her words with what she hoped was unmistakable meaning. "With. You."

Rolling over and going to sleep hadn't worked. He'd come downstairs looking for something to read, but Chas wasn't about to deny that he'd been hoping for a better outcome, for instance that he'd discover her there, unable to sleep, watching TV or hunting for something to read. That she'd see him and turn to him and they'd let nature take its course. Finally. But, of course, this was Miranda. Nature's course was never straightforward with her, and now he was trapped in a strange seduction, if it was one at all.

They stood a few feet apart, watching each other watch the other for a reaction. Despite having intended for this moment to happen, Chas admitted to himself that he didn't know what to do, hadn't known from the instant he'd heard the subtle, sexual huskiness in her voice when she'd said his name. He'd feigned sleepiness to give himself an extra second to strategize. And an unassailable strategy was what he needed, because, although his inner Neanderthal was aghast at the notion, his evolved side knew having sex would be the wrong way to end the night. He also knew there was no way he could get out of it. Practically from the moment they'd met he'd issued an open invitation, and now she'd accepted, which obliged him to follow through. He recognized the rare irony of lust and social etiquette conspiring against his better judgment.

Given their earlier conversation and her present wide-eyed stillness, he doubted theirs would be the passionate, uninhibited coupling he'd been anticipating for days; nor would it be tender and sweet, as it might have been an hour and a half ago. At this point, awkward was the best outcome he could predict.

He moved toward her slowly, hoping his reluctance

didn't show. Not knowing what to say, he remained silent and picked up her left hand, kissed it gently, then kissed her lightly on the mouth. Folding her hand into his, they walked up the dark staircases silently.

Once in his bedroom, he turned on some of the softer lights and then looked at her. She had crossed the room quietly and stopped near the foot of the bed. She looked as uncomfortable as he did, and the sheer absurdity of the situation made him want to laugh, to share the joke, but he didn't dare. He looked away casually as he began to unbutton the shirt he'd tossed on before going downstairs.

This is crazy.

There was no enthusiasm in the room with them. No passion, no breathless laughter, no buttons outwitting fingers made clumsy with anticipation, or clothes landing in scattered heaps on the floor. They were quiet and tense, and he hadn't been so conscious of what he was about to do since his first time. He glanced at her again.

The dark blue T-shirt he'd given her stopped mid-thigh, and the long, lean curves of her legs made some of his best intentions disappear—until his eyes flicked to her face and saw her gaze fixed on his hands as they approached the last button of his shirt. There was a tensile energy about her, like that of a cat about to pounce—or flee—and he let his hands drop, let the shirt hang open in case the act of taking it off triggered flight.

"Which side do you prefer to sleep on?" he asked just to break the tension.

Her eyes met his. They were cautious, not shy. It didn't reassure him. "Right, if you don't mind."

"Not at all," he replied with another false smile. "I'll be back in a minute. I'm going to turn on the alarm."

He left the room and made the unnecessary trip downstairs to give her time to decide if she was going to follow through—and himself time to come up with a way of getting out of the immediate situation without destroying its long-range potential. He hadn't ever slept with a woman he didn't want to sleep with, and he hadn't *not* wanted to sleep with a woman he was attracted to at any point since puberty. Yet here he was,

powerfully attracted to a woman who was just as powerfully attracted to him, on the verge of sleeping with her,
and knowing it was going to be a mistake, quite possibly
an irreparable one.

When he returned to his bedroom, he was greeted by
darkness. Pitch-black, inky, near-total darkness. The wall
sconces had been turned off and all the draperies closed.
Even the blinds on the skylights had been closed.

He walked carefully to the bed and slipped between
the sheets with his boxer shorts still on, feeling more
than a little ridiculous. That feeling disappeared almost
immediately as he felt Miranda's hands reach for him.
She smoothed her cotton-clad body next to his, molding
her warmth against him. Her mouth sought his and,
finding it, claimed it as her hands drifted over his chest
and arms.

His pleasant surprise at her assertiveness was dispelled
when his hands began to roam in kind, causing everything about her to tense. He broke their kiss and pulled
back slightly.

"Miranda," he whispered. "We don't have to do this."

She drew in a short, sharp breath. "You don't want
me?"

Great. "Shh. Of course I do. I just want you to be
comfortable, and if that means—"

"I want you, Chas."

He paused for only a heartbeat, then brought her
mouth back to his.

He let her continue to set the pace of their lovemaking, but her movements, her progression, seemed based
less on pleasure for either of them than on something
else he didn't understand. Something orderly and con-
trived. Passionless. After too little time spent learning
each other, she rolled onto her back. He traced her inner
thigh to its top, then tried to touch her higher, but she
murmured a small protest and he immediately slid his
hand away. It was the first sound she'd made.

Almost immediately after that, she slipped beneath
him—still wearing his T-shirt—and began to take him
inside her. He knew she wasn't ready and tried to postpone his entry, but she wouldn't let him, and she gasped

when he resigned himself to following the prompts of
her hands. He tried to keep his movements gentle, but
she rebelled at that, too, and moved beneath him relent-
lessly, bringing him to a swift, if reluctant, climax.

He rolled to her side feeling partly used, partly confused, but—he wasn't proud of it—physically satisfied.
Before he could catch his breath, she slipped out of bed,
and a moment later a ribbon of light appeared beneath
the bathroom door. A moment after that he heard the
shower come on.

She returned to his bed a short while later, damp and
fresh and warm through the heavy cotton T-shirt, and
slipped immediately into his arms, burrowing and snug-
gling against him. All the tension that had marked their
encounter was gone, and she lay relaxed and soft within
his arms, as silent as she'd been through the entire pro-
ceeding. He was on the verge of falling asleep when he
heard her whisper his name.

"Yes?" he whispered back.

"Thank you." She said it softly, sincerely, into his
chest. Then she laid her cheek on the spot where her
words still burned and fell asleep almost instantly.

Chas lay awake in the darkness, holding her tightly,
for a very long time.

The beeping of his alarm was the first thing Chas became aware of. The second thing was the warm, soft,
fragrant curves of a woman pressed against him. He
reached for his watch on the bedside table and turned
off the alarm, then opened his eyes. It was six thirty.
She'd barely moved all night.

As carefully as he could, he slid out of bed and went
downstairs to make a pot of coffee. While it was brewing
he emptied the dishwasher and threw in a load of laundry, anything to keep himself from reviewing the events
of the night before.

Coffee in hand, he closed the door at the bottom of
the staircase and continued up the last set of stairs quietly. He needn't have bothered. She was still deeply,
silently asleep in the same position she was in when he
left her.

He stood at the bottom of the bed, watching her sleep, knowing he should be mentally preparing himself for the meetings he would be taking part in an hour from now. Thoughts of last night took precedence, though. Thoughts of Miranda. She was beautiful and intelligent, which was always a potent combination. And she held fire inside her, and passion. He'd seen them both, felt them both—just not in bed, and that not only surprised him; it angered him.

He'd never experienced anything like last night. Not when he was sixteen and didn't know what he was doing, not at any point in time when he was with a woman who didn't know what she was doing. For him—for most people, probably—ignorance had never stood in the way of fun when it came to sex, and frequently it was the cause of some pretty intense fun.

Taking a slug of his cooling coffee, he walked over to one of the small sofas on the far side of the room. He sat down, leaned his head against the back of the sofa, closed his eyes, and fought the wave of anger that rose within him. At least now he knew where her early antagonism and lingering skittishness came from. Every time she looked at him, she probably saw her father. And the ex-boyfriend had done an excellent job of fucking up her head by teaching her to enjoy being used. Sex and fun obviously were mutually exclusive ideas to her.

He took a deep breath and let it out slowly. It had to have taken a lot for her to trust him. To go to bed with him. Granted, she'd been nervous, but she hadn't been afraid, not of him and not of sex. She had soft, experienced hands and a generous, skillful mouth, but she was more tense than a virgin in a—

He stood up and headed for the shower, shaking off the guilt that started to build and shutting down his thoughts before they could stray into dangerous territory.

It's not my problem. She's leaving in two weeks.

He had too much to do today to get wrapped up in Miranda's issues. The meeting with Joe's team was going to take place at his mother's house, so no one at the company would be alerted that there was a problem—

or a team in place to solve it. His mother had even given the household staff the day off to avoid any inadvertent leaks. Chas had to be there at eight, and it was already nearly seven. Traffic would be a pain in the ass.

After his shower, he crossed the room naked and pulled on his clothes, then went downstairs for a fresh cup of coffee for himself and one for her. When he came upstairs she was still asleep, still in the same position. A dark humor stabbed through him, and he wondered for a moment if the sex had been so bad that it killed her. He'd never known anyone to sleep so soundly. He hadn't exactly been silent as he showered and dressed.

"Miranda, wake up. It's getting late, sweetheart, and I have an appointment," he said softly as he crouched next to the bed and stroked the hair away from her face.

Her eyes fluttered open slowly, and she was smiling before she focused. She stretched and the T-shirt twisted around her, pulling tight across her barely existent breasts. Every remnant of last night's makeup had been washed away, leaving her skin shiny and tight. She looked younger than she had a right to.

"Why didn't you wake me up earlier?" she mumbled. "You're all showered and dressed."

He passed her a mug of steaming coffee. "You looked too comfortable."

She set it on the table after a tiny sip and, with a dreamy smile, snaked her arms around his neck. "I was. What time do you have to be at work today?"

"I don't. I have an all-day meeting." He kissed her on the tip of her nose, then disengaged her arms. "You can call me on my cell phone if you need me."

She lifted an eyebrow. "If I *need* you? Like if I have an emergency attack of writer's block or need a quick, inspiring roll in the sheets?"

She seemed totally at ease, which made him wary. He forced a smile. "Why do I have the urge to call you a vixen instead of a smart-ass?"

"Because you're channeling Cary Grant again, while I, on the other hand, am channeling Joan Collins rather than Doris Day."

"Glad to hear it." He nudged her over and sat on

the edge of the bed. "Are you busy tonight? Don't feel obligated to say no," he teased. "I was supposed to ask you on Sunday but forgot. My brother is in town tonight and my mother asked me to invite you to dinner. I don't want to pressure you, but if you leave town before she gets to meet you, I'm history. She'll change her will, change the locks, the whole nine yards. You'll be saving a life if you say yes."

She smiled uncertainly. "Really? I mean, she really wants to meet me?"

He nodded with a grin. "If not through me, then through Paxton, so don't read anything into it. She has every one of your books. In hardcover. I think she wants them signed."

"How can I say no to such a fan?"

"Excellent. I'll pick you up at six thirty." He made a move to stand up and she grabbed his arm.

"Wait a minute. What should I wear?"

He shrugged. "Something comfortable."

"Not good enough. A bathrobe is comfortable. So are high heels in the right situation."

He hitched an eyebrow. "Keep that bathrobe and high heels idea in mind. But for tonight, casual is fine. I'm not going to change," he said, indicating his jeans and golf shirt. He dropped another kiss on her nose and reached out to tuck an errant curl behind her ear. "Will you forgive me if I usher you out the door? I have to be in Greenwich in half an hour."

"I'll think about it," she whispered with a smile, and pressed herself against him, her lips soft against his neck. His hands automatically slid around her, tangled in her hair, but every muscle in his body was rigid. He'd seen that expression before, many times. It was the look of a satisfied, gratified woman, and it had always left him feeling pretty full of himself.

This morning it made him feel like a fraud.

CHAPTER
15

Miranda felt a little jolt when she pulled into her parking space a half hour later. She couldn't remember anything about the fifteen-minute drive through the city. Her mind was blank and her body deliciously achy. She hadn't felt this loose and relaxed and at peace with the world in years, maybe ever, and she wasn't in the mood to share her dreamy, mellow afterglow with anyone. Unfortunately, Paxton's Hummer was already there, parked with its owner's usual aplomb.

When Miranda walked in, pounding from the rear of the condo assaulted her ears, and the paint fumes made her cough. Paxton, standing mercifully alone at the breakfast bar, looked her usual, casual, easily elegant self as she flicked through a stack of invoices. Her eyes missed nothing as they scanned Miranda from the top of her hastily brushed hair to the bottoms of her decidedly evening-wear Ferragamos.

"Good morning. How long have you been here? Did you make any coffee, by chance?" Miranda asked, feeling buoyant.

Paxton tilted her perfect blond head in the direction of the full coffeemaker. "Ten minutes ago. I'm sorry to drop in like this, Miranda, but Liz wanted to meet one last time. We were supposed to meet at eight. I called you last night to tell you. You must not have gotten the message. Anyway, she's running late." She glanced at Miranda's rumpled skirt. "I'm glad to see you and Chas are getting along." Her dry, bitchy tone scraped at the surface of Miranda's mood.

Refusing to let it show, Miranda smiled as she walked to the cabinet housing the coffee mugs. "You could say that. Thank you again for introducing us."

"Did I?"

"What do you mean? Of course you did."

"You didn't meet at the paintball gallery?" Paxton's tone had gone from dry to acerbic, causing Miranda to put her mug down and turn to face her friend.

"No. That's the first place we saw each other, Paxton, but you introduced us. Until that moment in the restaurant, he was just some incredibly obnoxious cop who kept getting in my way. How do you know about the gallery, anyway? Did he tell James?"

Paxton returned her gaze to the stack of paperwork. "No. My mother told me, actually."

Surprised, Miranda hesitated before responding. "Your mother talked to Jane?"

"Yes," she responded stiffly. "It's hard to believe, but she did. Met her for lunch, actually, at some horrific little diner on that side of town."

The thought of the elegant, patrician Grace Shelby being served a patty melt and fries on a thick crockery plate was almost too much to imagine, and Miranda took a large sip of the steaming Italian roast to keep the smile off her face. "Why?"

"Mother's planning her fortieth wedding anniversary and decided that she wanted 'all the lambs back in the fold,' as she put it."

"Well, I'm glad, Paxton. I'm glad for Jane and for your parents. Aren't you? Even a little?"

"Hardly. Obviously I think Mother's abandoned her principles, but I'll be civil."

"It's been seven years, Paxton."

"Seven years without an apology, Miranda," she snapped, then instantly regained her icy calm. "I'm sorry. I think we should drop the subject." She glanced at the Day-Timer that lay open on the counter. "While

I'm here, I might as well go over the final schedule with you. Liz said everything will be finished by a week from Monday, which will give us that Tuesday to do a walk-through and fix any last-minute glitches. That Wednesday, I'm having a cleaning crew come in, Thanksgiving is Thursday, and the tour starts Friday. Are you sure you won't spend Thanksgiving with us? I really don't understand why you won't. We'd love to have you."

Miranda looked at her friend and recited her standard lie easily. "It's a family holiday, Paxton. As wonderful as your family has been to me over the years, I just don't like to intrude. Anyway, I have to get back before the end of the month. I have bills to pay and all that good stuff." She smiled and put a brisk tone in her voice. "At this point, I'm still planning on leaving town on that Wednesday morning. My revisions should be done before then. If my plans change, I'll let you know."

Paxton looked up and met her eyes. "I know I'm crossing an invisible line here, Miranda, but if that last statement is dependent on anything to do with Chas, there are a few things you'd better be aware of. He's a great guy. The best. But he's not into long-term planning. I've known him as long as I've known James, and every single one of his relationships has been a drive-by. I know you're over Josh, but you're still fragile. Don't let yourself get hurt."

"Thanks, Paxton. I appreciate your concern." Miranda forced a smile. "I guess it's a lucky coincidence that being a drive-by is about all I have the energy or inclination for these days."

"Point taken." The blonde snapped shut the Day-Timer and scooped the papers into the file folder.

"Paxton, honey," Miranda said wearily, "don't leave in a huff. Is it just that I happened to see him while I was with Jane that has you upset, or what? Because I swear to you that I didn't know who he was, and meeting him at the restaurant that night was a complete surprise. Jane never mentioned his name. So, after a few anonymous, completely annoying encounters, we actually ended up liking each other. Isn't this what you expected to happen? What you *wanted* to happen? I'm not going to kiss and tell, but a few days ago you said I needed a lover, and that's why you introduced us. Your attitude has me totally confused."

Miranda watched in surprise as Paxton hesitated, fumbled with her purse, then sank onto a bar stool. "Yes. I wanted you to meet. And yes, the whole Jane angle has me annoyed. But what I said is the truth, Miranda. I don't know what the deal is with Chas, but he's short-term material."

"So am I, Paxton."

"You deserve better."

Miranda let out a heavy breath and took a deep sip from her coffee, wanting nothing more than a long, hot soak in her tub. "Paxton, I don't know what I deserve right now, but I'm not sure a woman could get someone better than Chas. And if you ever quote me on that, I'll deny it."

"He's a *fling,* Miranda," Paxton said, looking at her with an urgency in her eyes. "I didn't expect you to fall for him. I really didn't. You're so different. I thought he would be a diversion."

"He is a diversion, and I haven't fallen in love with him, if that's what you think. I like him, and I think he's funny and smart and sharp and sexy as hell, and I can't believe I'm saying any of this to you, but we are not in love, and when I leave in two weeks it will be with good feelings and a warm glow and that's it." She paused for a breath. "I'll have no regrets, Paxton, I promise you. Please don't fret about it. If you're going to expend any emotion, direct it toward Jane. She's your sister, and despite everything that has happened between you, she loves you and she needs you."

Paxton stood up. "You can't possibly understand it, Miranda. She turned her back on everything and everyone and didn't care what the family thought when she married that . . . that old geezer. She essentially told us to go to hell. Why should I welcome her back? That's rhetorical, by the way. You don't have any family. You can't possibly understand. *She* left *us,* Miranda. Without a backward glance."

Miranda stiffened against the dagger of truth that slashed through her, and gave her friend a cold look. "That's not how she sees it, Paxton. Besides, she was twenty-two. And she loved him. So what if he was older?"

"Older? He was *three times* her age. And poor."

You stupid, rich bitch. Miranda longed to shout the words at her. Instead she lowered her voice. "I grew up poor, Paxton. It's not a character flaw. He loved her and he took care of her."

"He loved her trust fund," she snapped.

"You know better than that, Paxton. Or you would if you talked to her. Your mother has apparently gotten over it. Why can't you?"

"Why should I?"

Miranda set her coffee mug down on the counter a little too abruptly and glared at her oldest friend. "Because she needs you. It doesn't matter that y'all never liked him. He was good to her. She loved him and she was married to him for four years, living happily with him in a shack in the desert. Then he died. She moved back here to be near the only people she had left, Paxton. The only people she still loved. And instead of welcoming her back, and helping her to grieve, y'all treated her like she had leprosy. None of y'all contacted her when she lived in Manhattan, even though it's less than an hour away, and in the few months since she moved up here, you haven't gotten in touch with her once. I give her tremendous credit for coming back."

She stopped to take a deep breath and regain her composure, but the words refused to stop. "Frankly, I find your family's attitude awful. Just plain ugly. I'd give up everything I have and ever will have to have a family to run to, Paxton. But it's the one thing I'll never have no matter what I do, and to watch you squander yours makes me sick."

Her words shocked both of them, and Miranda left the room in a hurry.

"Miranda, wait."

Miranda ignored her and continued into the master

bedroom, where she flung her purse on the bed and walked over to the window to watch the sound batter the shore.

Amy's right. Dealing with all of this really is too high a price to pay for staying in the condo.

She heard Paxton come into the room and sit down on the bed. Then she heard Paxton sniffle, which was a sound she'd never heard before, and it made her turn around.

Paxton, beautiful, composed, perfect Paxton, sat on the edge of the bed with her mouth trembling, her face crumpled, her eyes red-rimmed and flowing. She looked lost and alone and utterly, utterly miserable. Miranda hesitated for a moment, debating whether to ignore her or not. Then, feeling like a heel, she crossed the room and sat down next to her. She was more alarmed than surprised when Paxton leaned into her and let out a heart-wrenching wail, followed by sobs that shook her lithe, toned, tanned body.

Having shut off her sentimental side fifteen years ago, Miranda's first inclination was to grab her car keys and head for the stairs, but she didn't. She couldn't. Seeing Paxton cry was like seeing a statue of the Madonna weep. It was nothing she'd ever expected to witness in her lifetime, hadn't even considered the possibility.

Awkwardly, Miranda patted the smooth blond head until the storm passed and Paxton was in the hiccuping stage. Finally she pushed away and faced Miranda, looking like a swollen parody of herself.

"Paxton, honey, what's wrong? It's not just what I said, is it?" Miranda asked gently, and instantly wished she hadn't.

Paxton shook her head and her face crumpled again. "I'm three months pregnant."

Miranda let out a slow breath of relief.

"And James is having an affair."

Miranda's jaw sagged and she nearly slipped off the bed. "He *what?*"

It took another ten minutes of soothing Paxton to get her back to coherency, but finally Miranda convinced her to wash her face and come downstairs to talk about it in the living room. It just seemed to make sense that a partner's infidelity shouldn't be discussed while sitting on a bed, but Miranda was punting on this one. Most of her girlfriends were either still single or already divorced, and she'd never been one for engaging in intimate discussions anyway. She was the one who always slipped out of the room and reappeared when the topic had changed. Now, however, she was stuck. Paxton was her oldest friend. She felt obligated to listen.

"Are you feeling better, precious?" Miranda asked gently, handing Paxton a cup of tea. *God help me if she wants advice. I'm going to have to cut and run.*

Paxton looked down at the cup, then into Miranda's eyes. "What's this?"

Miranda blinked. "Hot tea. I thought it would make you feel better."

Instantly back in control, as if her composure had never slipped, Paxton patted Miranda's hand and stood up. "Stay here, Miranda. I'll be right back," she said briskly.

She crossed the large open room, set the delicate china teacup and saucer in the sink with as much care as if they were made of plastic, and disappeared into the wine cellar. She returned to the living room a moment later with a dusty wine bottle and two small, exquisitely cut goblets.

Miranda looked at her with raised eyebrows. "Wine?"

"Sherry. It's fabulous." She set down the goblets, opened the bottle, and poured the fragrant wine into them. She met Miranda's surprised look with one of mild exasperation.

"Oh, for Christ's sake, Miranda. Don't tell me you've fallen for that nonsense. Do people think pregnant women put their brains in neutral for nine months? When she was pregnant with me, my mother drank martinis every evening and was told by her doctor to smoke cigarettes to keep her weight down. Do I look deficient?"

Miranda shook her head, and dared not defy her. Not

when Paxton was in what James called her "closing argument" mood. "I'm just a bit surprised, honey. It's only nine thirty."

Paxton settled onto one end of the couch, brushing away the logic with an elegant hand as she would a bothersome mosquito. "Midmorning pick-me-up. Prelunch aperitif. Whatever. Even the Victorians did it."

They sat there in relative silence for several minutes, listening to the hammering going on in what was becoming the projection room.

"Did I ever tell you how James and I met?" Paxton asked suddenly. Her back was to the sliding doors, and the sunshine pouring through them made it difficult for Miranda to see her face.

Miranda shook her head in answer to the question and took a sip of the sherry, sure the conversation wasn't going to be a short one, and equally sure she might not want to endure it completely sober despite the early hour. And Paxton was right: The sherry really *was* fabulous.

"I first saw him at a swim meet at the country club when I was ten. He was sixteen and wearing a Speedo. He was tanned and gorgeous and flirting with every creature that had the correct plumbing," she said in a matter-of-fact voice. "I fell in love with him that day, I think. And when I was twenty-six and on Wall Street, he finally noticed me. At that point I wouldn't have gone out with him if he'd paid me. He was a hound dog." She took a sip of the wine and a deep breath and fixed her eyes on Miranda, who took another sip and tried not to squint.

"He asked me out every time he saw me for a solid year. And then one summer night he and Chas showed up at a party at a house I was sharing in the Hamptons. To this day neither one of them ever told me who invited them. I think they crashed it. Anyway, Chas and I started chatting on the terrace, and then we wandered into the house and he asked me where the bathroom was. Before I knew it, I was in the bathroom handcuffed to James. Chas winked at me and told me he'd be back in two hours, unless I found him first." She shook her head with a tight smile. "They both knew I'd never be caught dead wandering around like that, so I locked the bathroom door and stayed handcuffed to James for two solid hours while he tried to persuade me to go out with him."

"And you finally said yes?"

"Of course I didn't."

"Why not?"

Paxton raised her eyebrows in surprise. "I didn't want to date him and have him dump me two weeks later. I wanted to marry him, Miranda." She took another sip of sherry and set the tiny glass on the table. "I'd done my research. I knew his family; I knew his friends. I even knew some of his girlfriends. I was only going to go out with him when he was ready to give up the rest of them and not before. The day after the party Chas called me and asked me what it would take, because he couldn't stand listening to James talk about me anymore. I told him that I wanted to be the last woman on James's list. That was when he told me James hadn't been on a date in four months. I said yes the next time he asked me and . . . well, you know the rest." She suddenly peered at Miranda as if through a microscope. "Why weren't you at our wedding? I know I invited you, and I know you said you'd come. But you didn't."

"Josh's appendix burst the night before I was supposed to fly up. I couldn't very well leave him in intensive care."

Paxton shrugged. "As it turns out, you should have. You would have met Chas then."

After a few moments of silence, during which Paxton seemed to be lost in thought as she rubbed her hand over her still-flat belly, Miranda couldn't take it anymore. She tossed back the rest of the sherry and poured herself a new glass. Only then, ensconced in a corner of the couch with her blood racing comfortably and her head getting mellow, did she dare ask the question.

"What makes you think James is having an affair?"

Paxton leveled her with a look, and Miranda brought the goblet to her lips as a shield.

"Credit card receipts, airline tickets, phone bills." She

let out a measured breath and looked away. "He purchased two tickets to Italy on his American Express card, Miranda. That bill usually goes to his office, but he brought it home for some reason, and I found it on the desk, underneath a pile of other bills that I usually pay. He had told me he was in London on business on those days. It was the first time he didn't ask me if I wanted to go."

"Were you busy?"

"Yes, but for London I'd cancel. He knows that," she replied imperiously.

"Maybe he had to go through Italy," Miranda said weakly.

Her look was scathing. "Did you flunk basic geography? Miranda, he went to *Italy*. There were hotel bills from a place in Tuscany near our new house, and some little town on the Amalfi coast, and another one outside of Rome. And they weren't the Intercontinental. They were two boutique hotels and one B-and-B. Little places that no one's ever heard of."

"That *you've* never heard of. Maybe he had business there."

"He's a bond trader, Miranda. He doesn't have business that takes him to Italy. Besides, I asked Mother if she'd ever heard of those towns, and she said she had. She said they're all very old and picturesque. Romantic."

"So what now?" she asked, trying to be as dispassionate as Paxton was at the moment.

Paxton picked up the glass in front of her. "I want you to ask Chas to talk to him."

Miranda stopped breathing. "You *what?*"

"You heard me. I want you to talk to Chas. If James has told anyone, it would be Chas."

"Who probably would have hauled his backside to jail or something. No way, Paxton. *You* talk to Chas. I don't want to get involved. I hardly know Chas. And I'm sure James wouldn't—"

"You already are involved, because I just involved you. And if I file for divorce everyone will know anyway."

Miranda felt her eyes widen in surprise. "You'd divorce him?"

Paxton fidgeted with her glass, and Miranda watched her eyes fill again. "Well, maybe. No. I don't know, but he doesn't know that. And I'd sure as hell threaten it. Why won't you talk to Chas for me, Miranda? Please?"

"You talk to him. You know him better than I do."

"Oh, for heaven's sake, Miranda, you're sleeping with the man."

"Well, that hardly puts me in a special class, does it? I mean, according to you." Miranda stood up a little too quickly but walked to the sliding doors anyway and opened them to take a deep breath of the cold sea air. She had to get out of Connecticut soon. Life was getting surreal.

"You really won't?"

Miranda turned and looked at her friend, who had relapsed from Wonder Woman into a teary Madonna cradling her belly.

Sweet Jesus, why me? She closed the door. "Paxton, what am I supposed to say? 'Hi, Chas, honey, how was your day? Oh, by the way, would you be a darling and ask James if he's having an affair, because Paxton is a mite curious?' "

"Well, yes. No. Chas will know what to do. He always handles things the right way."

Miranda rolled her eyes and looked back at the water.

Paxton let out a long, heavy breath and sniffed. Her voice, when she spoke, was strong again. "Let this be a lesson to you, Miranda, just in case you're getting serious about Chas. I don't care what your colleagues say; you can't reform a rake. I've never known one who could keep his zipper up for long. We've been married for five years. James didn't even have the decency to wait for the seven-year itch."

A rake? It took a moment for Paxton's words to register; then Miranda turned slowly to look at her. "Excuse me, did I just hear you right? You know what my colleagues say? By that I presume you mean *romance writers*?"

She watched Paxton enter the Grace Kelly zone, and

the temperature of the air in the room seemed to drop by at least fifteen degrees.

Miranda ignored it. "I can't believe you, Paxton. You've dismissed my career for how long? And the whole time you've been reading romances *behind my back*? And you've never read *mine*? How dare you?"

Paxton's patrician chin rose. "You write contemporaries. I read historicals. Occasionally."

"I can't believe you."

"Oh, for heaven's sake, Miranda, everyone reads them. And the only reason I bugged you about it is that it has always struck me that you should be writing something else. I don't know, something bigger. And don't start in about making *The New York Times* list. That's not what I'm talking about. Can we get back on point? The point being that my husband is having an affair and he doesn't even know I'm pregnant."

"You haven't told him?"

"Why should I? Why would he stick around? In another six weeks I'll be exploding out of my clothes. There's no way he'll leave some twenty-year-old waif for a thirty-two-year-old who's the size of a small house."

Surreal was too kind a word. Miranda returned to the couch and sat down, then picked up the glass of sherry and downed it in one large sip.

"You'd better be careful, Miranda. Sherry can sneak up on you."

"So can friends. And editors and agents and men and love and affairs and all sorts of shit that no one ever expects to sneak up on them," she muttered, and leaned back against the couch with her eyes closed.

Her comment was met with silence, and she glanced at Paxton, who had come out of the Grace Kelly zone and was back in the courtroom, eyeing her coolly.

"Oh, hell, Paxton, what now?" Miranda asked tiredly.

"You swore."

"I what?"

"You swore," Paxton repeated. "You said 'shit' and you just said 'hell.' You never swear. And you mentioned the word 'love,' which I've also never heard cross your lips before."

Miranda blinked. "Oh, no. We're not talking about me. If you're done discussing James, we can move on to the weather or decorating or names for the baby, but we are *not* talking about me." Miranda looked at the small, empty goblet and tried to remember how many times she'd filled it. It couldn't have been more than three times. She closed her eyes again as she heard the doorbell ring, followed by the falsetto voice of Liz the decorator. No wonder little old ladies loved it. Who would need Xanax if there were a decent amontillado in the house?

CHAPTER
16

When he arrived at his mother's house, Chas was surprised to see only two cars in the driveway. And one was an undercover car from the Stamford PD. He'd expected a minivan at least, given the size of the team Joe had said they'd assembled. He walked into the kitchen and found Joe sitting at the table with his mother and a young woman with strawberry blond hair and a sweet, innocent face. The mood in the room was relaxed, and they were laughing at something that Joe had just said.

"There he is," his mother said, getting to her feet. Joe and the other woman followed suit. "Sarah, this is my other son, Chas. This is Special Agent in Charge Sarah McAllister. She's part of the Computer Crimes team from the FBI. Your grandfather and Dalton are already in the living room with your colleagues."

Hiding his surprise, he shook Sarah's hand. Her grip was firm but feminine. "It's nice to meet you."

"The pleasure is mine. I've heard a lot about you from Joe," she said with a smile, and Chas thought again that she didn't look old enough to be out of college.

"Chas, why don't you grab a cup of coffee and bring it in? Then we can get started," his mother hinted.

"I'll be right there." The women left the room and Chas glanced at his brother, who was regarding him with cold blue eyes. "What?"

"The answer is no," Joe said flatly.

"What's the question?"

"Am I sleeping with her and do I mind that she's running the show? No to both."

"Glad we have that out of the way." Chas reached for a mug and filled it from the coffeemaker. "Does she know what she's doing?"

"She did her masters at Stanford and her Ph.D. at MIT. She's the best at the Bureau."

"How old is she?"

"She hasn't hit thirty yet."

"How the hell did she manage that?"

"Because I'm really, really smart, Detective Casey."

Chas nearly snapped his neck turning to the doorway in time to see Sarah stroll to the table and pick up the mug she'd left behind, probably on purpose. At least she was smiling.

"Please call me Chas. And I'm sorry. It wasn't meant as—"

She brushed the air dismissively. "I know you'll find it hard to believe, but you're not the first man to question my abilities. I had a heck of a time with your brother the first time we met. But don't let the letters after my name fool you. What Joe left out was that I dropped out of high school at fifteen and hacked professionally for a year. Felony trespass was as far as they got before they stopped looking. Too bad, because I was very good at being very bad." She smiled. "I got three years suspended sentence with the stipulation that I go to college and that I work with the LAPD Computer Crimes guys. I dragged myself through USC in two and a half years and the judge helped me get into Stanford. I took care of myself after that. So I know my stuff and I've already spent a lot of time on this investigation. We're moving very fast. I wouldn't be surprised if we make an arrest within days, but I'm not going to make any promises."

Chas looked at his brother, who was biting back a smile, then looked back at Sarah. "I know when I'm in the presence of greatness. I'm here as an observer, and I'm at your disposal."

"Thank you. Why don't we go into the living room and get started? Everyone else is already there."

Six hours later the group broke up. Sarah and Joe and all four members of the Stamford Computer Crimes Unit headed down to the suite of empty offices that had been leased on the third floor of the Brennan building. Since early morning, the rest of the interagency team had been down there setting up equipment, hacking into the firm's secure networks, and installing data line taps on targeted computers.

Chas and his mother remained in the house with his grandfather and Dalton Harrington, a member of the board of directors of Brennan Shipping, and Chas's godfather.

"What do you think?"

Let the games begin. Chas looked at his grandfather. "I think you're in the best hands you could be in. My advice is to answer their questions, give them what they need, and stay out of their way. They know what they're doing. Let them do it."

"Is that what you'll be doing?" Dalton asked with a grin.

"As a matter of fact, that's exactly what I'll be doing," Chas replied mildly.

"For how long?"

Chas swallowed his irritation at the thinly veiled goading. "For as long as it takes."

"What do you think of that girl, Chas?" his grandfather asked, getting up to stretch his legs. He walked to the fireplace and leaned against the mantel, standing beneath the portrait of himself. The contrast of Joseph Brennan captured in oil at the age of thirty, and living proof of a life well lived at just past eighty, was striking. He was still a vital, good-looking man. And as wily as they came.

"Special Agent McAllister is extremely competent, from what I see. Joe said she's the best at the Bureau," he said with a shrug. "You know Joe is a tough audience."

"I've already talked to him. I'd like you to work with her, Chas. Form an opinion."

This can only lead to trouble. "Why?"

"We've been working with her for a little over a week and we're all very impressed. I think I'd like to offer her the job you turned down," his grandfather said easily.

It shouldn't have bothered him, but it did. In fact, it felt like a sucker punch. *Probably because it is one.* Chas didn't let it show. "I think she'd be a great candidate. If you can pry her away from the Bureau."

"I'll handle that."

Chas nodded once. "Okay. What do you want me to find out?"

"How she works. How she thinks. If you think she'd be good in the position. You know what the job entails."

"I'll do my best. Are we done?" He stood up and looked at his mother, who had remained silent.

She glanced at him and smiled. "We'll see you tonight, won't we? With Miranda?"

Chas nodded.

"Lovely. Your grandfather and Dalton are flying back to Palm Beach at five. Drop by for drinks at seven."

He shook hands with the men, kissed his mother on the cheek, and left. He headed straight to the gym, where he intended to beat the shit out of something inanimate.

By four o'clock Miranda had powered through seventy-five pages of her manuscript, tweaking, fixing, and rewriting, before she'd called it quits. The carpenters had left and the painters had never arrived, so the condo was mercifully silent as she began to fill the enormous tub in the master bathroom. Her cell phone was turned off, and the nearest house phone was under a pillow on her bed. Nothing and no one was going to disturb this bath. For one thing, she needed to soak a few sore muscles that had gotten some unaccustomed exercise last night. And for another, she had to get herself in the right frame of mind to meet Chas's mother.

She slipped into the hot, silky water with a smile, closed her eyes, turned on the air jets, and let decadent thoughts take over. Decadent thoughts that related to herself for a change, rather than fictional beings and their fictional sex lives.

There really is something to be said for a broad chest and a pair of strong arms. For deep, dark eyes and a bad-boy smile. And a soft, gentle mouth. She sighed, letting herself relive last night moment by moment. By the time she'd gotten them into his bedroom, into his bed, her eyes were open and she was frowning.

Damn reality for being what it is, she thought with more than a little annoyance. As far as technique was concerned, Chas hadn't been all that different from Josh. She knew it was disloyal to both men to consider them so objectively, but the thought had been floating around unformed in her brain for most of the day. The fact that Chas *wasn't* different surprised her—disappointed her, to be perfectly candid—because he was *so* sexy out of bed, with those hot, dark eyes that could see straight into her soul and that smile that could make her forget . . . everything.

She had expected sex with Chas to be exciting, but it wasn't exciting and it still hurt. It hurt more, actually, because Chas was bigger than Josh in that respect. It just wasn't fair. Chas's *attitude* was so different. He seemed to genuinely like women. Not just her, but women in general. He'd been so gentle and sweet and hesitant last night, not rushed and demanding. He hadn't once told her what to do and when to do it like Josh used to. And afterward he'd held her and let her fall asleep in his arms. She closed her eyes again and sank up to her earlobes in the silken foam. It was probably a horrible thing for a romance writer to admit, even to herself, but she'd be happy to put up with the "during" just to get the "after."

The doorbell rang at six twenty-five. The sound wave vibrated every cell in Miranda's body. She opened the front door after taking one deep breath that came out slowly when she saw Chas standing on her doorstep smiling at her. Hungrily.

His jeans hugged him just right as he stood there, one hand in the pocket of his leather bomber jacket, the other flipping his keys around his finger. There was nothing particularly different about him. He still looked the

same, still smelled of the wind and the beach and soap
and shaving cream. But something made her look away,
and then she felt foolish because it had nothing to do
with last night. *Nothing at all. I'm not embarrassed; I
don't regret it—*

Without a word he slipped his arms around her waist,
walked her backward into the foyer, kicked the door
shut with one tennis-shoed foot, and kissed her as
though it had been days instead of hours since they'd
seen each other.

Feeling as heady as she had after a few glasses of
Paxton's sherry, she broke their kiss reluctantly. "That's
some greeting."

"You were blushing." His eyes weren't entirely
amused. Something serious lurked in their depths.

"I know," she replied, glancing down to focus on the
top button of his open-necked shirt.

"Why?"

"Chas." She rolled her eyes in mild exasperation.

"You're doing it again."

"Well, this time it's because you're embarrassing me,"
she said, bringing her hands from around his neck to
rest on his chest.

"What was the cause of it last time?"

"I thought you were a detective," she said, pushing
against him lightly.

He pulled her close, lowered his mouth to her ear. "I
am. And what I'm detecting is evasion. You're not allowed to feel awkward about last night, Miranda. It was
a great night," he whispered between feathering light
kisses along her neck. "But if you don't get that look
off your face, you might as well walk into my mother's
house with a placard around your neck saying, 'I slept
with your son.' Joe and my mother aren't exactly
stupid."

Sweet Jesus. "It's that obvious?"

He straightened, met her eyes with a grin, and nodded. "Try to think about other things for a while."

She grabbed her purse, and, after he made sure she
turned on the outside lights and had her keys, they left
the condo. He held the car door open for her, closed it

carefully, walked around to his side, and slid in. Then he leaned over to kiss her again. And again. All of her senses were trained on the hot, sweet, slickness of his mouth on hers.

"This isn't going to make us late, is it?" she murmured against his lips.

"Nope." He slid his hand around her neck, bringing her mouth back to his for one last, deep kiss that had her wanting to kick off her shoes and crawl across the gear console.

Eventually, with a groan, he broke away and brought the car's engine to life.

She leaned against the seat and took her time catching her breath as he drove toward the interstate. "Well, now that we've reestablished our acquaintance, what does your mother know about me, and what should I know about her?"

He glanced at her with a smile that undermined her attempts to regain her poise. "Interesting questions. Let's see, she knows that you're staying in Stamford to write a book set here and that you've been interviewing me. She knows you're friends with Paxton and Jane."

"Does she know them?"

"She knows Paxton. She and my sister went to law school together, then terrorized Wall Street together," he said with a grin.

"They worked together?"

"Against each other." He let his eyes drift over her face for a moment. "You are so beautiful," he murmured, then brought his eyes back to the road as fire flashed through her. "They both specialized in securities and finance, but Paxton went to work for a law firm and Julie went to work for the Securities and Exchange Commission." He grinned. "As a prosecutor. Every so often they'd have lunch together just to give half of lower Manhattan heartburn."

"Paxton didn't practice that long, though, did she? Why would she scare people?"

"Neither of them did. Paxton quit when she had Hunter, and Julie moved to Philadelphia when she got married. But Paxton's first case was some huge war between two large brokerage houses. She ended up being the architect of the deal and brought the opposition to their knees. Fast." He shrugged. "She can't talk about it, but I remember James talking about it, and that was before he realized who Paxton was. Could be an urban myth, for all I know, but it made Paxton's reputation. You've seen her in action. She's terrifying."

Miranda shuddered and looked out the window, remembering this morning. "You can say that again."

"How is it going in the condo?"

"The carpenters finished today. The painters are almost done. The wallpaper goes up next week, and then someone's coming in to reglaze some tile. New carpet in the living room, new furniture, and then I think she's done, bless her heart."

"I meant with her. You mentioned that she drops in unannounced occasionally."

"Constantly," she said, then glanced at him sheepishly. "I'm sorry. I shouldn't complain. She came over today and stayed for a few hours, poor thing, so I didn't get quite as much accomplished as I wanted to." She paused, wondering how and when to mention James.

He looked at her with raised eyebrows. "Poor thing? Are we still talking about Paxton?"

"What do you mean?" she asked guiltily, and she saw it register in his eyes.

"What did she want? You said she was there for a few hours," he said, carefully turning his eyes back to the road.

Great. He thinks I was telling her all about us. She cleared her throat. "She was kind of upset about something. She . . . actually, she wants me to ask you about it."

He glanced at her again. "Since when does Paxton use a go-between? The woman could take on an army by herself without flinching."

Miranda swallowed. They had gotten off the interstate and were driving along winding roads lined with stone walls that framed serene, understated estates and the occasional colonnaded superstructure. The aura of money was palpable, and she suddenly felt very unprepared to meet his mother.

"Miranda? What does Paxton want you to ask me?" He slowed down and pulled off the road into a driveway that presumably led to a house. She couldn't see one from where they stopped.

"Is this your mother's house?"

"No. It belongs to some friends of hers. They're in Arizona until May. I pulled over because I want an answer. What does Paxton want you to ask me?"

She met his eyes and hesitated, biting her lip as she tried to find the right words. "Okay. I'm not sure how to say this. I think she's crazy, but Paxton thinks James is having an affair."

Chas said nothing, but his eyes went neutral. *Not a good sign.*

She closed her eyes and leaned her head against the seat. "Oh, sweet baby Jesus. Chas, this will destroy her. She adores him. She's pregnant, for pity's sake, and hasn't even told him."

"He already knows she's pregnant. And don't jump to conclusions."

She turned to stare at him as her heart rate picked up speed. "You're his best friend. If anyone would know, you would. And you haven't denied it."

"I haven't corroborated it, either, Miranda. He's given me no indication that he's having one. Of course, if he did, I'd kick his ass into next year, and he knows it." He met her eyes. "I'm surprised that Paxton would even suspect him. He worships her, Miranda. I had drinks with him last week and he had the same look in his eye when he was talking about her then as he did when they were dating. Did she tell you what made her suspect him?"

"She found some receipts from hotels in Italy. Little hotels in little romantic towns . . ." Chas gave her a tight, unamused smile, and Miranda continued. "She also found a credit card bill with two tickets to Italy for the same day James told her he was going to London. And it was the first time he didn't ask her to go with him."

Chas shook his head in disgust, then put the car in

gear and pulled back onto the road. "I'll find out what the hell he's up to. But I'm not going to play go-between, and neither are you. This is between Paxton and James. We stay out of it," he said with finality.

"That's fine with me." Miranda looked out the window and let several minutes pass before she spoke again. "Have I ruined your evening?"

He shot her a smile. "Not at all. Has Paxton ruined yours?"

She smiled back, shaking her head.

"Good. Paxton lives in a world of her own making, and it revolves around her. I hope you realize that."

"I used to live with her, Chas." She let out a slow breath. "Tell me about your mother."

"You should be more nervous about Joe."

"I'm a Southern woman, Chas. I can handle men. But we'll get to him in a minute."

He raised an eyebrow and bit back laughter. "Whatever you say, Miranda. My mother is pretty easygoing." He glanced at her. "Remember when you repeated that crap you read about me, that I was the son of a cop and a socialite? Well, that's true on paper, but my mother is so far from the accepted stereotype of socialite—" He stopped. "When my mother got married and moved to New Haven, she gave up the 'Greenwich lifestyle.' They bought a small house and lived on my dad's salary. A lot of people wrote her off. When we moved back to my grandparents' house after my father was killed, a lot of her old pals tried to cozy up to her. That's when she wrote them off."

He turned off the road onto a curving driveway that swept across a wide lawn, beyond which sat a deceptively simple two-story white house with black shutters and a red door sporting a tasteful, shiny brass knocker. Three golden retrievers bounded up to the car as Chas slowed down to pull into a small parking area. Eventually, wearing a big doggy smile and sweeping the ground with the enormous golden plume of its tail, one of the dogs sat down in the middle of the place Chas was aiming for. The other two circled the car, yipping with enthusiasm. Tails hit the car's body with dull, rhythmic thumps.

Chas glanced at her with a long-suffering look and shut off the engine. "I forgot to tell you about them. No fear of dogs, I hope? Or allergies?"

She shook her head and attempted not to smile.

"They were my sister's idea. Four years ago she talked my mother into trying to become a breeder. The first two had puppies within two weeks of each other." He paused and took a breath rich with long-practiced patience. "She couldn't bear to split up the families, just as Joe and I had told Julie she wouldn't. So now she has nine."

"Nine? *Nine* golden retrievers? In the house?" Miranda strove to keep the incredulity out of her voice.

"Eight females and one eunuch who still hasn't figured out what hit him. And they're not so much *in* as *throughout*. But she had the house wired with that electronic fencing, so they can't get everywhere. When she turns it on," he added dryly. "Ready for the circus?"

"As I'll ever be."

He stepped out of the car, and instantly the dogs bounded toward him with tails beating the air. One gruff word from him and they sat down, but they were twitching with high spirits, and it was plain to see that their good behavior wouldn't last.

He came around to her door and opened it an inch. "We should probably make a run for it. Can you manage?"

No longer hiding her laughter, she nodded, hitched up her long, full skirt, and swung her legs out of the car. He helped her to her feet and they hurried to the side door. With the dogs bounding behind them, he pushed her through the opening and pulled it closed behind him as fast as he could while retaining a firm grip on her arm so she didn't fall.

When she stopped laughing and looked around, she realized a woman who could only be Chas's mother stood several steps up in a doorway that obviously led into the kitchen. She was leaning against the doorjamb with her arms folded across the front of a beautiful royal-blue sweater. Her hair, the color of steel shot with silver, was cut in a short, sleek style that accentuated high cheekbones and the bluest eyes Miranda had ever seen. And she was biting back laughter with an expression Miranda had come to recognize far too well from knowing Chas.

"Well, Chas, you've started with the cook's tour, I see." She straightened and moved elegantly down the three stairs, bringing her hand out as she drew near Miranda. "Miss Lane, I'm Mary Casey, mother of that young man who can't remember where I've left the front door. I'm so pleased to meet you. I'm a tremendous fan of yours."

Miranda smiled and slid her hand into his mother's. It was cool and thin but had a surprisingly firm grip. On second thought, Miranda wasn't surprised at all. It suited her.

"Please call me Miranda, Mrs. Casey. I'm very pleased to meet you. Thank you for inviting me."

"I'm delighted you're able to join us. And you must call me Mary. Keeps me young." Her eyes flicked to Chas, who bent to kiss her on the cheek and was rewarded with a warm smile. Then she tucked Miranda's arm through hers and led her through the kitchen, which held a heavenly aroma, through the enormous yet elegant dining room, to a small study at the end of a hallway. She casually directed Chas to fix them some drinks.

Miranda tried not to stare at the floor-to-ceiling wooden bookshelves, gleaming and ornate and filled with everything from enormous leather-bound tomes to ratty, well-read paperbacks. The couches and chairs were leather and comfortably worn. The art was understated and original. The warmth was genuine.

Shaking herself back to the moment, she reached into her purse and pulled out a small package swathed in layers of bright tissue paper and tied with long, curly streamers. She held it out to Mary Casey, who accepted it with a smile.

"I know flowers are more customary, but I ran into Paxton Clarke today and she happened to mention that you collect these. And then I was out running some errands and I saw this one. It was so unusual that I thought I'd risk it."

"Paxton Shelby? Sweet girl. Her mother, Grace, was a few years behind me at Smith. Have you met Grace?" Mary Casey paused as she unwrapped the gift and glanced at Miranda, who nodded. "Wildest girl I'd ever met, but then, in those days, that wasn't saying much."

"I didn't realize you went to Smith. I went there, too."

"Oh, I know that, Miranda. *My daughter* told me." She shot a meaningful look at Chas, who just grinned. "I figured that if you were not as charming as Chas has implied—because, of course, he actually *tells* his dear, old mother *nothing* of any interest—I figured we could always talk about Smith. Fortunately, I don't think we'll get that far."

While Miranda laughed silently at Chas's eye roll, his mother let out a little gasp of delight. She delicately unearthed from the tissue the small crystal disk sliced with myriad tiny cuts that formed a Celtic knot pattern. "This is exquisite. Thank you, Miranda."

She moved to one of the tall windows that flanked the fireplace and pulled back the heavy drapery. The window was hung with sun catchers of all descriptions, from flawless pieces of Baccarat and Waterford crystal to several lopsided ones made from Popsicle sticks and tissue paper. She draped the kelly-green satin ribbon over the window's latch and turned back to Miranda. "You have lovely taste. And not just in men, my dear."

"Mom, it's getting a bit thick in here," Chas said, handing both women heavy crystal goblets of white wine.

CHAPTER
17

"Since you're pouring, I'll have Glenfiddich, neat."

Miranda turned to the owner of the deep, amused voice that came from behind her.

So this is the other half of Team Hellion.

Whereas Chas was tall, broad and dark, and indisputably sexy, the man before her was taller by at least two inches, broader, and blond, with blue eyes that made every glance a heartbreaker, and a smile that could blind a girl not already under the influence of a Casey.

"You must be Miranda. I'm Joe," he said, directing that smile at her.

"I'm pleased to meet you." She reached out to shake his hand.

"Don't be so formal," he replied as that warm, strong hand pulled her gently toward him so he could plant a friendly kiss on her cheek.

Randi, honey, say hello to your next hero.

As the expression in his eyes began to change from friendliness to laughter, Miranda realized she was staring—and that Joe Casey was fully aware of the effect he had on women. A quick glance told her Chas was regarding her with the same level of amusement.

Oh, I can handle you, cupcake. She smiled back. "I'm so terribly sorry for staring, Joe, but I'm trying to catalog you. I think you may have to star in my next book," she

said in her best moonlit-magnolia voice, and was rewarded by seeing his smile fade.

His eyes darted to Chas, who was laughing openly,
then back to her. "I'm sorry. I don't quite follow you."

This is too good to be true. She gave him a long
blink. "Oh, I thought Chas might have forewarned you,
darlin'. I write romance novels. In fact, I'm nearly finished with one and will be starting another very soon.
I think you're going to have to be my next hero. Would
you mind?"

She doubted he would look more alarmed if she'd
asked him to parade down I-95 buck naked. Then his
face settled into an expression not unlike Chas's cop face
and he looked at his brother again. "She's joking, right?
I mean, you said she was a smart-ass."

"Welcome to the brotherhood."

Joe paused. "Does it hurt?"

"All you have to do is lie back and relax," Chas said,
clapping him on the back and handing him his drink.

"Well, I'd say Miranda won that round. Good girl.
You have my full permission to carry on. It's good for
them," Mary Casey said, sitting down in a large leather
wing chair. The three of them followed suit, Chas drap-
ing his arm around Miranda as they sat on the sofa.
The casually affectionate gesture brought warmth to her
cheeks. Neither Joe nor Mary even seemed to have noticed either the gesture or her blush, and it took her a
second to realize why. They were an affectionate family.
They were comfortable touching and hugging. That in
itself was a reality different from her own. She pushed
the thought out of her mind and brought her attention
back to the conversation.

"I'm glad you could join us, Miranda. Chas said that
you aren't going to be in town for very much longer,"
Mary said.

"Thank you. That's right. I'll be leaving in about two
weeks." As the words came out of her mouth, they
sounded hollow, and she took a sip of her wine. She
didn't look at Chas, and from the corner of her eye she
could see that he wasn't looking at her. But she could

have sworn there had been a minute flexure of the hand cupped around her shoulder.

"Do you come up this way often?"

Miranda smiled. "No, unfortunately, I don't. This trip was to see Paxton. Generally I only come up here for book tours or conferences. Mostly I just stay close to home in Atlanta."

"Great town. Did you grow up there?" Joe asked.

Miranda took a minute before answering, wondering how much, if anything, Chas might have told them. "No. My . . ." She hesitated. God, she hated even *thinking* of Walter as her father, much less referring to him that way. "My daddy was in the military, so we moved a good bit. I grew up mostly in Alabama, but there were a few stints that took us elsewhere."

There was a canine commotion outside the windows and, with a sigh, Mary looked at Chas. "I forgot to put the dogs in the kennel. Would you mind?"

Both men stood up and excused themselves, and Mary looked at her with a smile. "And they say women can't go anywhere by themselves. While I have you alone, let me congratulate you on rendering Joe the next best thing to speechless. I'm not sure that's ever happened before."

Miranda grinned. "I would imagine not. You have two very good-looking sons."

"Good-looking, talented, and trouble. Women get mesmerized by them. I know that's a strange thing for a mother to say, but I've seen it happen too many times. They've been doing it since before they could talk. You're different."

Not sure how to reply, Miranda just took a sip of her wine and kept her smile in place.

"I didn't mean to make you uncomfortable, Miranda. Did Chas mention that they had a band in high school and college? They're pretty talented, even considering I'm horribly biased." She shook her head with a smile. "It was terrible for their egos."

"What do you mean?"

Mary Casey raised a droll eyebrow. "There were so

many females flinging themselves at the two of them and the other boys in the band—one of whom was James Clarke, Paxton's husband—that they became awfully difficult to live with. Thought they were God's gift to women.''

Miranda smiled, thinking that their assumption might not be far from the truth. "It must have made for some interesting times."

Mary just rolled her eyes. "At one point Julie wanted to join them onstage. I absolutely put my foot down."

"Why?"

"For one thing, she can't sing. *At all*. For another, it was the late '80s. Do you remember what girls wore onstage in those days?"

"Spandex and glitter?" Miranda offered.

"Exactly. And not much of either."

"Spandex?" Joe repeated, returning to the library a few steps ahead of Chas.

"We were discussing your band. Remember when Julie wanted to join you?"

"I still don't know why you wouldn't let her," Chas said, resettling himself on the couch

"She can't sing," Joe stated flatly.

"Well, I know, but she was never going to sing," Chas pointed out. He glanced at Miranda. "We were going to put her center stage with a tambourine and a dead mike. A good-looking girl in a band brings in guys, who are the ones who drink the beer and make more money for the club. And if you bring in business, you get return gigs." He slid his arm around her again.

She smiled and glanced at him; then her eyes were drawn to the photograph on the table behind him. A young man, looking too much like Chas, stood beneath a spreading tree with two small, laughing, crew-cutted boys next to him, dangling from skinny arms that clung to a branch. An alien tightness tugged behind her eyes and she had to look away.

"On the other hand, every club you played was always packed to the gills with women, according to what I heard, and where women go, men follow. That's been a constant in the laws of nature since the days of Adam and Eve," Mary interjected. "I just didn't want my daughter onstage flaunting herself. I doubt she would have gotten into law school if she had."

"I flaunted myself onstage and I still got into law school," Joe replied with an expression that was far too innocent.

Mary fixed him with a stern look.

Miranda laughed and glanced at Chas. "Did you flaunt yourself, too?"

"Not as shamelessly as Joe. He was the drummer, so he could twirl his sticks or throw them into the air and catch them without missing a beat. I was on keyboards. All I could do was play standing up," he replied with a grin.

Miranda looked at Mary, who was watching her sons with amused pride. "You really did have it rough, didn't you?"

"Miranda, you have no idea."

They ate in the large dining room, clustered at one end of the elegantly set table. The silver gleamed in the candlelight, and the crystal flashed with every sip of wine. The pace of the meal was leisurely, the food was delicious and homespun, and the conversation never stopped. It was like being part of an upscale, East Coast, Walton family reunion, and Miranda was loving it.

After the meal ended and the pace of the conversation mellowed, Chas placed his napkin on the table. "Anyone up for a walk? We can take the dogs down to the stable and back and let them run off some energy."

He caught Miranda's eye and winked. She smiled, feeling a bit hazy around the edges from the wine she'd enjoyed before dinner and during. That haziness was the only reason she admitted to herself that Chas was dangerously under her skin and burrowing deeper every minute.

"That sounds like a great idea," Mary replied, and stood up. "Everyone bring something from the table and we'll clean up the kitchen later."

Ten minutes later the four of them were in the large mudroom off the kitchen rifling through the many jackets hanging on the hooks that lined two walls.

"Try this. It's Chas's. You'd be the first one to wear it," Joe said with a sly grin, tossing Miranda a Greenwich High School letter jacket. "He never let anyone get near it."

"Gee, Chas, I'm starting to feel like I'm your girl," she teased, slipping into it.

"It's about time," he murmured as he shrugged into a ski jacket with old tow tags still hanging from the zipper.

"Hats or mittens, anyone?"

"Mom, it's only thirty degrees outside and we're not six years old. Go," Joe ordered gently, aiming his mother toward the door and giving her a light push.

After the warm coziness of the house, the first breath of cold air seemed to freeze Miranda's lungs solid. She sobered up instantly.

"Now this is one thing I miss," Joe said lazily as he walked next to his mother with his arm slung casually around her shoulder. "Air that you can see in the summer and chew in the winter."

Miranda felt Chas's hand curl around hers, probably as much for affection as for safety. As soon as Joe opened the gate to the kennel, the dogs surged around them in one large mass of fur, tongues, legs, and tails. After some cursory sniffs, they raced ahead of the four humans and disappeared into the night.

The conversation was light as the four of them crunched through the stiffening grass. When they reached the stable, Mary went in to check on the horses and Miranda followed her, glad for the warmth. Joe and Chas stayed outside.

"She's cute."

Chas glanced at his brother. "More than cute. She's smart and she's tough. She's a black belt in tae kwon do. Don't piss her off."

Joe grinned. "Well?"

"Well, nothing. You heard what she said. She's going back to Atlanta in two weeks."

"How long have you been dating her?"

Not long enough. "I don't know that I am," he replied absently. "I met her ten days ago."

"Christ, that was fast." Joe shook his head.

"What the hell are you talking about?"

"In case it escaped your notice, Chas, you're whipped. Is she coming up for Christmas?"

"The hell I am," Chas replied, lowering his voice. "And I haven't asked her. I haven't even thought about it."

"You're going stay in touch with her, aren't you?"

"Sure."

"You'd be a fool not to. I like her, even if she did take me down with one punch." Joe paused. "She wasn't really serious about that hero shit, was she?"

"As a heart attack."

They stood in silence for a while, huddling against the cold.

"I'm heading down to one of those executive boot camps in the beginning of March, courtesy of Boeing. It's in southeastern Georgia, in a swamp, I think. Want to meet me in Atlanta for a little R-and-R when I'm done?" Joe asked.

"What are you doing that for?"

Joe shrugged. "I think they want us to throw some support behind a bill they want to get passed. Their chief counsel for government affairs invited me. I figured I'd go. After all, it's all defense contractors. I figure I'll get to play with some serious weaponry while wading through slime up to my ass and getting bitten by mosquitoes the size of F-16s. Are you up for it?"

"I might be. I'll have to see how things go. There's no point in pushing it."

"Do you ride?" Mary asked as they walked down the small center aisle to the second stall. A dark, shapely head swung over the low door at the sound of her voice.

"Not properly," Miranda said, scooping up a small pile of oats from the floor and holding them out toward the horse's velvety lips. "When I was in elementary school there was a farm next to the schoolyard, and after school, for a dollar, the farmer would let us plod around the paddock on his old workhorse. It wasn't much, but it was exciting at the time." She glanced at Mary with a smile. "You're studying me."

"Yes, I am, and I apologize for being so rude," she replied without a trace of embarrassment or, it seemed, any inclination to explain herself. "Let me make the introductions. That lady whose nose you're stroking is Esme, and her pal in the next stall is Jonesy."

Deciding silence was the best response, Miranda just gave the dark horse a final pat, then moved to the next stall, where a shy, gentle palomino whickered softly. "She's a beauty, too. Wouldn't you give anything to have eyelashes like that?"

"She is a beauty," Mary agreed. "We rescued her about a day before she would have become dog food. She'd been a show horse and had broken her leg so badly that she couldn't perform anymore and wouldn't even be able to support the weight of a pregnancy. A girlfriend of Julie's found out, and we drove over to outside of Pittsburgh to pick her up, then brought her back and got her some proper care. She can't run any distance, but she's perfect for my granddaughters. They're just learning how to ride, and this sweetheart knows how to teach them the ropes," she said affectionately, rubbing the horse's golden neck.

"Lucky horse. Lucky girls."

Mary met her eyes. "Lucky Chas, too. Let's get back to the house before that Southern blood of yours freezes."

Finally, after dessert and coffee and a late glass of port, Miranda and Chas stepped back into the cold, clear night. The moon was full and rising, and the wind was blowing just enough to send leaves cackling along the ground.

She looked over at him, desire stealing through her with a strength that threatened to leave her breathless. "It was an absolutely wonderful evening, Chas. Even the dogs were charming. I had such a good time." Placing a cool palm against his cheek, she leaned forward and let him gather her into his arms for a long, deep, satisfying, tongue-tangling kiss that ended only when she began to shiver.

He pressed a last kiss on her forehead as she heard the car's electronic locks click open. "Hold that thought. And fasten your seat belt."

CHAPTER
18

Something had to change. They'd come back to his house, and she'd remained warm and willing—until they reached the bedroom. That was when his carefully planned, slowly executed tactics were abruptly dismissed in favor of her silent, passionless, and not very enjoyable routine. At the moment, she was getting out of the shower. He'd just heard the water shut off.

His eyes had adjusted to the near-total darkness, and he watched her cross the bedroom, felt her slide in beside him and curve into him. She was soft and warm and damp and wearing one of his button-down shirts. She smelled like soap. It was nice soap. It was his soap. He didn't have a problem with the soap. He had a problem with the woman. His arm slid around her out of habit.

After making love to a woman, he wanted her to lie beside him damp, warm, and soft, feeling like a woman, smelling like a woman: salty and sweaty and been-made-love-to. Earthy and sexy, not scrubbed and sanitized. She'd performed this hygiene-patrol routine both times they'd been together, and, though he'd never really thought about it before, it *couldn't* be anything about him that made her want a shower. No *other* woman had ever leaped out of bed to scrub away all the evidence, all the warmth, all the intimacy. *All the possibility for another round.* But, of course, this was Miranda. As much as he liked her, he didn't have a fucking clue what went on in her head.

He turned as she lifted her face to his. Even in the darkness he could see that she was smiling. *She can't have enjoyed it,* he thought as he smiled back and leaned down to kiss her.

He lay there for close to an hour, feeling the slow rise and fall of her breast against his side. She'd fallen asleep instantly, as she had last night. She was lovely, curled up on her side with her long brown hair strewn across the pillows. Her face was relaxed and lacked the edge, the intensity that kept her eyes moving when she was awake, that kept her eyebrow cocked with doubt and her mouth pursed and ready to deliver a sarcastic comeback. He wouldn't miss that edginess if it stayed away for a little while. The idea of a soft Miranda, a sweet, warm, loving Miranda like the one she revealed occasionally, and only by accident, was appealing. Of course, he wouldn't want that one around all the time, because he would miss . . .

He left the thought unfinished and slid out of bed carefully so as not to wake her. Walking across the room, he sat down, leaned his head against the back of the small sofa, and waited for his pulse rate to return to normal.

All the time. Had he really even thought the words? He never had before, not ever, not with any woman. He'd never been tempted to. *Damn Joe and his insinuations.* He'd only known her for ten days. Chas shook his head like a wet dog but couldn't shake away the reality. It hadn't even been a decision. *It had been a given.* And that scared the hell out of him.

When his father died, Chas had been old enough to understand the basics. He remembered the funeral. The sea of dress uniforms. The folded flag. Moving away from their little house in New Haven and into his grandparents' house in Greenwich. But, eventually, he'd begun to forget about them as other things took their place. The small yard in New Haven and the rickety metal swing set was replaced by acres of fields and woods, and an in-ground swimming pool. Then Boy

Scouts and Little League, and later hockey, tennis, and golf, and eventually girls.

And *that* was when the loss began to resurface, when the guy talk evolved from bottle rockets to Spin the Bottle, from hanging out to going out. Memories had drifted back into focus. The look on his mother's face that awful day, that month, that year. The way, even years afterward, she would turn away to hide sudden tears. The way she placed photographs of his father in every room, never too prominent but always there, as if to let him watch them grow up. It was then that Chas decided he'd never put anyone in a position to mourn him or even to depend on him emotionally.

He'd honed the art of detachment as deliberately as he had every other natural talent. He was smooth, easy, honest, and the women came to him. He learned how to seduce slowly and depart gently, leaving them not hopeful but not unhappy, keeping himself fully intact. Until now.

Miranda was different. He'd known that the first time he saw her. She was intelligent, beautiful, successful, sarcastic, not easily impressed, but easily wounded if you knew where to aim. And he did, instinctively. She wasn't even any good in bed, but instead of making him want to move on, that very realization made him want to—

I am definitely not going there.

He stood up and walked back to the bed, and tried to slide between the sheets without waking her. But she opened sleepy eyes and blinked at him with a sweet smile that caused a distinct pain in his chest.

"Can't sleep?" she murmured.

"It won't last."

"Would you like me to rub your back?"

He paused before answering, just in case there was a better offer about to be made, but all she did was give him another dreamy, drowsy blink. "No. Thanks for offering, though."

She slithered up onto the pillow, and rested her head against the headboard. She was waking up slowly but surely. *It could be a good sign.*

"Want to talk?" she asked with a smile in her voice.

Definitely not *a good sign.* It was a question that always made him catch his breath, as if he'd been poked with a lit match. It was a question that never led to good times, but tonight that was only half of it. Right now, under the circumstances there was only one right answer. "Sure. About what?"

She yawned and shrugged. "My book. I've hit a rough patch and I need male input."

"Okay."

"I decided to try writing a love scene from a male point of view, but I don't know where to start." She smiled and he knew he was in deep shit. "I need to know what your fantasies are."

"Not gonna happen, sweetheart."

She started laughing. "Not *yours,* Chas. I meant that as a universal 'yours.' Just some standard male fantasies."

"I doubt there's much difference between mine and any other guy's. We're simple creatures, Miranda. We like our beer cold, our food hot, and our women naked." He slid up to a sitting position and leaned back against the headboard. As a diversion, he reached for the remote and opened the blinds covering the skylights. The moon was almost directly overhead and flooded the room with silver light. He glanced at her. She was looking at the remote in his hands.

She met his eyes. "What does that do?"

"It controls almost everything in the house." At the moment, discussing electronics was a damned sight safer than discussing male sexual fantasies. With a romance writer. In bed.

"What do you mean?"

He took it back from her and pointed it at the stereo across the room, which immediately started flashing. He shut it off before it could make any noise. "Up here, it controls the blinds, the lights on the walls, the stereo. The alarm system. I had the house specially wired. When I take it into the study, it controls the TV, the DVD player, the VCR. When I'm in—"

"The alarm system? For the house?" she interrupted. He nodded.

"But last night you said you had to go downstairs to turn it on." Her voice had gone quiet.

She was way too observant. "I didn't say I had to. I just said I was going to."

"Why didn't you turn it on from up here?"

He set the remote on the bedside table and slid his arm around her. It took a moment before she relaxed against him. "You seemed tense, and I didn't want you to think I was waiting here to devour you like some vulture," he said softly into her hair.

She was quiet for a full minute. "You're a nice man, Chas."

No tears. *Thank God.* "Thank you."

"So tell me about your fantasies."

You, naked, with the lights on and me driving the bus. "Um, Miranda, I really—"

She shook her head. "I don't want to analyze or understand the fantasies. I rate only on creativity, and the kinkier the better. It's just grist for the creative mill."

He gave her an amused sideways glance. "Well, since you put it that way, I have one."

"One?"

"Yes, one. You're sure you want to hear it?"

"Go ahead."

He let a silence build. "I've never slept with a blonde."

She blinked at him. "What?"

"Don't get offended, but I've never slept with a blonde. I suppose that sometime before I die, I'd like to."

She bit her lip and failed to hide her amusement. "Chas, there are tons of blond women around. It can't be that difficult to find one to sleep with."

He shook his head. "You'd think so, wouldn't you? But Miranda, I'm thirty-eight years old, and I've dated my share of women who I thought were blondes. But when it was time to view the evidence, the collar and cuffs didn't match." He shrugged. "I've never dated a natural blonde."

She laughed and tossed that silky fall of dark hair over

her shoulders. "What's the intrigue? Do you suppose they do it differently than brunettes or redheads?"

"I'm sure they don't, but you asked what my fantasy was, and that's it. What about yours?"

"I don't have any."

"Oh, come on, you can't say that. I just told you mine."

She shrugged. "Well, it's true."

"None at all? Not even the little house with two-point-four kids inside, a white picket fence outside, and sterling-silver handcuffs in the basement?"

She lifted an amused eyebrow. "No, I don't like white picket fences and I wouldn't know what to do with kids if I had any. And forget the handcuffs. I think I don't have any sexual fantasies because my characters are always getting wild."

She settled back against his chest comfortably, and he wrapped his arms around her, idly rubbing his chin along the top of her head. "They're not that wild, Miranda. Some of your ideas seem like fun, actually."

"Thank you. They're supposed to. Like I said, no one wants to read about reality."

"What do you mean by 'reality'?"

She twisted her face up to look at him, and laughed. "I know what you're trying to do, but I know what I'm talking about."

"You're saying that people don't act on their fantasies?"

"Oh, *come on,* Chas. Why do you think romance is fiction's largest market segment? It's safer and easier to dream about it than to follow through, and when you get right down to it, sex is sex. Bodies are bodies, and the options available to the average user are somewhat limited."

That could explain a lot. "Did you just say that 'sex is sex'? In other words, it doesn't matter who you're with or what you're doing?"

She paused, watching his face, then pushed away and spun around to face him, legs tucked beneath her. Her face was flushed, and the pulse at the base of her throat had started to flutter. "Oh, come on, Chas. That's not what I meant. You know that's not what I meant."

"That's *exactly* what you meant, Miranda," he said with a smile, gathering her rigid body back into his arms. He tilted her face to his. "Can I ask you a question that I've never asked a woman before and I never thought I would?"

Her eyes were wide and wary. "Okay."

"How many men have you slept with?"

She paused. "Why do you want to know?"

"Humor me."

"Two."

He hid his surprise. "You mean I'm the second?"

She waited a moment, then nodded.

What the hell was wrong with men in Atlanta? And everywhere else she'd ever lived?

"So you've had one lover before me. The professor."

"Yes, Chas. Is there something you're not comprehending here?" she snapped.

He smiled and smoothed a hand over her hair. "And we're indistinguishable in bed?"

"I didn't say that."

"Relax, Miranda. I'm not upset."

She stared at his throat for a long time, then met his eyes. "There's not as much of a difference as I would have expected there to be," she mumbled.

He swallowed a laugh. "You really have stopped lying to me, haven't you?"

Trying to hide a smile, she nodded.

"You're a brave woman. So here's another bad question that I don't want you to take offense at. Do you like sex?"

"What?" She tried to pull away but he held her snug against him.

"I'm not challenging you; I'm asking a question. What do you think of sex?"

"I can't answer that."

"Why not?"

"Well, for one thing, we just had sex."

"Did you like it?"

"I'm definitely not answering that."

"So you didn't."

"Don't put words in my mouth." She pulled away again. He let her go this time.

"So you did like it or you didn't?"

"Don't interrogate me," she snapped.

She settled opposite him on the bed and met his eyes. "Okay, you want an answer? I'll tell you. To be perfectly frank about it, I think it's overrated."

Nothing could have kept his eyebrows down after that answer. *"Sex?"*

"Yes."

"You think *sex* is overrated? Isn't that how you make your living?"

"I make my living writing about relationships, not sex," she replied coolly.

He held up his hands in surrender. "Okay, so it's overrated. Why?"

She folded her arms across her chest and met his eyes straight-on. "Well, since I'm obviously never going to have the privilege of sleeping with you again after this conversation, I'll be candid, Chas. I don't know what all the fuss is about. I, like the majority of women, prefer the cuddling to the action. There. Shall I go home now?" She made a move to get off the bed.

He reached out and took her arm gently. "No way. Keep talking. I think we're onto something."

"What's that supposed to mean?"

"Well, I've slept with a few more women than you have men—"

"How many?"

"Miranda, that's not important."

"You won't say? You made me say how many partners I've had."

"I didn't make you; I asked you. And I can't give you an answer because I don't know the answer. I quit keeping track when it stopped being a rare and glorious event."

"When was that?"

Looking into those eyes that had gone green with annoyance, he was tempted to dispense with his strategy and just get her naked. "My sophomore year in college. Can we get back on point?"

"What is the point exactly?"

"All the fuss about sex."

"Or lack thereof," she said sweetly. "Is this going to be a serious conversation?"

"Hopefully not."

"Great. Then I'd like to continue it downstairs." She slid off the bed and was halfway to the stairs before she glanced over her shoulder with an arch look. "I might want to take notes."

Sweet Jesus, take me now. I'll repent. I mean it this time.

Waiting for Chas at the bottom of the stairs, Miranda tried to keep at bay the stampede of bad thoughts rushing her brain. He arrived downstairs a moment later wearing the jeans he'd had on earlier. She let him take her hand and even kissed him back before they walked into the kitchen. He pulled out the bottle of port he'd opened the night before and poured some into a small goblet, and got himself a Heineken. And there they sat, half-dressed and across the kitchen table from each other at one o'clock in the morning on a Thursday in mid-November, about to have a candid conversation about sex.

Surreal. Definitely surreal.

She smiled tightly. "Fire at will."

Calm and relaxed, he smiled back. "You're tense," he said, and took a pull from his beer.

She raised an eyebrow. "I am not. I'm perfectly comfortable—"

"Not now," he interrupted. "In bed."

She didn't know what to say. He hadn't said it in an accusing way, or a negative way. He'd just said it. She chewed on the inside of her cheek for a moment. "What do you mean?"

"You're not relaxed. And you like to drive the bus."

That one stung. She took a breath and smiled. "You'd prefer to drive?"

He laughed and reached for her hand. "Yes. Not all the time, but I want to drive."

His words lit an unexpected fire in her belly, and she crossed her legs. Determined to keep her eyes off his face, she dropped them to his chest, which she had been looking at or leaning against for the better part of an hour. It was bare. Gloriously bare.

"Why am I the second?"

Her pulse jumped at the question, and her eyes shot back to his face. "You mean instead of the first?"

He lifted her hand and lightly kissed her palm. "I mean instead of the twenty-first."

"Oh. I just . . ." She shrugged. "I don't sleep around."

"But if the professor was the first, that means you waited until you were nearly twenty-five. That's kind of late, don't you think? I mean, you're beautiful and smart and personable. You weren't in a convent, were you?"

"I grew up in small Southern army towns, Chas, and Walter was a military police officer and a religious man, to boot. I wasn't willing to mess with him, and not too many boys were willing to mess with me. Walter wouldn't have tolerated a 'loose woman' in his house," she replied quietly. "And at Smith I had other things to deal with, like classes and being of the Southern, big-haired, feminine prototype among all the hairy-legged radical feminists. Then my mother died and Walter handed me his surprise. . . ." She shrugged. "My opinion of men dropped pretty low and stayed there. Then I met Josh and everything seemed all right."

Chas leaned forward to rest his forearms on the table. She glanced at him quickly, just to make sure he wasn't about to get all sympathetic and kind.

He wasn't looking at her. He was looking at his beer bottle. "That makes sense."

"I'm glad you approve."

He glanced up at her with serious eyes. "Come on. Don't snipe."

She looked away. "I'm just wondering if we're done so I can go upstairs and get some sleep."

"Not yet." He picked up his beer and took a long swallow. "I know we've only made love twice, Miranda," he began, looking straight at her with a teasing smile on his face. She flushed, but felt herself relax and even smile back. "But both times you only let me touch you certain places, in a certain order, for certain lengths of time. And when I enter you, you're not ready."

Damn him. "Yes, I am." She yanked her hand out of his and leaned back in her chair. A sickening mortification started to churn through her, and she braced herself for the criticism she knew would start soon.

He let a moment pass before he reached out and tilted her chin up. Wanting nothing more than to leave, to just disappear, she met his eyes reluctantly. To her surprise they weren't annoyed. They were concerned. Dark and soft and concerned.

"I don't know what went on between you and Josh, but sex isn't supposed to hurt, Miranda. It's supposed to feel good. For both of us. Just like in your books."

"It doesn't hurt," she said quickly, and felt her face get hot. *Why am I still sitting here? If I really need to humiliate myself, there are plenty of other ways to do it.*

He let out a controlled breath. "For Christ's sake, Miranda, it has to hurt." When she didn't reply, he continued. "If it doesn't hurt, why do you gasp?"

"I gasp?"

With one hand he tilted her chin up again and twined the fingers of his other through hers as if he knew she was a flight risk. And she would have been if her clothes weren't two floors up and her car across town.

"Yes. You gasp. It's the only sound you make." His eyes were warm and causing endless turmoil in her mind. "But I don't mind the gasp. In fact, if you spent the whole time gasping, it would be quite a turn-on. What I do mind is why you're gasping. I'm hurting you."

"That's not true," she whispered. "I'm enjoying it."

"Would you be willing to let me prove you wrong?"

She looked up at him. "What do you mean?"

He hitched an eyebrow flirtatiously. "Let me drive. Let me make love to you the way I want to."

She jumped as if touched with a live wire, and the warmth that followed the jolt didn't soothe. It wasn't that kind of heat.

"Consider it research," he continued. "I'm not like your ex in any other way, am I?"

"No."

"Then it follows that we shouldn't make love the same way either, right?"

Uh-oh. She nodded.

"Then let me make love to you the way I want to just to test that theory."

She took a sip of the port, and kept the goblet near her lips. "You're not talking about anything weird, are you? Because, frankly, I don't even like reading about that stuff."

He laughed and shook his head. "The negotiations didn't last this long when I bought my car." He squeezed her hand and grinned at her and that warmth flared up again. "Nothing weird, Miranda. Just standard, old-fashioned, plain-vanilla, missionary-style sex."

After a moment she shook her head. "Sorry, Chas. I trust you, but I'm a person who doesn't walk into a dark room without turning on the light first. You have to—"

"No problem. Here's the plan. Since you mentioned light, that's the first thing that will be different. There will be enough light for me to see what I'm doing. The next thing is that you will be naked. I will touch you. A lot. Everywhere. And you *will* have at least one orgasm."

Sweet Jesus. How could she have ever thought he was like Josh? She cleared her throat. "I have them."

He looked at her with his cop face, and her irritation spiked. "Did you have one with me?"

"Yes, couldn't you tell?"

"No," he said bluntly. "And if I couldn't tell, you didn't have one."

She was about to argue when he grinned. It both warmed and unnerved her. "So do we have a deal? We make love and I'm in charge?"

Miranda raised an eyebrow with a composure that was faked. "If I say 'stop' or 'no,' you'll stop?"

"No way."

Her eyes widened.

He shrugged. "Would you prefer that I lie?"

"Of course not."

He rubbed his thumb over her knuckles. "Well, okay, I might stop. It depends on how you say it, and when, and why. If I do something that scares you, or hurts you, or offends you, then yes, absolutely I'll stop. But if you're just afraid of going over some edge, or afraid of enjoying a new sensation, or you're just clinging to some old inhibition, then there's no way I'm going to stop. I'm driving *and* navigating. You're just the passenger this time. No backseat driving, and no other rules or conditions. Are you game?"

The look in his eyes made it difficult to breathe. "May I have some time to think about it?"

"No."

"Fair enough," she said with false bravado. "When should we start?"

"Half an hour ago." He paused, and the silence of the house seemed to throb around them. "Come here, Miranda."

With her heart beating as fast as it did during a storm, she stood up and walked around the end of the table. She let him pull her onto his lap. He draped his arms around her loosely, clasping them at her hip, and eased her against his chest. He didn't say or do anything for a long time, and she felt herself start to relax.

"You're a brave woman, Miranda Lane," he murmured into her hair eventually. "I know I've told you that before, but the longer I know you, the more you amaze me." His mouth moved gently to her temple and down her cheek to her ear. "I never know who you're going to be one minute to the next, and you drive me crazy," he whispered. "You're the sexiest, most frustrating woman I've ever known."

Miranda closed her eyes and let him seduce her.

CHAPTER
19

Finally.

Miranda, aroused, was warm and pliable and very, very responsive. Her eyes were drowsy with desire, and the rest of her was tousled and flushed. She was gorgeous.

Chas slowly set her on her feet and stood up, lifting her into his arms before she could take a step away. She wrapped her arms around his neck and her legs around his waist, laughing.

"I'm too heavy, Chas, or at least too tall. You're not going to make it to the staircase, much less up two flights of stairs."

"We'll see about that," he murmured, capturing her mouth as he adjusted her weight against him. He ignored the way she stiffened when his hands slid over her bare thighs. He casually caught his elbows behind her knees to give him added balance, then left the darkened kitchen.

"Looks like you were right, Miranda. I think I have to stop and catch my breath," he whispered against her mouth as they neared the staircase. He leaned her against the wall. Instead of setting her down, he slid his hands up her thighs until he reached a slick softness.

She tore her mouth from his. "Chas, don't."

He pulled his head back minutely and met her furious,

panicky eyes, but did not let his fingers rest. "Am I hurting you?" Her eyes were huge and dark and she was squirming to try to get away from his hands, but there was nowhere for her to go and they both knew it.

"No," she whispered.

"Scaring you?" She shook her head. "Offending you?" She repeated the gesture even as her eyes fluttered shut.

"We have a deal, Miranda."

"But—"

"Do you trust me?"

"Yes," she gasped softly.

"Then let me touch you," he murmured against her mouth, and moved his right hand minutely. She arched her back and her fingernails dug into his shoulders. He ignored the sharp stabs of pain and repeated the motion. A cry escaped her as she tried to move away, but he pressed her against the wall more firmly and moved his hand one more time to send her body writhing against him. Her panting cries ended only when he slid his hand away from her center and held her close. She was shaking.

"Are you having fun yet?" he asked as he felt her breathing slow.

"You're a bad, bad man, Chas Casey," she mumbled, burying her face in his neck.

"I'll try to be better next time." He continued his way up the stairs, her legs still wrapped around him.

They were halfway up the steep, narrow attic staircase that led to his bedroom when he stopped again and leaned her against the wall.

"You're slipping. Hang on," he said as he repositioned her.

She lifted her head. Mutiny was in her eyes. "Chas—"

His hands were already in place before she realized what he was up to, and she tried to squirm away again.

"No."

"Yes."

"No."

"Miranda—"

"We'll fall down the stairs."

"Only if you fight me. If you behave yourself, we'll be fine," he murmured with a grin.

"*Behave myself?* You—" She interrupted herself with a sharp breath, and when she spoke again her voice was a bit higher and a bit thinner. "I already—"

"Nope, you didn't. Sorry, sweetheart, that was only a warm-up," he replied, watching pleasure and panic and mirth chase across her glowing face. She was at the edge of control, and breathtaking because of it.

He moved his hands in unison this time and felt her nails dig into his shoulders once again as her body clenched and she tried to lift herself away from him. His hands followed her movements as he lowered his mouth to her long, lovely throat. When he increased the rhythm of his fingers, she arched her back and tightened her legs around him. A low moan tore through her, rising in pitch and volume to match the speed of his hands, culminating in a loud, panting cry that left her shuddering and rocking against him.

It took him longer to recover this time, too, and by the time he made it to the bed and laid her on it, his muscles were trembling from the strain of carrying her. He threw himself onto the sheets next to her and gave himself a minute to catch his breath before propping himself up on one elbow to look at her.

She was looking back at him with dark, half-lidded eyes and a languorous smile. It replenished his energy. Holding her gaze, he casually reached over to the top of his white button-down, which looked better on her than it ever would on him, and slipped the first button out of the hole.

She raised an eyebrow. "No time off for good behavior?" she murmured.

"Not a chance. You have an annoying tendency to change your mind, so I intend to make progress while you're—" he opened the next button "—relaxing."

She smiled and stopped his hand. "Before you go too far, Chas, there's something I have to tell you."

He shook off her hand. "Let me guess. You were faking and I need to try harder."

"I couldn't have faked that. I wasn't even expecting it," she said with a soft laugh.

He opened the third button and leaned down to take her left breast in his mouth.

She took in a startled breath. "Chas, there's really something you ought to know."

"Later," he murmured from around her small peak. He opened the fourth button, then the fifth.

"But—"

"Shhh." He lifted his head and met her eyes, feeling her go rigid as he undid the last button. He let his gaze wander down the long, slim curves of her torso outlined in silver—

His breath caught in his throat and he jerked his head back to look at her.

She was biting her lips to suppress laughter as she reached up to cup his cheek gently. "I told you there was something you should know about me."

"Would you care to explain this?" he asked in a voice that sounded a bit strangled to his own ears. He pointed in the general direction of her hips. "Is this . . . are those . . . real?"

She nodded.

"You're a blonde?"

She nodded again. "Really pale. Nearly platinum."

He blinked at her, at a loss for words. "Why do you dye your hair?" he asked finally.

Her hand slid from his cheek, her fingers threading through his hair. "Well, a while back I decided I was more interested in being taken seriously than in having more fun."

Recovered from the surprise, and more than a little turned on by it, he slid his hand down the smooth, taut skin of her stomach and beyond. "Are you still?"

"Not at the moment," she said, breathlessly.

"Good." He lowered his mouth to hers and gathered her into his arms, letting his hands roam freely and, eventually, his lips. It wasn't until his mouth had reached those golden curls that she tried to stop him.

"Chas. Chas, no," she said with enough urgency that he returned his mouth to hers without protest.

"Am I breaking our deal, Miranda?" he asked softly.

"You said plain vanilla," she said between breathy kisses. "That doesn't qualify."

"I said plain-vanilla sex." He let his mouth drift to the shell of her ear. "According to at least one public figure, that's not sex."

He felt her laugh, but she didn't relax, so he concentrated on kissing her and let his hands drift slowly toward her hips and points farther south until he heard her breathing change again.

"I want to taste you, Miranda," he murmured against her mouth.

"No. I'm not comfortable with that," she murmured back, and arched against him in response to his movements. He brought his hand up slowly, slid his slick fingers over her breast, and seconds later covered the same flesh with his mouth. He heard her sharp breath and knew it wasn't purely from pleasure. He slid his hand back to her center and then shocked her again when he brought his hand to her mouth and let his fingers drift across her lips.

"Chas," she said sharply.

"It's part of your essence, Miranda, as much a part of you and just as sexy as your eyes, your voice, your walk," he murmured against that protesting mouth. When he let his hand slide again, she grabbed it. Anger tensed the body that had been languid and soft moments ago.

"Stop doing that," she snapped.

He met her angry, mortified eyes. "Why?"

"Because I don't want you to do that, that's why."

"Do what?"

She gritted her teeth and closed her eyes, her hand still wrapped firmly around his wrist. She had a hell of a grip.

"You know what I mean. You're embarrassing me," she ground out.

"Miranda, look at me," he said softly, not continuing until she opened her eyes. They held a painful mixture of fear and shame and fury. "I'm not embarrassing you. Someone else did that to you but whatever he did or said was wrong. You're sexy and gorgeous and you make me crazy . . ." His whispered words faded into a kiss that had her moaning with pleasure, and ten minutes later he was back where he wanted to be—legitimately—devouring her with a restraint that he found amazing under the circumstances. Her responses weren't nearly as restrained as his efforts.

At last moving up her body, Chas slid his hips into place above hers. A dreamy, exhausted smile played across her face and in her eyes as she welcomed his mouth with hers and his body with her own. They moved together in an ageless, unchoreographed tumult, and Chas got as close to having a religious experience as he thought he ever would.

Miranda woke slowly, first becoming aware of aches in muscles she didn't know she had, then of the sun beating against her eyelids. She rolled away from the brightness and opened her eyes, blinking for a moment as she recognized her surroundings. *Chas's bedroom.*

Oh, God.

She looked to her left. *Chas.* He was on his back, a pillow over his face held in place by upflung arms. The sheet was twisted around his hips; one leg was uncovered. The shoulder and upper arm closest to her were crosshatched with crescent-shaped digs and long red welts. Some were faintly bloody.

She let her face drop into her pillow as mortifying heat engulfed her in rolling, echoing waves. *Please let it be nothing more than a really, really erotic dream.* But the shirt she'd worn last night was sprawled on the floor several feet from the bed. Chas had lobbed it there when it had gotten in the way of—

"Oh, God," she moaned, out loud this time, then lifted her head to see if Chas had heard her. He was just pulling the pillow away from his face. His smiling face.

His eyes found hers immediately, and she saw in them warmth and desire and laughter. She dropped her face back into the pillow. *I want him to leave me alone.*

But, of course, he didn't. She felt the bed move, then felt the long, warm length of his body press against her side. His hand slid across her bare back and over her bare bottom as his mouth found her ear.

"Good morning, Miranda," he murmured.

She didn't reply.

Faint laughter rocked through him, and he pushed her hair aside to let his lips drift down her neck. A minute later she felt his body cover hers, felt his legs against the back of her knees nudging them apart. She snapped her head up from the pillow and felt it connect solidly with his jaw. With a grunt, he rolled off her.

Glancing over her left shoulder, she saw him leaning on an elbow, rubbing his chin. "Sorry. Did I hurt you?"

"Let's just say you made your point. No nooky in the mornings. Got it."

She started to laugh and buried her face in the pillow again. This time he reached over and rolled her onto her back. The sheet tangled around her waist, and she knew he wasn't about to cater to her modesty. In fact, he let his eyes meander down her body, and it was all she could do not to cover herself with her arms against his open appraisal. Last night in the moonlight had been one thing. Bright morning sunshine was entirely another.

He spared her face a glance. "You look really, really embarrassed, and I don't think it's because you clipped my chin."

"Why, thank you for making me feel comfortable, Chas," she said, feeling her face grow even hotter than it had been a minute ago. "And here I was thinking you'd play nice."

He shook his head, clearly delighted with himself and wearing a grin that was pure trouble. "Sometimes I play nice and sometimes I play fair. Right now, I'm playing fair." He dropped a light kiss on her lips. "I refuse to let you pretend that anything that did happen last night didn't happen. So just in case you're intending to develop a ladylike case of amnesia, let me assure you that, yes, I saw you naked. I know what you look like, feel like, taste like, and what you sound like every step of the way." She reached up and covered his mouth with her hands, but he pulled them away and held them pressed to the mattress. "You writhe. You moan. You scream. You're sexy as hell. And you apparently mark your territory," he finished with a glance at his right shoulder. Then he looked down at their hands. And back to her face. "This could get interesting. It could be time you met my handcuffs."

She felt her stomach drop and her eyes widen, and when she opened her mouth to say something, nothing came out.

"Maybe another time," he said, openly laughing.

"Excuse me. The least you could do is allow me to retain a shred of dignity by not mocking me."

"You're perfectly dignified, Miranda. You're just naked. And I'm not mocking you; I'm laughing at you. I had no idea I could shock you so easily."

"You didn't shock me."

"Yes, I did." He lowered his mouth to her ear. "More than once. What surprised you the most, Miranda?" he murmured with naughty laughter still in his voice.

She counted to five, then met his eyes. "I'll tell you what surprised me the most, Chas. I never expected a white-bread Greenwich boy like you to be quite so earthy."

She expected his laughter but not his words.

"That wasn't earthy, Miranda. We haven't begun to approach earthy yet. But next time we're taking off the training wheels." He rolled off the bed and pulled her to her feet. "*Now* you're allowed to take a shower. But only with me."

CHAPTER
20

"What happened to you?" Amy demanded.

Satisfaction bloomed inside her, and Miranda smiled as she watched evidence of an early winter drift past her bedroom window. The carpenter was gone, the masons were gone, the dust was gone, and so, apparently, was her funk. A team of painters would arrive tomorrow to begin taping the study, and some sort of specialist was going to be applying real gold dust to the ornate stenciling in the dining room. But right now it was late Friday afternoon and blessedly *quiet*.

"Do you like it?"

"*I love it*," her agent stated flatly. "Andrew is wonderful. And I *love* the paintball scene. I sent it to Ellen for the Web site."

"Okay."

"Okay, now, the truth. These three chapters were great. When will you be finished with the rest of it?"

Miranda smiled confidently. "Five days at the most."

"You're sure that's going to be enough time? Even with the carpenters?"

"Positive. I'm dealing with painters now, and they're much less noisy. And after that it's carpet, and then the furniture and decorators."

"Okay, I won't bug you again. Keep in touch."

"I will. I promise."

Miranda ended the call feeling smug. She was humming. The story was humming. The characters were humming. Actually, the characters were bonking. Like bunnies. Because, for the first time ever, Miranda was having a good time writing love scenes. Her characters actually liked each other now. He had evolved and she had lightened up. Everyone's life was good. Her characters', her own.

Miranda leaned back and stretched her arms over her head, then stood up and went downstairs for some more iced tea. She hadn't seen Chas since he'd dropped her off yesterday morning, and wasn't likely to for another twenty-four hours. He was working nights and had had to be in court yesterday and today. She missed him after spending the last several nights with him, but she didn't mind. Not only was the book nearly finished but, more important, writing had become fun again.

Both Dirk the Dork and Randy Andy were gone, replaced by Andrew. Andrew the cop. *Detective Andrew*.

She smiled. Detective Andrew was sexy as hell. Whereas Dirk and Andy had just been jerks, Andrew was stubborn, but strong and rational. Andrew never lost his temper; he just glowered occasionally. He was tough but reasonable, and he laughed when her heroine—who was now Samantha—least expected it. And Samantha, it turned out, had studied ballet for years, so she was not only strong but *extremely* limber, which Andrew found *extremely* erotic. But then, he found everything about Samantha erotic, from the way her hand curled around a coffee mug to the way she brushed her hair.

Their first love scene had been a single kiss. The circumstances had been so sweet and he had been so tender that Miranda had gotten teary as she wrote it. But Samantha and Andrew were well beyond the kissing stage. At the moment they were in bed for the first time, and Samantha was in a state of suspended animation three-quarters of the way to *another* universe-bending orgasm. Although Samantha had known all along that Andrew was sweet beneath that crunchy SWAT-cop exterior, she hadn't realized he was quite so inventive. Or so naughty, like hot chocolate spiked with a shot of brandy. He bit, then soothed. Teased, then delivered. Straitlaced lawyer Samantha was having the time of her life.

So was her creator.

Miranda knew in her bones that this book was going to be a big seller. All the emotional turbulence that Chas and Paxton had inspired had been channeled into her characters, and she knew without needing to hear it from anyone else that this book was going to have the depth her others had lacked. These characters *mattered*. They mattered to her, they mattered to each other, and they would matter to Ellen Barber. But most of all, they would matter to her audience. Her readers would forgive her for abandoning her beta heroes when they met Andrew. Who wouldn't want what Andrew and Samantha had? They had everything: love, laughter, romance, emotional depth, and rocket-hot sex.

They had it because she had it with Chas, Miranda admitted to herself. Three-fifths of it, anyway. The laughter, romance, and—finally—hot sex. The other things she didn't have and didn't particularly want. Not when she was leaving in a matter of days. She lifted her chin as if to support the claim. She'd be crazy to become more deeply involved with him. Doing so would only lead to trouble.

Keeping control of her emotions had never been a problem, and she wasn't about to let it become one now. When she left Stamford, she'd drive away with good memories and enough inspiration to span the rest of her career. As Paxton said, this was just a drive-by romance. The warmth and the tug Chas caused inside her were just the effects of a well-documented syndrome known as intoxication by an overexposure to testosterone. The two days and a night without him had allowed her to regain her senses and reinvigorate her muse—and remind herself that she was leaving very soon. She'd miss him when she left, but . . .

But I'm not going to think about that now.

Shutting off the oxygen supply to that part of her brain, Miranda marched back to the loft, where her laptop lay waiting. Where Samantha lay waiting, breathless, aroused, and dangling over the edge of a precipice of passion. Miranda sat down, zoned out the rest of the world, and started typing.

It was hours later when, getting yet another refill of her tea, she heard a knock at the door and jumped. The tea splashed a trail down the front of her T-shirt and jeans, and a glance at the clock made her heart kick up a beat. It was half past midnight. It had to be Chas. Paxton would never come over this late. And she wouldn't knock. Miranda wasn't entirely sure she wanted to see him right now. The words were still flowing, and she didn't like messing with the magic.

Grabbing a Ralph Lauren dishtowel that would probably never see duty more hazardous than this, Miranda dabbed at the stain as she walked to the door. Resolved to stay cool, she took a measured breath and pulled open the door. He stood there, damp and windblown from the night, with a shadowed chin and hungry eyes, looking dangerous and flirtatious and lots of other words that rhymed with *luscious.* Never before had an armed man struck her as sexy or even particularly appealing. Trouble licked its lips.

She put her hand on one hip, and barred his way with the other as she kept her hand on the door handle. "What, no pizza this time?"

He smiled with his eyes first and then his mouth, and she knew remaining cool wasn't on his agenda. It was becoming less of a priority for her, too.

"I've already eaten."

Said the wolf to Little Red Riding Hood. She raised an eyebrow. "Flowers?"

"The stores are closed. I just ended my shift."

"A bottle of wine, then?"

He shook his head slowly, his eyes not leaving her face. "But I know where a few cases of good stuff are stashed."

She caught her lower lip in her teeth as she pretended to consider. "It's after midnight and you come over unannounced and empty-handed. I'm getting the impression you think I'm a cheap date, if not worse."

"Never let it be said." He ran his eyes over her, and she wondered how long it would be before the dampened stripe down the front of her clothes began to steam. "Having a food fight, were you?"

She lifted a shoulder nonchalantly. "I had to try it. I discovered it's no fun by myself."

"Not many things are, Miranda." He took a step forward, crossing the threshold, and slid his hands around her waist. His touch set off an adrenaline flurry. "Maybe my empty hands could be forgiven because of my impeccable timing."

Miranda felt a hint of delicious panic spark within her as he guided her into the foyer, his lips on hers. She felt him balance briefly on one foot, then heard the door click shut. That was when he really settled into the kiss, plumbing the depths of her mouth, drinking her in, dizzying her as he walked her backward until she was against the wall and his hands were roaming freely.

"I missed you," he murmured into her neck, running his lips up to her ear. "Did you miss me?"

"Some. I kept busy," she said coolly, trying to ignore the wicked surges his damp whisper incited.

"Me, too. It left me too tired to drive all the way home," he whispered as his lips slid across the front of her throat and stopped beneath her other ear.

She shivered as he nipped the sensitive flesh. Damp heat rose between them.

Get sensible. Don't let this happen. You don't need the complications. She slid her hands out of his hair and onto his shoulders, then his chest, and pushed, and kept pushing until he broke their kiss and his eyes met hers. Then she smiled politely and brought her hand away from his chest. She brushed a curl behind her ear just to break the high-voltage circuit buzzing between them. "Chas, I think we should stop right here. I really don't want to . . ." She paused for a breath. "I really don't want to do this right now."

He gave her his best bad-boy smile. "Forensic evidence indicates otherwise."

The only thing that could save her now was space—physical and emotional. She wasn't sure he'd allow her either. Not with that smolder in his eyes. She gave a little laugh that was far too breathless and dodged the issue. "I just wasn't expecting to see you tonight."

Her intent began to overpower his, and he lifted an eyebrow. "Am I interrupting something?"

She smiled. "Of course you are, Detective. You're interrupting my work." *And destroying my equilibrium. Shattering my resolve. Melting my kneecaps and hip sockets and turning the rest of me into mush.*

"Are you researching, or writing?"

"Writing."

"Damn the luck. If you were researching, I might be able to help." He slid his hands to her waist, then let her go and stepped back. "How's it going?"

She refrained from letting out a relieved sigh. "Really well," she said, and glanced away. "How have you been? Is the trial finished?"

"My testimony is," he replied, hunger still in his dark eyes. Then he fell silent and watched her fidget. "You really don't want me here, do you?"

She met his eyes again and offered an apologetic smile. "I'm not sure that I *don't* want you here, but if I ·said I *did* want you here, it would be a lie. A half-lie, anyway."

He shook his head in mild exasperation. "An honest woman and the male ego is a bad combination."

Her shrug was full of insincere contrition. *I'm almost home.*

A moment later he ran a knuckle lightly over her cheek, then walked to the door. "Good night, Miranda."

"Good night, Chas." She followed him to the door, and the first wave of guilt lapped at her feet. *What are you doing? He's your hero. You can't send him back into the rain.* She winced and tried to mollify her conscience.

Okay. If he makes another attempt, I'll concede. But he won't because he's a gentleman and understands that I have to work.

With the door open and his foot across the threshold, Chas turned and slid his arms around her, lowering his mouth to hers for one last deep, dizzying kiss. "If you let me stay, I'll let you drive the bus," he whispered against her mouth.

Save me, Jesus. She kicked the door shut with her foot.

"But that's not why I let you stay. I was joking," Miranda protested five minutes later.

Without giving her a chance to reconsider her rashness or to pass it off as flirtation, Chas had scooped her into his arms and carried her up the stairs as if she were a featherweight. Now they were in her bedroom with the lights off, the blinds open, and their clothes still on. She was in a state of mild panic. He was in a state much closer to euphoria, if the smile on his face was any indication.

She glared at him. "I've never driven the bus with you. I mean, your way. I don't need to drive the bus. I want you to drive the bus." *I'll make a complete fool of myself if I drive.*

"A promise is a promise." He grinned, then broke into a laugh. "I *want* you to drive."

"Chas, *I don't know how.*"

He set his hands lightly onto her shoulders, then ran them down her arms as he brought her into a close embrace. "There is no 'how.' You just do whatever comes to mind." He hitched an eyebrow. "You've read books. Hell, you've *written* books. And I've read them. Use that imagination. Be bad. Be very, very bad."

She felt heat surge to her face. "Chas. I. Don't. Want. To. Drive."

"Why?"

She couldn't even hold his gaze for very long before she had to look away. "I can't go from zero to sixty this fast. I don't know if I can get to sixty at all. I may get stuck at twenty."

"Twenty isn't bad. It's better than neutral." He paused and tilted her chin up so she had to look at him. "Are you afraid?"

Heat roared through the rest of her, swamping her confidence and charring what was left of her desire. Now she *really* wanted him gone. "A little," she admitted grudgingly.

He ran warm, strong hands over her back. "Don't be," he murmured. "Drive as slow as you want to. There's no such thing as a mistake, and you're allowed to make wrong turns. Sometimes those can turn out to be the best adventures."

She met his eyes, knowing that every miserable doubt and fear was there for him to see. His long, slow seduction the other night had allayed them, but this spontaneity had brought them roaring back to life. Every Bible-thumping lecture Walter had made her sit through. Every failed date. Every piece of sexy lingerie Josh had ever laughed at. And every delicious sin Chas had introduced her to. It was just too much to handle at once.

She looked away. "Please, Chas. I already feel like a fool. No amount of conversation is going to change that right now. I have to think about this."

Disbelief flashed across his face and was gone so quickly that she wondered if she'd imagined it. His smile seemed a little forced as he placed a light kiss on her forehead. "Okay, Miranda. I won't pretend I understand what's going through your mind, but I'll back off."

Standing there in the half-light afforded by the uncovered windows, Miranda looked flushed and agonized, as if she'd just run a marathon.

Damn it.

Chas refused to let his annoyance show. They had only a few days left together. He hadn't wanted to spend them arguing or apologizing—or reverting to being platonic—but they certainly seemed headed straight into one of those zones unless she came up with some marginally reasonable explanation for her behavior. After the last time they'd been together, he'd assumed it was clear sailing ahead. She'd required some persuasion, but . . .

But she'd had an hour of careful seduction behind her. He took a slow, deep breath and met her eyes, which were shifting from hazel to rich green and back, and he had to shake himself. She was mesmerizing.

"Miranda, I like you. I don't want to scare you. I don't want you to think I'm—" *I can't believe I'm about to say this* "—to think I'm some sort of pervert or lecher. I like you," he repeated, then shrugged. "If you need to hear it, having sex just for the sake of having sex ceased being a thrill for me years ago." Her chin had begun to sink to her chest, so he gently tipped it up again until they were looking at each other. Her color was getting better. "I don't sleep with every woman I meet, and I don't find any pleasure in hit-and-run dating. I just like to keep things simple." He ran his thumb over her bottom lip as an act of self-discipline. His lips would have preferred to take care of it themselves. "There's no one on my radar screen at the moment except you and I can't imagine there will be anyone else for a while."

His pulse rate kicked up a few notches, and the room seemed suddenly to throb with a shocked silence. *What the hell did I just say?*

It had to have shocked her, too, because as they stared at each other, he watched most of the blood drain from her face. Then she blinked and straightened and smiled, wrapping that Southern politeness around her like a cloak. He knew it was sheer bravado. She hadn't wanted to hear what he'd said any more than he'd wanted to say it, or even admit it. But unfortunately for both of them, it was true.

Just what in creation does he expect me to say to that?

A silent blink was the only reaction her body could produce as she stood there staring at him in a room so still she could hear the dust fall through the air. He looked a bit startled himself.

Under pain of death she'd never ask him why he said it, but the chance that he might offer additional unsolicited declarations or unwanted explanations convinced her that the best strategy was to drop the subject and hightail it out of the bedroom. Her mother had always said the best place to have a difficult talk was in the kitchen, because there was always something you could do to keep your hands busy, and keeping your hands busy was critical to maintaining composure.

She took a shallow breath and smiled. "Why don't we go get something to drink, Chas?" she said evenly, and headed slowly for the stairs. *Slowly* was the hard part. She felt like sprinting. Down the stairs, out the door, back to Atlanta. As soon as she arrived in the kitchen, she busied herself rinsing out her glass of tea and pouring herself a glass of wine.

"Miranda, I'm—"

She turned to face him calmly. "Why don't we just stop here and pick things up when we're a bit less . . . whatever we are?" she said with a smile that cost her a lot. After a moment, she stepped up to him and pressed a soft kiss against his mouth. "I'm never quite myself when I'm writing, Chas. I go into a different place and I can't always snap out of it at the drop of a hat. Let's talk tomorrow, okay, darlin'? When I'm not in my zone." She kissed him again. "I'll call you."

He searched her eyes until she was sure he could see clear back to the moment she'd been conceived. Then, with a tight smile and a quiet good-bye, he left.

As soon as she saw his truck pull out of the parking area onto the street, she went upstairs, crawled into bed, and pulled the covers over her head. She had too much to do in the next few days to fret over Chas Casey and the lunacy he inspired. She had to finish revising her manuscript, then proof it, print it, page-check it, and package it for Amy and Ellen. When she completed all of those tasks, she'd take a day for herself, pack her things, and drive home.

Now she was going to sleep, and hope that by morning the world would have righted itself.

Chas slammed the truck into gear and pulled out of the parking lot. *Great fucking way to end a couple of truly shitty days.* On top of pulling his regular night shift, he'd spent two full days in court testifying on a two-year-old case. He could have finished his testimony in two hours if it hadn't been for the damned defense attorney, who kept objecting to every damned question the district attorney asked. Those days in court had been preceded by those two nights with Miranda, each unforgettable in their own way. And then there was the bullshit that had just transpired, which was in a class all its own.

He took a deep breath and trained his eyes on the red light in front of him but lost that focus again in seconds. He was annoyed as hell. *On top of every other fucking hang-up she has—Men. Sex. Her God-damned father and the asshole ex-boyfriend—now she wants a commitment.*

He'd gone to her place not knowing what reception he'd receive, but he'd assumed that one way or another, he'd end up spending the night. That he would be teased then turned away—*twice*—had never crossed his mind. And the damnedest thing about it was that he was not only horny; he actually missed her company. He would have stayed without sex if she'd asked him to. Of course, by the time the thought of suggesting that crossed his mind, he would have seemed desperate at best. *Desperate.* He floored the engine and took off at the green light.

No fucking way, sweetheart. You're just not that memorable.

It wasn't even seven when Miranda woke up to the sound of the doorbell.

The painters.

She groaned and rolled out of bed, pulling on a sweatshirt as she jogged down the stairs to let them in. They were a nice crew of young guys, all much too healthy-looking and entirely too energetic that early in the morning. Like a bunch of playful puppies, they barreled through the door and began setting up their equipment in the living room. With a silent, more or less welcoming smile, she ducked into the kitchen.

Glancing out the window as she waited for the coffee to finish brewing, she acknowledged glumly that it was going to be another claustrophobic day. Swollen, dirty-white clouds hung low in the sky, woven with haphazard streaks of gristly gray.

It was a day that had "Paxton" written all over it. James spent every Saturday morning with the children, which meant Paxton would be at loose ends. Cup of

coffee in hand, Miranda headed upstairs to dress. She
had to get out of the house before Paxton arrived. For-
going even a quick shower, she shoved her laptop, the
adaptor for the car's cigarette lighter, and the extra
charged battery into her bag, grabbed her car keys, and
left the house. Minutes later she passed a surprised Paxton on the road and gave her a smile and a little wave,
then let out a huge sigh of relief.

The Starbucks in downtown Stamford proved to be
entirely too domestic a place on a weekend morning.
She needed solitude and focus, not engulfment by bevies
of impatient suburban mothers hissing at overindulged
toddlers intent on mindless destruction. She needed a
place that matched her mood gray for gray, and so
ended up parked at the public end of her private beach,
watching seagulls huddle as the rain left pockmarks in
the sand.

Finally, at four o'clock, after having nearly finished
her revisions from the cramped space inside her car, Miranda allowed herself to turn on her cell phone. There
had been five calls. All were from Paxton.

"Why would I expect him to call?" she asked out
loud. "I threw him out. He's my hero and I sent him
back into the cold, wet night." She closed her eyes and
leaned against the seat. "I'm such a bitch. The man is a
god and he wants me. And I sent him away. If ever he
talks to me again, I'll be lucky."

Opening her eyes, she punched in his cell phone
number.

"Hello, Miranda." His voice was friendly and easy.
Not a good sign. He should at least sound annoyed.

"Hi, Chas."

"What can I do for you?"

"Well, you're speaking to me. That's more than I expected." He laughed quietly but didn't say anything. The
sound soothed her, washing over her, as her mother used
to say, like the waters of Jordan over a sinner's soul.
"Are you working tonight?"

"My shift starts in a few minutes."

"Would you like to come over after you're finished?"

she asked, bracing herself as she heard him hesitate, expecting him to ask her why.

"Are you sure I won't be in the way?"

She winced. "I know I deserved that, Chas. But please come over. If nothing else, let me speak to you face-to-face."

"I didn't mean it that way. I'll call you when I'm leaving the building."

"Thank you," she said, her words followed by an awkward silence. "I'll see you later."

"'Bye."

Miranda laid her head against the seat again and closed her eyes, wondering if this was how people got sucked into masochism.

As weeks go, this one sucks. Chas sat as his desk staring at the report in front of him, not focusing on a single word. He'd gotten very little sleep last night. When he'd arrived home from the debacle with Miranda, there had been a long list of e-mails from Joe and Sarah McAllister about the investigation at Brennan Shipping. The bottom line was that it had stalled.

Their best leads had turned out to be dead ends, at least so far, and despite having taken down the network and plugged the obvious leaks, the security was still porous. The only good news was that they had discovered when the hacking had begun. Even that was a pyrrhic victory, because it had started a hell of a long time ago. Longer than the team's worst-case scenario. As a result, Sarah had returned to Washington this morning to brief and consult with the leaders of the interagency task force. As for his mother, she was keeping her nose out of it. Joe was being cryptic.

"I hear you and Randi Rhodes are quite the item."

God damn it. Murphy and his bullshit were the last things he needed. Chas gritted his teeth and looked up. "I thought we went over that last week."

Murphy grinned. "Things not going so well, Casey?"

"Do you have a point? Because I'm busy," he snapped.

"Just being friendly. See ya around." He sauntered off with an arrogant smirk.

Chas forcibly returned his attention to the reams of paperwork the Jensen case was generating. The case just kept getting bigger and every possible jurisdiction was trying to get a piece of it. Customs. ATF. DEA. FBI. Not to mention Bridgeport and Stamford, where the crimes had actually been committed. He and Gruber had been denied the fun of questioning Mrs. Jensen again. The U.S. attorney had asked her to surrender her passport while the case was being investigated and, in response to that, she'd hired a battery of lawyers, thereby guaranteeing the addition of serious pain to the process.

A moment later Gruber appeared in the opening of his cubicle. "Mrs. Jensen just found another partridge in her pear tree. This one's alive."

Chas glanced at his watch. Six o'clock on the nose.

"What the fuck is going on this week?" he muttered, locking his computer. He shrugged into his sport coat and followed Gruber down the hall.

It was nearly one o'clock in the morning when Chas pulled up in front of Miranda's condo, and he was still unsure of what he was supposed to say. "What the fuck?" wouldn't cut it. His temper was simmering below the surface. Few people had ever seen a display of it, and he had no intention of putting Miranda on that short list.

The first thing he noticed about her when she opened the door was that she wasn't defiant. She wasn't penitent, either. She wore a serious but soft expression that contained no hint of a smile, which was good. Anything else would have made him turn around and join the boys for a few beers at O'Grady's.

"Come in, Chas." She stepped back and allowed him to enter. She was wearing a long skirt and the same soft sweater she'd worn the night they'd met at the restaurant with Paxton. In fact, he realized with suspicion, everything about her was soft. Kittenish.

Okay, let's see where this goes.

"Can I get you something to drink?"

"A beer, if you have one."

She moved past him toward the kitchen and returned a moment later. After handing him an opened Heineken, she picked up a half-filled wineglass and leaned a hip against the breakfast bar. "How was your day? Or night, I guess."

"Lousy. How was yours?" he replied in as conversational a tone as he could manage.

She let a small silence build as she considered him from across the top of her goblet. "Just because of last night?"

He met her eyes with a half smile. "No, but that's close to the top of the list."

"What would you like to talk about first?"

His eyebrows shot up and he had a hard time not laughing out loud. *The woman actually expects me to tell her what's bothering me. Right.* "Why don't we start with last night?" he said, humoring her.

Miranda dropped her eyes to his hands, which were detaching his tie. "You wear a clip-on," she said, a small frown creasing her forehead.

"Yeah, if a bad guy wants to strangle me, I want to make him work for it. A real tie makes it too easy. Is that what you wanted to talk about?"

She flashed him a look of mild exasperation. "No. I need to confess," she said quietly.

Christ. Not again. "What have you done this time?"

She took a deep breath and let it out slowly, but she still didn't raise her eyes. "Last night you completely misunderstood what my issue was, and I let you because it was easier than admitting that I'm plumb crazy."

He tried to stifle a smile as he folded his tie and pushed it into the pocket of his sport coat. Then he leaned one shoulder against the wall and took a pull at his beer. "Plumb crazy, huh?"

She nodded. "You assumed that my . . ." She closed her eyes for a minute, and he could see a blush rising in her face. "My hesitation," she continued carefully, "was because I wanted some sort of commitment." She opened her eyes and finally met his in an agony of embarrassment. "That wasn't the case. It isn't the case. I don't want anything of the sort. I mean, we're just . . ."

This wasn't the conversation he expected. "Just what?"

"We're just enjoying each other. I know our lives are just intersecting, not meshing, and I'm fine with that. There's no point in getting tangled up. I finished my book tonight and—"

"Congratulations. We'll talk about that in a minute. Finish what you were saying," he said.

"My witless behavior last night was the result of . . ." She paused and shrugged. "I don't even know what to term it, Chas. Fear, embarrassment—"

Oh, man. "Miranda, stop," he said gently. His hands slipped around her waist and brought her closer until she placed resisting hands against his chest. Half expecting it, he stepped back immediately, loosening his hold but keeping her within his embrace. "Sorry. Look, whatever I did to cause you—"

"That's just it, Chas. You didn't do anything," she interrupted, on a hard breath that she tried to hide and couldn't. Her eyes were bright with a touch of panic, and her usual elegant motions had given way to abrupt, jerky movements that were more revealing than her words. "I was raised on a mixture of Walter's Southern Baptist Bible-thumping and Mama's halfhearted Catholicism. My mother extolled the virtues of 'waiting', probably because she didn't. I think Walter was terrified of raising the daughter of a fallen woman, so he scared the daylights out of me with his lectures of what happens to fast women. Going to Smith balanced some of that, but as I told you, those years weren't exactly spent in hot pursuit of my G-spot, and then Josh—" She stopped and closed her eyes.

He had to grit his teeth against the anger rising in him and an overwhelming need to hold her tight.

"Looking back, I think Josh was more repelled by sex than anything. I obviously was let believe that what we— I mean Josh and I—that what we had was normal, and I think I just didn't even want to challenge that." She opened her eyes, and he was relieved to see a hint of amusement flickering in their green depths and on her lips. "I have since learned the errors of my beliefs,

thanks to you, but, as they say, all that learnin' hasn't
settled properly yet." Her smile faded to a faint sadness.
"You don't pit a rookie against a pro, Chas. Last night
I just felt like you pulled the rug from beneath my feet.
And I didn't know how to tell you."

Christ. Could I have been a bigger ass? He slowly
brought her close to his chest, his arms tight around her,
and rested his chin on her hair. "I'm the one who should
apologize, Miranda. I should have paid more attention."

"Chas, I didn't tell you all that to make you feel
guilty," she whispered against his chest. "I just needed
to tell you that before I told you what I really want
to say."

Oh hell. There's more. He glanced down as she
glanced up. Her eyes were very green and . . . *wicked?*
He frowned. "What's that?"

"Let's go upstairs. It's time for driver's ed."

CHAPTER
21

Miranda smiled as she watched Jane scurry out of the huge converted warehouse that housed her paintball gallery, cross the sleet-slicked street, and bustle into the diner. Miranda's brief wave caught her attention, and Jane walked over to the table, calling hellos and her order for a cup of coffee to the waitresses behind the counter.

Sliding into the seat, she shrugged out of her heavy jacket and grinned. "It's good to see you. How goes the book?"

Miranda smiled back. "I'm done with the revisions and have begun proofing it."

"Well, I hope you celebrated in a big way."

Miranda smiled. *The party lasted for hours.*

"So are you happy with it? What's it about?"

"It's so much better than I expected it to be," Miranda replied quietly. "It's about a cop and a lawyer, and it's my steamiest yet. I told my editor the love scenes will melt her monitor."

Jane burst out laughing. "How much hotter can books get? Yours are a godsend to single women everywhere, at least in my humble opinion. Every time I get lonely, which is happening altogether too often lately, I reread the book about Reed and it gets me through it. Did you order?" she asked as a waitress ambled toward the table.

"No, I was waiting for you."

"Okay, well, here's a hint: If it's made with grease, they do a wonderful job with it. It's those items involving fresh veggies that never seem to work out. Isn't that so, Brenda?" she said to the waitress who was bearing down on them like the *QE2* coming into port.

"Girl, if you ain't in the mood for grease, what you comin' here for? We specialize. You want veggies, go to one of them places got ferns that's 'live." She jerked her pencil toward the ceiling, from which hung several baskets of Boston ferns. All of them had been dead for at least a decade. "You know you got good food when the cops keep coming back. And here they come." One hand anchored solidly on her generous, pink nylon–clad hip, Brenda turned her heavily but skillfully made-up face toward the door. "Well, if it isn't my little friend," she bellowed.

"Hey, Brown Sugar."

Laughing, Miranda looked toward the door. Her smile froze when she saw Detectives Murphy and Pellegrini walk through it. She glanced at Jane, who was too absorbed in the goings-on to notice her distress.

"Don't you call me that. I ain't your brown sugar. Thought I told you to get out, anyway. You nothin' but trouble. I oughta throw your skinny white ass out my door for what you said to me last time."

"Brenda, *cara bella*, last time I was here I asked you to marry me," Pellegrini replied with a huge grin, in a voice that carried to every corner of the restaurant despite the vintage Aretha blaring from the speakers.

"Yeah, and you said it in front o' my man. That didn't make for no happy home that night. Don't know why I don't throw your skinny ass out," she repeated with an emphatic shake of her head, which set dancing the myriad crystal beads woven into her elaborately braided and twisted-into-a-pouf hair.

" 'Cause you love me."

"Listen to you."

"Brenda, baby, you can do anything you want to me except sit on me. It's the one thing I'd never survive."

"Damn straight, little man. I'd squash you like a bug,

but you'd die happy." She lifted her chin and spun her considerable curves toward Miranda and Jane. "You girls know what you want?"

Miranda saw the cops' eyes light on her, and she smiled, if a bit tensely. By the time she and Jane had placed their order and Brenda had harrumphed her way to another table, Pellegrini was standing in front of them. Murphy stood behind him, studying her with an amused but disdainful intensity. It sent a chill down Miranda's back. She smiled and returned her gaze to Detective Pellegrini.

"Well, if it isn't Hotshot," he said with a grin. "What have you been up to lately? Terrorizing men, as usual?"

Miranda bit back her laughter. "I'm not that bad, Detective."

"Call me Tony." He slid his eyes to Jane, who, Miranda noted with interest, seemed flustered. "So, what's the deal, JJ? Did you bring her in as a ringer just to shake us up that day? Doesn't look like Chas has recovered yet."

"Oh, he will soon enough," Murphy said in a quiet, snide tone that Miranda didn't like one bit.

She kept her smile firmly in place and watched as Jane shook her blond head and glanced up at Tony Pellegrini. "No. I didn't even know she could shoot a gun, much less hit something." When Jane looked away, Miranda could have sworn she was blushing.

Tony nodded, not saying anything as he openly studied Jane's fidgeting hands; then he grinned again and glanced at Miranda. "Well, good seeing you again, ladies. Enjoy your lunch."

The men turned to walk away; then Brian Murphy turned back. "By the way, I liked the excerpt of your book. It's very, uh, realistic. I saw it this morning on your publisher's Web site."

Although he was smiling a bland, harmless smile at her, Miranda felt a cold thread of evil slide along her spine. "Thank you," she said automatically, and was rewarded by a conspirator's wink as he turned to walk to an empty table at the far end of the restaurant.

Jane looked at her. "What was all that about?"

"I'm not sure," Miranda murmured. "My editor wanted an exccrpt for the Web site, so I sent her one."

"What is it about?"

"Paintball."

"Like what happened at my—"

Miranda shrugged. "I modified it."

"Why would he bring it up in such a creepy way?"

"I think he and Chas don't get along very well," she replied. "He asked me out."

Janey's blue eyes widened. "Did you go?"

"I met him for coffee."

"And?"

"And nothing. He's what my mother would have called a dullard. Anyway, I'm not going to spend my time with *you* thinking about *him*." Miranda lifted her coffee cup to her lips. "Is there anything you want to tell me?" she asked over its rim.

"About what?" Jane asked, not meeting her eyes.

"A certain cute detective who made you blush a few minutes ago?"

"I don't know what you're talking about."

"Really?"

"Positive."

Miranda set down her cup and leaned against the back of the booth with a smile. "Sorry. Occupational hazard. I see the potential for romance where absolutely none exists. It happens all thc time."

"Does that include seeing it when you look in the mirror? Paxton let it slip to my mother that you haven't been home a few mornings when Her Highness came to call."

"*She told your* mother? Good Lord." Miranda looked up to see their waitress bearing down on the table, arms laden with plates of food guaranteed to clog even the cleanest arteries. "What perfect timing. Here comes Brenda."

Miranda lifted her head from the back of the chaise lounge, where she lay cocooned in a luxurious mohair throw. The weather had returned to being what autumn should be. It was cool and breezy and clear for a change.

Shading her eyes against the setting sun, she glanced at the tiny screen on her cell phone and clicked onto the call with a smile. "Hello."

"How are things?" Amy asked, getting straight to the point as usual.

"Excellent. It's finished. I'm putting it in the mail tomorrow."

"How's the sex?"

Miranda blinked at the question, then laughed. "Fabulous. Tell Ellen to wear asbestos gloves when she handles that envelope."

"I'll pass on the message. Are you happy with it?"

"Very."

"Why?"

"Because it's the best thing I've ever written. The other ones hummed. This one sings, Amy. It's a full-throated aria that bounces off the rafters."

Amy laughed. "Good girl. I'll read it as soon as I get it and send it on to Ellen right away. Now, what are you going to start on next? Use simple words. I'm a simple woman."

Miranda smiled. "I'm not sure what I want to do," she said at last. "I'll try to put together a proposal for a follow-up to this one, but I think I want to write something big."

"Big as in a thousand pages or big as in best seller? Or both, like Diana Gabaldon? Big issues, big words, what? Don't go artistic on me."

Miranda squinted into the sunshine. "I'm not sure," she repeated. "The ideas are still just dust motes. Let me think about it while we see how everything settles."

"Okay. So when do you head back to Atlanta? Are you staying around to spend Thanksgiving with the barefoot contessa?"

"No way. The contessa is not only barefoot, she's pregnant again. I'm not sure what I'm going to do once you have the book. Catch up on my sleep, maybe. I'm still intending to leave on Wednesday." As she said them, the words sounded hollow in her ears. Today was Sunday. *Three days.* Thin, dark fumes of disappointment spiraled through her good mood. "I'm sorry. What did you say?"

"I asked you if you were serious. Why would you leave on Wednesday? It's the busiest travel day of the year. Every schmuck in Brooklyn heads to Jersey to Grandma's house, and every schmuck in New Jersey heads to Aunt Tilly's on Long Island. It's a nightmare. It will take you eight hours to cross the George Washington Bridge. And the turnpike will be madness. Leave on Thursday. Or Friday."

"I can't. I don't have anywhere to stay. This place is being cleaned on Wednesday, and the tour starts Friday."

"Oh." Amy paused. "I have another call that I have to take. I'll talk to you soon."

Miranda hung up the phone and rested her head against the cushion. Two planes moved across the sky, their contrails forming a large X right over her head. The winds diffused them and they widened, expanding the point of intersection. The planes kept moving forward.

Just like Chas and me.

She pushed away the thought and forced herself to smile. *I've finished the book from hell. I'm free of the rewrites, free of the deadline, free of the funk. Free to get pulled under by the riptide of his magnetism for the next three days.*

In the past ten days Chas had gone from being a specimen under a microscope to a living fantasy. She had nothing to complain about other than that the fantasy was coming to a close. They'd had two nights of amazing sex. Three if she counted Tuesday, which had been sex but not amazing.

And she had three more days with him. And three nights. Then a smile and a wave and a long drive home. An uncomfortable tightness pricked behind her eyes and she blinked against it. *It's a fling,* she reminded herself firmly. A nice, sexy, romantic vacation fling that she'd known from the start would end practically before it began. She had no claims on his time and wanted none.

She was more relieved than surprised when she saw the door slide open and Paxton step onto the deck. At least she wouldn't be allowed to wallow in utterly ridiculous, pointless, immature, and self-defeating thoughts.

"What are you doing out here?" Paxton asked. "It's freezing."

"I'm breathing air that doesn't smell like paint fumes. And celebrating the fact that I have proofed, printed, and packaged my manuscript," Miranda replied with a deliberately lazy smile.

"Congratulations," Paxton replied, sitting down in the chair across from her. "I'm not sure whether I should thank Chas, or kill him."

"I can understand that. What has he done?"

Paxton set her supersize Kate Spade handbag on the deck with a small crash and leaned back, fixing her ice-blue, laserlike gaze on Miranda. "He set us up."

"Who?"

"James and me."

"Set you up how?"

Paxton paused ominously. "He set us up on a blind date," she said pronouncing each syllable and every consonant with razor-sharp precision. "Last night." She let out a tight breath. "He called me Friday afternoon and asked me to meet him for dinner at the Ritz-Carlton at eight because he wanted to talk about James. And he told James to meet him there at seven forty-five because he wanted to talk about you. We both should have figured something was up, but it was a hectic day and we didn't, so I walked in and there was James at the table instead of Chas. Then the mâitre d' comes over and hands him a handwritten note from Chas that said, 'Paxton thinks you're having an affair. Work it out.'" She let out a harsh breath that ended in a reluctant laugh. "The dessert arrived with a key to a room."

Chas Casey, you are a wonderful man, Miranda thought as a deep warmth built within her.

Paxton tilted her head against the back of the chair and smiled a bit sheepishly. "Poor James. He was so stunned he actually had tears in his eyes. He couldn't believe I would think he was capable of it. Of course, he did lie about London, but apparently he went over there with the architect to find some things for the house and to find someone to fix the fountain. It was supposed to be a surprise, because he'd told me when we bought the place that it would cost too much to fix it." She shook her head with a smile. "I'm such an idiot. For your information, the condition is called progesterone poisoning, it lasts for forty weeks, and you'd think I'd recognize the symptoms, since I've had it twice already." She sighed. "So how are you doing? Are you still planning to leave on Wednesday?"

"Of course," she replied with a false smile.

"You don't want to, do you?"

Miranda lifted her glass of tea to her lips and took a sip to hide her surprise at the question. "Of course I do. Atlanta is home, Paxton. It's where my life is. This was just a vacation."

"And Chas is just a fling?"

Miranda stiffened against the pang that ricocheted through her chest. "I'd rather not discuss it, if you don't mind."

Paxton nodded, then tilted her head toward the doors. "It's coming along nicely, don't you think?"

"It doesn't look like the same place I walked into three weeks ago," Miranda replied. There was no point in telling Paxton that she preferred the warm, foresty tones of the original decorating scheme to the vibrant, sleek design that had taken over.

"No, it certainly doesn't," Paxton murmured. "I must be getting old, because, personally, I wouldn't be able to live here the way it is now. It's gone from cozy to sterile. But lushly sterile, if that's not too oxymoronic."

"No, I know what you mean. It's kind of like an operating room done in tropicals. But the transition from soothing to blinding has been kind of interesting. The chaos in the house and in the color schemes has made life seem tame by comparison."

"By comparison?" Paxton lifted an eyebrow. "What else is going on?"

Ain't chasin' that rabbit, honey. She smiled. "Oh, nothing, really. I hadn't expected this to be quite such a working vacation, that's all. I've hardly seen you or Jane."

Paxton's silence was an indictment in itself, and Miranda cringed inwardly.

"Well, I'll get out of your hair," Paxton said a moment later, then stood up. "We should try to have lunch before you leave."

Miranda walked her to the door. "I'd like that. Pick a day."

"I'll get back to you," Paxton replied, and pulled the door shut behind her.

"We haven't done anything to celebrate the completion of your book," Chas said, fighting a yawn as they sat on the couch in the living room watching the fire. It was two o'clock in the morning. He'd just arrived.

Miranda glanced up at him with tired amusement. "We haven't done anything to celebrate the completion of your shift either. I've finished lots of books. It's what I do, Chas."

"But this was a real trial for you." He yawned again. "I'm sorry. I'm wiped out. Let's go to bed."

She stood up slowly and stretched, and together they walked through the condo turning off lights.

"Will you be in town for Thanksgiving?" he asked after they were in bed and curled into each other. Her whole body stiffened, which didn't surprise him.

"No. I'm leaving on Wednesday," she replied, her voice tight and wary.

"You're not going to make very good time, you know. The roads will be clogged in every direction. Why not stay over and leave on Friday? Actually, Sunday would probably be better. Think of how many shopping malls there are between here and Atlanta."

She squirmed to change her position, and looked up at him with a frown. "What in the Sam Hill are you talking about?"

All of her movements served to awaken parts of him that had been nearly asleep only seconds before. He let his hand drift across her back. "Wednesday is the biggest travel day of the year, and Friday is the biggest shopping day of the year, so you're screwed either way. The only time traffic will be moving all weekend is on Thursday afternoon. Why not stay over until Monday?"

She laid her head back onto his chest, not entirely relaxed. "Because I don't have any place to stay. I have to be out of here on Wednesday."

"There's room in my bed," he murmured, letting his hands smooth over the warm length of her thigh and back again.

"It's better if I stick to my original timetable. I thought you were tired."

"I was. Things change," he said against her mouth. "What's waiting for you in Atlanta on Friday?"

"Nothing," she replied warily.

He concentrated on teasing her until he heard her breathing change. "Then why don't you stick around for a while? Just for a few extra days. I have Tuesday, Wednesday, and Thursday off. We can play."

"This is totally unfair," she said breathlessly, trying to keep his hands at bay. "If I stay, things will get messy, Chas."

"Why?"

"Because a few days could turn into a week, and suddenly I'm dealing with mud pies in summer."

"What does that mean?"

She sighed. "There's no way to handle them without getting sloppy. Thank you again, Chas, but I really can't stay."

"Won't."

"That's right. I won't." She rolled away from him and turned on the bedside lamp. Her eyes were soft with remorse but lit with determination. "I know I sound ungrateful or at least ungracious, Chas. But I'm neither. To be perfectly blunt about it, holidays are not my best time of year, and I'm not good company. My mother died the day before Thanksgiving. I've gotten used to not having anyone around on holidays, and I don't want to mess with that." She stopped and looked away. Her voice was softer when she continued.

"There's a reason writers tend to be recluses, Chas. As a whole, we're not only crazy, we're superstitious.

Changing things too much upsets the muse, or makes us lose our mojo, or something. I already know I'm going to beat myself up over falling for you in the first place. I can't set myself up for round two. Please understand." She met his eyes with a smile as brave and painful as any he'd ever seen. It wrenched something loose in him he'd always considered secure.

"No promises. I have three days to make you change your mind," he said, sliding his hands through her hair and guiding her lips to his.

CHAPTER
22

It was late on Tuesday morning when Miranda looked around the condo's master bedroom for the last time. She'd gone through every drawer and closet in the place twice, and had checked under every piece of furniture to make sure she wasn't leaving anything behind. Pulling the zipper shut on her duffel bag, she felt the first wave of her departure wash over her. It was a bit premature and she knew it, but leaving anywhere she'd enjoyed herself always gave her a pang. She'd remained adamant about not extending her stay, but had conceded to staying at Chas's house tonight. She was going to leave Stamford whenever they woke up, and that was final. Of course, before that happened, she had to get through tonight.

She glanced at the doorway. He filled it, smiling and watching her with an affectionate warmth that she wished she could misinterpret. "You're blocking my only escape route."

"I know. I'd have handcuffs on you already except that it would make it difficult to drive separate cars," he said with a grin, walking toward her. He ran his hands down her arms in a way that had become familiar, and right now it chased away her shivers, leaving her warm inside.

She looked into his deep, dark eyes and wished her

feelings weren't so visible, wished her emotions weren't so mixed. Wished she was sure she could talk without getting upset.

He shook his head in mild exasperation. "You're making me feel like I should apologize for something, Miranda. Come on. It's time," he said. Picking up her duffel bag in one hand and her hand in his other, he led her out of the room.

"So where did you learn to cook?" she asked as they stood in his kitchen a few hours later. The quick trip to his house had been followed by a decadent and leisurely afternoon in bed, which didn't end until the sun had set and real hunger had set in.

He glanced at her with one eyebrow raised. "Small talk? After—"

"Okay, fine, darlin'. You choose the topic," she interrupted with a laugh.

"If you grew up with a cop for a father, why did you need to interview me?"

Memo to self: Do not ever let him pick the topic again. "Policing a military installation in the Deep South a few decades ago and being a detective in a Northern city in a post–September eleventh world are pretty different things. Wouldn't you agree?" she replied, trying to keep a chill out of her voice.

"Of course, but you wanted to know how being a cop affected my personal life. I doubt that has changed much in—"

"Some memories are best left undisturbed, Chas."

He didn't reply, and neither of them spoke for a few moments.

"At what point did Miranda Lane become a brunette?" he asked eventually, a teasing note in his voice.

She smiled and felt her shoulders loosen. She hadn't realized she'd tensed them. "How long have you been harboring that one? It sounds rehearsed."

"A week, give or take a few hours."

She rolled her eyes. "Miranda Lane has always been a brunette. Miranda Burrows was a blonde, but she ceased to exist."

"You changed your name?"

She shrugged. "I had no reason not to. Walter didn't want any part of me. Turnabout is fair play. I decided I didn't want any part of my old life."

"Why did you choose Lane?"

"It was my mother's maiden name and the only name that means anything to me." She looked down at the lettuce she was tearing. It was in amoeba-sized pieces. She set it aside and rinsed her hands. "Look, Chas, if you need to hear the ugly truth, here it is: As far as I'm concerned, I don't have a father. A man contributed to my conception and a man helped raise me, but neither are what I'd call a father."

"Miranda, knock it off," he said sharply.

"Knock what off?" She heard the acid creep into her tone. "For all I know, I could be the result of a one-night stand, or a rape, or a romance gone wrong. I'll never know, and there's nothing I can do about it now, anyway. I don't have 'family,' Chas. There's no one I can ask questions of, no one who's going to tell me the truth or even pretty lies. I don't expect you to understand. You can't possibly. You knew your father, and he was a hero not only in your family but in real life."

He didn't respond. She reached for the tomatoes and started slicing.

"Do you think your mother was going to tell you someday?"

"Like when I was twenty-five?" she snapped. She put down the knife she was using and looked at him, using a deep breath to keep her emotions from slipping into her voice. "I'm sorry. I was eighteen when she died, Chas. I'd already moved away from home, about as far away from the Deep South as a girl can get. I was at *Smith*, for God's sake. It took me a while, but eventually I realized that I was never meant to go back. She raised me and pushed me out of the nest. If she had lived, I never would have fit in at home again. My mother and Walter were good people, Chas. Decent, hardworking, righteous people with hearts and consciences who lived by a moral code." She heard her voice break and stopped, looked down. "I'll never have any idea why she wanted me to go to Smith, and I'll never understand how on this green earth she got me there. But that's what happened. Can we please not talk about this anymore?"

"Sure," he said quietly.

She knew that if she walked out of the kitchen to blow her nose or compose herself, she'd fall apart. *There is nothing like an audience to keep one in line.* She closed her eyes for a moment, then picked up the knife and continued slicing tomatoes. The repetitive task gave her strength, and she was thankful that he didn't try to give her a hug, as Josh might have done, or refuse to drop the subject, as Paxton might have done. He just let her be.

It felt late, but it was only eight-thirty when Chas and Miranda finished the dishes and sat on the couch. She curled into his side, holding his left hand as he idly channel-surfed with his right. Neither was interested in watching anything on television, but going to bed was out of the question for the moment. She was still wound up from their predinner conversation, and he was lost in thoughts of his own.

Some of his old rules no longer applied, and he wasn't comfortable investigating new terrain at this stage in his life, at least not on a deadline. Unfortunately, Joe's off-hand comment from the other night was haunting him. It *was* too soon to let her go away. There was too much about her he wanted to learn, and no time left to learn it. Chas didn't know how much longer he wanted her to stay, but just longer would do for the moment. He was braced for a fight, prepared to say or do anything within reason to make her stay. As to knowing what "within reason" meant, he was going to have to go with his gut.

He turned to find her watching him with a smile, her hair fanned out against his arm. Dropping the remote, his hand found hers and raised it to his lips.

"So why are you a cop, Chas? Really?" she asked softly, bringing his hand to her lips.

Where the hell did that come from? "What do you mean, 'really'? I've told you why."

"You told me it was because your father was a cop, but I don't think that's it."

He shrugged. "A man's got to do something."

"Why not investment banking, then? Or consulting? Why be a cop?"

He gave her a smile that was deliberately indulgent and patronizing. Despite her softness, he knew she was trying—consciously or not—to pick a fight. He also knew why. An angry departure was easier than a sad one, and she had a long drive ahead of her, after all. Dealing with New York drivers hard on the heels of an argument could keep her adrenaline flowing until she hit Philadelphia.

If she left.

"You ask too many questions. Why romance writing, Miranda?"

Her gaze flicked over his face as the softness faded from her eyes. "The short answer is because I type fast, I can do it from home in my jammies, and I like the buzz. The business answer is that I have a good imagination, a distinctive writing style that people seem to like, and I can make people believe in fantasy. And the marketing answer is that my readers tell me I do noble things that I never intended to do, like give them respite and hope and the courage to try."

"That's more than a lot of people can say."

She smiled. "I know, and it's one of the best-kept secrets of the sisterhood. We may be laughed at by snobs and sneered at by intellectuals and ignored by *The New York Times Book Review,* but I doubt John Grisham or Tom Clancy or James Patterson get nearly as many letters from people saying their books soothed a troubled soul or healed a breach or changed a life."

"Is your book going to change mine?"

Her look became guarded and she sat up straight. "Only if you let it, Chas."

"What if I said its author already had?" He asked the question easily, attempting lightness so as to not take her too much by surprise, but he knew within seconds that he'd made a mistake. A huge mistake. This was

Miranda, after all. The woman could not be trusted to respond conventionally to anything, particularly something she viewed as a threat.

"Don't do this to me, Chas. Don't ruin this night for me," she replied in a voice so low it almost shook with the strain. She didn't say anything more, just turned to look at the television. She didn't let go of his hand, though, and he wondered if she realized how tightly she was gripping it.

Why had he said it? What good did he think it could possibly do? What reality could it possibly change? Miranda was as tense as an overwound spring; a word, a breath away from a twisting, spinning emotional frenzy that would take her someplace she did *not* want to go. She didn't like being out of control in any instance, but tonight of all nights, out of control would be the worst thing to be.

If she was going to make it through the conversation and the lovemaking and the leave-taking, *she* had to be the one to control the situation. When he flicked off the TV and stood up after twenty minutes of silence, she wasn't sure whether she was glad to leave the suffocating confines of the study or if she wanted him to keep flicking from channel to channel just to postpone the inevitable. Her mother had always told her there were only two ways to deal with deep water: you could go through it or you could go around it. As Miranda accepted his outstretched hand and stood up, she swore she could feel her feet get wet.

Their silence continued as they walked through the house turning off lights. When they returned to the bottom of the stairs, he dropped a kiss on her lips, then paused and did it again. They walked upstairs to his bedroom slowly, and once there he lit the gas fireplaces, led her to the couch farthest away from the bed, and pulled her onto his lap. It was so reminiscent of their first night together that the knowledge of what they'd shared since then seemed to be on the verge of crushing her.

She brought her hands up to his chest, met his eyes. *Torture.* "I don't want to talk, Chas."

"Miranda," he began softly.

"I don't want to talk," she repeated. "Make love to me."

He was watching her, studying her with his cop face in place, and she knew that tonight was going to be worse than she had imagined. He was looking for an advantage. He was playing to win. He would persuade or reason or even counterattack, but Chas intended to win.

So did she, and it was her game, her call.

She slid off his lap and tugged gently on his hand. He stood up, and together they crossed the room. They were almost to the foot of his bed when he kissed her. It was a strange kiss, chaste and passionless and calm. His hands were slow as they began to undress her, and the knowledge that this might be punishment for leaving him threatened to break the slim thread of her control.

A breath dangerously close to a sob escaped from her as his warm hands rounded her waist, and the sound transformed her tension into rage.

"No, Chas. Not like that," she whispered harshly. She slid her hands from around his neck to his shirtfront and ripped it open, sending buttons scattering. She pushed it off his shoulders and dug her nails into the flesh she'd uncovered, demanding wordlessly that his tenderness become ferocity, insisting silently that his gentleness become power.

"Damn you, Miranda," he said against her lips, his voice fierce and unrestrained.

Their mouths met again in a passionate clash of wills. Clothes were discarded roughly and their bodies fell together onto the bed as if there were no time left for gentleness. They had hard, hot, primal sex that catapulted her outside herself into a realm that was both dark and light, hot and cold, and neither safe nor secure, and afterward they both fell back, silent except for ragged, shuddering breaths.

Limbs tangled, chests heaving, they lay facing each other, and she knew the raw, aching need inside her had

been set aside, not satisfied. She lifted an arm, still heavy
with remembered exertion, and slid her fingers through
his hair. They came away wet, slick with sweat. She drew
them down his cheek, across his lips, his shoulders, down
his arm. His eyes, dark with a burning eloquence, never
left hers, even when he moved forward and captured her
mouth. She moved against him, let his hands claim her,
possess her again, slowly this time. It was quiet, gentle.
Erotic. And they held each other afterward, stroking,
soothing, still not speaking. As if, Miranda thought, he
knew that words would destroy her.

She awakened instantly, not sure how long she'd been
asleep. Through the skylight above her she could see
that the night sky was still dark, displaying no signs of
dawn.

"Miranda."

The repeated word was more a breath than a question,
yet she knew what lay within it. She didn't turn to him.
She didn't need to see his face to know the look he
wore. "I can't stay, Chas."

"Why?"

She knew she could get through this without getting
emotional. She had no emotions left. "Do we have to
talk about it? It's going to be difficult enough to say
good-bye in a few hours without having lots of other
words to remember or regret," she said softly, aiming
her words at the ceiling.

"I think we have something to talk about."

"You're part of this chapter of my life, not the next,
darlin'." She leaned up on one elbow and placed a finger
across his lips. "I taught myself long ago not to lean too
heavily on anyone, and I know you well enough to know
you'd let me lean. I need to know I can do this alone."

"Do what?"

"Live," she said after a moment.

"I'm not talking about a lifetime."

She gave a silent laugh. "A lot of women would be
offended by that comment."

"You're not like any other woman. Stay, Miranda.
Just for a few days."

"Just to keep you company?" She smiled. "Chas, I really like you, but it's over and I have to leave. There's no point in staying." She reached up and smoothed her hand along his face, willing her fingers to remember its contours and texture. "From a purely practical stand-point, what would I do with myself?"

"Work on that proposal you came up here to write." He rolled onto his back. They weren't touching any-more. Not a stray leg or an idle brush of a hand. "I like you," he said after a moment. "I like you a lot. I care about you."

"They're lovely words, Chas—"

"I want to know you better."

She closed her eyes and clenched every muscle in her body against the onslaught. "To what end?" she asked, keeping her voice easy. "I don't want a commitment, but when I eliminate the standard options, I don't find what's left too appealing. I'm not interested in a casual, long-distance thing."

He caught her fingers and brought them to his mouth, flirted with them, nuzzled them. "Why not?"

"Because I don't do casual well. Obviously." She pulled her fingers away. "Being in a casual relationship with you would keep me in limbo, and that's one place I don't want to be. I like the idea of monogamy, but I realize it's an acquired taste. You're not a long-term guy. And I don't mean to imply that I want you long-term anyway." She gave a light laugh that cost her a lot. "I know that sounds awful. What I mean is that I don't want you to change, and you don't want to change. I like security, Chas, but I don't need or want someone else, a man, to give it to me. I like to be settled by myself. You unsettle me, and while it's been a glorious sensation for the last few weeks, it's not something I want to experience for any length of time." She sat up. "I think we just need to end it here, Chas. I don't want you coming down to Atlanta on your weekends off, or inviting me up here. That would be entangling." She paused, and when he didn't respond, she drove it home. "There's no room for negotiation, Chas. I've enjoyed every minute I've spent with you, but whatever we've had will be over in a few hours. If anything happens in the future, it will be something different."

He leaned back on his pillow to watch her, arms beneath his head. His eyes were carefully neutral. "So it just ends? You don't even want me to call you?"

She smiled sadly and nodded. "What would be the point?"

"Keeping in touch."

She shook her head. "That would just make me miss you more, Chas, and I'm going to be doing enough of that without any help."

"Miranda, this is ridiculous. Why should we . . . ?"

She swallowed hard and clamped down on the emotional churn within her, refusing to give in to the tears that ached at the back of her eyes. "Because there's no point to continuing. Telephone calls are going to end with invitations. Invitations will lead to meetings, and meetings will lead to wonderful things, but they'll also lead to more good-byes, and eventually one will be permanent. I don't want to do that to myself. I'm not like you, Chas. I wouldn't be able to date a guy for a few weeks and then say to him, 'Oh, an old friend is coming into town for a few days; I'll give you a call next week,' and then spend the next few days in and out of bed with you."

She stopped and took a breath, trying to get her voice under control. Her words were coming too fast and sounding too urgent. She had to stay cool to get through it. "Frankly, I wouldn't be able even to go out on a date with another guy, because I'd know I was being unfair to him, and that would be unfair to me, and I just can't do that to myself."

He hadn't moved since she'd started talking, hadn't changed his expression.

She took another deep breath, wrapping her arms around knees that had been pulled against her chest. "Look, Chas, it's not like you'll ever be in a position to move to Atlanta, and there's no reason I'd ever move here. For one thing, I couldn't afford it, and for another, it's full of Yankees. For another, the dating situation would be no different. I don't do casual and you don't do commitment, and neither one of us is looking for a spouse in any case." *Please just agree with me. We both know I'm making sense.*

"So this has been a vacation fling."

"Don't say it in that tone of voice."

"But that's what it is."

She breathed in his annoyance and fed on it, let it calm her. "You're upset because you can't have what you want, Chas, and you're not used to that."

"So I'm a child, too. Wonderful."

"You know me better than that. I'm rarely subtle. If I wanted to insult you, I'd get right to the point." She let a smile glimmer on her lips before continuing softly. "I just mean that you're the fix-it man, and this can't be fixed because it's not broken. This is just the way it works."

They fell silent. He fixed his eyes on the ceiling and eventually she slid next to him. She felt herself begin to drowse again in the dark silence and willed herself to stay awake.

"What about Walter?" he asked.

The word triggered a blast of adrenaline that woke her up instantly. "What about him?"

"Are you going to do anything about him?"

"Like what?"

"Like try to find him." His voice was hard and cold.

"No."

"You're not curious?"

"Not that curious," she said quietly.

"Would you like me to do a rundown?"

Portents of darkness crept to the edges of her mind and crouched there, waiting. "Why? What could you find out?"

"His home address, for one thing. Whatever you'd like to know."

She closed her eyes and took a slow, deep breath. "When did you do it?"

"Yesterday. The file is over there."

"I wish you hadn't."

"Why?"

She paused as anger and helplessness mingled and

rose within her, and waited for them to subside. "It's my life. It's my story. You're interfering."

"You don't have to look at it."

"I know I don't, but now I know it's there. Why did I ever even do this?" she muttered.

"Do what?"

"Tell you anything," she snapped, knowing her words would sting and, perversely, looking forward to watching them hit their mark. "You're the one looking for your father, Chas, not me. I don't want to find mine, and finding yours is all you can think about. To the exclusion of everyone and everything else."

A muscle in his cheek twitched. Other than that small clue, he gave no indication he'd heard her. "You told me because you wanted someone to know. Maybe because you really *do* want to know."

"I want to know what? That Walter still doesn't care?"

Enough was enough. She swung her legs out of bed and reached for the tidy stack of clothes she'd left on top of her duffel bag earlier in the evening.

"No. Why he did what he did."

"He told me why he did it, Chas. Three hours after I buried my mother, he told me," she hissed. "I was a burden he never wanted."

"Those were his words?"

"Close enough."

"What did he say exactly?"

"Why do you care?" She pulled on her jeans and reached for her heavy cotton sweater.

"Because I do. And what does it matter if I know, since we're never going to see each other again?" His words hung in the air, thick and ugly.

She swallowed, her back still to him. Before they formed, the words made her throat swell and close, made her voice rough. "Since you put it that way, Chas, I might as well tell you. He said, 'You were your mama's girl, Miranda. Always just your mama's girl. And now she's gone.' " The image of Walter flashed into her mind. As if he were alive in front of her, she could see his strong, corded arms folded across his broad chest, his wide-legged stance, his unsmiling face, and his eyes. Those hated eyes, so blank, so cold and dark, so disinterested in her pain. She fought the memory with a shudder.

"That's hardly—"

"You weren't there, Chas," she shouted in frustration, viciously blinking back tears she was *not* going to shed. "I told you. Now drop it."

"No. Let's not."

She swung her head to face him, feeling the heat rise up in her, the anger kindle and threaten to explode. "Then I'd rather talk about *you,* Chas. And your search for a father that you somehow think is *not* going to end up under a gravestone." The silence echoed between them as he stared at her with impersonal eyes. She wanted to claw at them. "How much longer are you going to be a cop, Chas? You and I both know that carrying that damned badge is noble but it's not what fulfills you. It's not what makes the lights come on in you. Have you ever stopped to consider why you're doing it?"

She stalked around the room, picking up last night's clothes from where they lay strewn across the floor. His eyes followed her, causing a chill wherever she went. *Damn him and his training.*

"There's no denying your story is tragic, Chas. Rich or poor, if you lose the father you love, you lose the father you love. Trust me on that one." She whirled and stabbed him from across the room with an anger that indicted. "But you're trying to be the man you think your father would have wanted you to be, despite the fact that it breaks your mother's heart and has made you decide to cut yourself off from a side of life you revere. You're a family man to the core, Chas, but having one of your own is the one indulgence you won't allow yourself. I'm beginning to think you're less of an enigma and more of a plain old mess."

"Are you finished?"

"No. No, damn you, Chas Casey, I'm not," she said in a voice low and cold. "What do you think you're going to find, Chas? Do you even know what you're looking for?" she demanded cruelly, wanting to see his face change, wanting to see a reaction. Wanting him to hurt. "Redemption? Salvation? Approval? Everyone thinks the world of you already, Chas. What more could you possibly want? You spend every minute of your life making things better for everyone else." She took the bundle of clothes in her hands and jammed them into the duffel. "You're the perfect son and perfect brother and perfect friend and perfect lover, and the savior of neighborhoods and marriages, and you fight crime in your spare time. You're a God-damned superhero. And none of it is enough, is it? You've still got to keep searching for something you will never find *because it doesn't exist*." She met his cold eyes. "*He's dead, Chas.* And the longer you keep denying that, the longer you'll keep twisting that knife in your mother's heart. You put her through your father's death again every day you wear that badge. Every single day she has to face the possibility of losing you because you want the Holy Grail. Putting yourself in the path of a bullet won't right the wrong, Chas." She turned and bent down to pick up the bag.

"You're running away?" he asked in a voice that was unmoved.

"Not running, just leaving. Good-bye, Chas." She turned and walked down the stairs.

CHAPTER
23

Chas lay in bed, watching her go down the first set of stairs, hearing her descend the next. Eventually he heard the alarm start beeping and he knew she'd walked out the door. He reached over and shut it off using the remote control.

Following her wouldn't do any good; neither would throwing more words at the situation. They'd both said more than was necessary to wound each other, more than enough to make him want her gone. *Then why am I lying here with my gut aching and my body rigid, trying to breathe in every lingering trace of her?*

In a show of calm meant to fool only himself, he folded his hands behind his head, looked up at the ceiling, and tried on the experience of being rejected. It was an awkward fit, painful and full of self-loathing. He'd come on strong deliberately, expecting to win after she put up a good struggle, never expecting her to sink as low as *he* had, never expecting her to execute his worst-case scenario. He'd known from the minute he met her that any weapon in her hands was dangerous because she'd be unafraid to use it. He was an idiot for playing his angle the way he had, for thinking he was immune or out of range. Now he'd not only lost the battle; he'd lost most of his options. The only one that remained

viable was to wait, because he wasn't going to chase her.
Not down the stairs, not across the country.

Why would he? She didn't want to see him or hear
from him. She wanted only to cache him like any other
vacation memory. Make him a pleasant reminiscence.
And the fault was entirely his, for assuring her so convincingly that everything between them was casual when
it was anything but. Now, because of all that, he was
thoroughly fucked.

Miranda had left Chas's house at close to four in the
morning. Anger had counteracted her exhaustion for
about two hundred miles, then perseverance and really
nasty New Jersey Turnpike coffee had fueled her for 150
more. When she pulled off I-95 in Alexandria, Virginia,
she was nearly delirious with fatigue and had no energy
left for rage. She pulled into the parking lot of the hotel
she'd stayed in during her last book tour and was allowed to register even though it was only ten o'clock in
the morning. She walked into the room, then dropped
her bags on the floor and herself onto the bed.

It was two o'clock in the morning when she woke up,
stiff and still dressed. The glow of the street six stories
below her window cast the room in a gray half-light, and
after a few minutes of remembering where she was and
why she'd stopped, she also remembered that the hotel
had twenty-four-hour room service. She ordered something greasy and comforting, then walked into a bathroom that made her nearly limp with delight. Dropping
her clothes where she stood, she stepped straight into
the shower.

The hot water, creamy soap, and jungle-flower shampoo removed all traces of Chas Casey from her body,
but every sleek rivulet that ran over her skin anchored
him more firmly in her mind. And it was there he remained after her hair was dried, her oldest, grungiest,
most comfy sweats were on, her meal had been devoured, and she was curled up on one side of a bed
made for two. That was when she confronted them: the
ghosts of their last hours, the echoes of their last words.

That was when she relived every kiss, every touch. He'd led her to the cliff wall of sanity and over the edge.

She pushed away the memories and began to gather up her belongings. Sitting alone and thinking about him would do no good.

Alexandria was quiet at four thirty in the morning, although the interstate was already starting to gear up. It wasn't until she stopped for gas in Richmond that she turned on her cell phone to check for messages. There were two from Paxton, one from Jane, and one from Amy. None from Chas, and she berated herself for even imagining he'd call. She retrieved Amy's message and was relieved to hear the bittersweet news that Ellen was thrilled with the manuscript. Then she started up her car and got back on the road.

Late that afternoon, Miranda pulled into one of the guest slots near her front door, turned off the engine, and let out a breath heavy with both relief and sadness that she was home under the late-afternoon rays of a Southern sun. The key fit easily into the lock, but the reprieve she'd hoped to feel as she crossed the threshold didn't occur. Nothing had changed in her condo. Her furniture was in it, her prints were on the walls, her clothes in the closets, but it looked smaller and sadder than when she left it. Dustier. And it held a silence so complete it was roaring in her ears, smothering her. After only an hour she had to leave. Still in her sweats, she got back in her car and drove to the grocery store.

The knot of tension in her neck began to loosen as she sat in traffic at the entrance to the strip mall under the shade of a massive magnolia. The parking lot was jammed with last-minute grocery shoppers, yet the pace was easy. There was no chaos, no pandemonium. *Because I'm in the South,* she thought with a sigh. It was civilization. It was home. There were no rude drivers or cold rain to deal with, and there were loads of parking spaces.

She moved up a car length as the minivan in front of her made the right turn into the lot, and she saw the reason for the orderliness. She should have known, should have prepared herself for the eventual sight of the young, sun-burned Atlanta police officer waving her into the vehicular thicket surrounding him. But she hadn't, and the sight of him brought a lump to her throat.

By the time she arrived home with some basic necessities and a few luxuries, she had reached the edge of her emotional chasm and was hanging over the side staring into the yawning darkness of post-traumatic Chas syndrome. Armed with a glass of milk and the small wrapped package of fried chicken and hush puppies she'd gotten from the deli counter, Miranda walked onto her small balcony, opened the package, and inhaled the scents of heaven. Leaning into the soft evening air that held a crisp hint of autumn, she watched the lights of Midtown come to life on Thanksgiving night.

Over the next few days she sent Jane, Paxton, and Amy brief e-mails to let them know she'd arrived, but that didn't stop them from calling, and the last unanswered call from Jane had definitely been a concerned one. Her local friends, too, had begun calling to see if she was back, but she didn't feel like talking to them, either. They'd want to hear about her trip, and she didn't want to get into any of it. Didn't want to see the questioning eyes if she played it straight, which she wouldn't, or the grins and nudges if she bluffed, which she would. It was easier to shut off the phone, close the blinds, and let the world pass her by.

Wednesday morning at ten o'clock, however, the world came looking for her, literally. Miranda pulled open the door and squinted into the sunshine.

"Good Lord, Miranda, what in the Sam Hill did those Yankees to do you?" The honeyed, West Texas twang of her friend and fellow author Molly Crandall held laughter and incredulity, neither of which Miranda thought was warranted under the circumstances.

"Nothing. I just woke up."

"That's not what I mean. You look like you've been rode hard and put away wet a couple of days in a row, bless your heart," Molly remarked, breezing through the doorway in a perfumed swath of made-up, coiffed, and color-coordinated Southern womanhood. "When did you get back? I've been leaving messages."

"I know. I'm sorry for not getting back to you. I just needed a little time to regenerate. It was a long drive."

"You mean recuperate."

"No, I don't," Miranda mumbled as she shut the door.

"Regenerate what then?"

My life. Miranda shrugged silently and walked past her into the kitchen.

"When did you get back?" Molly repeated.

"Thursday afternoon. Want some coffee?"

"I'd prefer sweet tea, thank you, if you remember what that is." She paused. "It's Wednesday, Miranda. People don't take that long to recover from malaria, much less a thousand-mile drive." She followed Miranda to the small kitchen, tapping across the floor on tiny, high-arched, mule-clad feet. "What have you been doing since you've been home? Please don't say cleaning, 'cause I'll be forced to call you on a lie."

Miranda shot her a look. "Obviously not. I've been sleeping."

"Sleeping? For six days?"

"It was a taxing time up there and a long, tiring drive home." Miranda slid a tall glass of sweet tea across the counter.

"Thank you. We have a book signing tonight, my dear, in case you've forgotten." Molly's eyes flicked over her critically. "You only have six hours or so to get ready, and it's going to take you nearly that long, if I'm any judge. Get started. We're meeting Wendy for lunch in Virginia Highlands at twelve thirty," she said briskly.

"Did you come over just to make me feel good?"

Molly swallowed her dainty sip of tea. "Actually, I came over to find out if there was a bad smell coming from beneath your door and identify the body if there was. Just how much weight have you lost?"

"None. And I don't really feel like—"

"This is a command performance, sugar," Molly interrupted with a smile. "She signed another three-book deal two weeks ago and has held off celebrating until you got back. You go take a shower. I'll wait."

*   *   *

Lunch lasted forever, and was followed by some serious shopping on her friends' part. At the moment Miranda couldn't afford to set foot in Phipps Plaza, much less actually shop there. Not until she got the other half of her advance, anyway. And that would have to tide her over until her next proposal was bought. Of course, she reminded herself glumly, a proposal would have to be written first, and an idea would have to be born and grown before *that*. Just the thought of it made her want to crawl back into her unmade nest of a bed.

The book signing was moderately successful, and the requisite smiles and small talk with fans were therapy of sorts. Most of Miranda's books were still in print, even if they weren't exactly recent, which made it even more important to maintain visibility if she wanted to maintain her audience. The trouble was, she didn't want to do any of it. And Molly and Wendy finally wormed that sorry fact out of her over dinner after the signing.

"Honey, we all know that writing isn't a job; it's a disease. And if you're a writer who doesn't want to write, you're depressed. The question is, over what?" Molly sat back and shifted her knowing eyes from Miranda's to Wendy's.

The communication between them was fast and furious, and innately female. Miranda dropped her eyes to her coffee cup. They'd known her for five years. They were smart, savvy, happily remarried women. They knew men and understood life. She sighed. "I fell in love. I think I did, anyway. He's perfect, and I left him."

"What did you just say, darlin'?" Wendy demanded after a moment of stunned silence.

"Miranda? Did I hear you right?" Molly asked as a follow-up.

She nodded.

"Keep talking, shug. I'll order us another bottle of wine."

"I don't really want to get into the gory details, if you don't mind, and I don't need any more wine. But thanks just the same." Miranda offered them a tight smile. "The high-concept synopsis is that he doesn't do commitment and I don't do casual. That's in addition to the problem of geography."

"Geography isn't a problem; it's an adventure," Wendy corrected her, leaning forward conspiratorially. "And as for the commitment thing, sugar, we can tackle that. It's what we do best. Isn't that a basic trait for every hero we write about?"

Miranda gave a silent laugh. "Of course it is, but we make our living telling pretty lies. If our story lines worked out in real life, we wouldn't be novelists; we'd be therapists." She avoided looking at Molly, whose tastefully highlighted head was tilted in her direction.

"I don't think commitment and geography are the only plot devices in play," Molly said quietly. "You slept with him, obviously. Did he ask you to stay?"

Miranda took a deep, controlling breath and nodded, feeling a cloud of wild butterflies take flight in her stomach.

"Did he ask you to marry him?" Wendy asked.

"No. I think I don't want to talk about this anymore. Let's change the subject," Miranda said, and reached for her cooling cup of coffee, feeling rather than seeing the look her friends exchanged. Wendy, a truly incurable romantic, was about to go all soft and sympathetic. Molly, who was a firmly grounded realist behind all that Texas hair and perfect makeup, would not let that happen.

"I agree. You tell us more when you're good and ready," Molly said briskly, signaling for the check. "In the meantime, child, you work it off. You set that alarm clock, get that behind out of bed, and park it at your desk for a few hours a day. You've got bills to pay and books to write, and none of them are going to get taken care of if you're asleep."

Starting the next day, Miranda put herself on a schedule. In the absence of creativity, a little discipline went a long way toward keeping her on track and at least marginally productive. When the alarm went off at seven, she dragged herself into the shower. She wrote for four hours, then ran errands, worked out, and did her chores in the afternoon. By seven o'clock in the evening, she was back at her laptop, pounding away. Nothing she was writing was any good, but she was filling pages and keeping her mind off Chas.

That schedule worked without interruption for a month. Molly had taken to stopping by or calling at least once a day. She said it was just to catch up, but Miranda knew it was to check up on her. At first it was to ensure that she wasn't retreating back under the covers. Now it was to make sure she was writing. Miranda was ready for some privacy as the reality of life without Chas began to settle in her mind.

On a Friday afternoon dangerously close to Christmas, Miranda had been successfully edging Molly to the front door when the doorbell rang. By the time Miranda returned to the living room with three FedEx envelopes in her hands, Molly was back on the couch with a fresh glass of iced tea in her hand.

"My, my, who loves you so much?" Molly asked, glancing at the thick packets.

"Ellen Barber," she said, looking at the address label on the first. "Obviously my galleys, which I have two days to review." She flipped it up and against her chest. "Cover flats." She lifted the second out of the way and her heart stopped as Chas's handwriting confronted her on the third.

"What?"

The question sounded faint, dimmed by the thudding of her heart, which echoed in her brain. "Oh, um, a proposal. Amy said she was going to send it back with Ellen's comments," she lied. "I didn't expect it so soon, bless her heart."

"I didn't think you had any proposals out to her."

Miranda looked up with a smile and shrugged. "It was an old one that she'd been sitting on," she said. "I'll be fine, shug. I promise. Thanks for checking up on me."

"I'm not checking up on you, Miranda. I'm just being social," Molly protested, and stood up slowly. "Besides, you haven't been yourself since you got back."

"I wasn't myself when I was there, either. I know I've

been a basket case, but I'm done with all that. You run on home and I'll call you tomorrow."

"Call tonight if you need me."

"I will."

Miranda hugged her tight, which surprised them both, then shut the door behind her. She went straight to the packet from Chas and tore it open. It was a slim manila file folder with a note paper clipped to the front.

I came across this yesterday and thought you should have it in case you change your mind someday. Regards, Chas.

The warm flutter of unrealistic expectations died and cold dread settled in her stomach like a chunk of dirty ice as she stared at the folder without opening it. It was the report he'd run on Walter. It had to be. She closed her eyes for a moment, telling herself that she might as well grind this day to dust right now rather than put the report aside, only to spoil a different one.

She took it over to the couch and sat down, opening it on the coffee table. One computer printout and three sheets of a legal pad covered with Chas's clear, strong handwriting were all it contained. She picked up the printout and began to read.

When she was done, she opened her laptop. Eyes closed, fingers flying, she emptied her soul onto a silicon chip.

CHAPTER
24

Chas glanced at the calendar on the wall of his mother's kitchen. She'd been gone for a month. A month he'd kept filled with women, and work, and working out. And overtime and meetings like this one. He brought his attention back to Special Agent Sarah McAllister.

"We finally got a break at about four o'clock local time this morning," she said. "A script kiddie in an Internet chat room started boasting about getting some classified material. It happened to be a site one of our surveillance teams was monitoring for another investigation. Luckily the kid had more ego than sense and responded to the agents' questions. He was picked up for questioning several hours ago at his parents' home in New Orleans. He's seventeen and in the mood to cooperate. I'll be flying down there later today." She smiled tiredly. "It looks like the hackers are in Marseille. We've contacted the French authorities and are working with them to take suspects into custody as quickly as we can. Now, on this end—"

Chas glanced down at the gently vibrating cell phone clipped to his belt and checked the screen. He excused himself despite his mother's and brother's raised eyebrows and walked toward the library as he took the call from his captain.

"Casey," he said abruptly.

"Got a minute?"

"Yeah. What's up?"

"The chief just released the commission's decision. You didn't get it. Murphy did." The words were as blunt as the voice and hit Chas like a fist in the gut.

Anger and adrenaline surged through him. He clamped down on the reaction immediately and closed the library doors behind him carefully before replying. "Is this some sort of joke? It was practically a done deal. How the fuck did this happen?"

A slow, heavy breath preceded the captain's answer. "It's no joke, Chas. The chief changed his recommendation. I thought you'd want to hear it from me."

"What?" Chas stared in disbelief out the window, not seeing anything beyond it. "He . . . What the hell did he do that for? When?"

"About the time you started helping that writer."

The irony in the older man's voice was unmistakable and replaced the hot anger in Chas's veins with a hard freeze. "What does Miranda have to do with anything?"

"Oh, for Christ's sake, Casey. What do you mean, what does she have to do with it? The chief turned her down. You did an end run around him, and that lazy fuck Murphy made sure everyone knew you did. It's on her Web site, for Christ's sake—"

"Stop. I don't know what you're talking about. The chief turned her down for what? What's on her Web site?" Chas interrupted.

The captain paused for only a second before answering. "She called Prescott with a request to interview a detective from Persons. The chief said no once he found out what she wrote. Didn't want the department to end up looking bad." He paused. "How the hell did you not know? Didn't she tell you?"

A sudden flicker caught his eye and he looked out the side window, his gaze landing, as it always did lately, on the intricate sun catcher Miranda had given his mother. The pendant moved again, sending a shard of blinding light across the room as fast as a conspirator's wink.

Memories of their first date came into sharp focus in his mind's eye. Her pointed questions and teasing eva-

sions. Her carefully maintained distance and deliberate
refusal to get personal.

*God damn her. She knew what she was doing. And I
walked into it like a pussy-whipped fool. How the* hell
could she have done this to me?

"We met through mutual friends. My being a cop
didn't come into it," he replied tightly, staring at the
piece of sparkling crystal with an intensity that should
have melted it back to silicon.

"That's not the way Murphy tells it. Hey, I don't know
from Adam, okay? Murphy said you met her at the
paintball place, and Gruber and Pellegrini corroborated."

"Nobody asked me. Hell of an oversight," he snapped.

"Nobody had to, Chas. You were talking about it that
day. To me. And she put all of it into her book, and
that part of it is sitting on a Web site right now." His
commanding officer's voice had taken on an ominous
trace of annoyance. "Bottom line is that you acted with
blatant disregard for departmental policy. You on
tonight?"

"No."

"Just as well. Go work it off." The captain ended the
call, and Chas slowly closed the flip-phone and placed it
back on its belt clip.

*No wonder she refused to stay. She's a liar and a cow-
ard on top of everything else.*

He heard voices coming toward the library and realized the meeting had ended. Taking a deep breath, he
met the group in the foyer.

"Chas, it's been a pleasure working with you," Sarah
McAllister said with a smile, extending her hand.

He shook it and returned her smile. "Thanks for all
of your help. Let me know if you need anything else."

"I'll be back. I'm going to drop her off at the airport
in White Plains," Joe said, giving him a penetrating look
that told Chas he wasn't hiding his anger well enough.
"Will you be around when I get back?"

Chas nodded and watched them leave, then turned to
his mother and grandfather. "Well, it's over."

"So it is. Now we get to tally up the cost. Would

anybody care to give an estimate?" his mother said dryly as she walked toward the library. "Four years of top-secret research and development sold to the highest bidder on the open market."

"Don't jump to conclusions. We won't know anything until the bad guys talk."

"So what did you think of her, Chas?" his grandfather asked, crossing a path of weak sunlight to settle in one of the leather chairs.

Chas sat in the other chair, his back to the windows, and tried to keep his mind on the conversation. "Sarah? She's smart. Professional. Knows her stuff. Well respected in the industry, from what I've been able to find out. She'd be an excellent choice."

"Do you think she'd take the job?"

Chas met his grandfather's eyes. "Not a chance. She's had offers before. Excellent offers, but the jobs are too tame. She lives for the chase."

"Do you?"

He leaned his head against the back of the chair, his brain still fogged with anger and betrayal—and his own inability to have seen it happening. "I wouldn't say that, but I agree with her that the job seems tame. It's all defensive strategizing and implementation."

"Obviously it isn't, Chas. This wasn't the first time we've had trouble, and it won't be the last," his grandfather replied.

Chas stood up. There was too much adrenaline running through him to sit still. "Joe's the right person for the job," he said flatly, and began to walk to the door.

"Who was on the phone?"

He stopped and looked at his mother in mild surprise. "Captain Maloney."

"With news about your promotion? The commission was supposed to make a decision this week, wasn't it?"

"Murphy got it."

Both his mother and grandfather looked shocked. Neither spoke for a moment.

"Did he give you a reason?"

He remained silent for a moment, securing his anger in a safe place. "Apparently I acted with blatant disregard for departmental policy when I helped Miranda with her book."

"Good God, Chas. You can't be serious—" his mother began.

"She had requested permission to interview a detective, and her request was denied. It was a small fact she never bothered to mention, and it never occurred to me to ask if she'd gone through official channels. Excuse me, would you?" he replied tightly, leaving the room without a destination in mind. He didn't much care where he went, but he wasn't going to sit around while they worked out just how thoroughly she'd made a fool of him and just how easily he'd let her.

"What am I doing here?" Miranda whispered as she sat in her car in the hot parking lot staring at the sprawling, nondescript building. It was tan brick fronted with erratic plantings of azaleas and the occasional struggling bush magnolia. They were still green in the late-winter gloom, and the whole effect reminded her of jungle camouflage gear. It was fitting for a Veteran's Administration hospital, but sadly out of place in the dusty, unseasonable warmth of rural Alabama.

Walter was in there somewhere, according to Chas's report. Or at least he had been seven weeks ago. Not knowing what she wanted to learn, Miranda took a deep breath and pushed herself out of the car.

The drab, utilitarian lobby was filled with careworn people talking in quiet, hopeless whispers. The sickly-sweet miasma of disinfectant, age, and illness assailed her senses, and she nearly turned and walked back through the automatic doors. But she hadn't spent several sleepless nights and four hours in a car to get this far and fail. She walked up to the desk.

"Excuse me, could you tell me where I might find Walter Burrows?"

Half an hour later, after having convinced a hospital administrator that she was Walter's long-lost daughter, she stepped off the elevator on the fourth floor and thought again about leaving. The floor's common area was a grim place full of wandering old men in faded bathrobes and shuffling slippers. Blinking Christmas lights glowed cheerily weeks beyond their season. Strung above the banks of windows, they were an awful parody of the monitor lights attached to the mobile IV poles dotting the interior landscape. The lively country music playing softly in the background was at odds with the visual sterility.

Miranda scanned the faces for one that might be familiar as she made her way to the unit desk, only to learn that Walter was too sick to leave his bed. From the doorway of his room she could see six beds. Privacy curtains were half pulled around most of them. A different radio station provided a low hum punctuated by the steady cadences of three different electronic beeps.

She recognized him immediately, and the resentment she had been trying to kindle, or at least keep alive, faded. The handsome, robust man who had taught her to ride a bike and to shoot, and to fight her own battles, had become gaunt and shrunken, and drowsed openmouthed against a stack of flat white pillows. As she stepped farther into the room, pity and fear burning in her chest, she saw a woman sitting near the top of his bed, absently holding his hand while she read a paperback novel. A romance novel. Miranda swallowed hard and cleared her throat.

The woman looked up at the sound and met Miranda's eyes. "Hello."

Miranda fought the panicky churn inside her and managed a smile. "Hello. I'm terribly sorry to disturb you, ma'am. Are you Mrs. Burrows?" *God, the name sounds strange after all these years.*

The woman nodded and gave her a faint smile. "Yes, I am."

She swallowed again. "Ma'am, my name—"

"Well, damn, child. Where you been?"

Miranda's head jerked up at the voice, so familiar and so haunting. Her eyes met his—still bright blue, if a bit unfocused—and she saw recognition. "You know me?" she asked with quiet disbelief.

"What in tarnation did you do to your hair, M'randa? Does your mother know? Helen," he bellowed.

Miranda felt the precursor to tears scorch her throat and glanced at the woman, who was staring back at her in dull surprise, the paperback forgotten. "I—"

"I wasn't sure if you really existed, darlin'. You or Helen. I mean, your mama. Could we chat for a minute?" His wife stood, then turned to pat Walter on the hand. "We'll be right back, precious. You just stay right here and be good."

When they were outside the door, the woman turned to her with resignation in her eyes instead of the anger and hurt Miranda expected. "You're Miranda?"

She nodded, still too shaken to speak.

The woman held out her hand. "I'm Barbara. I married Walter twelve years ago."

Miranda clasped her hand in both of hers. "Ma'am, I'm so sorry to have surprised you like this. Please forgive me. I don't know what I was thinking. I only found out a short while ago that he was—"

"Don't, honey," she said gently. "I first heard about you a little over a year ago, when he started to get sick. He'd start talking about you and your mother. It was a shock. I didn't even know he'd been married before." She gave a silent, mirthless laugh. "After thirteen years, I thought I knew everything about the man." She met Miranda's eyes again. "When he started talking about you, I tried to find you."

"I changed my name a long time ago," Miranda replied quietly, for the first time feeling shame for not confronting him, for letting him slip away, for letting him steal her past. "How is he?"

The woman hesitated and took a deep breath, but instead of regaining her composure she seemed to shatter and buried her face in her hands. Gritting her teeth at her own stupidity and her inability to find even a false but comforting compassion, Miranda patted the woman's shoulder awkwardly and led her to a cluster of chairs near the nursing station. "Miss Barbara, I'm so sorry."

Barbara shook her head and sniffled, pulling a wadded-up, embroidered handkerchief out of the hip pocket of her tunic-style shirt. "I'm sorry, darlin'. I just met with the doctor an hour ago. Your daddy's not doing so well. They stopped doing chemo a month ago. The last round of tests showed it didn't do much good, so they're not going to do any more. It's just time now, they said. Just time and God's will."

"I'm so sorry." Her words sounded weak. Hollow.

Barbara sniffled again and took another deep breath, which seemed to have the desired effect this time. "You go to him now, darlin'. His mind wanders a fair bit these days, but he might remember some things. And it will mean a lot to him. He talks about his little girl all the time. So proud of you. He must have been some kind of good daddy." She patted Miranda's hand kindly and gave her a watery smile.

Miranda nodded automatically as emotion closed her throat. After a moment she slowly rose to walk back to Walter's room. He was staring at his hands as if he'd never seen them before. She sat down next to the bed.

"Did I ever get around to teaching you how to shoot?" he barked, his deep Alabama drawl slowing down the intensity of his question.

She nodded and produced a smile. "Yes, sir, you did. I'm still a pretty good shot."

He nodded. "Now I remember. You always was a good shot. Better'n those Prixley boys. I always said they could shoot the O out of a can of Old Milwaukee at twenty yards, but you could dot the I." He looked up at her, his eyes focused and clear for a moment. "How you been, M'randa?"

She had to force the words out. Had to force herself to slip her fingers under his large bony hand and give it a gentle squeeze. "I've been fine, Daddy. How are you feeling these days?"

"I'm fine, but these damned doctors don't know diddly. They won't let me leave and won't tell me why I have to stay." He blinked and looked through her again. "How's your mama? She ain't been to see me lately."

"Mama?" She waited until she could trust her voice. "Mama died, Daddy. She took sick and died a while back."

"Damn. Can't remember anything some days," he mumbled. "She was a good woman."

Miranda nodded. "Yes, she was. The best. Miss Barbara seems very nice, too."

He blinked. "Oh, yes, she is, too." He sat quietly for a moment, then dropped his gaze to their hands. Five minutes passed, and Miranda was sure he'd fallen asleep. As she began to slide her hand out from beneath his, he tightened his grip.

"She wasn't supposed to die without tellin' you, M'randa."

The slow, hushed words froze her in place, and she had to strain to hear the rest.

"She asked me to take care of her and you. And I did it 'cause I thought it was the right thing to do. But when the Good Lord took her, M'randa, I just got scared. I didn't know what to do but tell you what." He stopped talking and stared at her, shaking his head in a rhythm slow with age and helplessness.

It took a moment for her brain to absorb his words, to identify the gaps and assemble questions. Phrasing them without anger took longer. "Why did she need you take care of us, Daddy? What—?"

He began speaking again as if he hadn't heard her. "I know I did you wrong, M'randa. I tried to find you later. To set things right between us. I tried but didn't know where you'd got to. I'm glad you found me."

Miranda stared at the ceiling for a long time, trying to blink back the tears, trying to quell the merciless burn in her throat, to ease the searing pain in her lungs. By the time she formed the words and found her voice, she heard a gentle snore. She set him gently against the pillows and pressed a kiss to his forehead. "Me too, Daddy."

Numb, shaking, Miranda returned to the chairs where she'd left Barbara, who looked up from idly thumbing a dog-eared magazine.

"Poor thing, you look worn out and stretched thin. Did he remember you, darlin'?"

Miranda nodded and sank onto the chair next to her. "He's asleep now."

"Talking wears him out. Most everything wears him out." Barbara hesitated. "Is there anything I can tell you, honey? He's been talking about you for a year. I guess I know just about everything about you. When you were little, that is."

If there was something left to learn, she didn't want to learn it from this stranger. There would be other ways. She'd find them.

Miranda looked into the woman's kind, troubled eyes and made herself smile. "He's a good man, Miss Barbara, and he was a good daddy to me. He taught me well."

Barbara reached over and squeezed her hand. "I know what he did to you, Miranda. He told me," she whispered with tears welling in her kind eyes. "He thought he was telling Helen, actually. He apologized for treating her baby so badly. And he cried. I told him Helen forgave him, precious. I told him you did, too."

The cold force clenching her heart gave a vicious squeeze, and Miranda looked away, breathless. "You did the right thing. Thank you for telling me. I'm glad he met you."

After many false assurances to Barbara that she was perfectly fine, Miranda exchanged contact information and made as graceful an exit as she could. She proceeded to sit in her car through a brief rainstorm that left the parking lot steaming with a fog as thick as the one in her head. Closing her eyes and resting her head against the seat, she wondered how long it was going to take before she could think about today without being attacked by nausea or suffocated by a poison cloud of remorse.

She jumped a foot as something rapped at the window next to her head. It was Barbara, looking worried. Miranda rolled down the window.

"I knew you weren't right, darlin'. It's coming on to suppertime. Why don't you come back home with me? I'd sure enjoy the company, and I have some things of Walter's that you might want to look at."

The words her mother had instilled in her as a child flowed off her tongue without conscious thought. "Thank you, ma'am. If you're sure it's no trouble. Shall I follow you in my car?"

"I took the bus here this morning, so a ride would be a pleasure. It's not too far."

Miranda stashed her purse and her file of notes in the backseat and waited for the older woman to climb in.

Her apartment was small, immaculate, and painfully cheerful, with silk flowers and throw pillows covered in bright, crocheted covers. Barbara bustled in and immediately got Miranda settled in the best chair with a glass of sweet tea and some store-bought cookies. She excused herself and returned in a moment carrying an ordinary cardboard box, which she set at Miranda's feet.

"I'm just going to get a few things started for supper. You take your time and look through that, Miranda. Let me know if you find anything you'd like to keep. I don't have anyone else that might want it and, well, I just know that if Walter was still himself, he'd want you to have it."

Miranda stared at the box for a few minutes, as if touching it would somehow be a betrayal. But of whom or what she wasn't sure. Her mother? Herself? Or just her anger? For years she'd fantasized about tracking him down and screaming at him, telling him what she thought and how she felt. Then she'd just tried very hard to forget that he existed, that he ever had. But every image of him she'd held in her mind had been of him in his prime, when he was good-looking and powerful, with an easy smile and a protective streak a mile wide. She'd never imagined him old or ill or deserving of any human kindness, much less her sympathy. Or love. Yet here she was, finding it difficult to feel anything else.

Knowing Barbara wouldn't understand if she came back in the room to find the box untouched, Miranda bent down and opened it slowly. Some books and plaques and a set of old-fashioned photo albums lay near the top. Denying her curiosity, she moved those aside to see what lay below them. Smaller mementos of his army years were in a clear plastic box. She lifted the smaller box to her lap and snapped open the cover. The contents were a loose jumble of pins and ribbons, his dog tags, the stripes and chevrons he'd earned, a few odd reminders of some of his postings. His discharge papers lay folded at the bottom. Beneath them, she saw the ragged, darkening edges of newspaper clippings.

She lifted them out, and a small object slid out from between the crisp, aging sheets. It was a pair of gold bands, strung together with a piece of string. She didn't need to look to know that they were engraved on the inside with the date he'd married her mother. Looking at the simple bands cradled in her palm, Miranda let out a slow, unsteady breath. Keeping them in her hand, she unfolded the clippings.

The same picture she'd seen, framed, on Walter's dresser all through childhood stared back at her: her mother's face, young, sweet, unlined. Happy. Miranda's eyes drifted to the words beside the photograph.

Mr. and Mrs. Earl Watson announce the engagement of their son, Jimmy Joe, to Miss Helen Miranda Lane of Monroeville, daughter of the late Mr. and Mrs. Roy Lane. The maid of honor will be the groom's sister, Miss Eleanor Watson. The best man will be Private First Class Walter Burrows. The wedding date has been set—

A sick fear began to spread through her like thick, choking fog. Miranda flipped to the next clipping. It was dated one week later.

Local Boy Injured

Jimmy Joe Watson, son of Earl and Susan Watson of Tyler, was critically injured Saturday night when his car spun out of control on Highway 4 during a rainstorm and ran into a telephone pole. Also injured were passengers—

With shaking hands, she slid the next clipping from beneath the article. It was Jimmy Joe's obituary, dated two days later. Seven months before the day she was born. Three weeks before the day her mother married Walter. The words faded into a blur and the churn inside her became almost frantic. *She asked me to take care of her and you. And I did it 'cause I thought it was the right thing to do.*

Pulling in huge lungfuls of air in an attempt to maintain control, Miranda shut out the weak, raspy voice playing in her head and focused all her attention on reordering and refolding the fragile pieces of newsprint, only to let them fall back into the box. Setting the box on the floor, she reached for the crocheted afghan draped over the back of the chair beside her and wrapped herself in it to ward off the bone-deep chill that had settled inside her. The faded but colorful yarn smelled like it had been dried in the sunshine. Miranda hugged it around herself and closed her eyes, letting the hot rain of tears fall where they would.

Filled with a dull, aching mixture of sadness and relief, Miranda pulled into her parking space the next afternoon. Barbara had given her two boxes of things to keep, and over dinner and dessert they'd covered a lot of topics. How she and Walter had met when he became chief of police in a small town where she worked for the district attorney. How he used to be before he became so sick, what they had intended to do once they retired, and how fast everything had changed. How she'd had to sell their house so she could be closer to him once they moved him into the VA hospital. What was going to happen to her after he died.

They laughed, and Barbara had cried some, but mostly they just talked, and then Barbara offered her the couch for the night, and Miranda accepted. They parted affectionately, with promises to keep in touch.

. Exhausted, Miranda carried the boxes into her condo and set them in the corner of her office, needing to give herself some distance from the turmoil. But the turmoil didn't allow it and found her wherever she tried to hide. By nine o'clock that night she gave in to it and sat down at her laptop and released the torrent of emotion that had built up over the last few days.

It was hypnotic in a way, she realized after the frenzy had stopped and she'd crawled into bed. She'd been writing with her head thrown back, eyes closed, letting the thoughts flow straight from mind and heart to fingers without stopping to consider what they looked like on the screen. Without stopping to consider how well the sentence was constructed or what some outsider might think about it or how an editor might change it. It had been so long since she'd indulged in the uncontaminated act of just writing, instead of writing *something* for some-one else. This was just for her. After she'd gotten going, everything had started to flow like a drizzle turning into a storm and then a mudslide. It had been pure. Organic. Unstoppable.

The one thing she'd thought at the outset that it might be—which was *helpful*—it wasn't. Not at all, she thought, staring at the lights moving across the ceiling as cars pulled in and out of the complex's parking lot. Writing down her wishes and feelings and lies gave a voice to the anger and the rage and the pain, but it didn't fill the gaps. It didn't diminish the need.

That need was something she'd never acknowledged before, but now it was there all the time, laughing at her, taunting her. Making her realize that she hadn't been whole; for a decade and a half she'd only been hiding the holes, looking past them instead of into them, skirting them instead of fording them. Now they were all she could see. Gaping maws of blankness that didn't hurt and didn't scare her. They just echoed.

CHAPTER
25

Chas stared at the bronze liquid as it swirled against the sides of the heavy crystal tumbler. It had been two months since Miranda left. Two months. The first had been awkward. The second had been fucking excruciating, having to deal with Murphy's gloating at getting the promotion and the reactions of the other guys to the news. Of course, nothing had been said to his face, but Chas knew they were saying plenty behind his back. And as difficult as it was for him to believe that it could have, the whole experience had changed the way he thought about the job. About life.

He'd become restless in a way he'd never been before. His attitude toward the job wasn't the same. The energy was gone. The thrill of it, the adrenaline rush, the drive to find the answers, to make the collar—it had all changed. His enthusiasm had diminished and, more significantly, his edge had dulled, and that scared the hell out of him. For his own sake and the sake of the guys who depended on him to be focused, he had to shake it off.

It wasn't just losing the promotion that was feeding his discontent. It had more to do with losing Miranda, and with the words she'd flung at him the night she left. They'd made him start questioning himself, his motives, his decisions.

He'd been able to ignore it for a while. Christmas and

New Year's had come and gone with all the requisite galas and dinner parties to keep him occupied. And crime scenes, just to complete the spectrum of experiences. But now the doldrums of January had settled over the town and his life. The weather had turned really shitty, with lots of snow and record-setting cold. It kept even the bad guys indoors.

Pellegrini and Jane had finally gotten together and were still in the inseparable stage, and Paxton and James were doing some serious cocooning. Even Gruber had found a girlfriend. But for the first time in his adult life, Chas didn't want a woman hanging around.

No. That wasn't quite right, he thought as he brought the rich, smoky Scotch to his lips. He did want one. The one who had brought his career to a standstill, the one who had shredded his ego in private and his reputation in public. And that was the most fucked up thing about the entire situation. Despite everything, he still wanted Miranda.

His car, his truck, every room in his house held a memory of her. He could conjure her eyes, her smile, at will, and could imagine her response to a situation. He dreamed about her. It was all dubious pleasure. The woman had no heart and no conscience.

He missed her like crazy.

"You're spending an awful lot of time lost in thought these days, Chas," Paxton said as she swept back into the living room after relieving the nanny and checking on her children. James was out of town and she'd asked Chas to accompany her to a charity ball she hadn't wanted to miss. She picked up the flute of Champagne from where she'd left it on the low table and curled herself elegantly onto the love seat that mirrored the one on which he was lounging. Her hand fell naturally onto the slight but discernable bump at the front of her evening gown.

He met her eyes. "How would you know? You've been hibernating for weeks."

"I have friends." She smiled. "You haven't been yourself since Miranda left. When are you going to admit it? And then do something about it?"

"Admit what?"

Her blue eyes were soft and knowing, and highly amused. "Do you really want to know?" she asked, and took a slow, drawn-out sip, never taking her eyes off him. "What, I've been asking myself, could make Chas Casey turn moody and celibate—"

"I haven't."

"—turn moody and celibate," she repeated deliberately, "other than falling in love? After all, Chas, being moody, being celibate, and being in love are three of the few experiences you've never endured before."

"That baby is feeding off your brain."

"I know you think she trashed your fast track to glory," she said bluntly. "But you've always believed that there are two sides to every story. Why aren't there two sides to your own? Don't you want to find out if she actually did anything at all? Call her. Ask her why she did it."

Her words stung, but he didn't let it show. "Ignorance isn't a defense, and failure to disclose is a form of lying. It doesn't matter why she did it, Paxton. She did it," he said over the rim of his drink.

"Then why haven't you confronted her?"

He said nothing and sipped his Scotch.

"I've known Miranda a long time, Chas. She's as honest and candid as you are. If you asked her why she did it, she'd tell you. And if you really believed she did it, you wouldn't hesitate to confront her. Yet here you are, stewing," she said. "You're the type of man who surmounts obstacles, Chas, not the type who's stopped by them. What happened with her? Did you have a fight before she left?"

"I'm not going to discuss it."

"Find her, Chas. Say whatever has to be said and then marry her."

He gave a harsh laugh. "She's poison."

"So what? You face death every day anyway. In fact, you thrive on it," she said. "Have you ever stopped to consider that maybe you're an emotional coward? That you know it's easier to face a bullet than a broken heart?"

"You're out of line," he replied as guilt, anger, and

hot, sweet denial rushed through him. He set his glass on the table and rose to his feet.

"Yes, I am, but you're still listening." She paused and raised a cool, assessing eyebrow, then stood up and walked around the table. She stopped in front of him, and when she raised her eyes to his, he was shocked to see them bright with unshed tears. "Get over yourself, Chas. You want her so much that it scares the hell out of you. Welcome to real life," she said bitterly. "Love scares the hell out of most people, and it never stops. You just saved my marriage because I was too scared to save it myself. And yet your stupid pride won't even let you look for the truth in your own life."

When he was sure she was finished, he gave her a cold smile that belied the festering wound her words had ripped open. "A lovely time was had by all, Paxton. I'll see myself out."

"Don't be pigheaded. Over the years I've watched a lot of women try to get past that layer of polite indifference you maintain so well. Miranda is the only one who made it," she said as he crossed the large foyer. "You need her, Chas."

Like I need a hole in the head. He closed the ornate wooden door gently behind him.

He kept the music loud, the windows open, and his mind deliberately blank as he drove home. He swung the Porsche into his driveway and pulled it into his garage, and as soon as the music stopped, the thoughts took over.

Okay, maybe I did fall in love with her. Everyone makes mistakes. It won't happen again.

He walked into his kitchen and tossed his keys on the table, loosening his bow tie as he headed for the refrigerator and a bottle of water. A few minutes later he flicked through the pile of several days' worth of mail his cleaning lady had left on the counter. At the very bottom was a thick, flat FedEx envelope. He flipped it over and stopped short. It was from Miranda.

He stared at it for a moment, then turned away and headed for the study and some brain-numbing television. Whatever she had to say could wait. *Forever.*

At four o'clock in the morning he was cursing and stomping his way down two flights of stairs to the kitchen. He snatched the unopened folder off the table and went back upstairs. With a motion more violent than required, he ripped open the envelope and pulled out a thick sheaf of papers held together with a rubber band.

Her book.

What kind of sick, vicious streak does she have? I ought to burn the damned thing.

The top sheet was a loose piece of crisp stationery with her name and address embossed across the top in a funky, pink-tinted font.

Dear Chas,

he read, frowning, as he lowered himself to the couch.

I hope you're well and staying warm. Paxton complains about the cold and snow every time we talk. Thank you for sending me the file on Walter. I went to visit him.

He stopped and raised his eyebrows. *That's it?* He leaned against the back of the couch and continued reading.

I've enclosed the completed manuscript that I was working on while I was in Stamford. I am hoping that if you have time, you could read it and correct any technical errors related to police procedure, etc. If you don't have time, I'm sure what I have will suffice. I'll make sure to put a disclaimer in the acknowledgments that all errors are mine. Naturally, I'll be thanking you in the acknowledgments, as well. Please let me know if you would prefer not to be mentioned by name. You can contact me via e-mail, or you can try my cell phone. If I don't hear from you, I'll assume that everything checks out and that using your name is agreeable to you.

Her handwriting seemed to change as she began the next paragraph. Her smooth script became cramped and her letters became spiky, as if she'd been holding the pen too tightly.

> *I can't tell you how much you helped me with this book, Chas. Or how much I enjoyed the time I spent with you. Take care of yourself.*
> *Love,*
> *Miranda*

He stared at the note, reread it. Realized his fury had abated without any good reason for it to do so. He glanced at the note again. There was no evidence of gloating. There was nothing between the lines except—*I am* not *going there. Words are her weapon of choice.*

He put the note on the low table and walked away from it as he massaged the back of his neck, which had suddenly gone tight. As he retraced his footsteps and began a new circuit of the room, he passed the table and glanced at the note again.

Love.

Either she had more balls than he ever imagined or she had no idea what she'd done. It was a set of options he didn't want to think about.

Miranda and Molly met for coffee in Midtown and ended up walking through Centennial Park with their to-go cups in hand. It was a chilly, brilliantly clear late winter day.

"I like Atlanta best when no one's here," Molly sighed from behind her large, retro-80s sunglasses.

"They're here; they're just doing what every sensible Southerner does when there's frost on the sidewalk. They're staying inside."

"Good thing we've never been accused of being sensible," Molly said with a grin. The laughter was gone but the lightness remained in her voice when she continued. "Are you doing okay?"

Miranda nodded and took a sip of coffee, deliberately not meeting her friend's eyes.

"I called you Wednesday."

"I called you back."

"On Thursday night," Molly pointed out, coming to a stop in front of a bench. She sat down and snuggled into her coat.

"I was in Alabama," Miranda replied, sitting down next to her.

"Doing what?"

"Research."

"On what? I thought you were writing Yankees now. Alpha Yankees, bless their hearts."

Miranda turned to her. If nothing else, Molly would give her a reality check. "It wasn't book research, Moll. It was personal. I saw my father. Walter."

Molly's eyebrows rose but she said nothing, only lifted the steaming cardboard cup to her lips and waited for elaboration.

Miranda closed her eyes and gave a silent laugh. "You know I don't get soppy, and don't go thinking I'm changing my ways, darlin', but I think I love you. Anybody else would have been hugging me about now and cooing Oprah-isms in my ear. Not you, with your heart of concrete."

Molly started laughing, and Miranda felt some of her internal clouds lift.

"He's not well. But he remembered me and we talked a bit. I met his wife. I stayed over, actually, and she gave me a few things that were his." She paused and looked to the skyline. "He apologized."

"I'm glad, Miranda," Molly replied quietly. "You needed to hear it."

"That's not all. I found some newspaper clippings." Miranda stopped talking until she was sure the shakes were gone from her voice. "My mother was engaged to his best friend, who was killed in a car accident coming home from his bachelor party a week before the wedding. Walter eloped with her three weeks later." She paused for a slow breath. "My mother asked him to because she was pregnant with me."

Miranda kept her eyes aimed toward the skyline, though she couldn't see it for the blur. From the edge of her field of vision, she saw Molly take off her sunglasses and dab a discreet tissue to her face.

"Well," Molly said a moment later with a quiet, forced lightness in her voice. "We call those kind of men 'heroes' down here, shug. What do you suppose they call them up North?"

I really love you, Moll. "Same thing, I imagine."

"You needed to know, darlin'."

"I suppose I did. At least I have some answers now."

"And more questions."

Miranda turned to look at her best friend, who knew her mascara was smudged but wasn't fussing about it for the first time ever. Not that she needed a sign that momentous to know Molly was aching for her. She smiled tightly. "A few, and they'll never be answered. I suppose that's life, isn't it?"

"That's what they say." Pausing, Molly slid her sunglasses back onto her face and her attitude back into place. "Are you doing okay?" she repeated in a brisk tone.

"You know, Moll, I can't say as I'm okay or not anymore. I've spent so many years keeping everything together in such perfect order, and it's all coming undone by itself just now. Some days I can't even think straight."

"Is that bad?"

Miranda smiled. "I'm not even sure about that anymore either. That's how crazy I am. Let's keep walking."

Miranda arrived back at her condo, and by the time she'd done some laundry, tidied the kitchen, and settled herself in front of her laptop, it was midafternoon. As she waited for her writing application to load, she scrolled through the myriad e-mail messages—mostly spam—that came in through her Web site. Her eyes widened and she did a double take as she scanned the list of senders. *Chas.* She sat back in her chair, her heart pounding, her mouth suddenly dry.

"Be sensible, Miranda. You sent him your manuscript and asked him to get back to you with comments," she whispered to herself. "That's all it is."

Still, she had to close her eyes, count to ten, and take deep, calming breaths before she clicked on the message.

Miranda,
I read through your manuscript. Good story. Very different from your other ones. You nailed all the technical information. The only thing you have to change is my rank. List me as Detective, not Lieutenant.
Regards,
Chas

She stared at the message, feeling as though her brain had stalled in neutral.
He didn't get the promotion?
She took a shaky breath. *No, not possible. Maybe it just isn't official yet and he doesn't want to be presumptuous.*
That would be just like him, she decided, and walked into her kitchen for a glass of tea. While there, she glanced at her calendar. It was the middle of January. He'd said he'd be a lieutenant by the new year.
There was only one way to find out what happened. Before she could second-guess herself or talk herself out of it, she grabbed the telephone and punched in his cell phone number.
"Chas Casey."
The sound of his voice sent warmth sluicing through her like a wave against the shore. It retreated just as quickly.
What in the name of all that's holy am I doing? She smacked her forehead in hope of rousing what was left of her asleep-at-the-wheel sanity, knowing she couldn't hang up. He'd already seen the number and her name above it.
Closing her eyes, she swallowed hard and tried to smile. "Hello, Chas, it's Miranda."
"Hello."
She took a deep, openmouthed breath before attempting speech again but the words came rushing out anyway. "I'm not getting you at a bad time, am I? Should I call back? Are you on duty? I never could keep your schedule straight."

"No, this is fine. It's not a bad time," he replied, a familiar amusement in his voice. "How are you?"

She felt her cheeks grow warm and was glad there were a thousand miles between them. "Fine. Keeping busy."

"I'm glad to hear it. What can I do for you?" he asked, his voice back to neutrality.

"I got the file you sent me. Thank you."

"I didn't know if you'd left it here by accident or design, so I wasn't sure if you'd want it. I figured neither one of us had anything to lose if I sent it."

The quiet words sliced into her heart with a clean rapier thrust. She gripped the edge of the countertop and tried to ignore both the pain and the words. *Smile.* "I read it," she said, striving to keep her voice light. "In fact, I went to see him."

"That's what your note said. That took a lot of courage. How did it go?"

"I don't know about courage. Maybe it just took a whole lot of stupid." She gave a nervous laugh that ended with a deep breath. "He's not well. He's dying."

"I'm sorry, Miranda." His voice had softened, and the sound of it brought an unwanted lump to her throat.

"Thank you. It was a good visit. I'm glad I went," she said, shocked at how shivery her voice had become. "But that's not why I called, Chas," she continued in a rush as she heard him get ready to say something. Anything sympathetic would send her over the edge. She brushed the icy glass of tea across her forehead with a shaky hand. "I just received your e-mail about my manuscript. I was surprised to read the corrections you made to your title."

The silence that ensued grew too long to be casual, and, newly breathless with dread, she leaned into a corner of the counter. It was secure. Her knees weren't.

"I didn't get the promotion." His words were delivered in a carefully neutral voice.

"What?" she whispered, her heart beginning to pound in disbelief. "Chas, I can't believe that. What happened?"

"Murphy got it."

"*Brian Murphy?* But he doesn't have your record. He doesn't have your scores. You said it was a sure thing, Chas—"

"An incident occurred that I wasn't prepared for, Miranda," he said abruptly. "I acted in violation of department policy."

This makes no sense. "What policy? I can't believe that you'd do something like that, Chas. Not with all of your rules of conduct. What happened?"

"It's not important, Miranda," he said firmly after a pause.

"That's ridiculous, Chas. Of course it is. Tell me what happened," she demanded, her stomach churning at his desire to evade her questions. It was out of character. "Does it have something to do with me? It wasn't that ticket you made disappear, was it? I'll pay it. I swear I will. With interest. They can't—"

He let out an abrupt, quiet laugh. "No, it had nothing to do with the ticket."

"But it had something to do with me?"

A short silence ensued; then she heard him let out a heavy breath. "Yes, Miranda. You never told me that you were denied permission to interview someone," he said quietly. "By helping you I knocked myself off the list."

His calm words pulled the air right out of her lungs. Closing her eyes as the world started to spin around her, she slid down the cabinet fronts to land on the floor with a thump.

"I cost you your promotion?" she asked when she remembered how to breathe, how to talk. "Oh, God, Chas. I didn't . . . We met through Paxton and I didn't . . . Oh, Chas." Then the full realization hit her, and her voice caught on a sob that ripped through her vital organs like a filthy, jagged blade. "You weren't going to tell me. Do you despise me that much, to not even tell me?" The words were choking her. Tears ran down her face hot as fresh blood. "I didn't do it on purpose, Chas. I swear it. I'm so sorry. What can I—"

He interrupted her in a voice that was low and restrained. "Nothing, Miranda. There's nothing to be done."

"I didn't—"

"I believe you, Miranda," he said quietly. "Let's leave it there. Good-bye."

The flat tone buzzing in her ear snapped her back to reality, and she threw the phone onto the couch across the room. Burying her face in her hands, she cried as she hadn't in fifteen years, raging against all the hurt, all the anger, all the need that was pulling her under in a riptide of pain. She couldn't deny anymore that the one thing she wanted more than anything at all was Chas. She wanted to hear his voice muffled in her hair, to feel his lips against hers, to feel his arms around her body.

She knew without question he was the one thing she would never have again.

CHAPTER
26

A week after his conversation with Paxton, three days after his conversation with Miranda, Chas drove to the Brennan building and took the elevator to the eighteenth floor. As he walked through the quietly humming corridors, he returned the surprised greetings of the few people who knew him and felt the curious stares of the many more who didn't. The first of his mother's assistants glanced up with a smile and offered him a seat while she made a quick call to the executive assistant, who appeared in the doorway of her office immediately.

"Chas," she said, closing the space between them and extending her hand. "This is a surprise. I didn't see your name on your mother's—"

"I'm not on her schedule, Anne," he reassured her. "But I'm hoping I can see her for a few minutes. Is she free?"

"She's just on a conference call with your grandfather and Dalton. It should be ending soon. I'll let her know you're here."

Ten minutes later his mother opened her office door with a smile as she slid her glasses off her nose. "What are you doing down here?" she asked, motioning for him to enter. "Too bad you didn't come earlier. We could have gone to lunch."

"Hi. Do you have a minute?"

"For you, I have lots of them. Take as many as you need. What's up?"

He grinned to hide the nervous churn in his stomach and waited until she had seated herself before sitting down on one of the brightly upholstered wing chairs opposite her desk. Her office was small, not much larger than her assistant's, and the late-winter sunlight streamed through the many sun catchers hanging in the large window behind her desk. She'd always said she preferred to watch the light play off the walls of her office than be impressed by the view of the city and the sound beyond it. He wondered how many other CEOs of Fortune 500 companies could say as much.

He met her eyes, which were watching him with patient curiosity. "I want to ask you something."

"Okay."

"Something big."

She leaned forward, bracing her elbows on her desk, her chin on interlaced fingers. "Okay."

"How much do you hate the fact that I'm a cop?"

Her clear blue gaze never wavered. "A lot," she said without hesitation. "You know that."

"Is it just because—"

She shook her head minutely, and Chas stopped.

"I'm very proud of you, Chas. You know that, too. You're a wonderful son and a wonderful man and an excellent police officer. I've always been proud of you," she repeated. "But, yes, part of me hates what you do because I lost one man I loved due to his career choice, and I don't want to lose another. Because every day you carry that badge I relive the worst day of my life. Because you became a policeman for the wrong reasons. Because you're trying to live up to an expectation no one ever had for you."

Chas stared at her, struck silent by her calm, ready litany, by the contained flash of temper in her eyes.

"What surprises you, Chas? That I had an answer ready? I have more, if you'd like to hear them. I've been waiting for that question for fifteen years. Thank you for finally asking it." Her voice was cool and firm, but he heard the hint of a quaver in the background. "Your father had put in his notice a week before he was shot. He was going to go to work for my father as head of security. He'd had enough of police work. He loved it but he wanted a change, and he'd proven to himself and to my parents that he didn't need their money, their name, or their backing."

Her quiet words exploded in the room like a halon bomb, leaving it airless. "You never told me any of that."

His mother stood up and leaned against the window that sparkled in joyous contradiction to the dense, depleted atmosphere in the small room. Her arms were folded protectively across her chest. With deliberate and controlled nonchalance, she lifted a shoulder. "I know that. You didn't want to know. You probably would have thought I was making it up if I'd told you all of this when you announced your intention to go to the academy. But I have the letter he wrote to the chief, if you'd care to see it."

"Of course not." His voice was hoarse, and shocked. His mind was blank. Silence puddled around him, lapping at him in waves that mingled regret and guilt and a humbling sense of profound and misplaced arrogance.

"May I ask what brought this on? The promotion?"

When he focused and found her eyes, they were filled and overflowing. Soundlessly.

"Not the promotion. Miranda."

"She's back?"

"She may never be back."

"Then why bother with this?"

"Because while she was here, she asked me why I was a cop. None of the standard answers fit anymore."

She nodded slowly, as if the answer made sense to her. He wished it made sense to him.

"What now?" she asked.

"I've got two letters drafted. One's to you. When I leave here, I'm heading over to the chief's office."

"You're coming to work for us?"

"Yes."

"Why?"

He met her brimming but unyielding blue eyes. "Because I want to."

She closed her eyes. A moment later her shoulders slumped and her slim frame began to shake with sobs that Chas knew had been too long suppressed. He walked to her and wrapped his arms around her, feeling her tears wet his shirt. He'd never felt so empty.

Chas sat in his kitchen at seven thirty on a snowy morning in early March. He didn't have anywhere he had to be, didn't have anything particularly pressing to do. It had been roughly a month since that startling conversation with his mother, three days since he'd worked his last shift and turned in his badge. It would be two weeks before he moved into his new office. He lifted his coffee mug to his lips and reared back as the liquid scalded his mouth.

Having nothing to do was a strange sensation. He didn't know what to call it. Not freedom, not liberty. To say it was either of those things would imply he had been somehow imprisoned. He hadn't been. Well, if he had been, it had had nothing to do with the job.

It was only three days, but he'd figured it would have set in by now. Not that he knew what "it" was or what to expect, but surely there had to be something. So far, he missed only the external things, like having the reassuring weight of a Glock resting against his hip and having a heavy badge in his wallet. The routine.

That couldn't be the end of it. There had to be some other kind of response to leaving a job he'd loved for fifteen years. He'd expected to experience some void, some emotional—

"Christ. It's been three days and I'm starting to think like a fucking wimp. Next I'll be watching *Dr. Phil* and eating Häagen-Dazs for lunch," he muttered. He took another pull from his mug of coffee and burned his mouth for the second time in less than a minute.

"God damn it." He slammed the mug onto the table. *Okay, that's one big fucking reaction to leaving. My concentration is shot.* He stood up and walked to the sink, then poured the coffee down the drain.

He knew what part of the problem was. Having nothing else to focus on left him too much time to think about that conversation with Miranda. Even now, every time he thought about it his heart damned near shredded at the memory of her voice, hushed and thick with pain.

Helpless. That was how he felt, for maybe the second time in his life, and he couldn't do a damned thing about it.

But damn her for pushing the subject. Once he'd decided she was innocent, he'd made the decision not to tell her about losing the promotion. He'd decided that she would never know she'd been a suspect. *Big fucking heroic decisions.* He shook his head. They hadn't been that tough to make: He never thought he'd talk to her again. But then she called and she asked and he realized that she deserved to know.

When he told her, she sounded as if he'd just destroyed her. She'd started to cry. The woman had barely shed a tear the night she'd told him what Walter had done to her. She hadn't even gotten misty-eyed the night she left him, but she started to cry over his promotion.

How the hell could I have thought she'd do something like deliberately destroy my career?

"Because I'm an asshole," he admitted, then paused and looked around the empty kitchen. "Christ. Now I'm talking to myself."

This has to be what hell is all about.

He walked to the front of the house and grabbed a jacket from the closet in the foyer. Keys in hand, he set the alarm and walked out the door, his eyes automatically sweeping the neighborhood for unusual activity before he caught himself. With a deep breath, he slid into the driver's seat of the truck. He put the truck in gear, cranked up the stereo, and let some vintage Van Halen pound his brain into temporary blankness.

He pulled into his mother's driveway shortly after eight for lack of a more interesting destination and was just fending off the dogs when his cell phone rang.

"What's up?" he asked, recognizing Joe's cell phone number on the screen.

"Listen, I'm done with this executive boot camp bullshit and I'm flying up to Atlanta tonight. Are you coming down for the weekend or not? If you're not, I'm going to make other plans." Joe's voice held more than an invitation; it held a challenge. One Chas was very tempted to accept.

Entering the house through the mudroom, he shrugged off his jacket and smiled a greeting at his mother's housekeeper as he headed for the coffeemaker. "Thanks, but no. There's no point."

"Oh, fuck that, Chas. It's been months." Joe let out an exasperated breath. "So don't call her. Just come down for a change of scenery. Atlanta has more beautiful women per square mile than any city on earth other than LA. You haven't left town in months, and a few weeks from now you're going to bury yourself in an office."

"Thanks anyway," he said flatly, not trying to keep the irritation out of his voice.

"By the way, you're a chickenshit."

His mother walked into the kitchen with a smile, and gave him an affectionate pat on the back as she walked past him and poured herself a cup of coffee.

"You have to stop hanging around college bars. Your vocabulary is getting fairly narrow," Chas said into the phone.

"Bite me."

"I have to go. Have a great time," Chas said dryly, and ended the call.

"So how's Joe?" his mother asked with a grin.

"Heading to Atlanta," Chas replied.

"Are you joining him?"

"He wants me to."

"You're not interested?"

He gave her a look. "Not particularly."

"See if this doesn't change your mind," she replied, and slid a dust-jacketed hardcover across the countertop. "I just got it in the mail. It's Miranda's book."

"I didn't realize it was out already," he said, not looking at it.

"I preordered it. Anyway, here it is. It's a cute cover, isn't it?"

Troubleshooting was splashed across the top of the cartoonish cover, which featured the lower half of a tennis-shoe-wearing, jeans-clad man with a gun at his hip. Those legs were in pursuit of the miniskirted lower half of a long-legged, high-heeled woman with a briefcase. *Randi Rhodes* was draped in lush script across the bottom of the book. A pair of handcuffs formed the O and lowercase D of her last name. He picked it up gingerly and read the quote that ran across the top of the cover. *"Randi Rhodes has reached new heights on the Richter scale of sassy, sexy fun!"*

He rolled his eyes and smiled. "Yeah, the cover's definitely 'cute.' "

"Look at her picture."

After a sideways glance at his mother, he flipped over the book and looked at the inside back flap. The picture of her in the magnolia was gone. In its place was a headshot of her resting her chin on her hand, smiling dreamily into the camera. Her hair was short and very pale blond. He frowned. It was quite a change. She looked great. It was perverse, he knew, but part of him wanted her to look miserable. As miserable as he felt.

Closing the book, he set it on the counter and refused to let himself wonder why she'd done it. He knew the very thought would reopen that sucking *Lifetime Channel* wound that was bleeding his brain dry of all its testosterone. He glanced up at his mother, who lifted an eyebrow.

"You're welcome to read it before I do, if you'd like to," she said lightly after a pause.

He folded his arms across his chest. "Thanks, but I already read it. She sent me a copy of the manuscript a few weeks ago so I could review the technical stuff."

She smiled.

It didn't reassure him.

Then she put a hand on her hip and leaned against the counter. "She what?" she asked, taking a sip of her coffee.

"She sent me a copy. It wasn't bound or anything, but it was the finished manuscript."

"Did you read it?"

"Yes. She asked me to."

"And you didn't let *me* read it?"

"I thought you'd want to buy a copy and boost her sales," he replied with a shrug, and turned to refill his mug.

"I'd do that anyway." She let out an exasperated sigh. "What did you think of the dedication?"

"It was fairly standard. She told me she was going to thank me by name," he replied absently.

"I'm not talking about the acknowledgment," she said crisply. "I said 'dedication.'"

He glanced up at her. He could hear Miranda's words echo in his head as clearly as he had heard her utter them that night in Paxton's condo. *I don't dedicate my books to anyone. Ever.* "She dedicated it to someone?"

His mother paused and pursed her lips thoughtfully. "If I didn't know any better, Chas, I'd say she dedicated it to *you*." She straightened up and put her coffee cup in the sink, then kissed him lightly on the cheek and walked toward the mudroom. "I have to get going. See you later."

Chas remained where he was, staring at the book, his heartbeat kicking up a notch. Reaching for the book, he thumbed the pages until he reached the one bearing the dedication.

This book is dedicated with love
to the man who showed me what it means
to live a life of truth and honor.
He is a man who is a gentleman first,
and he will always be first in my heart.
I owe you so much that I can never repay.

He put down the book and walked toward the library, where he knew his mother's computer was booted up and logged on to the Web.

It was time to arrange a trip to Atlanta.

Looking away from the completed but unsent e-mail message on her screen, Miranda picked up her phone and held it in shaking hands. Staring at the keypad, she hesitated to touch it, wondering if she had the courage. She'd spent countless hours since she'd come back from Connecticut pouring every experience, every thought into her laptop. The process had changed, though, just in those few weeks since she'd seen Walter. She'd come to realize that the mental downloading had evolved from being a catharsis to a project.

A project she was about to send to Amy.

She'd realized that for all those years when she was shutting out the pain, she'd been leading a shadow existence, living in the shadows of life. Of family. Of loving. Of ties that bound the heart, that could stretch infinitely thin and still not break. And when she'd stepped out of those shadows, with her imagination frozen out of the picture and reality overwhelming her at every turn, she'd begun writing again, writing from her soul. Not writing from her head, as she did with her novels, and not just hurling fifteen year's worth of pain and memories and gaps and emotions at a keyboard, as she'd begun to do after she'd seen Walter.

She'd begun crafting something, something that had taken on a life of its own. Something completely different from anything she'd ever written. A diary, a chronicle of the journey she'd put off for all those years and was finally undertaking. And the conversation with Chas a month ago had let her understand where the journey was leading.

With a dry mouth and damp palms, she clicked the send command on her keyboard and then punched in a familiar number on the phone. Her agent's voice mail took the call.

"Amy? It's Miranda. I just e-mailed you something. It's . . ." She hesitated, and thought briefly about just hanging up. "It's different. It's . . ." *Hell and damnation.* "I want to do more than entertain this time." She closed her eyes in frustration. *Screw the explanation. There isn't one that fit.* "Oh, hell, Amy. You know I don't ask for favors too often, but I'm asking for one now. I just e-mailed you something, and I want you to read it and tell me what you think. Put it at the top of your slush pile, okay? Thanks." She ended the call and walked onto her balcony, dropping the phone onto the cushioned chair next to her leg and breathing in the pine-scented warmth of an early Atlanta spring.

Just what sort of crazy have I become?

It was close to midnight when Miranda heard faint chirps on her balcony, and then only because she was passing in front of the sliding doors on her way back to her office with her sixteenth cup of coffee.

"Hi, Amy," she said, picking up the chilled, angrily chirping phone. It had been a gorgeous day, warm and clear. The night sky was just as clear, and brilliant with moonlight and stars, but the air was cold and brittle.

"What's wrong with you? You ask me to drop everything and get back to you *and then you don't answer your phone?*" her agent snapped. "I've been calling you since four thirty."

Miranda winced. "I'm so sorry, darlin'. I left the phone outside and never went back for it. But I'm glad you kept trying. Did you read it?"

"Of course I did. How soon can you have it finished?"

Her agent's words generated a short, surprised laugh, a feat Miranda didn't think possible, given her mood of late. "Well, I hadn't thought about it. I just came up with the idea of sending it to you today, so it's all pretty new—"

"What do you mean, you haven't thought about it? You sent me a twenty-page synopsis. How much do you have written?"

"About a hundred and fifty pages of a rough draft and about thirty pages of notes."

"Are you working on anything else?"

"No—"

"How many pages are you going to hit?"

"I don't know. Three hun—"

"Could you finish it in a month?"

"A month?" Miranda repeated. "I doubt it. What's the rush?"

"After I finished reading it, I sent it to my new best friend, Ellen Barber, who had called me this morning in hysterics. One of her lit-fic authors dropped a bomb in her lap and left her with a hole in her publication schedule the size of Ground Zero. She wants to fill it with this."

"What? When?" A double punch of elation and panic hit her full strength, and Miranda sat down, sucking in a deep lungful of the cold, dark air. "This isn't fiction, Amy. And I doubt it's literature."

"Doesn't matter. She's already walked it up to the forty-second floor and has gotten a blessing on it from George Almighty, but only if she can have it in five weeks, max. Are you game? I told her I'd call her tonight."

Breathe. Think. "It's midnight."

"And that means what? You think she fell asleep waiting for my call? She's called me every hour on the hour since seven. She's still at the office." Amy let out a harried breath. "Look, Miranda, you're the one who put this on a fast track with that voice mail of yours. Take all the time you need to give me an answer, but I'm not letting you hang up until I have one."

Miranda sank against the back cushion. "Okay," she said weakly.

"You're sure? Because if you don't deliver, she'll probably kill you. She mentioned something about a one-eyed uncle named Vito who lives in Brooklyn."

Miranda sent the moon a wan smile. "He'd have to get through a lot of two-fisted Bubbas to find me, darlin'. Yes, I'll do it. I'll have a draft for her in about three weeks."

"Miranda, I think I love you. You get back to that keyboard, kitten. I'll get a contract FedExed to you in a couple of days."

The first streaks of light were just striping the sky as Chas finished his two-mile run by jogging up the steps to his front door. He walked through the house to the kitchen rather than heading for the shower. He waited until his breathing slowed somewhat, then picked up the phone and punched in Joe's cell phone number.

The ringing stopped, and he heard his brother fumbling with the phone. Chas glanced at the clock and grinned. *Too damned bad.*

"I'm flying into Hartsfield at four o'clock this afternoon," he said in response to his brother's sleepy grunt. "Will you pick me up or should I get a car?"

"What? Chas? Christ, what time is it?"

"Six thirty."

"Christ. Just a minute." Chas heard a muffled conversation before his brother's voice came back on the line a moment later. "Okay. What?"

"Enjoying yourself after ten days in the swamp?" he asked dryly.

"Damned straight," Joe replied quietly with a grin in his voice, and Chas could tell he was up and walking around. "So you're coming to Atlanta. What changed your mind?"

"Miranda."

"She called?"

"No. I decided I want to see her."

Joe was silent for a moment. "Does she want to see you?"

"I'll ask her when I get there," Chas replied tightly.

"I thought she doesn't like surprises."

Bastard. "She doesn't."

"Holy Christ." Joe started laughing. "Hell, yes, I'll pick you up. I wouldn't miss this for the world. Call me later with your flight information."

Chas heard the soft click and stared at the damned thing for at least a full minute before setting the phone back in its cradle. A moment later he headed up the stairs for a shower that would no doubt end up having to be a cold one.

CHAPTER
27

"Joe, would you quit bitching about Southern women? It's all you've been doing since I got in the car. We're in the *South,* you moron, and we're from the *North.* Making fun of their women is a really stupid thing to do," Chas snapped. He glanced at his watch. It had taken them only half an hour to get from the airport to Midtown, despite the fairly heavy traffic. It didn't surprise him. Not with Joe behind the wheel.

"I'm telling you about her, not broadcasting it on bubba-dot-com."

"Well, shut up. I'm tired of listening to you."

"And it's not Southern women in general; it's this one in particular. What the fuck she was doing there I'll never know." Joe snorted as he moved into the left lane, put his foot to the floor, and roared up Interstate 75 through the heart of Atlanta. "It was for executives, and she doesn't seem capable of finding her ass with both hands in a crisis. And she's damned lucky she's still got that very ass attached to her legs, because if I hadn't been there, she wouldn't. She said she dropped her GPS transceiver while outrunning an alligator." He shook his head in disgust.

"Both of you were in a swamp in the middle of the night, right?"

"All the more reason not to lose your GPS system,"

Joe muttered. "She had a flare gun. *If* there was an alligator, she could have blown it up."

"Besides the fact that I think they're still an endangered species, why didn't she?"

"She said she didn't want to give away her position."

"Makes sense to me. Blowing up several hundred pounds of gator with a magnesium flare would get some attention."

"She was fifty yards outside the zone to begin with, and she didn't know what her fucking position *was*. Why the hell would she care about giving it away?" Joe demanded, swinging onto one of the exits that would take them to Buckhead.

"Sounds like you saved her life. Good thing you were tracking her," Chas replied sarcastically. "Tell me again *why* you were tracking her?"

Joe let out a heavy breath. "I wanted to bring her in. She'd been bugging the shit out of me since I arrived. Uppity little . . . one of the guys who know her said her father is some retired air force general who pulled strings to get her a job. He'd have to have, because she's all tits and no brains. The thought of her running around D.C. with connections like that scares the shit out of me."

In other words, Joe's brand of Neanderthal charm hadn't worked on her. Chas liked her already. He bit back a smile and looked out the window. "She lives in D.C.?"

"Apparently."

"Where'd she go to school?"

"Undergrad and masters' out of George Mason," Joe muttered.

"Yeah, it must've been Daddy who got her the job. Who did you say she worked for?"

"Department of the Navy. Procurements."

"Naturally. Those navy guys love doing favors for the air force."

"Okay, I got it," Joe snapped.

"Apparently you didn't get *anything*," Chas said under his breath.

The brothers were silent for a moment before they both started laughing.

"Is she cute?" Chas asked.

Joe rolled his eyes. "If you like short-ass, spun-sugar types, I suppose."

"Do *you*?"

"Shut up." Joe turned from a Peachtree onto another Peachtree and flicked an index figure toward the windshield. "I'd say that's the place. Are you sure about this?"

Chas looked at his brother in disbelief. "You're asking me *now*? Of course I'm not sure about this. You're the one who suggested it."

Joe shrugged. "I just can't believe that you agreed to it," he said, steering the rented SUV into the strip mall parking lot.

Looking through the front passenger window, Chas bit back all the colorful curses that came to mind. After picking him up at Hartsfield, Joe had announced he was driving straight to the bookstore where, according to her Web site, Miranda would be signing books until five o'clock with a few other romance authors. It was ten minutes to five right now.

What in the name of Christ am I doing here?

The woman hated surprises, and he was going to pull one, a big one, in public when she was surrounded by friends and colleagues?

"I can't believe I agreed to it either," he muttered, glancing at his brother, who wasn't trying very hard to keep a grin off his face. "What's plan B?"

"Plan B is that you wimp out and we spend the night doing either beer and hockey, martinis and titties, or Scotch and cigars." Joe slowed and pulled into a parking space a few rows from the front of the store.

Chas looked out his window, only to see a familiar green Mini Cooper right next to his door. It had the same decal in the back window, the same little prism hanging from the rearview mirror. "Shit. That's her car."

"Well, I'll be damned. I think it's a sign from heaven. It's showtime, Chas." Joe's laughter was thoroughly unsympathetic. "Nervous?"

"Hell, yes, I'm nervous. I'd rather be under sniper fire," he muttered.

Joe laughed again and punched him in the shoulder. "Better you than me."

Miranda glanced around the store again, her "I'm an author, buy my book" smile fixed on her face. *Troubleshooting* had been out only a week, and so far both her reviews and her sales were pretty good. And she'd sold thirty-five copies today, which was better than Wendy, Molly, and the other three writers who were signing with her.

She brought her eyes back to the table in front of her, and looked down at her hands. She was trying to manipulate her pen the way Chas could. She'd been trying to do it since she'd returned from Stamford, but still couldn't get the hang of it. Probably because her hands were too small. His were much bigger than hers, and his fingers were longer and much more limber from all that piano playing.

Do not think about his hands. Do not think about him at all or you'll start to cry again.

She could scold herself for eternity, but it was hopeless and she knew it. Loving him from a distance was the perfect blend of heaven and hell, and it kept her in silken knots. It was only fitting that she would spend the rest of her life—

"Oh, my granny's garters. Would you ever look at that?" Wendy's soft gasp shook Miranda out of her daydream and she followed Wendy's gaze to the front of the store.

"Oh, fuck," she whispered, causing all five of her co-signing colleagues to drop their jaws and stare at her.

She didn't care. She grabbed Molly's hand under their table. "That's Chas and his brother," she whispered fiercely.

"Oh, honey, you have some *serious* explainin' to do," Molly drawled under her breath as all six pairs of writers' eyes remained fixed on the two men making their way down the open center aisle of the store.

Miranda knew her colleagues were appraising the brothers with sex and mayhem on their minds. She, however, was in a state of near panic.

Chas looked tired and tense but indisputably gorgeous in well-faded jeans and an unzipped leather bomber jacket over a simple white button-down. His hair had gotten longer, and he—

"I do hope you're going to introduce us, Miranda," Susannah Davis murmured as the men drew closer.

Chas's gaze was locked on Miranda, and she could feel a small trickle between her breasts from the unsmiling intensity of it even though he was still fifty feet away.

I'm going to melt if he doesn't turn down the heat in those eyes.

Joe, she noticed out of the corner of her eye, was giving her the smile of the sun god. Swallowing hard, she stood up, and tried to wipe her damp hands against her skirt unobtrusively. She stepped to the front of the horseshoe-shaped table as the men came to a stop.

"Well, look what the cat dragged in," she said, hoping her voice didn't really sound that high and trembly. Her knees were about to give out, as was her heart if she didn't get a grip on herself. "This is quite a surprise. Hi, Chas."

"Hello, Miranda." He leaned forward to give her a kiss on her cheek and, nearly dizzy with the sight and scent of him, she almost fell against him, but he stepped back, steadying her with hands that he removed immediately. She blinked, then looked away.

"Hi, Joe," she said in a voice more recognizably her own. "Looks like you've been in the sun," she added inanely. It was impossible not to notice his deep tan against his sun-bleached hair. His blue eyes were electric.

"Don't be so formal," he said, giving her a teasing smile that nearly blinded her as he enfolded her in a tight, lingering bear hug and planted a resounding kiss on her cheek. "What did you do to your hair?"

She stepped back, breathless and laughing, and glanced at Chas, who was not at all amused at his brother's very deliberate display of affection. Miranda bit her lip and met Joe's wicked eyes. "Well, as you can plainly see, I got rid of most of it, and I stopped coloring it," she said with a laugh, running her fingers through her short blond curls.

"Yeah, yeah. Likely story. So, what are you up to?" he said, glancing at the other women behind the table. Clearly too intrigued to remember their most basic manners, all five women were watching the three of them openly. Miranda knew by their wide eyes and tense postures that they were all committing the scene to memory. She wondered whose book it would show up in first.

"We're just finishing a group book signing. These are some of my friends," she said, and introduced the women individually. "This is Joe Casey, and this"—she took a step back and slid her hand around Chas's arm to bring him forward—"this is his brother, Chas. I interviewed Chas when I was researching *Troubleshooting*."

Seven pairs of incredulous eyes swerved toward her, topped by seven pairs of raised eyebrows as if to say, *That's all?*

She smiled nervously. "He was my hero."

Big mistake. Five pairs of mascaraed eyelashes fluttered down simultaneously as Chas looked up to the ceiling, perhaps for divine guidance. Only Joe kept his eyes trained on her.

He covered his laughter with a cough, then turned to Molly. "I'm pleased to meet you, Molly," he said, glancing at the nameplate in front of her on the table. "What do you write?"

Molly's big brown eyes were sparkling like a teenager's. "Why, the pleasure is all *mine,* Joe Casey. I write romantic suspense. All of my heroes are corporate lawyers," she purred in a voice smoother than Georgia moonlight.

With Joe obviously providing a foolproof diversion, Miranda felt Chas's hand encircle her elbow and tug her gently toward the nearest stacks. She eyed him nervously, unable to read a thing in his face. A glance back at her friends assured her they wouldn't miss her. Not with six feet, four inches of broad, blond trouble flirting with them, wearing a "tempt me" smile below a set of smoldering, bad-boy baby blues.

The minute they were out of sight of the table, Chas backed her up against the stacks and put a hand on either side of the shelves behind her head, then looked her straight in the eyes. He still hadn't cracked a smile, and he wasn't quite close enough to kiss.

Breath was awfully hard to find, and she really wished he'd step back, but she knew he never would. She swallowed and made sure she maintained eye contact, even if his look was singeing her. His eyes were nearly black. That had never happened outside of bed.

"Am I the man?" His voice was low and slid along her nerves like a well-oiled hand on sun-warmed skin.

"What man?" Her voice was more of a breathless squeak than anything.

"In your book. The dedication. Am I the man to whom you dedicated the book with love? To whom you owe so much you can never repay? The one who will always be first in your heart? That man."

She licked her lips and glanced away. *How can he be so calm while I'm fit to explode?* "As a matter of fact, you are," she whispered.

He looked down and let out a pent-up breath. A moment later, their eyes met again. "I'm sorry to blindside you like this—"

"Apology accepted."

"—but we need to talk, Miranda. Are you almost done?"

Fully cooked. She licked her very dry lips again and looked away from the dark fire in his eyes. "We only had to stay until five. I can leave now."

"Good. Let's get your things." He straightened up immediately and grasped her hand, leading her back to the table.

She didn't have to make excuses. In fact, she realized, she could have taken off her clothes and danced naked on the table for all the attention her girlfriends were paying to her. Joe was leaning against the table with his arms folded across that linebacker chest answering their questions and generally charming the Jimmy Choos off them.

"'Bye, y'all," Miranda said quietly, grabbing her purse and jacket.

Joe immediately stood up. "Ladies, I can't remember a more pleasant afternoon. But my ride is leaving. Feel free to call me with any other questions," he said to a flurry of protestations as he handed Molly a few of his business cards.

The three of them were crossing the parking lot in seconds, and as the warm, early evening air cleared her head, Miranda stopped in the middle of the traffic lanes. "Hold it," she ordered over a flustered laugh. "Why do I feel like I'm some celebrity being hustled away from the scene of a crime?"

The brothers stopped and glanced at each other before training their eyes on her. She nearly crumbled from the intensity, but she wasn't Southern for nothing. She shook their hands off, folded her arms, and stuck out her hip as her gaze flicked between them, and she waited for a reply.

"Our car is over there. Next to yours. I thought we could talk there more privately," Chas said simply, shrugging.

She lifted an eyebrow and gave him a slow blink. "Oh, you did, did you? Well, precious, this just all seems a bit too well-rehearsed for my taste. I feel like I'm being kidnapped. How about y'all just come clean right now and tell me what's going on?"

"Nothing," they said in unison, much too innocently.

She rolled her eyes. "Your mother stopped falling for that when you were about three years old, Chas. And I'm no fool."

"Miranda, would you please just come to the car with us? We're blocking traffic and there's a cop over there who's watching us," he said quietly.

She bit back a smile and lifted her chin. "Big whoop. You can just flash your badge and tell him I'm being taken into custody or some such nonsense."

Joe looked at Chas. "I like that idea. I'm an officer of the court. And what the hell, I'll admit it. Damned if

I don't have some handcuffs with me." He reached to the back waistband of his jeans and pulled out a pair of handcuffs, dangling them in plain sight.

Miranda dropped her attitude and snapped to attention. "You will do no such thing, Joe Casey. Put those things away right now. People know me around here. And that police officer is getting *mighty* interested in the three of us all of a sudden."

Joe smiled back at her, enjoying himself way too much. "Then, Miranda, I suggest you quit holding up traffic and come with us quietly." He slipped the handcuffs into his jacket pocket, and the brothers waited for her to make a move.

Mildly annoyed at having walked straight into this little mess—having created it—she continued to walk as gracefully as she could across the roadway with them flanking her, and didn't stop until she was next to her car's rear bumper. "I'm not going one more step until you tell me what's going on."

"That's fine with me, sweetheart, because this is our car," Joe said, slapping the big, black SUV next to her Mini. "There's a music store over there that I'm going to wander around in for a while. In the meantime, I think it would be a good idea if you two got reacquainted." He tossed the set of car keys to Chas, who caught them. As Miranda watched them hit the palm of Chas's outstretched hand, she felt cool, heavy metal encircle her left wrist and heard an ominous grating click.

With a gasp, she looked down to see a handcuff bracelet around her wrist, and then heard another click. Her head snapped up to see a surprised Chas staring at a grinning Joe.

"I suggest you climb into the backseat, kids, before someone sees you. After all, people around here know Miranda," Joe said with a wink as he turned away and sauntered toward the music store.

She whipped her head around to face Chas, who looked equally chagrined and a little sheepish. "Did you know he was going to do this?"

"Miranda, the man has just spent ten days in a swamp. Who the hell knows what's going through his mind?"

She turned away to try to regain her composure and instead nearly lost her reason. Molly and Wendy had parked near her and were walking straight toward them, too engrossed in conversation to look up.

"Let's get in the car."

"What?"

"Let's get in the car," she repeated through clenched teeth. "My girlfriends are headed this way, and if they see us like this I will never be allowed to forget it."

Miranda insisted they crouch on the floor with their heads below seat level just in case her friends looked in when they walked past. That was when he knew for sure there really was a God. Between her high heels and tight skirt, the handcuffs, and the incredibly tight space between the front and back seats, Miranda had no choice but to lean against him. He'd maintained his control in the store—barely—but there was no way in hell he was going to behave himself now. His left hand snaked up through her short, soft hair and brought her head to his. His lips met hers. Tentatively.

She didn't put up a struggle.

She pushed him back against the door and nearly devoured him.

When she eventually pulled her mouth away from his a long while later, she looked dazed. Her eyes were wide and lit with a dark green fire he hadn't seen in too damned long, and her lips were full and wet. Her eyes were wet, too.

"Marry me, Miranda."

His whispered words shocked them both. Not that he hadn't planned on saying them some time in the next few hours. He had. He'd just planned on doing it with some Champagne and candlelight and the ring he had in his carry-on—

"Absolutely not," she said with mutiny in her eyes.

Shit.

"I'm not only disappointed in you, Chas Casey, I'm furious at you," she continued. Her voice was so cold it might have frozen his balls blue if they hadn't been blue from disuse already.

"What for? You weren't a minute ago." It wasn't the response she was looking for. He met her eyes, now spitting fire, and slid out from under her and up onto his own side of the seat.

"I'm allowed the occasional lapse in judgment," she snapped. "It doesn't make me crazy all the time, and that's what I'd have to be to marry you. And don't you 'what for' me. You know what for. For putting me through—"

"Miranda, stop. Let's start over. I didn't mean to ask you that. Right now, anyway. I'll ask you again later, but right now we need to talk. Actually, I need to talk and you need to listen," he said firmly, keeping his eyes on her face to monitor how well his attempt to gain control of the situation was working.

"I don't think so, Chas. You're in the South now. Ladies first."

Placating her seemed like a good idea. "Of course, Miranda. Please, go ahead."

From her own side of the cramped space she glared at him, letting a silence build like a good head of steam in a teakettle. Finally she leaned forward and spoke in a low, dangerous voice. "Fine. You talk."

He wasn't about to question her. After a second's hesitation, he shrugged. "I'm an idiot, Miranda. There's no other excuse for letting you leave Stamford without telling you that I love you. How much I love you. And that I fell in love with you the moment you walked up to us in the parking lot and gave me that look."

"Oh." She dropped her gaze to their bound hands. "What look?" she asked after a long silence.

"The look that told me everything I needed to know about you. That you were fearless and strong and true. I was a fool, Miranda. I let myself believe that you could betray me and walk away. But I was a bigger fool to let you leave in the first place." He paused. "There's no good reason you should forgive me for being such an ass, but I hope you'll come up with one, because life just isn't the same without you."

Neither of them said anything for a long time. A *long*

time. By the time she finally spoke, the sky had gone from late-afternoon blue to being filled with twilight streaks of purple and orange.

"I tried not to fall in love with you, Chas," she said simply. "I really did. I couldn't help it, though. And when you told me about—" She stopped and closed her eyes. When she lifted her eyes to his again, dampness striped her face, silvering it in the half-light.

His free arm went around her, held her tight. After a moment she pushed herself away from him, wiped her eyes, and looked out through the windshield at the parking lot. "The thing is, Chas, I'm not as good a person as you think I am, and I don't deserve to hear what you just said about me. You see, I did exactly what you thought I did. I made a decision not to tell you about the chief's refusal."

Her words registered like a blow to his heart.

A moment later she turned and met his eyes. He saw fear and sheer determination behind the wet sparkle, and the chaos inside threatened to engulf him.

"I mean, I realize now I should have told you that very first night that I'd asked for permission to interview someone," she continued in a voice that shook. "But I didn't because it never occurred to me that I'd be denied. Then I really did mean to tell you the night I had you over to dinner, but it was difficult enough to keep my mind on the questions I was asking, what with you getting all romantic and my breasts falling off . . . Anyway, I just forgot. And we just went from there, didn't we? The very next night you just . . . we just . . ." She took a deep breath and met his eyes. "How bad is it? Having Brian Murphy outrank you?"

"He doesn't. I retired."

Her eyes widened. "Because of—"

"No." He brushed away a streak of tears on her face. "What you said to me the night you left started me thinking about things that I'd never wanted to think about. You were right. Not about everything," he added with a deliberate grin, and was rewarded by seeing a watery smile cross her face. "Seeing Murphy get the promotion made me realize that I wasn't on the force for the reasons I thought I was. Then Paxton . . . Look, we can talk about this later. Will you marry me?"

She let a long pause build, during which a troubling gleam came into her eyes. She leaned against the door. "I don't know, Chas. You don't have a job. I do. If I say yes, I don't want you hanging around the house all day getting underfoot. What are you going to do with yourself?"

He couldn't hold back a grin. "I'm going to work for my mother," he said sheepishly.

She lifted an eyebrow. "As what?"

"Chief security officer."

"Based on the look on your face, I was expecting you to say 'mailroom clerk,'" she said, starting to laugh. "And I wouldn't blame her for doing it to you, after what you've put her through. Are you looking forward to it? Because if you're not, you can't be coming into my office whining. I have deadlines to meet."

"Yes, I'm looking forward to it. I've already picked out furniture for my office and hired three assistants."

"Are they cute?"

"Adorable. They're triplets."

"Are they really?"

"No."

She lifted an eyebrow playfully. "They're blondes, aren't they?"

He took a deep breath, but it didn't help get rid of his smile. "You're the one and only blonde in my life, now and forever. So listen up, you smart-ass. I'm going to ask you one more time. Will you marry me, Miranda?"

Her smile faded to a soft, serious look. "You still want me to? After what I just told you?"

"That makes me want you even more."

"Why?" she whispered.

He lifted his free hand and brushed her hair back from her brave, beautiful face. "Because you didn't have to tell me. And in those few seconds you taught me a hell of a lot more about truth and honor than I've ever taught anyone."

She smiled, her eyes sparkling wetly again, and lifted her free hand to cup his cheek. "You are one crazy Yankee, Chas."

"Can I take that as a yes?"

She nodded. He slid his hand around her neck and brought her mouth to his.

A sharp rap on the window made them spring apart a few minutes later.

"I hate to break this up, but I'm hungry and I'm freezing my ass off out here," Joe shouted through the closed window.

Chas reached over and lowered the window a few inches. "I don't care," he replied, then turned back to Miranda. "Where were we?"

She pushed him away, laughing. "Chas, unlock the car and let the poor man in. It's the only way we'll get rid of these," she said, holding up their joined hands.

Outside the window, Joe doubled over with laughter. Chas glanced at Miranda, whose eyes had narrowed with suspicion. He looked away as he pressed the button to unlock the doors.

"Christ Almighty, Chas," Joe said, laughing, as he climbed into the driver's seat.

"What?" Miranda demanded, nailing Chas to his seat with her glare.

"Go on, Chas, tell her. I'll protect you. *Maybe.*"

"Tell me what?"

Without saying a word, Chas dug into the front pocket of his jeans and pulled out a small set of keys, with which he unlocked the handcuffs.

Miranda's eyes widened. "You had the key all this time?"

He nodded. "They're my cuffs. I thought they might come in handy in case you said no and I had to persuade you."

"You said *yes?* No way," Joe exclaimed as he brought the engine to life. "Congratulations, Chas. You are one lucky but undeserving son of a bitch. Miranda, welcome to the family. Now, if you don't mind, could you both get out of the car? Just in case what you've got is contagious."

"Good idea," Chas said, not taking his eyes off her face. Seconds later they were standing in the emptying parking lot, wrapped in each other's arms against the chill of a spring evening.

"Your place or my hotel?" he asked between kisses as they leaned against her car.

"It doesn't matter to me, darlin', as long as we get one thing straight."

"What's that?"

"Tonight, I'm *driving."*

All your favorite romance writers are
coming together.

SIGNET ECLIPSE

One wedding.
Three bridesmaids.
Four sexy tales of modern-day romance.

The Bridesmaids Chronicles

Now available
First Date
by Karen Kendall

Coming July 2005
First Kiss
by Kylie Adams

Coming August 2005
First Dance
by Karen Kendall

Coming September 2005
First Love
by Julie Kenner

**Available wherever books are sold or at
www.penguin.com**

S155

Coming Soon in Paperback

"Karen Brichoux writes with
such delightful insight, she reaches
past the heart and tugs at your very soul."
—DONNA KAUFFMAN, Author of
Dear Prince Charming

A NOVEL

THE GIRL
SHE LEFT
BEHIND

Karen Brichoux

AUTHOR OF *SEPARATION ANXIETY*
AND *COFFEE & KUNG FU*

New American Library

Penguin Group (USA) Inc. Online

What will you be reading tomorrow?

Tom Clancy, Patricia Cornwell, W.E.B. Griffin,
Nora Roberts, William Gibson, Robin Cook,
Brian Jacques, Catherine Coulter, Stephen King,
Dean Koontz, Ken Follett, Clive Cussler,
Eric Jerome Dickey, John Sandford,
Terry McMillan...

You'll find them all at
http://www.penguin.com

*Read excerpts and newsletters,
find tour schedules, and enter contests.*

Subscribe to Penguin Group (USA) Inc. Newsletters
and get an exclusive inside look
at exciting new titles and the authors you love
long before everyone else does.

PENGUIN GROUP (USA) INC. NEWS
http://www.penguin.com/news